SEASON OF LOVE

"Have you ever been with a man before?" Lone Wolf
asked.

"What if I have?" Catherine gasped.

Lone Wolf's hand slipped under her petticoats, his
fingers brushing lightly against her legs. They moved up
her ankles and her calves; they whispered behind her
knees and up her thighs. Catherine's body was burning
so, she could hardly speak. She turned her head and lifted
her face, as Lone Wolf lowered his lips to hers for a short
warm kiss. Then his lips traveled over her face, sending
tremors of delight through her body.

"I think I shall be the first man to be with you," Lone
Wolf mused, his lips toying with the throbbing pulse
point at the base of her throat. He chuckled, the sound
rich and mellow, a sedative to Catherine's ragged nerves.
"You may fight me," he granted, "and you may try to
escape, but I promise you Catherine, you *will* love
me. . . ."

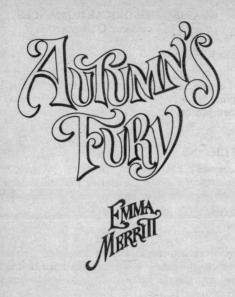

AUTUMN'S FURY

EMMA MERRITT

ZEBRA BOOKS
KENSINGTON PUBLISHING CORP.

ZEBRA BOOKS

are published by

Kensington Publishing Corp.
475 Park Avenue South
New York, NY 10016

First printing: February 1986

Printed in the United States of America

To Paul LaVerne with all my love

Prologue

*The New World in what is now North Carolina
Autumn, 1587*

The flames of the campfire danced in golden flickers over the sculpted features of the two Roanoac braves who sat talking. Their voices were low, their conversation serious. One was dressed entirely in buckskins and the other wore a linen shirt, leggings, and moccasins. The first had shaved his head on both sides, greased and painted his cockscomb red, and decorated his scalp lock with feathers; the second had his thick, black hair cut short in the European style. Wanchese was a war chieftain; Running Bear, a peace chief.

"Will Dare is different," Running Bear argued. "He does not speak with a forked tongue, nor is he a coward to be prodded to unwise action by his council."

"But he is not the governor of the colony," Wanchese countered. "Not even the acting governor. What authority does he have?"

"He has great authority, my friend. Although his older brother, Ananias, is the acting governor while John White is in England getting the needed provisions, Will Dare is the strength and voice of the colony." When

7

Wanchese made no immediate comment, Running Bear continued. "Will wants peace, Wanchese. Come and talk with him. Let him know that you and your braves did not kill George Howe. He is a just man and fair."

Wanchese's head jerked up, and he glared at his friend. "We have done nothing to apologize for," he growled. "And certainly not to a paleface. This is our land, Running Bear, not theirs." His voice thundered across the clearing. "And if I can prevent it, our land will never belong to them."

"You are fighting a losing cause, my brother," Running Bear sadly pointed out. "The few Roanoacs who remain are scattered. Our villages are burned to the ground, and our people have taken refuge with other tribes. Our confederacy is destroyed, and our old allies, the Croatoans, now led by Manteo, have agreed to a peace alliance with the palefaces." He waited for a moment before he said, "Come back to the settlement and live in peace with the palefaces."

Instead of answering, Wanchese slid back into pleasant memories of times past. "Do you remember how it used to be, my brother, before the palefaces landed on our shores? When the Croatoan and Roanoac lived in peace together, when they were a strong confederacy? You, Manteo, and me."

Running Bear nodded, a smile of remembrance curving his lips. How well he recalled those halcyon days of youth. How easily he was led down the path of memory as Wanchese talked. Manteo, Wanchese, and he had grown up together, played together, and had finally earned their first feather together. The three of them, young men and proven warriors, had been fishing together on the shores of Roanoke Island when the first English explorers had set foot on American soil. They were the ones who had rushed forward and greeted these strange men. Gladly they had befriended the palefaces,

8

quickly becoming their guides and interpreters, and soon their advocates.

That summer in 1584 the three chieftains had sailed to England with the explorers. They had been treated as nobility because they were native princes, and as wards of Sir Walter Raleigh they'd been tutored by the most knowledgeable scholars in all Europe, Master Harriot having been one of their instructors. They were taught to read and to write English; they were taught to cipher. In every way they were exposed to the grandeur and sophistication of English custom and civilization.

Running Bear spoke, his question piercing the heavy silence that hung over Wanchese. "You never liked England, did you?"

"No," Wanchese admitted frankly. "Civilization and progress didn't appeal to me then and they still don't. I did not like the wooden cities with streets so narrow one could hardly pass through them, nor did I enjoy having the compound pots emptied on my head, the stench and filth, the paleface diseases, the rivers full of the green slime, the forked-tongue talking in the council of the woman werowance. I liked none of that, my friend."

Running Bear chuckled, pointing out, "But you are remembering only the bad things. We had fun there, remember." He smiled as he said, "And you must admit it was quite an honor to be presented to the Queen herself."

Wanchese smiled lamely. "For you it was an honor, my friend. For me it was torture. I never learned to endure all those binding garments the palefaces wear." He chuckled. "Furthermore, the paleface chieftain liked you the best. Remember the way she smiled when you recited one of our songs about Elder Sister, the Moon?" Wanchese's soft chuckle burgeoned into gusty laughter. "She thought you had written it about her and for her. She wouldn't let you out of her sight after that." He looked across the flames and asked, "Do you still have the desk she gave you?"

"I do," Running Bear answered. Then both of them slipped into a moment of introspective silence. Finally Running Bear reminisced softly, "Do you remember the way people would gather at the river to watch us as we canoed by?"

"I remember," Wanchese sighed. "But those days of happiness are gone, my brother. They ended when Manteo and I returned the following summer. If only . . ." The last two words were wrung out of the agony of his soul, and they hung in the air, his wish never to be reconciled. "But you cannot know," Wanchese sighed. "That summer two years ago, when Manteo and I returned to our land with the second group of Englishmen, you stayed in England to complete your studies."

"But I do—"

"No." Wanchese shook his head. He was the calm before the storm. "You've heard what the palefaces and Manteo told you, but you don't know." His voice vibrated with anguish and thundered with fury. "You did not view their cruelties at first hand as I did." He paused, bitterly adding, "Manteo saw it all; he knows, but he has become a paleface himself. He no longer speaks like an Indian, but I, Wanchese, werowance of the Roanoacs, tell the truth."

Pensively Running Bear angled his face and looked at Wanchese. Carefully he spoke, "I have learned, Wanchese, that even truth is relative. Each of us has his own way of looking at and speaking the truth." He smiled, knowing his friend had to talk to cleanse his soul of the bitterness and hatred that festered there. "But speak, I will listen. I will weigh your words, and I will judge for myself."

"From the beginning, my friend, I did not like Sir

Grenville. He was caught up in his own importance, and from the moment he set his feet on our shores he was determined to make our people see him in the same light as he saw himself. Using Manteo and me as his guides, he visited three of our villages, Secotan, Pomeiooc, and Aquascognoc. All went well until Grenville returned to his fleet and discovered that one of his silver cups was missing. He couldn't believe that he had lost it. Immediately he accused the Aquascognocs of stealing it and sent a runner back demanding the return of the cup. Because the people of Aquascognoc didn't give it to him, he and his soldiers marched back to the town, scattered the people, and burned the village to the ground. For one small drinking vessel"—Wanchese snarled contemptuously—"Grenville destroyed all the belongings and food stuff of an entire village because he had lost one small cup."

"We have sometimes warred with other tribes over matters as small, my brother. Shall we condemn the palefaces for doing what we have done?"

Wanchese did not respond to Running Bear's question. His hatred was a festering sore, his words the seepage from this inflamed wound. His voice, hard and callous, bespoke no leniency or yielding.

"Still Chief Wingina did not retaliate. He listened to Manteo's defense of the palefaces, and he accepted their reasoning and their excuses for this wanton destruction. He granted permission for the paleface soldiers under Governor Lane to build their settlement and their fort. That day, my brother, the palefaces came between Manteo and me. I returned to my Indian life, taking up residence in Dasamonquepeuc, while Manteo stayed with the palefaces, in their settlement.

"One summer later, led by Manteo, the treacherous Governor Lane with twenty-five armed soldiers came to Dasamonquepeuc on the pretense of speaking with the

11

great Werowance Wingina. Thinking the paleface spoke the truth, we received him into the village. We spread out mats of friendship, we organized games to entertain, and our women cooked a feast. All this, Chief Wingina did in their honor."

Wanchese closed his eyes, reliving the horror of that day. "The games had been played, and the winners honored. I was sitting beside our chief when I heard Governor Lane shout: *'Christ, our victory.'* Not words of peace," Wanchese cried, the sorrow wrung from his heart. "Not words of worship to their God, but words of war—words that signaled a massacre. From all around the palefaces fell on us, shooting, throwing their spears, and swinging their swords. We jumped to our feet and ran into the forest. I barely escaped; Chief Wingina did not. A paleface pursued him, determined to kill him."

Wanchese was quiet for a few seconds before he sighed deeply and continued to speak. "Killing Wingina was not enough; the soldier cut his head off and paraded it through the village, my friend. They laughed and mocked our great chief, yelling for all to hear that now he couldn't find rest in the land of Manitou because he had no head. They slaughtered innocent women and children." He lapsed into silence before he added softly, "My braves and I swore revenge. Fearing for their lives, the palefaces and Manteo returned to England several moons later."

"Some palefaces are bad like Governor Lane," Running Bear agreed, offering no excuses for the unnecessary cruelties of the palefaces. "But some are good. Thomas Harriot, John White, and Will'am Dare."

"None are good," Wanchese declared vehemently. "And they do not change. Your governor, John White, is like the rest of them. Two moons ago he and your settlers marched into our village after the death of George Howe with the intent of killing all of us. If I had not persuaded

12

our people to flee, the palefaces would have massacred all the Roanoacs that remain." His laughter was a hollow snort. "They massacred Indians all right. But they killed no Roanoacs. They killed their allies, the Croatoans, who had come to our village to get the food we had left behind." Wanchese unsheathed his European knife and lightly ran his thumb along the sharp iron blade. "War, not peace, is my answer."

Running Bear sighed his disappointment and shook his head. Leaning forward and taking the knife from Wanchese, he held it up and looked at it for a long time, turning the blade in his hand. He was fascinated by the reflection of the fire on the metal. A shining silver one moment; a shadowed dimness the next. A tool to sustain life one moment; a weapon to take life the next.

"My brother, you have just cause to be angry and bitter. I can understand your feelings, but fighting is not the answer," Running Bear said. "Our knowledge is too far behind theirs, too limited. We can't fight them with weapons of war. We must learn from the palefaces how to make their tools of peace. We must use what we have learned in England the past three years to educate our people. We must build schools, and we must teach them to read, to write, and to cipher. We must work to create an alphabet, so we can do these things. Only through knowledge can we battle the paleface and win."

"I remember well the lessons we learned from the palefaces, Running Bear. You and Manteo are the ones who have dim memories. Remember those who settled on the shores of the Chesapeake long before the Englishmen. The ones who wore the black robes, carried the crossed sticks, and prayed to the beads. They would not be happy until we accepted their dead god who lay on the sticks; even then they were not satisfied. They wanted to make slaves of all of us. They took the honor out of war, my brother. In order to know how many of our enemy we

13

had killed they demanded that we bring back scalps. Not only the scalp locks of the warriors whom we had slain honorably, Running Bear, but the scalps of old men, women, and children." Wanchese spat contemptuously. "For these cowardly deeds against our own we were paid in beads, my brother. Paleface beads in exchange for a man's life and his honor."

Silence enveloped the two men, and they stared at one another across the fire. Each knew the truth had been spoken.

Wanchese finally asked, breaking the lengthy silence. "Do you, like so many of our people, believe the palefaces are gods with strong magic? Do you fear them too, my brother?"

Running Bear handed the knife to his friend, and he stood, walking away from the fire into the shadows to look pensively and longingly into the thick North Carolina forest, the land of his birthright twenty-five winters ago. He folded his arms across his chest and leaned against a tree trunk, lifting his head to gaze at the star-studded sky.

"No, my friend who is closer than a brother, I am not afraid of the palefaces in the sense that you mean. And, yes, I am afraid." He paused for a moment before he explained. "Like you, I fear the change that is going to come into the lives of our people, yet there is nothing we can do about it. It is not within our power to paint time another color, my brother. Only the Grandfather of Time has the brush that can do that. The palefaces are going to bring their wooden cities, and they are going to take our forests for their homes and ships. Our wilderness will be no more. For this . . . I am afraid. More, I am sad."

Wanchese didn't let the haunting words fade into silence before he growled, "I still say war." His anger and bitterness merged into a consuming desire to rid the Indian lands of the invaders. Hurriedly he rushed on, his words tumbling out, "We will walk in your magic, my

14

brother. It is strong." He smiled hopefully. "It always has been."

Looking over his shoulder, Running Bear saw the despair that racked his friend's face; he heard his desperation; and he wanted to agree with Wanchese. He turned and smiled as he walked back to the fire. He laid a hand on Wanchese's shoulder. "It will take more than my magic for us to win, my friend. It will take more than your skill as a warrior. It will take more than the palefaces' weapons." When Wanchese opened his mouth to protest, Running Bear said, "I know that you are a great war chief, but there are times when you should listen to the peace man, Wanchese, no matter how hard his words may strike your ears. And this is such a time."

Wanchese leaped to his feet and cried, "You are no longer an Indian, my brother. Like Manteo you have become a paleface."

"Being an Indian, Wanchese, does not lie in dress or hair style," Running Bear explained, his voice quiet and deep, "nor in being an enemy to the palefaces. Being Indian is much more than that. It is loving your land and your people so much that you are willing to make any sacrifice necessary for them. It is protecting them at any risk."

He returned to the fire and picked up the white buckskin jacket that both of them recognized—the Coat of Peace. As was the custom of the Eastern Indians, each village of the tribe sent a square of buckskin to the peace chief's wigwam, and his mother lovingly stitched the patches together, embroidering them with colored porcupine quills. As she sewed, the peace chief's mother called upon Manitou, the Creator, to bequeath much magic to her son, and she prayed for Manitou to send his spirit helpers to assist him. She knew that the path of a man of peace would be a hard one, an inglorious one.

Running Bear pulled the Coat of Peace over his head and straightened it across the broad shoulders that he squared proudly. "I am the peace chief, my brother, and I wear the coat of peace. Forever I walk the path of peace; yet forever I fight for my people. I shall learn the palefaces' ways, and I shall teach the palefaces our ways."

"You are not fighting the palefaces," Wanchese jeered. "You are joining them."

"I have spoken, Wanchese. Think what you will." Running Bear's tone was kind, yet he refused to be intimidated or mocked, to give way to anger, or to budge from his stand.

Late into the night the two friends talked—argued— each trying to persuade the other. But each was adamant in his resolve. By dawn nothing had been settled, yet they had to part.

"What have you decided?" Running Bear asked as he watched Wanchese ease his quiver over his head, shifting his right shoulder so that the stiff buckskin carrying case hung upright against his left shoulder blade.

"I shall walk in your wisdom," he said. "I will meet with your Will Dare to let him know that my braves and I were not responsible for the death of the paleface settler, George Howe."

"That is good, my brother," Running Bear replied. "I shall give him the news when I return to Roanoke."

"Shall I walk with you?" Wanchese asked. "I don't know if it's safe for you to be traveling alone in Scupperongac country."

Running Bear shook his head. "No, I'll be all right." He pointed to his shirt, but he looked at Wanchese, bestowing a rare and mischievous grin on his childhood companion. "Safety is one of the advantages of being a peace man. Not even the powerful Scupperongac will take my life as long as I wear the Coat of Peace."

Slowly Wanchese nodded his head, and then he walked to the edge of the clearing. He paused to turn back, lifting his hand in farewell before they parted. "Your words

16

were wise, Running Bear. I shall try to live by your wisdom."

"Not my words," Running Bear quietly denied, "the Creator's. We must hear him if we're to survive." Then he asked, "Where are you going from here?"

"To persuade the inland tribes to trade food to the English. If they don't, I fear the English will retaliate, taking it anyway, destroying villages and killing innocent people in the process." Wanchese took a step; then as if he thought better, he turned back, looking at his friend.

Running Bear held his hand up and signed farewell. "We shall meet back here in two days' time?"

Wanchese nodded, disappearing into the forest.

Wanchese stood at the edge of the clearing for a long time before he pushed through the heavy undergrowth. He knew something was wrong. The silence was ominous. Nothing—absolutely nothing—was stirring, and Running Bear hadn't answered any of his calls. Cautiously the war chief walked through the silent camp, stopping at the black ring of ashes. Holding his bow in his left hand, he reached over his shoulder with his right and whipped an arrow from the quiver. He cooed again; all the time his moccasined feet quietly and carefully moved through the camp, his eyes darting all around him, his head never moving. Then he saw Running Bear . . . hiding behind a tree! Wanchese relaxed, emitted a long sigh of relief, and dropped his guard. Grinning, he lowered his bow and sneaked toward his friend.

Playing games was like old times; it carried him back many summers and temporarily he forgot his heavy concerns. How often he, Manteo, and Running Bear played hide-and-seek, he thought, chuckling softly.

"Will you never outgrow your childish games?" he asked, his hand touching the shoulder that protruded from behind the trunk.

The words were no sooner out of Wanchese's mouth, his hand was no sooner on Running Bear's shoulder than he rounded the tree. His jaw went slack, and his face blanched. A spear pierced Running Bear's body, pinning him face forward to the tree.

Wanchese stood for a moment, the blood rushing through his veins so fast that his head roared. A knot formed in his throat, and anger banded his heart so tightly it interfered with his breathing. Running Bear was dead; someone had violated the sacred law of the Indian by killing a peace man.

Dead! Running Bear is dead! The thought kept running through Wanchese's mind as he laid his bow down and unpinned his friend's body. *My friend is dead! Our peace man is gone!* Wanchese gently laid Running Bear on the ground, softly chanting the agony of his soul. He ran his fingers over the delicate stitches of the patchwork coat which announced to everyone that Running Bear was a peace man. Any Indian would have known who he was. Then Wanchese looked at Running Bear's right hand. It was clenched into a fist. He saw the crumpled sheet of parchment.

When Wanchese pried Running Bear's fingers open, a broken necklace dropped to the ground, but at the moment Wanchese wasn't interested in the jewelry. He unfolded the parchment and looked at the writing—the paleface knowledge that Running Bear had wanted for their people. Although Wanchese viewed that knowledge as contemptible, his eyes, sparkling with unshed tears, ran over the characters of the alphabet that Running Bear was creating. This had been the life and soul of his friend, his driving ambition. As if the paper itself were sacred, Wanchese carefully refolded it and tucked it into his pouch.

Then he picked up the broken necklace and dangled it in the air. It looked as if it had been jerked from someone's neck—perhaps the killer's. Wanchese's fingers touched the four teeth centered between the two rows of pearls, and he brought the necklace closer to his face. The pearls connoted wealth and station. The fangs? The wolf fangs! Only one Indian in the forest boasted wolf fangs as his totem. Lone Wolf, war chief of the Scupperongacs, the man reputed to be one of the most valiant warriors of the Great Forest tribes. The warrior whom Running Bear was to meet!

Wanchese's expression set, and his eyes narrowed with purpose and resolve. He would revenge Running Bear's death . . . but first he must bury his friend. He dropped the necklace into his pouch and turned his attention to the matter at hand.

Wanchese walked through the forest, gathering herbs, berries, and bark. When he was through, he went to the bank of the river. First he built a small fire; then he began to mix his concoctions, all the while lowly chanting his grief, all the while planning his revenge. Using the water as a mirror, he drew the string on his pouch and, using bear fat, smeared colors over his face and upper body. When he was through, he stood and threw back his head, crying to the Creator.

Finally Wanchese lowered his head, the wailing chant dying on his lips. He stamped heel and toe, he stalked, he crouched, and again he stamped. His buckskin-moccasined feet shuffled to the left; shuffled to the right. He yowled his anguish; he howled his bitterness and his revenge. When he stopped his death dance, he cupped his ear with his hand, then cried aloud in his despair, *"Ai-yee! The Spirit cannot hear me."*

From his heart came the bitter question, "What does he hear?" The words had no sooner passed his lips than his deep resonant voice affirmed the answer, a stolid and monotonous death chant. Wanchese was promising retribution for the death of the peace man; he was promising more. . . .

19

Later, Wanchese returned to the death-quieted camp. Stooping, he lifted Running Bear in his arms. "Naked you came from Earth the Mother. Naked you return to her. May a good wind carry you."

He began the long journey to their village. Though a brave who boasted many feathers on his scalp lock, Wanchese grieved over the loss of his childhood playmate, and his lifelong friend. The valiant warrior mourned the loss of the peace man's wisdom. As Wanchese walked, he chanted out his anguish, and his soul cried as tears ran down his cheeks.

"I will revenge your death," he promised Running Bear.

Wise One, the great chief of the Scupperongacs and village chief of Scupperong, sat cross-legged in the middle of the townhouse in front of the sacred fire which burned at all times. Circled around him, passing the sacred pipe of tobacco one to another were the elders of the tribe. In prayer Wise One lifted his face, letting the moon massage his rigid form with her silver fingers. He didn't understand the recurring vision, nor did it frighten him. He was sure it was Manitou speaking to him. Believing this to be the voice of the Great Spirit, Wise One was filled with a sense of urgency; therefore, he had summoned the elders of the tribe.

An aged woman rose to her feet, puffed on the pipe, then spoke. "I am old, my chief. The wind of sixty winters has turned my black hair white as the snow. Much wisdom is lodged in my head which even the winter winds cannot blow away. Speak your dream, and I will listen."

"I have felt the winds of more winters than you, woman called No-am-ee, and I now feel another wind blowing. Soon it will be time for me to begin my journey to the land of Manitou, the Creator. But he has spoken to me and promised that I will not leave until another comes to take my place as peace man."

"No one has spoken to me about a vision of the peace man, my chief," No-am-ee said. "Perhaps to some of the other elders the chosen ones have spoken, but not to me."

Wise One's gaze swept the circle, but none nodded an affirmative answer. "I thought not," he said sadly.

"Tell us your vision, Great Chief," No-am-ee said. "We will listen, and we will explain if we can."

Closing his eyes and lifting his face to the smoke hole, Wise One softly chanted the song of his vision:

One comes in the autumn.
The sunset in her hair,
The forest in her eyes,
The glorious sun her face,
This is Autumn Woman.

On her back is a quiver filled with arrows.
In her left hand a bow,
In her right hand a war club,
This is Warrior Woman.

She walks toward me.
Laying her weapons down,
She reaches for the Coat of Peace.
She wraps it around herself.

She stretches her arms to the people of the forest.
She calls for all tribes to follow.
She is our peace woman.

"Tell me, old woman," Wise One said, when the wailing chant echoed through the wigwam no longer. "Tell me, one who has felt the wind of sixty winters, what does my dream mean?"

21

Chapter I

Standing by the table she had shoved to the side of the cabin earlier, Catherine Graystone held her muddied hands over a bucket of clay she was using to daub the cracks between the logs. Her younger sister, Ellen, was on her hands and knees, polishing the plank floor. Having worked since early morning to get their two-room cottage ready for the harsh, coastal winter, Catherine and Ellen had abandoned their farthingales and ruffs, and were wearing only petticoats beneath their linen gowns.

The rounded neckline of Catherine's dress was partially unbuttoned, and damp tendrils of auburn hair escaped the white linen coif to cling to her forehead and cheeks. Not wanting to get any dirtier than she already was, she lifted her arm and, with bended wrist, wiped the perspiration from her forehead.

"Oh, Kate, I do wish we could have afforded to bring some servants with us," Ellen grumbled, rocking backward and waving her hands in the air. Her beautiful, young face was wrinkled in disgust. "Just look! My hands are ruined. Sweeping and scrubbing and polishing." Following her own command, the sixteen-year-old began a detailed survey of her dainty hands, mumbling, "And I don't know if I have enough ointment to keep them from getting red and ugly."

"Stop grumbling!" Catherine admonished her lightly, her eyes scaling the walls for any cracks she might have missed. "I gave you a choice, and you were the one who wanted to polish. You didn't want to get your hands muddy, remember."

"This isn't anything like Governor White said it would be," Ellen complained, totally disregarding her sister's rebuke. "Remember, Kate? Remember what he told us when he was persuading you to invest our inheritance in this venture? Remember all those letters we read? They described a fertile land with an abundant food supply. Remember how beautiful it was supposed to be? Like the Garden of Eden!"

"Perhaps it's not quite what Governor White said it would be," Catherine conceded easily, "but it's not all that bad either." She chuckled. "For all we know, Ellen, this may be the way Eden looked."

Ellen refused to laugh at Catherine's joke. "It is all that bad and more," she maintained, half-heartedly swiping her cloth over the floor as she talked. "Just think, Kate, we don't have enough food to last the winter. We'll probably all die of starvation."

"So far we haven't gone hungry and we probably won't. Will and Manteo are seeing to that now," Catherine calmly returned, although she was becoming irritated by her sister's constant faultfinding. "If they can get us enough food to make it through the winter, we'll be all right come summer."

"If we make it through the winter," Ellen mimicked, her words coming out in huffed phrases as she picked at the beeswax mold with her fingernails. "And our making it through the winter depends as much on the attitude of these savages as it does on food." She dropped the wax and picked up her rag.

"They're not savages," Catherine quietly countered.

23

"No!" Catherine's apparent calmness goaded Ellen into retaliation. "What do you call them then? Have you so quickly forgotten what happened? How they riddled George with sixteen arrows and bashed his head beyond recognition with their war clubs!"

"George was a foolish man," Catherine retorted dryly. "Despite what we were told, he deliberately wandered two miles from the settlement by himself. Then he left all his weapons on shore and waded, half naked, into the water to fish. When you take all that into account, his end is not quite so scary." Catherine returned to the table and picked up her daubing bucket and paddle. "Now stop whining and get to work."

Snorting her anger, Ellen gripped her polishing rag with both hands and attacked the floor. Several minutes of dedicated vengeance, however, took their toll. She soon dropped her rag and flipped over to watch Catherine who stood on tiptoe upon a chair, daubing some of the cracks close to the ceiling. Finally Catherine dropped the paddle in the bucket and began to smooth the mud mixture with her fingers.

"You just don't worry about anything, do you?" the younger girl taunted.

"Worrying won't change a thing," Catherine said absently, flattening her feet on the chair bottom and lowering her arm. "Besides Running Bear told me the other day that we're not the Indians' primary interest right now. Internal problems are occupying most of their attention."

"And you'd believe anything Running Bear told you, wouldn't you, Kate?" Ellen snickered. "I agree with Aunt Rose; you're a fool where these savages are concerned. Since you and Running Bear met in England, you've been inseparable. You *really* do like him, don't you?"

"I more than like him." The answer was firm, and a

24

touch of anger had replaced Catherine's irritation. "I admire him. He's a man totally dedicated to peace and to the welfare of his people. His one desire is to open schools so he can educate them."

"You share that dream also, Kate," Ellen said idly, her words more reflective than reproachful. "Like father, you've spent all your life learning—reading, writing, ciphering." She laughed mockingly. "Even weaponry and sports. You were reckoned quite a bowman, much to Aunt Rose's despair. Not many women—in fact, not many people—can boast of the education you have. Why you can speak two languages besides English: French and Spanish." Her memory jogged, she mocked, "Nay, Kate, you speak another. You have learned to speak Running Bear's language quite well."

"Aye, and to make the signs as well," Catherine returned, refusing to rise to Ellen's bait. She rose onto her toes again and reached for a crack that was very high up.

Slouching on the floor, Ellen watched Catherine a long time before she said, "Perhaps you should have married John Turner, Kate. He wasn't such a bad person."

"Not so bad!" Catherine's tone was scathing. Almost falling from the chair, she spun around to peer down at Ellen.

"Because of your friendship with an Indian you defied Aunt Rose and Uncle James, you refused to marry a perfectly decent man—"

"A perfectly decent man!" Catherine howled. "Don't you sit there and fault me, Ellen Graystone. You know perfectly well that John Turner was old enough to be my grandfather."

"Because of those savages you invested *our* fortune in this plantation venture."

"Nay," Catherine firmly replied, barely restraining her anger. "My friendship with Running Bear was not

25

the only reason I stood up to Aunt and Uncle. I did it for you and me. I don't want others dictating our lives for us."

"Maybe for you, but not for me," Ellen bounced around, propping herself up on one elbow. "I was perfectly happy in England. You're the one who wanted to sail for the New World."

"I seem to remember your insisting on coming to the New World with me after you met Will'am Dare," Catherine taunted, hurling the gauntlet of accusation right back at Ellen.

Admitting her guilt by gesture but not by word, Ellen dropped her head. She mumbled, "For yours and the colonists' sake, I hope Running Bear can convince the Indians to live in peace, Kate. I hope he can persuade Wanchese to talk with Will." She paused; then announced defiantly, "But even if he can, I won't like the New World any better."

She was selfishly stating what she felt as a child would, with no thought of the consequences of hurt feelings; her wants overrode any twinge of conscience.

"I certainly don't intend to spend the rest of my life here, and I won't."

Because this was the first time Ellen had voiced her feelings and because she was unsure of the effect doing so would have on Catherine, she warily watched her older sister as she said, "You've squandered our inheritance to bring us over here, but I'll find a way to get home, Kate. I promise you."

Catherine slowly dropped her arms and carefully stepped from the chair. Walking to the table on the far side of the room, she set the wooden bucket down and raked one side of the paddle across its rim then the other, cleaning off the caked mud. Then she laid the paddle on the table.

"I agree," she finally said. "If that's the way you feel

26

about it, you can return home on the ships that bring our supplies."

Irritated because Catherine hadn't reacted as she had anticipated, Ellen tossed her head and cried petulantly, "That's the way I feel."

Catherine was exhausted—getting the cabin ready for the coming winter involved a great deal of work—and she was irritated. Ellen had done very little except pout and whine since they had arrived. Catherine was tempted to lash out at Ellen, but she refused to give her the satisfaction of knowing how upset she was. For the past thirteen years, since their mother's death, Catherine had been friend, sister, and mother to Ellen. She loved her younger sister and she couldn't begin to imagine what life would be without her, but she was not going to allow a selfish sixteen-year-old to bully her.

"I suppose you'll be glad to see me leave." Ellen's small voice whispered across the cabin.

Love in her eyes, Catherine looked at the small figure huddled in the middle of the floor. Sunlight lingered in Ellen's hair, spinning the yellow strands into pure gold. The length of it was coiled into a knot, but loose curls formed a natural halo for the girl's innocent face. Her brown eyes were like those of a fawn, innocent and gentle. Her lips were naturally red, and her cheeks had a healthy glow.

As Catherine stared at Ellen, she instantly regretted her anger and irritation. She could understand Ellen's desire to return to England. Ellen was soft and gentle; she was the kind of woman who needed to be petted and coddled. She was destined for silks and satins and court life, not for the wild, rugged life of the frontier.

Lifting a hand to push strands of hair from her heat-flushed face, Ellen asked in a small voice filled with self-pity, "Are you never sorry that we came, Kate?"

"Nay." The soft reply sighed into silence. "My only

regret is that I allowed you to come with me." Dipping her hands into the basin of water, she slowly washed them. "For me, anything was preferable to marrying John Turner, and if I had stayed in England, all of us would have been miserable because I wouldn't have married him to please Aunt and Uncle." She picked up a piece of cloth and dried her hands. "But I should have given more thought to your coming. I should have known."

"I thought it would be different," Ellen mumbled. "If only father . . ."

If only father . . . Catherine silently agreed. If only Father had lived, all would have been well, and she probably would never have invested their inheritance in this colonial venture. John Graystone had enjoyed his children. He'd adored Ellen because she was so much like his beloved wife, Annie. Kate, as he'd called Catherine, he'd loved and admired because she was intelligent and spirited. He'd delighted in her learning. He'd marveled at her determination, which others had often called defiance. Indeed, John had pampered Catherine, never quibbling when she'd flaunted convention. He'd laughed when she'd refused to marry because it was a social and religious custom. A romantic at heart and a bit of a rebel, John Graystone had wanted his daughters to marry for love.

Laying the drying cloth aside, Catherine walked to the window and stared at the forest that surrounded them. "Here, I am my own mistress, Ellen, and as soon as we relocate on the Chesapeake and build the City of Raleigh, I shall build my own plantation." She turned to look at her sister, her voice dreamy and soft, her eyes starry. "I'm happy. The land is beautiful; it's exciting. I like it because it's new and untouched."

Both women lapsed into silence. The dream of one was the nightmare of the other. Catherine continued to stare out the window, and Ellen resumed her polishing. Finally, however, Catherine turned, picked up the daubing bucket, and set it outside the door. Returning to the center of the room, she placed both hands on her hips and slowly turned around, her full skirt billowing around her long, slender legs. She was quite proud of their cabin.

Still wallowing in self-pity, Ellen spoke, her voice misty with unshed tears. "It seems like England never was, doesn't it?" Her voice broke. "I hate this, Kate. All this work and what have we got?" She flung her arms out in a desperate gesture, fanning her hand across the room. "A building that serves as meeting place, church, and dining hall. The Governor's Mansion"—she laughed scathingly—"it's only claim to elegance is that it has four rooms. The rest of us, depending on our social standing and the amount of money we were able to invest in the venture, live in one- or two-room cottages."

"But this is just our temporary home," Catherine reminded her gently. "We're going to have a beautiful house one of these days, one that is much larger and grander than the one we left in England." Catherine walked to Ellen, and kneeling on the floor, she wrapped her arms around her young sister. "Life is whatever we make it, darling. Good or bad. So let's make it good, shall we?"

Ellen suddenly had an ominous premonition of things to come. "Kate!" she cried, "please, let's go home. As soon as Governor White returns, let's go home. Both of us."

Catherine hugged Ellen tightly and spoke soothingly. "Ellen, listen to me." She paused, carefully searching for her words. "I can't go home because I am home." As soon as she had uttered the words, Catherine felt their full impact; she knew the truth of her statement. "My destiny lies in this land."

"Mine doesn't," Ellen quietly and emphatically

responded, her words setting the course for her future. With a dignity and resolve that was out of keeping with the childish outburst she'd indulged in only moments ago, she returned to her polishing.

Wisely Catherine said no more; instead she picked up an extra rag and the mold of beeswax and helped Ellen with her chore. By late afternoon they had finished their tasks and had moved the furniture back into place. Standing, Ellen placed her hands in the small of her back and stretched her aching muscles. Then she walked to the basin and washed and dried her hands. "Do you need me for anything else, Kate?"

"Not right now. There's nothing more that I'm going to do until the daubing dries. Why?"

"I think I'll go see if the men have returned or if they've sent word back."

Catherine nodded. "Would you stop by Dyonis's and see if the shutters are ready? If they are, tell him we've finished with the daubing and are ready for them to be hung. And while you're that close, go to Eleanor's and tell her that I'm almost finished with her set of ruffs and laces." Pulling her coif from her head, Catherine tossed it on the commode and, dipping her hands into the basin, wrung out the washcloth.

"I hope the men have returned safely," Ellen murmured, her thoughts centered on Will'am Dare.

"If nothing else, perhaps Ananias will have sent word back to Eleanor," Catherine assured her.

"Or perhaps Ananias will be back himself." Ellen's lips twitched in a mischievous grin. "Remember how many excuses he made to keep from going with the men."

"Aye." Catherine chuckled with her. "He was frightened."

"It's hard to imagine Ananias and Will being brothers, isn't it?" Ellen asked as she quickly unrolled her hair and recombed it. "They're so different."

30

Sitting down in the rocker near the door, Catherine pressed the wet cloth against her flushed cheeks. "That they are," she agreed. "Will is the younger by fourteen years, yet he is the wiser. He was the first to volunteer to go with Manteo in search of food, and Ananias the last."

While Ellen secured her thick coil of hair at the nape of her neck, she and Catherine indulged in desultory conversation, comparing the two Dare brothers. But once Ellen had donned a clean coif, she skipped to the door and waved a goodbye. Long after Ellen left, Catherine sat, alternately pressing the damp cloth against her face and fanning herself. Eventually she stood and pulled a linen towel from a peg on the wall. During the short time that she had been in the New World, she had learned from the Indian women the pleasure of bathing in the cool, clear water of the river. Now, unnoticed, she walked down the narrow path that led to her particular hideaway beside the stream, a spot that was not too far from the settlement.

Once Catherine was secreted in her bower, her fingers deftly undid the buttons and ribbons of her gown, and hidden in the shadows of the trees, she shrugged out of her clothes. Draping them over a low-hanging limb, she walked to the water's edge and gingerly dipped the toes of one foot into the stream. She laughed softly as the cool water surged over her heated flesh. Daringly she took one step after another, getting both her feet and ankles wet, then her knees. Her hair burnished to copper and her skin glowing golden as the setting sun touched her, the naked twenty-three-year-old played in the water with the abandon of a child.

Her soft, tinkling laughter caught the warrior's attention. Having taken time to rest from his long journey, Lone Wolf was kneeling beside the river when he heard the happy sound. His curiosity aroused, he concealed his canoe and disappeared into the thick

31

forest. Then, from the cover of trees, he watched the paleface woman as she bathed.

His breath caught in his throat as he gazed at her. Standing in ankle-deep water, she presented a picture of loveliness. Her breasts were firm and uplifted. Her midriff sloped into a small circle of waist, and her stomach was flat, narrowing into the dark triangle that bespoke her femininity. Her legs, long and slender, were beautifully proportioned. Her whole body was gilded by the glow of the sun on her water-sheened skin.

Then Catherine had that eerie feeling—the shiver of apprehension that prickles the spine when one is being watched. She felt the obsidian eyes on her as they peered through the forest. She sensed Lone Wolf's presence. Poised as if to take flight, she hesitated for a second that stretched into eternity and looked in the direction where the Indian was concealed. Then, like a skittish colt, she tossed her head, her auburn curls flying in wild abandon about her face and shoulders, and her eyes darted anxiously back and forth along the banks of the river.

She saw nothing except the forest. Yet she couldn't dispel the feeling that she had been visually touched; she couldn't help feeling that her privacy had been invaded. Her pleasure cut short, she waded ashore and headed toward her bower, quickly drying off and dressing. Just as she dropped her gown over her head, she heard Ellen's worried call.

"Catherine! Where are you?"

"Over here, Ellen. I'm . . . I'm over here . . . taking a bath." Not wasting the time to put her shoes on, Catherine picked them up and ran through the forest to meet her younger sister.

"Oh, Kate!" Ellen cried out, relief replacing her frustration. "You shouldn't go off by yourself like this. You know we've been cautioned about wandering around alone. There's no telling what the savages might do.

32

Don't be as foolish as George Howe."

"I'm all right," Catherine assured her sister, with more confidence than she felt. Her eyes darted around, and the prickle of apprehension still tapped her spine. She knew the intruder hadn't gone, for she still felt that penetrating gaze. She dropped an arm over Ellen's shoulders, and the two of them walked toward the clearing.

"Don't go off by yourself like this again, Kate," Ellen pleaded, her voice becoming more accusing as her fear changed to relief. "You don't know how worried I was before I found you."

"I'm sorry." Catherine apologized in a low voice, her hand tightening around Ellen's shoulder, but she couldn't stop the shudder of fear that racked her body, nor could she still the panic that raced through her blood and accelerated her heartbeats. "I didn't mean to make you worry. I just wanted to get away for a little while, to relax and think. I knew once you were with Eleanor you'd visit awhile."

"I did," Ellen concurred, relaxing now that she knew Catherine was safe. She smiled. "I also checked with Dyonis about the shutters, and he was a step ahead of us. He'd already sent Billie to hang them."

"Any news of the men?" Catherine asked.

Ellen shook her head, her eyes darkening with concern. "Nothing yet."

Catherine squeezed Ellen's shoulder again. "Don't worry, dear. He'll be all right."

As they walked, the two sisters lapsed into silence, Ellen thinking about Will, Catherine about the disturbing presence she had felt at the river. When they stood in front of their cabin, they heard the first bell for the evening meal.

"Look at you," Ellen shrieked befeore the sound had died away. "It's time for us to be in the hall, and you're

33

not even ready."

"Since you're already dressed, why don't you run on," Catherine suggested. "I'll be along later."

Ellen's lips curved into a beautiful smile, and she lifted her skirt with both hands so she could skip unimpeded down the dirt path. "You don't mind?"

"No."

Catherine stood for a second longer, watching her sister scurry away. Finally she turned and, pushing the heavy door, entered the cabin. More from habit than conscious effort, she dressed; then she combed her hair and tucked it into a clean kerchief. As the bell sounded the second time, she walked toward the large building in the center of the compound. Smiling and exhanging pleasantries, she joined the converging crowd. When she entered the hall, she spied Eleanor sitting at the head of the table, holding her month-old daughter in one arm and waving frantically with the other.

"Ananias and Miles have returned," Eleanor called out before Catherine had time to sit down.

"And the food?" Catherine demanded, her face lighting up at the good news. "Did they find us some provisions?"

"Aye," Eleanor answered, nodding her head vigorously. Her smile grew even wider. "Ananias will be here directly to tell us all about it. He's—"

"Ananias!"

The jovial greeting boomed through the room, interrupting Eleanor. Everyone's gaze shifted to the slight man who stood in the door. Ananias, feeling the importance of his temporary position, cocked his chin arrogantly as he strutted out of the doorway, then swaggered the length of the hall to take his place at the head of the table. There, he stood, impatiently waiting for all the planters to assemble.

Disgust clouded Catherine's eyes as she watched

34

Ananias. She had never liked him. He was a weak man with shifty eyes and twitching hands, and he was indecisive. His short, gray hair, which belied his thirty-nine years, was combed back from his face, only small tufts of it showing beneath the slouching, plumed hat that he wore at a jaunty angle. His small mustache and pointed beard had been trimmed and brushed, and he nervously drew a perfumed handkerchief through his gloved fingers.

As he gazed at the crowd, he never seemed to look directly at anyone. Instead his glance fell between people. Catherine reflected that when Ananias was asked a question he never answered it directly either. When everyone was seated, he held his hand up for silence, his small, thin lips curving into a smile of sorts.

"We have indeed been fortunate." Ananias' thin nasal twang shrilled through the unfinished hall. "Because of our Indian friends, we found tribes who were willing to barter goods in return for food. However, we did not get enough provisions to see us through the winter, so it was decided that we should separate. Some of us would return to the settlement. Others would proceed further. Manteo came home with Miles and me, but he will be leaving again tomorrow to join Will and Stafford who are traveling northward."

"Northward did ye say?" several colonists mumbled in unison. "Will's traveling to the North Land?"

"That's—that's where the Lumbroans are," Ellen cried with a start, fear's ghastly tentacles clutching her heart. "And they're definitely hostile to us."

"Not exactly hostile." Manteo stood in the door. With agility the tall, lean brave quietly moved to his place at the table. "The Lumbroans are just less than friendly. Because they and the Scupperongacs are discussing a treaty, I do not think we have cause to fear any trouble from them . . . presently."

35

Frightened of the impending dangers that surrounded them, Ananias desperately clung to Manteo's reassuring words. He smiled tightly, and the rigors of his journey overtaking him, he said, "Now, shall we eat? During the meal I will give you a detailed account of the expedition and answer your questions."

Awaiting no affirmation, Ananias sat down and nodded at the chaplain, who said grace. Then the meal was served. After eating, the men migrated to the large fireplace at the end of the hall to discuss, in minute details, Ananias' trip and the colony's impending move to Chesapeake Bay. Meanwhile, the women washed, dried, and put away the dishes. Not until the candles burned low, did the small group disperse for the night.

"Kate"—Ellen's voice was even smaller than usual as the sisters walked toward their cabin—"I'm worried."

"I know," Catherine whispered. At the moment words seemed ineffective.

"I—I think I love Will, Kate."

Catherine laid an arm over Ellen's shoulders, drawing her closer. "I think you do too." She laughed softly. "And I think Will loves you."

"You do?" Ellen squealed, her head jerking around. Wide-eyed, she looked into Catherine's moonlit face. "You really do?"

"I do," Catherine repeated. "And I know everything's going to be all right. I promise. Will shall return unharmed. And I will be very surprised if you and he don't marry and have a houseful of children."

"I would like that very much," Ellen admitted. "I've always been fond of children. And you, Kate," she asked, "wouldn't you like to be married and to have children?"

Taking Ellen's elbow and guiding her into the cabin, Catherine said, "Aye, someday I'll be wed." Then she laughed lightly. "But not now, so let's hush up and go to bed."

36

Catherine lit a candle, and in the flickering light, they undressed and donned their nightshirts; then they lay down and talked. Just before the flame fizzled out, they recited several scriptures and sang a hymn.

The song over, Ellen snuggled under the covers. "Good night, Kate," she said sleepily. "I'll see you on the morrow."

"Good night, Ellen."

Catherine silently hoped Running Bear was safe; then she turned on her side, curled into a ball, and nestled her head in the soft bolster. A smile curved her beautiful lips as she drifted into dreamland. . . .

Spring had come to the woodland, clothing the trees, the bushes, and the grass in verdant richness. Catherine, dressed in a robe that was loose and flowing, stepped out of the forest into the clearing where an Indian stood, his back to her. Although she couldn't see his face, she knew he was Running Bear. He was wearing the white Coat of Peace. She paused for that fraction of a second, enjoying the anticipation of waiting. Then as if he sensed her presence, the brave turned. Still Catherine didn't move. But when he held an arm out, and called "Come Catherine," she raced toward him.

His voice joined the song of the wind, gently touching her ears. He smiled—that soft, special smile—and he spoke. "I thought you'd never get here. I've been waiting." She reached him, and he caught her hand in his; his gentle squeeze was reassuring.

"I came as soon as I could," Catherine replied. "I had many things to do before I could leave. I had to be sure that Ellen and Will were safe."

"I know. I've been taking care of many things too."

Held together in the close bonds of friendship, they stood in nature's cathedral. Their steeped roof was a canopy of trees; their choir the song of the forest creatures. Running

Bear turned to her, his soft, ebony eyes piercing her vivid green ones.

"*Are you truly my friend, Catherine?*" His eyes were shadowed with a sadness that Catherine didn't understand.

"*Aye.*"

"*You fully understand what must be done?*" His eyes delved to the very essence of her soul, and when she nodded, he quietly said, "*I think you do.*" He paused, still gazing into her eyes as if he sought something more, something he had found lacking—an answer perhaps. "*You alone understand that the Indian and the paleface must work together.*" He spoke so softly that Catherine leaned forward, furrowing her brow as if it would help her hear him better. "*Only then can we give our people the best of both worlds— the new and the old.*" Running Bear gently tugged her hand. "*Come, Catherine, let me show you the forest. Let me introduce you to the beauty of my world.*"

They walked down flower-gilded pathways, by rivers that sparkled with clear, clean water. They watched birds flutter from tree to tree; they listened to their melodies. They watched squirrels scurry from limb to limb, deer grazing nearby.

"*All this the Grandfather has made, Catherine,*" Running Bear declared, his hands reverently touching the trunk of a tree. "*And he made it good. If we take care of it, it will take care of us. If we allow it life, it will give us life.*" The soft, ebony eyes continued to search Catherine's face. "*Do you understand?*"

She nodded, and again she wondered why he was looking at her so strangely, so deeply; she wondered at the sorrow she saw mirrored in his eyes.

"*I have spoken what the Grandfather placed in my heart, but that is not enough. Now I must take a long journey.*"

Catherine didn't understand. "*Let me go with you,*" she suggested eagerly.

Running Bear caught both her hands in his. "*I wish you*

could go with me, Catherine, but the path I must walk now is not wide enough for both of us." His grasp tightened, and as his obsidian eyes locked with hers, Running Bear seemed to flow into her. "You must stay, and you must teach our people to walk the path of peace together."

"No," Catherine cried. "That's your task. You're the peace chief." But even as she uttered the words, she knew that Running Bear was leaving. "You can't go," she screamed.

Without saying a word, Running Bear leaned nearer, touching his lips to her forehead in a sweet, tender gesture of farewell. Then, turning, he walked away.

"You can't leave me alone," Catherine called out desperately, her eyes misting with tears. Still he didn't stop or turn back. "What about your school?" she shouted, her voice wavering. "What about your people? Are you going to abandon them? Are you going to leave them without a peace chief?"

Now Running Bear stopped; he turned around. "The Coat of Peace is hard to wear, Catherine. It is easier to win the feathers of war; it's much easier and more glorious to walk the path of war than the one of peace." He ran his hand down the front of his jacket. "See. It's held together by tender threads that are easily broken and pulled apart." His hands grasped the hem of the garment, and he pulled it over his head. Bending, he laid it on the ground.

"What are you doing?" Catherine ran to the jacket. "How can you take it off and throw it down?" she asked accusingly.

Running Bear chuckled. "I'm not throwing it down, Catherine. This is the way the Creator wants it to be. You see, whoever wears the Coat of Peace must willingly pick it up and put it on."

"You're never coming back," Catherine whispered as she bent, her fingers reverently touching the soft buckskin.

"No," Running Bear replied.

39

Catherine lowered her head and gazed at the coat for a long time. Finally her fingers closed over the skin, and she picked it up. Tears streaked her cheeks. "Then—then I'll wear it." The words were defiant; they were accusing. "I'll walk the path of peace," she gulped, "and I'll guide our people."

Before she knew what was happening, Running Bear had slipped the coat over her head and had straightened it across her shoulders.

"Manitou will guide you, Catherine. He will show you where to go and tell you what to say." Running Bear lifted both hands and cupped her chin. "You will be the peace woman. You will teach our people to walk the path of peace." Without taking his eyes off her face, Running Bear backed away, a sad smile haunting his visage. At the forest's edge, he lifted his hand in farewell.

"No," Catherine screamed. "No, Running Bear. You can't leave me. Stay awhile longer and teach me to be a peace woman," she pleaded.

She wanted to run after him, but she couldn't. Her feet were too heavy; like a tree they seemed to be rooted to the spot.

"Don't leave me alone, Running Bear."

"You won't be alone, Catherine. Manitou will send a warrior to walk with you."

"I don't want a warrior," she cried. "I want you."

"And I want you, Catherine, but that is not the way it is to be. Each of us must walk a different path."

Slowly Running Bear faded into the forest, and Catherine stood in the clearing. She looked down at the Coat of Peace and ran her palms over it.

It felt different—it looked different. Her eyes widened with surprise.

Running Bear's coat had changed. It was no longer too big for her; it fit perfectly. Rather than being a man's buckskin shirt, it was a woman's robe. She walked to the river

40

and leaned over, looking at her reflection. Her hair was parted in the middle and hung in two thick braids over her shoulders.

And the robe—it was no longer Running Bear's coat. Now it was hers, and it was more beautiful than she could have imagined. It's white form-fitting bodice, softly molded her breasts, and its three-quarter-length sleeves billowed into graceful fringes. The garment was cinched around the waist by a wide belt, the full skirt softly swirling about her legs. Below it Catherine wore moccasins and leggings that were laced to her knees. Colorful quills, worked into an elaborate design, decorated all her garments.

She was a peace woman.

. . . Catherine awakened and sat on the edge of the bed. As the third generation first-born daughter, dreams and premonitions were not new to her, but this dream was different. Running Bear was dead; the thought frightened her. She knew her destiny was irrevocably bound to this new land and its people, but suddenly she felt alone—all alone. With a heavy heart, she moved to the window, unlatched the shutter, and threw it open. She welcomed the brisk autumn air that touched her flushed skin as she pondered the dream. Who would the warrior be?

Chapter II

Disconcerted by her dreams, Catherine was unable to go back to bed. She stood at the window for a long time, staring into the blackness. Finally at dawn, she decided to go to the river and bathe. Not wanting to awaken Ellen, she fumbled for her dressing gown, hastily pulling it over her nightshirt. In her hurry she tied only the ribbons at her waist as she slid her feet into the soft buckskin moccasins that Running Bear had given her. Tiptoeing through the cabin, she quietly closed the door and sped across the compound to her secret bower by the river.

A golden silhouette, Catherine stood on the shore, watching the newborn sunbeams as they ribboned across the horizon, casting their rich color on the rippling surface of the river. It seemed so peaceful and tranquil, she thought, looking at the water; yet its appearance was deceptive. It was treacherous, the Croatoans had warned them as they had pointed out safe areas for bathing and swimming. Still the river fascinated Catherine; she returned to it time and time again—when she wanted to be alone, when she wanted to daydream. Crossing her hands behind her back, Catherine closed her eyes and leaned against the gnarled trunk of a massive oak tree. Her thoughts again strayed to the strange dream.

She was a mass of contradictory emotions. When she thought about Running Bear's tender farewell, she wanted to cry. When she considered his admonition and charge, she was puzzled. How could she, a paleface and a woman at that, lead his people in peace? Yet at the thought of the beautiful robe, peace flowed through her entire being. Nonetheless, she shivered with fear when she remembered Running Bear's prophetic utterance. What had he meant when he'd said God would send a warrior to walk by her side? What did it all mean?

Then an ominous foreboding enveloped her; the silence hung too heavy. She opened her eyes as apprehension coldly ran along her spine. She felt the same presence she had sensed yesterday when she was bathing; eyes were on her again. *Someone was watching her!*

Frightened, she pushed away from the tree and hurried to the cabin, finally breaking into a full run. Her heart was beating loudly and wildly; it was pumping so hard her chest seemed about to burst. When she almost stumbled on a root, she lowered her head so she could watch where she was stepping, and she grabbed her skirt in both hands, lifting it up. She hadn't gone far, however, before she saw fringed buckskin leggings and two moccasined feet firmly planted in the sandy loam, blocking her way. Then she collided with the hard wall of a masculine chest.

Catherine's head jerked up. She opened her mouth to scream, but the Indian reacted more quickly then she. Laughing quietly, he covered her mouth so that only a muffled sound came out. Flailing her arms and grunting imprecations, Catherine twisted, trying to free herself from the fleshy prison, but the Indian easily subdued her.

"At least you have spirit," he growled in his own language, a glint of praise shining in the depths of his raven black eyes. To calm her he said in English, "Friend,

43

paleface woman. Friend."

At the familiar words, Catherine ceased fighting and stared at him, puzzled. Lapsing into his own language, a dialect which Catherine didn't understand, the Indian continued to talk to her, the husky timbre of his voice oddly soft and soothing. Eventually when her breathing returned to normal, when her eyes lost that wild, haunted look, he again said, "Friend." Then he slowly inched his hand from her mouth.

Catherine stumbled away from him. She wanted to scream, she wanted to run; but she did neither. Fear rooted her to the spot, yet it didn't stop her from looking. Never had she seen a man like this bronzed creature of the forest. It was hard for her to determine how old he was, but he was no callow youth. She would guess that he was at least thirty. He possessed a ruggedness and a strength that most of the men Catherine knew lacked, even her Indian friends. There was a primitiveness about him that she found frightening. His bearing and expression were harsh and uncompromising.

This brave didn't look like the Croatoans or the Roanoacs with whom Catherine was familiar. His shining black hair was parted in the middle and hung in two thick braids over his shoulders. His cinnamon skin, bronzed by the wind and the sun, was smooth, and he looked as if he had been sculpted from stone. His angular face was unyielding, the jut of his chin arrogant and determined. His cheeks were smooth with high, prominent bones, and his ebony eyes were shaded by a heavy fringe of blue-black lashes. But his lips, those firm, sensuous lips, compelled Catherine's attention.

Aware of her blatant perusal, Lone Wolf smiled and held out his hand, but Catherine didn't smile, nor did she take his hand. Instead, she whispered in a sandpapery voice, "Do—do you speak English?"

His expression never changed, and his large hand

44

remained extended, palm up. He didn't reply by word of mouth or by gesture. Because he didn't lie, he wouldn't tell her no. But he couldn't tell her the truth either. Because of the unrest in the Great Forest among the Scupperongacs, the Lumbroans, and the Iroquois, he didn't want her to know that he understood her language.

Probably he had spoken the only words he knew, Catherine thought fleetingly, remembering the fifteen men who had been left several years ago as caretakers of the colony. Evidently this Indian had come into contact with them and had learned a few words of English. She repeated her question in Running Bear's dialect.

Although Lone Wolf did not respond to her question, he was not surprised when she spoke the Algonkian dialect. He had heard about the Indians who had been living with the palefaces in the land over the water.

By this time Catherine had become too immersed in the man to think about the answer to her question. Fascinated by his masculine beauty, she lowered her eyes, visually tracing the column of his massive neck to his shoulders. Naked to the waist, he wore fringed buckskin leggings and moccasins, brightly decorated with quill embroidery; over his right shoulder hung a bearskin blanket which, during autumn and winter, was as much a part of his garb as his moccasins or breechclout. When forced to sleep on the trail, it served as his blanket. During the coldest months of winter, he used it as a robe.

Ordinarily, Catherine would have been interested in the stitching and design of the brave's buckskin clothes, but today she was too aware of this warrior's body. Never having been so close to the partially nude body of such a virile man, Catherine was totally enthralled by the beauty of this brave's physique. His smooth chest, adorned with several necklaces, rippled with muscles, whereas the soft fawn-colored buckskins contrasted with

45

the dark color of his skin and softened the harshness of his gaunt strength.

Lone Wolf, aware of Catherine's bemusement, moved closer to her with effortless grace, and Catherine, too preoccupied with her discovery of him as man, made no effort to ward him off. As he looked at her, he was inundated with emotions he had long thought dead, emotions that had seemed to die with his wife and son so many summers ago. More important, he was angry and disgusted because this paleface woman could elicit such a response from him, not the maiden whom he had finally chosen to be his second wife.

As he looked at Catherine, he felt an awakening of desire—a hunger he hadn't experienced in many summers. He would like to make this paleface his woman. Perhaps he would take her captive to share his lonely wigwam. Suddenly he felt more light-hearted than he had in a long time. He silently laughed as he came up with the answer to his problem. With such a one to share his sleeping platform, a loveless marriage could be endured.

Catherine hadn't moved nor did it enter her mind to call for help. For some inexplicable reason she knew the Indian meant her no bodily injury; and from the way he was returning her gaze, she sensed what he wanted. Tingling with the first poignant awareness of her womanhood, she responded to this Indian as she had never responded to a man before. His gaze touched her, compelling her to come nearer to him. His eyes, burning with interest, lingered on the gentle mounds of her breasts; then they slowly, pleasurably, moved upward till her gaze was locked to his.

Catherine couldn't help but be aware of his scrutiny, and she was painfully aware of his amusement. Not understanding what was happening to her, never having experienced passion in all her three and twenty years, Catherine felt her entire body tingle to life beneath his

46

heated gaze. Desire raced through her limbs. Embarrassed at her wantonness and afraid of the current of emotion that blazed through her, she wanted to lower her face, to break the visual bond, but those eyes, cold and calculating, caught and held her softer ones, refusing to let her go. She had no chance against the assault of his eyes.

"Your eyes remind me of the leaves in spring." He spoke softly in Scupperongac, his voice casting a spell over Catherine. Understanding the caressing softness of his tone and seeing the passionate persuasion in his eyes, she willingly allowed Lone Wolf to bewitch her.

Lone Wolf smiled, and Catherine watched with fascination as tiny friendly lines splintered from his eyes, as his lips curved into that special gesture which mirrored the amusement of his soul. As his smile turned into a low chuckle, jet-black eyes caressed her clear, creamy skin, slowly moving to the silken curtain of hair that hung loosely around her face. Catherine's auburn tresses were beautiful. They blazed fiery red in the rays of sunlight, reminding him of the forest in the fall.

"Your hair is the color of the autumn leaves." Lone Wolf's eyes lifted, and again he gazed into her face. "There is a fire that burns in the depth of these eyes, and there is courage there also." His hand rose, and his fingers gently touched her cheeks. "And I think I see more." He smiled, the gesture starting in his eyes and slowly moving to his mouth. "I think perhaps I see the small fires of desire." His voice lowered then. "And I am the one who shall fan them into a large blaze, my Autumn Woman." He chuckled. "I am the one who shall be warmed in that blaze."

Understanding full well Lone Wolf's intent and promise, Catherine's face fused with soft pleasure, causing desire to wing through the man's body. As his whole being was absorbed by her presence, so was she by

47

his. He lowered his arm, and his hand touched her breast, pushing her dressing gown and nightshirt aside. When his warm flesh touched her skin, Catherine reflexively jumped from his clasp, her eyes widening with apprehension.

"Don't be afraid," he murmured in his own tongue; then he added in English, "I'm your friend."

Catherine, forgetting to wonder at the ease with which he spoke English, was lulled into a false sense of security by his soft, placating words. Then when she least suspected it, his hand darted out and cupped her neck, dragging her closer to his body.

"Get your hands off me," she hissed, twisting and flailing in his arms.

When his clasp tightened, she cried out in pain and looked fearfully into his face. His eyes were flinty with purpose and resolve. He extended his other hand and ran it through her hair, his fingers tenderly, almost worshipfully, touching it and grazing her breast as he fondled the silken tresses.

"Let me go," she threatened defiantly, "or I'll scream and awaken the settlement. The soldiers will kill you."

Forgetting she had on moccasins, Catherine raised her leg and kicked the Indian's shin, the impact hurting her more than it did him. Oblivious of her futile attempts to free herself, the brave laughed at her frailty, but he was wise enough to clamp a hand over her mouth. Then he saw what he hadn't noticed before: the satin smoothness of her creamy skin compared to the bronzed tan of his. So different. So white. So delicate. He forgot her promise to cry out. He forgot everything but his fascination with her beauty.

Lone Wolf removed his hand from her mouth, and he ran his fingertip across the tiny splattering of freckles that teased the bridge of her nose where she had been kissed by the sun. He looked at the beautiful eyes,

48

sparkling with life, hinting at just a touch of apprehension, and his soul smiled compassionately as he saw the questions and the doubt in them. Then his lips curved sensuously as he saw the innocence.

Although Catherine knew convention demanded she should lower her head and tie the ribbons of her bodice to cover her nakedness, she did neither. Although she knew that propriety demanded modesty from her, she felt no immediate shame; she knew no embarrassment. Rather she felt as if she had met an integral part of herself. Somewhere in the periphery of her mind she knew that she had met her destiny. Proudly she lifted her head higher, jutting her chin a little more. And when she did, she automatically squared her shoulders, thrusting her breasts forward.

Masculine eyes slowly crept down Catherine's body, savoring all the beauty of her slender frame. He admired the creamy lines of her neck and the proud arch of her breasts that tapered into a small waistline. His hand traced a hot path of desire down her cheeks, down the slender column of her neck, across the collarbone. Catherine shivered at his touch, but she couldn't have—she wouldn't have—stopped him. She had been waiting for this touch all her life . . . all her life she had been waiting for this man!

She heard Running Bear's soft words, *"Manitou will send you a warrior,"* and she was caught up in a magical spell which defied man and time. She recognized her warrior. . . .

Catherine wasn't surprised when she and Lone Wolf moved that fraction of an inch that put them into one another's arms. She welcomed his touch this time, and she shivered when his lips came down on hers, tasting the virginal delicacy of her mouth.

Never having been kissed before, Catherine was lost to the swirling emotions which pulled her beneath their

49

current. When Lone Wolf's hand slid down the line of her back to curve around her buttocks, when his other hand touched her breast, Catherine sighed and melted in his arms. When his tongue stroked her lips, Catherine didn't know what he was asking or demanding, but she knew he was evoking an emotional response that would be her undoing. She had to fight this man!

Summoning her errant resistance, she clenched her teeth and she tensed in his embrace. But the brave was not to be put off. If he took no more, he had to have this small taste. His arms tightened around Catherine until she cried out, and his mouth slanted, pressing harder against hers. Still Catherine didn't open her lips. But her resistance wasn't all defiance. A novice at lovemaking, she had no idea he wanted her to open her lips; she didn't know how to respond.

Lone Wolf slid his thumb between their lips, gently prying her mouth open. Then when her mouth was filled with the moist warmth of his tongue, his lips moved softly over hers, burning her with the intensity of his passion. Her lower body, aware of its void, trembled with need. Her hands slowly crept up the muscled warmth of his chest, locking around the nape of his neck, and she pressed closer to him, her body aching with its emptiness.

One of his hands lowered, moving across her stomach, his fingers running underneath the dressing gown, singeing her skin through the thin material of her nightshirt. When he touched her maidenhood, Catherine tensed and would have pulled away from him again, but he murmured endearments in her ear. She relaxed, giving herself to the rhythm of his love strokes, the reflexive movement of her hips exciting him further.

Lone Wolf groaned low in his throat. Not since Morning Star had he wanted a woman as he wanted this paleface. His hand lifted, gently fisting around her auburn hair, and he pulled her head from his, breaking the kiss.

As quickly as their lovemaking had begun, it ended. The warrior, still holding her in the tight circle of his arms, lifted his head and looked about him. He had heard the soft faraway call—a summons Catherine didn't notice because it blended with the sounds of the birds that chirped about them. When he heard the call a second time, he whistled softly, a bird call cooing through his lips.

Catherine stared at him as she heard the coo, and the enormity of what she had done hit her. Burning with shame, she thrashed out wildly, pushing out of his relaxed arms. Patiently amused, the man stepped back, easily avoiding her flailing arms. He looked into Catherine's face—her lips swollen from kissing, her eyes passion glazed. Then he smiled tenderly, but he didn't fully release her; one hand still banded her wrist.

He thought of abducting her, of taking her with him. But as quickly as the thought entered his mind, he dismissed it. She would be in the way right now. He had a mission to perform—an important one that required speed and expediency. He needed to get to the tribes in the north, and he needed to talk with the Lumbroans before they and his people were walking the path of war. This woman would only slow him down. He smiled. In more than one way this captive would impede him.

Furthermore, he admitted, it would be unwise to anger the palefaces at this point. They had powerful weapons that thundered fire, weapons he must learn about before they engaged in battle. Until he knew more of them and their war strategies, these palefaces could be formidable enemies. He must learn their traits, their strengths and their weaknesses, before he dared incur their wrath.

Catherine twisted and squirmed, trying to free her hand from his clasp. Then, as suddenly as he had caught her, the brave turned her loose, and she stumbled

51

backward, falling against a tree. Leaning on the trunk and rubbing her wrist, she stared at the warrior who rested his hands on his hips, a pleased glint in the depths of his eyes. Under his steady gaze, Catherine slowly pulled her nightshirt to, and with fumbling fingers, she tied the laces of her dressing gown.

"Goodbye," he murmured in English, his voice blending with the song of the wind. He moved, lifted a hand, and grazed her cheek with the tips of his fingers. When he spoke again, he lapsed into his own language. "I want to take you with me, but I can't. I'll be back for you. I promise."

Her breath caught somewhere between her throat and her lungs, and Catherine could only manage a whisper. "What—what is your name?" She had to know; she couldn't let him leave without knowing something about him. Perhaps he knew enough English to understand the question—she prayed he did.

He smiled, but he didn't reply. He also wanted to know her name, but he didn't want her to know his. He pretended that he didn't understand her.

Catherine lifted her hands and signed as Running Bear had taught her, speaking first in English, then in the Algonkian dialect. "Catherine. I am called Catherine." She moved her hand, touching his chest. "What are you called?" Desperately she repeated. "Who are you? What is your name?"

Lone Wolf was delightfully surprised. Not only did she speak one of the many forest dialects, but she could sign as well. He chuckled, acting as if they were playing a game. Still he didn't let her know that he understood English. His fingers gently touched the smooth skin above her breast.

"Catherine." Liking the sound, he said it again. "Catherine."

She nodded excitedly. "That's right. I'm Catherine."

"Catherine," he murmured again, smiling at her exuberance. The name seemed to fit his autumn-haired woman.

Catherine glowed. "Yes," she cried, "that's right." A second time her fingers touched the sun-browned smoothness of his chest, and she spoke, signing at the same time. "Who . . . are . . . you?"

After what seemed an eternity, the Indian relented, speaking his name. "Lone Wolf." Then he added in his own language, "I am Lone Wolf, war werowance of the Scupperongacs."

"Lone Wolf," she repeated, and he nodded his head.

She looked him fully in the face. Never had Lone Wolf seen such beauty in all his life. Her eyes were sparkling like deep green pine needles that had been touched by the dew, and her lips were rosy from having been thoroughly kissed.

His fingers lifted a necklace of pearls and wolf fangs from his neck, and he gently circled Catherine's head with them. "I give you this. Forever you will know the Lone Wolf," he signed. The pleased murmur which he added was in his language for his ears alone. "Now you are mine."

Not understanding that the necklace was a brand of ownership, thinking it only a gift, Catherine smiled, lowering her head and watching as he smoothed the shining fangs and pearls over her breasts.

"Thank you," she whispered.

He never acknowledged her words in English; he continued to speak in the Scupperongac dialect. "Everyone who sees you will know that you belong to the Lone Wolf. No harm will come to you by my people." His voice softened, belying the gravity of his promise. "I shall kill anyone else who touches you."

He heard the bird coo again; it was closer this time. He knew he had to go, but he would be back. Quietly he

53

moved, making no noise that Catherine could hear. Softly he cooed, and out of the covey of trees behind him lumbered a large wolf, one of the most magnificent animals Catherine had ever seen. The huge beast's coat glistened silver and gold in the sunlight. Its ears were erect, its head high, its shoulders squared. As the wolf stood beside his master, its tawny eyes, watchful and alert, were targeted on Catherine.

When she finally tore her gaze from the animal and centered it on Lone Wolf, he was smiling—a special smile that made Catherine feel as if she were the only woman in the world for this particular man. He waved. Then he turned without another word, and both he and his wolf disappeared in the dense forest. For a long time Catherine stood, her eyes gazing into the woods, her fingers absently touching the wolf fangs—the only evidence of her meeting with the great war chief. Finally, however, she stirred and moved slowly toward camp.

As she walked, she tucked the necklace inside her nightshirt. If Ellen or any of the settlers were to see it, they would weary her with endless questions, questions for which she had no answers. So it was better that Lone Wolf remained her secret.

Several weeks had elapsed since Catherine had met Lone Wolf, but not a day passed that she didn't think about him. She remembered his shining black hair and his obsidian eyes; she remembered his strength. Even more, she remembered his tenderness and warmth. Hanging around her neck, safely concealed beneath her gown was the wolf-fang necklace. No one but Ellen knew she wore it, and even Ellen didn't know Lone Wolf had given it to her. In fact, Ellen had evinced no curiosity about the necklace at all. Since Catherine habitually traded her needlework to the Indian women for their goods, Ellen assumed Catherine had bartered for it.

"How much more mending do you have?" Ellen asked one morning as she and Catherine worked in the sitting room of their cottage.

"The laces on two petticoats," Catherine replied, pulling her thread through the two layers of material. "How's the broom coming?"

"Not bad, considering," Ellen returned, tying a bundle of straw to a broomstick.

But Ellen had time to say no more; the meeting house bell tolled. Stopping their work, the two women stared at each other for one spellbinding moment before they simultaneously stood, dropped what they were doing, and ran to the door.

"Maybe it's the men come home." But even as Ellen gasped the words, she knew the bells weren't tolling the safe return of the men.

"I don't know," Catherine returned, lifting her skirt with her hands so she could move faster. "We'll find out when we get there." Her words were lost in the noisy din of the gathering crowd. Following the settlers into the hall, Catherine and Ellen sat on benches near the entrance.

Catherine could tell immediately that the news wasn't auspicious. Ananias, wringing his hands, stood in front of the assembled group. Standing next to him was an Indian—one whom Catherine didn't immediately recognize. Grotesque painted designs distorted his features, making his visage harsh and cruel. His cockscomb was greased a vibrant red and thickened with deer bristles. Many feathers decorated his scalp lock. In his left hand, he clutched a bow, in his right a spear.

When Ananias finally quieted the crowd, he said, "We . . . uh"—he cleared his throat nervously—"we . . . have some unfortunate news." Ananias was not only nervous, he was frightened. "Wanchese, chief of the

Roanoacs, has—"

"Wanchese," several of the more militant settlers cried in unison, rising to their feet. "What's that murdering devil doing in this room?"

Ananias held out shaking hands to silence the uproar. "Wanchese's Indians have surrounded the settlement and have cut us off from the fort," he said, his voice getting shriller by the second. "Two . . . two of his braves are holding Eleanor and the baby as prisoners until Wanchese joins them."

"Unlike you palefaces we will not harm the woman and the child," Wanchese interrupted, elbowing past Ananias to stand in the center of the room. His stilted English sounded in every corner of the big hall. "As soon as I have spoken and have returned to my people, she will be released."

His eyes, cold and hard, moved across the sea of expectant faces. Several he recognized; they had been with the Lane colony. The others were strangers. He saw Catherine, and some of the harshness was smoothed from his countenance. He liked her. She was different from most of the paleface people whom he knew.

"This is the last time I come to you in peace," he announced. "And I do this for my friend the peace man who was killed ten suns ago."

A stunned silence fell over the group, the most militant wilting on the bench.

Catherine heard Wanchese say ten suns ago, but she heard no more. Ten nights ago she had dreamed about Running Bear. She had dreamed about him the night he had died. But even with her previous knowledge of Running Bear's death, Wanchese's announcement placed a large, heavy weight on her heart. She drew in a sharp breath, and the pain of confirmation speared through her body. Her heart was hurting so badly she could hardly get her breath. Her tears, shed more for herself than for Running Bear, were heavy; spasms of grief racked her body. Leaning closer to her, Ellen wrapped her arms around Catherine, trying to comfort her.

"What did you do with the body?" one of the settlers asked.

"I carried it back to our village, for burial," Wanchese answered. "That is what Running Bear would have wanted. Although he was staying with you, he was a Roanoac warrior, belonging to the Roanoac Confederacy, and he received a warrior's burial."

Catherine stood. "How could anyone kill him?" she cried. "He was a peace man."

"I do not know," Wanchese replied, touched by the woman's sincerity. He pulled the wolf-fang necklace out of his shirt, and he held it up. Because he knew Catherine cared for Running Bear, he said, "I found this necklace in Running Bear's hand. A pearl and wolf-fang necklace—the totem of Lone Wolf, the war chief of the Scupperongacs."

"Their . . . their war chief," Catherine gasped, her voice dropping to a hoarse whisper. Her hand automatically flew to her breast.

Wanchese dropped the fangs into the pouch. "All the forest people know the pearls are a token of authority and honor. They also know that wolf fangs are Lone Wolf's personal totem."

Catherine's fingers curled into the soft linen of her bodice, the heel of her hand pressing pearls into tender flesh.

"So"—a gloating voice from the back of the room, taunted—"an Indian killed him."

Wanchese's expression didn't change. "I do not know that an Indian killed him," he replied. "It could have been one of you. An Indian respects and honors the men of peace."

"How dare you," one of the settlers snarled, jumping to his feet. "How can you point a finger at us seeing how you killed Howe—"

"Don't speak to me about my crimes," Wanchese retorted, not a whit remorseful, "until you have repented of your own. You massacred our village, killing innocent women and children. And your John White came with flowery words of peace, but when Howe was killed, he didn't treat us as equals. Taking the word of a Croatoan, he decided that my followers and I were guilty of the murder. Highhandedly he demanded that we come to your settlement to discuss your terms of peace. When we didn't obey, you"—Wanchese's eyes touched the countenance of each person who was sitting under the sound of his voice—"you decided to punish all Indians by showing them who was in authority. Forewarned by a Croatoan, we deserted our village. But you had no idea that we were gone, so when you came with your arquebuses you marched in, firing and killing. You didn't care who you killed as long as you killed. Again you slaughtered innocents—this time your allies—Croatoan women and children who had slipped in to salvage food supplies that we had left behind." His words echoed into a heavy silence, and he dared them to refute his words.

Finally a man called out, "If you're not going to do something about Running Bear's death, we will. He was our friend."

"Aye," another chimed in. "Exactly what are you planning to do to find out who murdered Running Bear?"

"That is none of your concern," Wanchese replied. "I have informed you of Running Bear's death because he was your friend and he lived with you. I could do no less for my friend. But revenge for his death belongs to us, not to you. I have spoken. Now I will leave." Walking down the long aisle toward the front door, Wanchese said over his shoulder, "I will send your wife and baby back to you, Ananias, as soon as I have reached the safety of the forest."

Wanchese was hardly out of sight when a colonist bounded to his feet and thundered, "Let's kill that devil."

"No," Ananias countered, his voice unusually calm and controlled. "We cannot take any chances. Eleanor's life is in danger. Wanchese may be our enemy, but I must assume that he's a man of his word. If we allow him to return to his people unharmed, he will send Eleanor and Virginia back to me. Otherwise, I may never see them again."

Catherine didn't want to hear any more of their talk. She wanted to be by herself. Breaking out of Ellen's arms, she pushed to her feet and stumbled out of the building, making her way to the cabin. She unbuttoned her dress and pulled the necklace out of hiding. Running her fingers over the fangs, rolling her fingers around the pearls, she let her tears flow freely.

Was Lone Wolf the murderer? Had he killed her dearest friend?

Chapter III

"Do you want me to come in with you?" Ellen asked the next morning as she and Catherine stood in front of Running Bear's cabin.

"No," Catherine returned quietly, "I won't be long, and I'd like to be by myself."

She shoved the door open and stood in the shadows for a long time before she walked across the room to the window. As she unlatched the shutters and threw them open, letting the bright sunshine stream through the window, she thought about how much she and Running Bear had enjoyed being together. He had always been kind and gentle with her, never excluding her because she was a woman.

She had first met him in England when Master Harriot had engaged her to teach "three intelligent young Savages to read and write." Manteo and Running Bear had immediately liked Catherine, and their friendship had extended beyond the class room. Wanchese, however, was different. He had liked Catherine, and he had applied himself as a student, learning to speak and to write English, but his heart had been elsewhere, not in what he was doing. He had maintained a distance from anything even faintly English.

Soon Running Bear and Manteo were teaching Catherine the ways of the woodsman, and she readily learned them. Because she was an avid sportsman like Manteo and Running Bear, she joined in their fun, even when they got Sir Walter's permission to build a dugout. The braves showed her how to fell a tall tree and trim off the branches; then they rolled the log to the house. Once it was dried, the three of them removed the bark. Then they built a fire and lined burning embers along the top of a log.

As the wood charred, Manteo, Running Bear, and Catherine scraped it away and placed more burning embers on the log. In this way, they slowly hollowed out its center, making a deep, narrow canoe, long enough to accommodate two or three people. Then they covered the outside of the canoe with pine pitch to make it waterproof, and they laid blankets over the charred bottom. Finally, they whittled two paddles. In time Catherine became quite skillful in handling the dugout. And she and Running Bear spent many a happy hour canoeing up and down the river Thames.

They also enjoyed other games of skill. Catherine taught Running Bear to fence and to shoot the arquebus, and he taught her the art of throwing the spear and the tomahawk. Both of them already knew archery. When she outscored him, which she did on a few occasions, Running Bear could laugh about it. He admired and appreciated her skills.

As the days grew into months and the months into years, Catherine and Running Bear developed a deep bond of friendship—one that transcended any relationship Catherine had ever had with a man. When he admired one of her necklaces, a gold locket suspended on a chain, she gave it to him. Later when they were in London, she had his name engraved on the back of the case. As she clasped it around his neck, he promised her

61

that he would never take it off.

Now, turning away from the window, Catherine moved to the desk. She rubbed her fingers over the beautiful finish. Running Bear had been so proud of this piece of furniture. It had been a personal gift from Queen Elizabeth herself. She had been so pleased when she'd learned that Running Bear was going to educate his people that she had sent him the desk as a token of her approval.

Catherine looked at Running Bear's papers—so neat, so methodical. She ran her finger around the ink well; she touched the quill. She picked it up and looked at the dried ink on the frayed point. Sitting in the chair, she opened the small leather chest and spread his parchment out. With the tip of her finger she traced every letter that he had written. Running Bear's death she hadn't understood, but she had accepted. The death of his dream she couldn't accept.

Catherine unconsciously lifted her hand and touched the smooth pearls and the polished wolf fangs. Why hadn't she told the colonists about her meeting Lone Wolf? she wondered. Why hadn't she taken his necklace off? Because she didn't believe that he had done it! Because she didn't believe he would sacrifice his honor as a warrior to kill a peace chief!

She returned the pearls to their hiding place beneath the material of her bodice, and she stacked Running Bear's papers in the leather chest. Closing the lid, she latched it and tucked the box under her arm. Then she walked out of the cabin. As she stood in the open doorway, she turned, taking one last look, saying her farewell. Softly she spoke.

"I heard you speak the other night, Running Bear, and I'll do what I can to carry on your work. If no one else will do it, I'll teach your people myself. I'll see that your school becomes a reality."

Catherine took Running Bear's papers to her cabin and lovingly placed them in her trunk, carefully protecting them with layers of material. When Governor White returned and the settlers relocated on the Chesapeake, she would get Manteo to help her open a school.

During the coming days, Catherine performed her duties out of habit. When she wasn't thinking about Running Bear, she was thinking about Lone Wolf. Sometimes both of them were on her mind. The one brought peaceful, serene thoughts; the other turbulent, fiery remembrances. She couldn't forget Running Bear's warmth and gentleness; she couldn't forget his speaking to her in the dream. Yet Lone Wolf's touch and his smile haunted her. She remembered the passion he had awakened in her, thought of the day her heart had burst within her when she had heard Wanchese say he had found Lone Wolf's totem clutched tightly in Running Bear's fist.

One afternoon as she and Ellen mixed more daub for the town hall, Ellen finally tired of Catherine's preoccupation. "Kate," she exclaimed, pouring her bucket of water into the flat wooden trough, "You've got to come out of this. You haven't been yourself since Running Bear died. I have to repeat myself to you several times before you answer, and when you do, you don't reply to the question I've asked."

"I know, and I'm sorry," Catherine apologized. She stopped pushing the wooden shovel through the clay-and-straw mixture, and she leaned on the handle. "I guess I'm just tired, Ellen. We've been working long hours, getting the fort and houses ready for the winter." She sighed. "My arms and shoulders are hurting from mixing the daub."

Knowing Catherine didn't want to talk about Running Bear, Ellen nodded and flexed her shoulders. She, too, was getting tired. When she hadn't been filling cracks, she had been carrying water from the river or dragging saplings to the fort to repair the palisade. "Perhaps we should exchange tasks for a while?" she suggested, holding the bucket out. "You get the water, and I'll stir."

Exchanging the shovel for the bucket, Catherine walked toward the river where the women and children were working. Since Running Bear's death, none of the villagers had ventured away from the settlement alone, Catherine included. They feared the Roanoacs; they feared the Scupperongacs, and they knew they were being watched by one or both. Everyone walked about, casting fearful glances over his shoulder, looking backward more than forward, starting at every sound. Even now Catherine was peering anxiously about. When she noticed a slight movement, she stopped walking, turned, and stared. Involuntarily she cried out.

"Indians."

The women and children screamed and ran toward the fort. Catherine dropped the bucket she was carrying and lifted her skirt with both hands, moving as quickly as her feet would carry her, but she couldn't outrun the fleet-footed savage who burst from the cover of the trees. His arms darted out, one hand grabbing Catherine's coif which, tied around her neck, acted like a noose. As he yanked the kerchief from her head, the laces bit into Catherine's throat, choking off her screams. Letting go of her skirt, she lifted both hands and clawed frantically at her neck as she struggled to run, to jerk her neck out of his grasp, but her foot caught on a root and she fell to her knees. Her body was propelled forward, her neck arched, and her head snapped backward.

When Catherine looked into that strange face streaked and distorted with paint, when she saw the arm drawn back, the hand clutching a macelike war club, she screamed, throwing her hand over her mouth. This Indian was fierce, and he was painted for war. His

64

features were grotesquely colored, and his black eyes gleamed out of whitened sockets. His cockscomb was greased a vibrant red; his scalp lock was decked with feathers. When she heard the blood curdling yell that sprang from his lips, she shivered with fear and went into shock. She saw him, but she couldn't see him; she heard him, but she didn't hear him.

After he had gagged her with a piece of rawhide, the Indian's hand banded around Catherine's arm and he yanked his captive to her feet, jerking her behind him as he swiftly moved through the forest. He was walking so fast that Catherine couldn't keep up with him. She ran until she couldn't pick up her feet; then she fell to her knees, and he dragged her. When he tired of this, he gave her another yank, almost pulling her arms out of their sockets. Again she struggled to her feet, wondering how long she could endure such mistreatment.

Then Catherine got her second wind; she wasn't going to be that easily subdued. Although the forest was swimming around her, she dug her feet into the ground. She gulped deeply, filling her heaving chest with needed air. Then she anchored herself to the spot by wrapping her free arm around a small sapling before she pulled against the Indian. He stopped walking, and he turned, glaring at her. His eyes were black and fathomless; she could see nothing but hatred and contempt in their depths. He jerked on her arm; still Catherine wouldn't turn loose of the tree. Pulling back his free arm, he slapped Catherine across the face, and she staggered back, reeling from the blow. The sharp pain that started in her jaw made her nauseous. Tears washed her eyes, and a small trickle of blood ran down her chin.

Having thus crushed her resistance, the brave dragged Catherine through the forest, finally reaching the sound where another brave waited with the dugout. When the second Indian saw Catherine and her captor, he growled his disapproval.

"So this is what kept you, Red Fox?"

Quickly he raked the branches off the canoe and pushed it away from shore. Then he eased himself into the bow, putting his paddle in the water and resting it against the canoe.

"What will the palefaces do when they learn we have taken a captive?"

"That is my concern not yours, Strong Bow," Red Fox barked. The two men looked at each other for several moments before Strong Bow inclined his head in agreement and turned his back to his friend.

Red Fox pressed Catherine into the bottom of the canoe and laid his paddle in the stern. He gave the craft a powerful shove and jumped in. Holding on to the sides, he shifted his body, evenly distributing his weight, and as the canoe sailed smoothly away from shore, he picked up his paddle and with one powerful stroke turned the dugout toward the bay. Insensible to her surroundings, Catherine wasn't sure how far they traveled or how long. Hurting and exhausted, she lay quietly in the craft.

When they reached the mainland, Strong Bow and Red Fox carefully concealed the canoe. Then they parted. With a sinking heart Catherine watched Strong Bow disappear into the forest, leaving her alone with Red Fox. Moving in an opposite direction, Red Fox pulled her through the woods. Catherine's hair caught on the thick undergrowth and slowly uncoiled, tangling around her face and shoulders, and her clothes and flesh were torn by the bushes.

Hardly able to take another step, Catherine finally collapsed at the foot of a tree. She raised her hand and pushed her hair out of her face. Then she breathed raggedly, filling her hurting lungs. Roughly the Indian shoved her into a sitting position and tied her against the tree. By the time he was through, she couldn't move at all. Then his hand touched her chin, and he tilted her face up. His eyes fed lustfully on her features. Frightened but disgusted, Catherine jerked her head out of his clasp. Her eyes mirrored her hatred.

The brave laughed, doing nothing when she lowered her head so that she wouldn't have to look at him. Then something else caught his attention. He walked into the clearing, looked around, and cooed softly, the call blending into the sounds of the forest around them. Catherine watched him curiously, wondering what he was doing. She'd heard no unusual noises, seen nothing unusual. But Red Fox's ears were keener than Catherine's. He had heard the summons; now he heard the answer. In a few minutes two more Indians emerged from the thick woodlands.

Because Catherine was out of view, the newcomers didn't see her immediately, but when they did, she became the center of attention. They danced around her, snarling and growling, tormenting her with their fierce cries. Their raucous sounds of pleasure filled Catherine with fear. She wanted to cry, but she blinked back her tears. Remembering something her father had taught her long ago, she began silently to recite her favorite verse of poetry, saying it over and over again to herself. Sullenly she stared at her captors, refusing to let them know how deeply they were affecting her.

Finally the braves returned to the clearing. Sitting in a circle, they talked in low, hushed voices, and when the sun was setting, streaking the sky orange, purple, and red, and casting a golden shadow on the earth, a fourth Indian walked out of the forest. Catherine felt his presence at the same time that her captors did, but she didn't turn to look at him. He was just one more Indian to taunt and torment her.

Then she heard the voice; she recognized him. Lone Wolf! When she twisted her head, pain seared through

67

her body. She tried to spit the moistened rawhide out of her swollen mouth, but she couldn't. She tasted the blood where the thong that held it had cut into her tender flesh. She tried to squirm, but she was tied too securely to move; she couldn't even thrash her legs about to draw attention to herself.

She watched Lone Wolf shrug the bearskin blanket from his shoulder and let it drop to the ground. She watched as he and the Lumbroans went through their greetings, as they ate and later smoked the pipe. She heard their low voices; she heard their laughter. Finally she dropped her head, and tears ran unchecked down her cheeks. When her crying was over, Catherine sniffed and opened her eyes. She started, and her heart felt as if it were in her mouth. She was staring into the golden brown eyes of the wolf, inches away from hers. His teeth were bared. For the second time in one day, she instinctively voiced her fear, the garbled sound defying even the rawhide gag.

"What is it, Wolf Friend?" Lone Wolf called, standing and quietly moving to the tree where Catherine was bound. The wolf growled softly, low in his throat, but he never moved.

Lifting her tear-stained and bruised face, Catherine stared into Lone Wolf's visage. Although her eyes were filled with hatred and contempt, they also begged the Scupperongac warrior for help. The war chief evinced no emotion, nor did he show any sign of recognition. He knelt, hiding Catherine's body with his. Gently he touched the dried blood on her chin, he touched her swollen lips, he looked at the bruise which blackened one side of her face. But he said nothing. He lowered his gaze, and he looked for his necklace. When he didn't see it, he unbuttoned her dress, roughly pulling the material aside. When he saw his wolf fangs, his obsidian eyes once again touched hers. He didn't speak a word, yet his eyes spoke volumes.

Catherine could see the triumph that glittered in their black depths, and she wished she had ripped it from around her neck the day Wanchese had told her about Running Bear's death. Lone Wolf buttoned her dress and sprung to his feet. Turning swiftly, he looked Catherine's captor in the face.

Speaking in the Lumbroan dialect, Lone Wolf asked, "What are you doing with the paleface, Red Fox?" The dead calm of his voice warned Red Fox of his anger. "Do you not realize how important our mission is?"

"I know how important it is," Red Fox responded defiantly. "But she is my captive, and I am taking her back to my village."

"No," Lone Wolf barked softly, his fingers smoothing the ruff at Wolf Friend's neck, "you're not. You're going to take her back to her people." Red Fox shook his head. "Once the palefaces find she is gone, they will be angry; they will go to war." Lone Wolf looked at the Lumbroan earnestly. "We are not ready for that yet, Red Fox."

Perhaps you're not, Red Fox thought, but we are. However, he said nothing. Instead he looked at the Scupperongac war chief; carefully he measured him. "We are not afraid of the people who come from over the water. Our magic is stronger than theirs."

"Give her to me and let me take her back to her people."

Red Fox laughed. "Could it be, Lone Wolf, that you desire this woman also, that you want her for yourself? What will you do to her on the path back to the paleface village?"

"We have been acquainted many summers, Red Fox," Lone Wolf said, ignoring the taunt. "We have been warriors together, fighting the Five Nations. Let no woman come between us or our people."

Knowing Lone Wolf's prowess as a warrior, Red Fox had no desire to fight him. On the other hand, he wanted the paleface. Even when he tired of her, she would be

69

valuable for bartering.

"You are the one letting the woman come between us," Red Fox countered. "According to our laws, my brother, the captive belongs to the captor."

"I have already claimed the paleface."

"If she is yours," Red Fox asked, "where did you find her and why do you not have her with you?"

"I found her many suns ago by the river that flows by the paleface's village," Lone Wolf said, his eyes never leaving Red Fox's face. "I claimed her then. I left her because I have important business to attend."

"I do not believe you," Red Fox snarled, forgetting the peace mission.

"You are saying that I speak not the truth," Lone Wolf returned, his voice softly challenging. "She wears my totem. Let me show you." He knelt beside Catherine and pushed the material aside to reveal his necklace. Looking up, he smiled his triumph. "She is mine, Red Fox."

Recognizing Lone Wolf's totem, the other two Indians grunted their approval, but Red Fox couldn't give Catherine up this easily. When Lone Wolf ungagged her, Red Fox said, "Leave her alone, Lone Wolf. I am not going to let you have her."

Lithely Lone Wolf sprang to his feet, turning to face Red Fox. "With your accusation you have severed the tie of friendship between us, Red Fox. Now your stubbornness is going to sever the tie between the Lumbroans and the Scupperongacs. Surely you are not going to let a paleface further separate our people, possibly cause us to walk against each other on the path of war. Can you not see this is what the Five Nations and the palefaces want—one Algonkian tribe to war against the other?"

His lust obscuring his reason, Red Fox refused to hear the truth of Lone Wolf's words. "I want the woman, and I shall have her. You may have placed your wolf fangs around her neck," Red Fox taunted, "but you were not warrior enough to take her captive. You left her for me,

Lone Wolf. I took her, so she belongs to me."

"You are speaking foolishly, Red Fox. You have shamed your people and the Grandfather. You have made many charges against Lone Wolf, war chief of the Scupperongacs. You have forgotten that your duty is to your people, and you have laid your honor aside because of the lust you feel in your body for the paleface."

Red Fox lifted his right hand, holding his spear above his head for a breath-stopping minute. Then he threw it, the flint blade slicing into the ground, the shaft vibrating the challenge. The other three Indians never took their eyes off the weapon. Mortal combat it declared. Wide-eyed, Catherine watched all that was going on. Although she had never witnessed such a challenge before, she knew what it meant. From the few words she had understood, words that were similar to the Roanoac she had learned from Running Bear, and from the anger which emanated from both men, Catherine knew they were going to fight for her.

"Are you sure this is what you want?" Lone Wolf asked. He did not fear Red Fox, though he reckoned him a valiant warrior, but peace between their tribes was tenuous and Lone Wolf knew the death of either of them would mean war. Once again the attempt for an Algonkian confederacy would be foiled.

"I am sure." Red Fox looked at his spear. "Are you going to accept the challenge, Lone Wolf? Or are you a coward? Are you afraid to fight me in an honorable duel to see who will get the paleface?"

Though his expression never changed, Lone Wolf's heart sank. Wise One, the peace chief of the Scupperongacs, believed in Lone Wolf's magic, and he had trusted him to carry out this mission. Wise One had a vision of the Algonkian tribes uniting for the betterment of their people. With the coming of the palefaces, Wise One desired such a union even more. He believed that it was up to the Lumbroans and the Scupperongacs, long time

71

enemies, to end the warring between their tribes and to start walking down the road of peace. Because of his valor, his reputation, and his swiftness on foot, Lone Wolf had been chosen as the ambassador for the Scupperongacs.

Red Fox broke the silence that stretched between them. "Perhaps the songs and dances celebrated in honor of your valor, Lone Wolf, are a thing of the past. Perhaps you are getting too soft to be a war chief. Perhaps you are becoming fond of the palefaces." His taunts were brazen.

Lone Wolf's hand circled the shank of Red Fox's spear; he pulled it out of the ground. Raising his leg and bending his knee, he broke the weapon and tossed it at Red Fox's feet.

"So be it!"

Red Fox and Lone Wolf motioned one of the other Indians to tie their left wrists together. In his right hand each brave grasped the hilt of a knife, and at a whoop from one of the Lumbroans, they began to circle, their hands lowering as they fended off each other's blows.

The two men shuffled in a circle, slashing then jumping to avoid the deadly blades. Their blood curdling battle calls sent shivers of fear down Catherine's spine. Sweat beaded on their brows, and their wrists bled, the raw flesh swelling as they pulled against the bonds. Lone Wolf, the more agile and the swifter of the two, slashed deep crisscross cuts on the Lumbroan's chest. Red Fox, the heavier of the two, knew he couldn't outmaneuver Lone Wolf as long as they were standing. In order for his weight to aid him, Red Fox had to get the Scupperongac on the ground.

With a forceful lunge, Red Fox hit Lone Wolf's arm, knocking his knife out of his hand. At the same time, Red Fox kicked Lone Wolf from behind, throwing him off balance. As Lone Wolf buckled, Red Fox brought his knee up, smashing the Scupperongac warrior in the face, cutting his lips and causing blood to run from his nose. To keep from screaming out, Catherine bit her lower lip until it bled.

Red Fox, taking advantage of his opportunity, used his weight to throw Lone Wolf on his back. Breathing deeply from the exertion, the Lumbroan pushed Lone Wolf's left hand to the ground, and he lay over him. Holding his right arm up, his hand a tight fist around the hilt of the knife, Red Fox made that final lunge, going straight for Lone Wolf's heart. But Lone Wolf swung his legs into the air, ankles first, levering his torso up, and he flipped Red Fox aside. Quickly Lone Wolf jumped to his feet, wiping the blood and dirt out of his eyes.

With a growl, Red Fox lumbered to his feet. Concentrating all his strength in his left, he pulled Lone Wolf close to him. The Lumbroan's blade found its mark, cutting the Scupperongac warrior deeply under the ribs. Grunting his pleasure, Red Fox pulled his arm back, again aiming for the death blow. Exerting all his strength, Lone Wolf lifted his leg, bent it, and jabbed his knee into Red Fox's stomach. When Red Fox doubled over, Lone Wolf, using the side of his hand, hit his opponent across the back, knocking him to the ground.

While Red Fox was dazed by these blows, Lone Wolf made a desperate sweep for his knife, but Red Fox rallied. Rolling over, he stabbed Lone Wolf in the lower thigh. The war chief of the Scupperongacs grimaced with pain, and his body momentarily tensed. His outstretched hand, palm down, closed, digging up a handful of soil. Catherine's eyes widened with fear, and her breath caught in her chest. Dear Father, she prayed, don't let him die.

With a quick movement Lone Wolf raised his hand and flung sand into Red Fox's eyes. Although blinded, Red Fox brought his powerful hand down over Lone

73

Wolf's stomach, but the Scupperongac's fingers closed around the Lumbroan's wrist. Nevertheless, Red Fox outmaneuvered Lone Wolf; he pushed him back and fell on top of him.

Their battle cries ceased as both men collapsed in the dirt. The whoops turned into ragged grunts. Catherine strained against the cords that bound her to the tree, but all she could see was the prone body of Red Fox. Neither combatant moved; none of the onlookers moved. Then Red Fox, using his right hand, pushed up, one last death-defying cry wailing from his lips.

"No," Catherine screamed. "Dear God, no!"

Red Fox looked at her, his face ugly and fierce. His wild eyes raked her body, and his lips twisted in a leering smile. Then he fell. After what seemed to be an eternity, Lone Wolf slowly moved from under his lifeless body, rolling it over. Blood dribbled from Red Fox's mouth, and the knife protruded from his sternum. Lone Wolf pushed to his knees, spitting out blood, heaving deep gulps of air into his lungs. Finally he reached for his knife and cut himself loose from the dead brave. He stood, looking down at Red Fox.

"Take him and go." He spoke to the Lumbroans in a quiet, emotionless voice. "Tell your chief and your council the truth. Werowance Wise One and I will meet with them soon."

Lone Wolf walked to the tree and knelt, cutting the cords that bound Catherine. He lifted his hand and wiped the blood from his nose and the corner of his mouth. His eyes were hooded; his visage set. He sprung to his feet and watched as Catherine stiffly moved her arms and tried to stand on legs that were numb from impeded circulation. He offered her no help. Catherine stared at his impassive face.

She signed. "What are you going to do with me?"

He didn't answer her; he just continued to stare.

Nervously she began to finger-comb the tangles out of her hair. He hadn't hurt her before. Perhaps he wouldn't now.

Again she signed. "Take me home."

Lone Wolf stared at her, never uttering a word, his expression never changing. Thinking perhaps he hadn't understood her, Catherine bent and picked up a stick. She began to draw the picture of the settlement in the sand. Looking up at him, she pointed to one of the cabins; then she pointed to herself.

"My home."

With his foot, Lone Wolf rubbed the drawing away. Nothing was left but the smooth surface of the white sand. Squatting beside her, he took the twig from her hand and drew a picture of his village.

"Home," he said in English, pointing to one of the wigwams. "My home." He looked at her. "Our home."

He dropped the twig, and his fingers curled around the wolf-fang necklace that circled her neck, pulling upon it until her face was almost touching his. Softly he began to speak to her in his own tongue.

"I left you the other day because I had business to attend, but now that is over. I've fought and killed a brave because of you, and I have ruined the peace talks between the Lumbroans and the Scupperongacs. Because of you I have placed my warriors in a position to be killed; I have failed as a war chief. I have left the path open so the Iroquois can come in the spring and summer to loot, to murder, and to take our young men, our women and our children. Had I taken you when I first claimed you, none of this would have happened."

He paused, looking into those green eyes that reflected her fear. "I promise you this won't happen again because I'm taking you to my wigwam now." He pointed to his drawing once again and again said in English, "Home."

"No," Catherine cried, shaking her head.

75

Lone Wolf's hand clamped around her upper arm, and he jerked Catherine to her feet. Dragging her behind him, he walked across the clearing, stopping only long enough to pick up his blanket and to sling it over his shoulder.

"I don't want to go to your home," she cried. "I want to go to mine."

Lone Wolf was oblivious to her pleas. For hours, it seemed to Catherine, they silently walked through the forest. Finally he stopped, shoved Catherine to the ground, and built a fire. Then he walked to the river, and when he returned, he had discarded his leggings and was wearing only his breechclout. Sitting across the fire from him, eating the corn meal that he'd given her, Catherine saw the swollen, proud flesh of his left wrist; she saw the angry gash across his chest; she looked at the inflamed wounds under his ribs and on his lower thigh. Although he had daubed a concoction on them, Catherine visually traced the red marks that streaked his leg.

He gave no indication of pain or discomfort, but Catherine knew he was suffering. Even in the firelight she could see the dullness in his eyes; she could see the flush of fever as it crept into his face. She had been aware of his flagging steps as they'd walked. Eventually he stood and moved out of the circle of light, returning with handful after handful of pine needles which he used to make a mattress. Covering the pallet with his bearskin blanket he extended his hand, motioning Catherine to join him.

Swallowing the fear that knotted in her throat, Catherine shook her head. Lone Wolf growled his irritation. He moved suddenly, the action jarring his pain-racked body as his hand caught hers and he dragged her around the fire to the bed. He shoved her down first; then he stretched on his back beside her. Trembling, Catherine lay there, wondering what was going to happen. Finally, however, Lone Wolf dropped into a

76

fevered sleep, fitfully turning during the night.

But Catherine could not sleep. During the night, she got up and put more wood on the fire, and finally she touched Lone Wolf's brow with the tips of her fingers. He was burning up with fever. She lifted her gown and ripped her underskirt into strips. Then she scooted down the pallet of needles. Just as she was about to stand, however, Wolf Friend began to growl low in his throat.

Catherine's heart beat faster than it ever had, and she gulped. "Wolf," she whispered, "one of you has to use good judgment. Your master can't, so it's up to you." Speaking softly to the animal, she eased herself to her feet and walked away.

Her first inclination was to run—run as fast as her feet would carry her—run to freedom—escape this savage. But she couldn't leave him; she couldn't let him die. After all, he had saved her from Red Fox. So she spent the rest of the night placing cool compresses on Lone Wolf's face. At dawn she washed his wounds and noticed that the red streaks were receding. Later his fever broke, and he lapsed into a more peaceful sleep. By afternoon she knew that he was going to be all right, and she knew it was time to leave. Her fingers curved around Lone Wolf's necklace. She hesitated for a fraction of a second; then she pulled it over her head and dropped it beside him.

After she changed the compresses on Lone Wolf's forehead a last time, she stood, looking down at him. Then she slowly backed away. He was in no condition to stop her now. Wolf Friend growled and would have stopped her, but in his sleep Lone Wolf threw out his hand and touched the wolf on his head. Wolf Friend lay down beside his master and watched as Catherine disappeared into the woods.

"It's all right, Wolf Friend," Lone Wolf murmured, one hand petting the wolf, the other closing around the necklace. "The autumn-haired one is stubborn. She

77

doesn't yet understand that she belongs to Lone Wolf." He chuckled softly. "She will be back soon if she does not kill herself first."

Lone Wolf lay quietly for a long time before he rolled over and pressed his ear to the ground. "We have company, my friend," he muttered to Wolf Friend as he weakly pushed himself to his feet, "and I'm not sure if it is friend or foe." Quickly he slung his quiver and bow over his shoulder; then, always protective of the forest, he squatted beside the fire, dousing the blaze thoroughly. He stood, scattering the pine needle mattress with his feet, and folding the blanket over his arm, he moved into the shelter of the forest, the wolf at his heels.

Because they had stopped to sleep not far from the place where Strong Bow and Red Fox had hidden their canoe, it didn't take Catherine long to find the craft. Although it was larger than the one she had been taught to use, she felt confident that she could handle it. Tucking the skirts of her gown and her petticoats around her waist and slipping out of her shoes, Catherine dropped them onto the bottom of the dugout.

Feeling as if she were being watched, Catherine threw her head over her shoulder and looked one last time into the mainland forest. She saw no suspicious movement, and she felt no alarm. Saying a silent goodbye, she picked up the double-bladed paddle and laid it in the stern. Then she gave the dugout a shove and jumped in, holding on to the sides until she evenly balanced her weight. This done, she picked up the paddle, and with a remembered, practiced stroke, she propelled the smooth-sailing vessel toward Roanoke Island.

A lone figure, hidden by the forest, silently watched the paleface as she paddled away. He would have given chase, but he had no canoe. Smiling inwardly, he trotted more deeply into the forest, headed toward the Northland. He would return.

78

Chapter IV

Catherine sat up in bed, clutching the sheet under her chin with trembling hands. Closing her eyes, she leaned against the wall. She breathed deeply, trying to still the erratic pounding of her heart. She unclenched a fist and wiped the thin sheen of perspiration from her face.

Rousing, Ellen mumbled sleepily, "Is anything wrong, Kate?"

"No, dear," Catherine said. "Go back to sleep. Everything's fine."

But that was a lie. Everything wasn't fine.

Nothing had been the same for Catherine since she'd returned to the settlement two days ago. She hadn't lied, but she hadn't told them the whole story either, not even Ellen. Catherine's ordeal was something she didn't like to remember, and she wasn't going to talk about it. Deeply imprinted on her mind's eye was Red Fox's contorted face just before he'd collapsed in the last spasm of death, blood gurgling from his twisted mouth, the flint knife jutting out of his chest. And every night since she had left Lone Wolf, she had been plagued by the same nightmare, forced to relive the horror of that awful day, awakening to terrible war whoops every night.

Drenched in perspiration, she dropped her tear-streaked face into her hands. Her shoulders shook as she silently cried out the misery of her soul. Not only was she contending with horrible dreams, she was struggling with her conscience, wondering how Lone Wolf was, wondering if he had recovered from his wounds. Finally spent from crying and chilled, Catherine lay down again, snuggling under the covers to eagerly await the morning. She never escaped that nightmare, but daylight lessened its horror. When the first rays of light peeked through the cracks in the shutters, she slipped out of the bed and called Ellen. Quickly they built a fire and bathed.

They hardly had gotten dressed before a booming knock sounded on the door and echoed through the sitting room. Neither woman had time to move before the door flew open, and Will Dare came bounding in. Wasting no time on etiquette or social graces, he strode across the floor, and meeting Ellen in the doorway between the two rooms, he enveloped the petite woman in his arms and cradled her to his massive frame.

In the short time Will Dare had dwelt in the new land, he had dropped the lifestyle of the European courtier. He wore a white linen shirt, fringed buckskin leggings, and a pair of leather boots that reached to his knees. The linen material that stretched across his shoulders was damp with perspiration, and his collar was open, revealing a vee of crisp dark hair.

He was tall and lean, almost a savage himself with his thick black hair and his raven-colored eyes which flashed with arrogance and a zest for life. His whipcord body was in excellent condition, sinewy and muscular. During his twenty-five years, his eyes and his hair had caught many a maiden's eyes, and the handsome, witty Will Dare had not been averse to such attention. In turn he had caught the maidens, giving them no more than a quick tumble in bed. Aye, he was a scoundrel and a rake.

"Dear God! Sweet Ellen, I didn't think I should live to

see you again."

He lowered his head and unmindful of the amused older sister, his lips for the first time touched Ellen's. But it wasn't a deep, lingering kiss. Rather, he fluttered quick butterfly kisses all over the young woman's small face, ending on the tip of her upturned nose.

"Oh, Will!" Ellen was so overjoyed at his safe return that her voice quivered. "I'm so glad that you're home."

"And so am I for what it's worth," Catherine softly added, watching the happy reunion.

"I was so frightened. I thought something had happened to you," Ellen cried, pushing as far away from him as the circle of his arms would allow. Her eyes touched every inch of his face, then swept down his body to make sure he was all right.

"Not hardly." Will laughed.

"Did you hear about Running Bear, Will?"

"Aye," he said. "Communication in the Great Forest is quick. A runner reached us not long after it happened."

"And Catherine," Ellen cried, "did you hear about her? Did the Lumbroans send a runner to tell you that she had been captured?" Will shook his head, his dark eyes darting to the older Graystone. "They captured her, Will, but they couldn't hold her. She managed to escape."

Will looked at the fading bruises and cuts on Catherine's face. "Did they hurt you?" His question implied more than mere physical abrasions.

Catherine shook her head. "No."

"What happened?"

Catherine swallowed. In a low voice, she succinctly described her capture and her subsequent release. Not once did she mention Lone Wolf's name.

Satisfied that he would get no more from her, Will lowered his gaze, his eyes now centering on Ellen's sweet

81

face. "As much as I want to stay and"—he winked at her, smiling at the sudden rush of color in her cheeks—"talk, I can't."

The bell tolled through the small settlement, its clang ominous and heavy.

"A meeting." Ellen sighed dully. Inadvertently she looked out the window. "Ananias is calling another meeting!" Turning her head back to Will, she cried, "Oh, merciful God, Will, we've had so many of these the past few days. And now something else is wrong."

"Aye," Will answered, "but I don't have time to explain. I need to talk with Ananias before the crowd arrives." Pushing her away, he looked over her head at Catherine. "The two of you get there as quickly as you can."

His boots snapped as they hit the wooden floor, and the door thudded closed. Will was gone, leaving the woman alone to face new worries and concerns. Hurriedly they ate a bit of dried meat, and soon they were walking toward the large building in the center of the compound. As they joined the gathering crowd, Catherine nodded and smiled, exchanging the usual greetings, but she sensed an air of preoccupation. No one was really seeing or hearing the others; rather, everyone was wondering what had prompted the unannounced call for yet another assembly. When Catherine entered the building, she headed to where Eleanor sat.

"Have you talked with Will yet?" she asked in an undertone.

Eleanor shook her head. "Nay. As soon as he and Manteo returned, he stormed into the house, demanding to speak with Ananias. The two of them closed themselves in the study and talked; then they rushed to the hall." She lifted large, soulful eyes to Catherine. "You know men and their secrecy."

Catherine's gaze shifted to Ananias who stood in the

center of the room, facing the solemn assembly. His eyes flitted over the crowd resting on no one in particular, and he nervously plucked at his breeches with his fingers. Finally he sighed and pressed his trembling hands on the table to keep others from seeing his fear. He was too weak a man to cope with the enormity of such a situation. First Running Bear. But the consequences of the Indian's death hadn't fallen on his shoulders. The Croatoans and the Roanoacs were handling that. *Now this!* There was no way he could evade this, Ananias agonized. His gaze fell on the man who sat in the front row. If only he hadn't listened to Tom. . . .

When Will entered the building and saw Ananias' emotional state, he immediately joined his brother. He spoke softly but bitterly. "Under the circumstances, Ananias, I think perhaps it would be better if I conducted the meeting." Thankfully Ananias nodded his head and collapsed onto the nearest chair. Lifting his shaking hands, he wiped the perspiration from his face.

With a snort of disgust at his brother's reaction, Will turned to address the settlers. "As all of you know, we left here several weeks ago in the hope of bartering with the mainland Indians for enough food to last us until Governor White returns from England. We didn't have much success, however, because the Lumbroans are exacting food tribute from the smaller tribes in the surrounding area. After we managed to trade for some provisions, Manteo and I decided to travel farther inland. We also decided that it would be best for some of the men to return to the settlement in case hostile Indians attacked."

Will couldn't keep his cold, ebony eyes from the fidgeting man in the front row or from his brother's bowed head. "But Tom persuaded Ananias to let him and several others explore on their own. Ananias and Miles came on to the compound, but Tom and his group

83

traveled southward for several days, finally taking refuge in a small, friendly village. The next morning as Tom and his men were paddling away, they spotted movement on the banks. Without investigating, Tom fired his arquebus, killing an Indian woman who had come to the river to get clay for her potting." Will paused long enough for his words to sink in.

"Never having seen or heard firearms before, the frightened Indians fled to another larger village for protection. Taking advantage of the Indians' absence, our men looted the village, taking all the food they could find. Then they burned the wigwams to the ground, without even bothering to move the body of the dead woman. As they traveled up the river," Will continued in an impassive voice, "the Indians regrouped and ambushed them, killing Spencer and Butcher. Tom managed to escape."

Will's eyes earnestly scanned the group, slowly moving from one face to the other. "Evidently we haven't learned anything from the military operation Lane carried out two years ago. In order to survive in this land, we've got to live in peace with the Indians." The colonists murmured their disagreement until Will raised his voice. "When Manteo learned that the Scupperongacs were seeking retribution, I took matters into my own hands. I traveled to Scupperong, their tribal seat, and as the spokesman for the colony I placed us at their mercy."

"You had no right to do that," one of the men yelled out indignantly. "Indians ain't nothing more than savages. In the absence of Governor White, Ananias is our spokesman. Furthermore, one of them uncivilized beasts murdered Running Bear."

"If I hadn't done it, Hayman," Will growled, "there would have been no need for a spokesman at all. Our colony would have been wiped out before it began."

"So what are the savages gonna do?" someone else called.

Standing, legs straddled and hands on hips, Will said, "The woman who was killed was to have been the second wife of one of the chiefs of the Scupperongacs. As strange as it may seem his first wife and son were murdered also." Will waited for the importance of his words to sink in before he spoke again. "For savages," he said dryly, "the Scupperongacs have a fair system of justice. They informed me that according to their laws they may either demand a life be given for the one taken—they may demand a death for a death—or they may levy a fine against the guilty party."

A sigh of relief seemed to flow through the assembly, and all of them visibly relaxed, several saying simultaneously, "Levying a fine don't sound none too bad, Ananias."

"No," Will agreed in weary tones, "that's a wonderful alternative, and it's the one they seem to be leaning toward. However, the council is vacillating between levying a fine and demanding a captive."

All eyes turned and centered on Tom who jumped to his feet, his gaze locked on the acting governor's face. "You can't let 'em take me, Ananias," he shouted in a high, shrill voice, his thin face gaunt, his hands shaking with fear. "After all, you gave me permission to go, so you can't turn me over to those savages. They'll kill me."

Although Tom addressed Ananias, Will answered. "Is that any worse than what you've done, Thomas? You killed an innocent Indian woman needlessly, turning the wrath of these Indians against us. It's not enough that we must worry about the Roanoacs and the Lumbroans. Now we must worry about the Scupperongacs."

Tom's blue eyes turned pearly, and his voice was no more than a growl, his words a testimony to his cowardice

85

and inhumanness. "She wasn't nothing but a savage, Will. Consider her just one more dead savage. One less to worry about. Furthermore, how was I to know that it were a woman. She were hiding in them bushes."

"You didn't take time to see what or who it was," Will barked. "You were too all-fired ready to kill."

John Carpenter rose to his feet, pointing a gnarled hand at Tom Small. "I'm not of a mind to turn you over to them savages, Tom, but look what you've done." His arm waved across the small crowd. "If'n they don't decide to fine us, there's not hardly enough of us to put up a fight of any sorts. Them Scupperongacs are one of the most powerful tribes here." He looked at his wife who sat quietly on the bench beside him. "Why didn't you consider the womenfolk?"

"The Scupperongacs wouldn't have Tom anyway!"

Will's blistering words echoed through the room like the rap of a judgment gavel, hushing the argument but opening a flood gate of questions. The hall was filled with the hiss of murmured confusion. Each person turned to those seated nearby. Everyone was whispering, no one was listening. Will held his hands up, and he motioned for both men to be seated.

"Under no condition do they want the man who killed the woman because they consider him to be a coward. According to them a coward isn't good for anything—not as a captive, not even for torturing." The colonists waited with bated breath for Will to continue. "If they take a life, they want us to replace the Indian woman with one of ours."

"One of our women! A white woman to go to those savages!" Incredulous cries came from all corners of the room.

As if they had not spoken, Will continued, "She will become the property of the chief."

"No, Ananias," Dyonis Harvie shouted, his fists clenched at his sides, his face ashen with anger and fear.

86

The bench grated against the floor as he leaped to his feet. "You can't let Will make this decision for us. We can't let them have one of our women." His gray eyes lowered, and he looked at his wife, Margery, and at the month-old son she held in her arms. Hatred gleaming in his eyes, he then looked at Tom Small. "I could kill you with my bare hands, Tom Small." His snarled threat echoed the thoughts of all the colonists.

"I don't think any of you married men has to worry at this time." Will's deep, husky voice flowed through the large hall. "According to Manteo, the Indians never indiscriminately take married women captives except in cases of open warfare. Since we have admitted our crime and have honored their laws and customs, the Indians will do the same for us. If they should decide to choose a maiden, they will select from the unmarried ones. However," Will's voice grew louder and firmer, "I don't believe the Indians want a captive. At the moment they would rather have tools and weapons."

Catherine pushed the bench back, stood, and spoke, her voice unusually low and quiet. "But there is that chance that the Indians might want a woman?"

Will nodded and answered. "There is."

"What will happen to the woman if the Scupperongacs should happen to choose her?"

The question hung in the air. Because only Manteo could answer, all eyes centered on him. His gaze moved across the assembly, but his eyes were enigmatic, his emotions carefully and deliberately hidden. He spoke slowly in crisp, concise English that merely hinted at his Indian heritage.

"Women captives are well treated by the Scupperongacs, and if the one who is chosen pleases her owner, she will be adopted into his tribe. She will be given a name and fill the place of the maiden who was killed by Tom Small."

"What does that mean?" Catherine asked.

"According to Indian custom this adoption brings the dead person back to life in the eyes of the relatives. If the captive is adopted, she will become a member of the tribe, and she will assume the dead maiden's position and her duties. In this case, she will become the daughter of a powerful clan chief of the Scupperongacs." Manteo's wise eyes swept to Ananias. "In such a position this woman would be a great asset in keeping peace between your people and the Indians. Eventually she will have a place on several councils—the clan and the tribal." His eyes twinkled with a subtle, quiet humor that was characteristic of the Indians. "It's not impossible that she should become a chief."

"What if she ain't pleasing?" someone called.

"She will not be adopted and is considered property. Her owner can do with her as he wishes. Make her his concubine, sell her, repay a debt of honor with her, or hand her over to the women so they can torture her."

"Surely we have an ally in the Croatoans," a colonist eventually muttered. "Perhaps we can fight our way out of this."

"We have an ally in them," Will confirmed. "But the Scupperongacs are a much stronger and much larger tribe. Manteo informed me that even with the help of the Croatoans we would stand no chance against their superior forces."

"It is true, my friends, against them you will stand little chance. You would be outnumbered a thousand to one." Manteo paused, then said, "Also the Croatoans are torn between two loyalties. True, they have sworn to be your ally, but they are also allied with the Scupperongacs." Manteo waited for the murmurs to cease. "As all of you know, after Governor Lane massacred Dasamonquepeuc and killed Chief Wingina, the Roanoac Confederacy was broken, and the few remaining Roanoacs were scattered. The Croatoans, who had been in a loose alliance with the Roanoacs, feared attack by the Lumbroans; therefore, they made an agreement with the Scupperongacs."

"But if Lone Wolf killed Running Bear . . ." the words of the settler hung in the air.

Manteo hesitated before he answered. "Running Bear was a Roanoac not a Croatoan. His tribe will seek revenge for his death. In any case, neither the Roanoacs nor the Croatoans will paint for war until they are satisfied that Lone Wolf is guilty, and they won't judge him until he has spoken in his defense."

"We can whip the Scupperongacs," one of the planters declared. "With our arquebuses, pistols, and cannons, I figure one of us can easily take a hundred of them savages."

"Perhaps you could if the Scupperongacs were to fight according to your battle plans," Will replied scathingly, irritated by the stupidity of these yeomen. "Don't any of you understand?" The hard leather soles of his boots clicked against the smooth, wooden floor as he walked back and forth across the front of the building, looking into the faces of the planters. "These warriors are in better physical condition than the majority of you. Not only are they planters like you, but unlike you, each one of them is a warrior. And"—his voice grew louder—"they were not trained to fight as our soldiers are." He stopped talking, dropped his hands to his hips and surveyed the meager crowd with a derisive scowl. "I don't think there's time to teach them the basic rudiments of fighting according to European standards, nor do I think they're interested in learning."

Manteo smiled, amused by Will's grim but truthful outburst. "They don't have to fight at all." His eyes again flickered across the crowd. "All they have to do is continue to surround you, and you will starve to death one by one. They know that you are marooned on the island with few provisions, and they also know that it will take several months for Governor White to return with more. Besides," he added, "I think you have nothing to fear." He smiled, thinking of the Scupperongac chief who felt nothing but loathing and contempt for palefaces. "The Great Chief is not looking for a paleface captive or daughter." He paused. "Perhaps it would be good for them to choose one of your women. It would certainly have its advantages."

A subdued murmur ran through the room, and all visibly relaxed. But Catherine was still curious. "What assurance do we have that once the Indians have made their decision and have exacted punishment, they will leave us in peace?"

"The word of the council," Manteo returned evenly. "That have no need to lie. They are so powerful and numerous, they could come tonight and take all of you captive. Will has presented your case, and I spoke for him. The council has listened, agreeing to give you a chance to right the wrong which has been done to their people. They are willing to live in peace if your people are. Right now war with you is what they want least."

"You believe they will keep their word?"

"Yes."

"What makes you think they will keep their word when it is possible their war werowance killed a peace chief?"

"I have heard no one charge Lone Wolf," Manteo replied. "I think perhaps it is a trick of the Lumbroans to start intertribal warfare."

"So you think we ought to accept the judgment of the Scupperongacs?" a stocky man at the rear asked.

"I do," Will responded. "Manteo assures me that Great Chief Wise One speaks the truth and will honor his word."

Eleanor, placing the baby's head on her shoulder and

rocking back and forth, asked, "When will we know their final decision?"

"In the morning."

"If they should decide on a woman, are you in favor of letting 'em have one without putting up a fight, Ananias?" The man's voice was tense.

Since the question was put to Ananias, Will didn't bother to answer. He stepped aside and looked at his brother. But as usual Ananias didn't have the nerve to voice his opinion directly. He clutched the seat of his chair with both hands and wished he could shrink through a crack in the floor. But there was no way he could escape. Ashamed to look the settlers in the face, he dropped his head. If it were left to him, he would walk the path of least resistance . . . but he didn't dare voice these words.

When Ananias didn't speak, Will said, "My answer would be nay. But it is something that we will have to vote on when the time comes. Right now I suggest that we wait to see what the savages are going to demand. Let's not get the cart before the ox. The Indians are as desirous for peace as we are."

"Kate"—Ellen's voice was even smaller than usual as she leaned toward her sister—"I'm frightened."

Catherine laid an arm over Ellen's shoulder, drawing her closer. "Everything's going to be all right. I promise."

"It's only right that Tom should give his life," Ellen exclaimed.

"He should be the one punished," Catherine quietly agreed, "but evidently the chief doesn't want him." She added, in jest, "And I can understand why. Tom doesn't cut such a fine figure for a man; I don't imagine he would be a replacement for the chief's daughter, nor would he be apt if the chief wants a new bed partner." She grinned at Ellen and squeezed her shoulder. "Hush now, and let's

91

listen to Will."

When Catherine returned her attention to Will, he was saying, "I think we should be prepared for the worst." He paced across the front of the room. "The Indians won't do anything until tomorrow, but Manteo has assured me that we're being watched. Therefore, we must be careful. Let's begin moving all our things to the fort. Here's the way we'll do it to keep the savages from suspecting what we are doing. . . ."

The rest of the day passed quickly. Following Will's and Manteo's instructions, the women cooked the feast they would serve the tribal council, and the men prepared for battle. Though the settlers put up a brave front, there was an undercurrent of anxiety and apprehension. Each wondered what the outcome of the conference would be. After the evening meal in the main hall, the women went to their cabins, and the men migrated to their usual place at the far end of the room and in hushed tones discussed their plans.

As the lamp burned low, both groups began to disperse, heading for their cabins and beds—all but a few men who talked with Will and Manteo into the wee hours of the morning. Finally, however, even they doused their lamp to apprehensively await the new day.

Chapter V

Early the next morning both Catherine and Ellen dressed carefully before they joined Will, who looked dashing and primitive in his Americanized garb. His hair was brushed in full waves from his handsome face, and his eyes glowed as he looked at Ellen. A woman on each arm, he proudly escorted the Graystone sisters to the town hall where the tribal council was waiting. The seven council members, six men and an old woman, sat on benches on one side of the building, the colonists on the opposite. Both groups, separated by a large aisle, faced each other. Displayed on the table in the center of the room was a fine array of weapons and tools.

Although the Indians seemed oblivious to the flurry of activity, Catherine was aware that their eyes blatantly raked over her and Ellen as Will led them to their seats. She was, however, determined not to let her nervousness show. When Will left them to take his place beside Ananias and Manteo in the center of the room, Catherine sat down, holding her head high and her shoulders erect. Acting as if she didn't have a concern in the world, she fluffed her ruffles and pressed the wrinkles out of her gown. Then she leaned down to dust an imaginary fleck of dirt off the toe of her brocade slipper. When she straightened, Catherine turned her head, and with a touch of the audaciousness so deeply ingrained in her, she leveled a long, unhurried stare at the Indians, her eyes slowly moving from one to the other.

She didn't lower her face until she had looked at all of them, but it was pride, not courage, that kept her gazing at this hostile group of people. Finally she slowly lifted her hands, pulling her veil over her face, covering her forehead and eyes. The Indians looked so cold and hard that if she hadn't known better she would have thought them to be sculpted from stone. Their eyes were deep and fathomless. Their expressions were formidable; their backs and shoulders straight set.

Wise One, the tribal chief and the spokesman for the Scupperongacs, stood; he walked up and down the building, looking curiously at the palefaces who had come from the Land over the Water. He had seen such strange-looking men before; there were several who had taken refuge in villages north of Scupperong, but this was the first time he viewed their women. With all that clothing to hide them, he wondered, how did one know what they looked like. He gazed at the veils which covered their faces. How did they see?

Halting in front of Catherine, he stared for the longest time. Though frightened, she returned his gaze, her eyes never wavering. This is a brazen one, the old chieftain surmised, and a fighter. His dark, inscrutable eyes penetrated layers of lace to see those partially obscured feisty green eyes. He was impressed with Catherine's demeanor. When he saw her nervously finger the ruffle of her dress, he almost smiled.

Slowly his gaze shifted, and with the same careful scrutiny, he studied Ellen, who scooted closer to Catherine, burrowing her face into her sister's shoulder. A weak one, he thought, and a frightened one. But she is the younger of the two, the more malleable. Without a word, without a change in expression, Wise One finally pivoted on his heels and walked to the other council members, quietly speaking to them.

At Will's prodding, Ananias stood, greeting the Indians and setting the conference in motion. Each of the council members reciprocated the greeting with lengthy speeches which Manteo interpreted. Finally Wise One addressed the topic of the meeting. Catherine, having heard all the details of the crime told and retold many times during the past few hours, closed her eyes and sighed. She was tired of the endless oratory, of the echoing translations by Manteo. She wished they would get down to the crux of the matter.

As if Ananias had read her mind, he spoke. "Here is a selection of our finest knives, swords, and hatchets, Great Werowance Wise One. We honor the law and customs of the Scupperongacs. We wish to live in peace with your people and are willing to do whatever it takes to bring about such an end. We would like to make a lasting bond of friendship with you and your people."

Wise One heard Ananias out, but he didn't so much as acknowledge one word the acting governor said. Instead, he walked over and ran his fingers lightly over the weapons. When he reached the head of the table, he stopped; then he lifted his head and looked at the man standing in the door. Quietly he strode to the entrance, and he stared at the arquebus. The stick that thundered! Tentatively he reached out and touched the barrel. Still he didn't speak; rather he returned to the council. After he spoke softly to them, he crooked his fingers and they followed him to the table. They picked up the weapons and held them, brandishing them through the air. Looking at each other, they grunted their approval, quietly conversing.

After the examination, the Indians laid the weapons down and Wise One again addressed Ananias through

Manteo. "You know that according to our law . . ." His deep, mellifluous voice reverberated through the unusually quiet assembly as he recited the Scupperongac laws, listing the alternatives of repayment for the life taken. When he had concluded, he said, "The family is allowing the council to make the decision." He leveled those penetrating eyes on Ananias' twitching hands first, then on Will's calm, impassive face. It was to the younger Dare that he spoke. "I am in favor of taking the weapons, but we wish to confer longer before we announce our decision."

When Manteo's voice trailed into silence, a murmured protest rippled through the hall, and Ananias slumped in his chair. Hiding his irritation and disconcertion behind a composed façade, Will moved forward and spoke for his brother.

"How long will it be before you can make this decision, Werowance Wise One?"

"As long as it takes," Wise One replied bruskly and dismissively, and he promptly turned and walked toward his tribe's representatives.

The small group of Indian chieftains huddled together for a long time, their voices hushed as they debated their answer. The agitated colonists, watching the Indians, squirmed on their benches and whispered one to the other. Whereas Ananias showed his nervousness, wiping his brow and sighing deeply, Will didn't. He stood patiently beside Manteo, feet apart, arms folded across his broad chest.

When Wise One stood, he moved front and center, facing Will. Before he could say anything, however, a shadow fell across the room. As if a deity had appeared, a reverent silence fell across the room. Talking ceased; all movement stopped. Catherine, like everyone else, felt the awesome presence, and like the other settlers she shivered in the ominous quiet. Momentarily stunned, she looked from Will to Manteo, both of whom turned a shocked face toward the door. She looked at the council members who were quiet but not perturbed. She looked first over one shoulder, then the other. The settlers sat, transfixed, their eyes on the door. Finally, her gaze swept down the aisle to moccasined feet, and she saw the brindled wolf. The air caught in her lungs, and she stared. She couldn't believe her eyes.

Lone Wolf!

His gaze contemptuously raked over the assembled group of settlers as he walked deliberately down the wide aisle between the palefaces and the Indians, the wolf beside him. Only the soft thud of Lone Wolf's moccasined feet and the tap of the wolf's claws on the floor could be heard; only the broad width of Lone Wolf's sinewy shoulders could be seen. When he reached the table, he looked from Ananias to Will. The one he dismissed as being of no consequence; the other he admired and recognized as a warrior. At the head of the table now, Lone Wolf commanded the wolf to lie down. Then the war chief walked to where the other council members sat. He spoke to them in hushed tones.

Catherine watched as they looked at one another. She saw them voice questions, sensed that they disagreed. She heard Ananias nervously ask, "What's wrong, Manteo? Who is this savage, and what does he want?"

"Can't you tell?" Will grated. "Take a look at that wolf that's watching us. Look at that pearl and wolf-fang necklace hanging around his neck."

Answered by implication, Ananias cowered further into his chair. "What does he want?" he gulped, his voice relaying his apprehension.

The uncertainly of dealing with these savages was taking its toll on Ananias. He couldn't endure much more. He reached into the folds of his doublet, took out his handkerchief, and wiped his face with shaking hands.

"Make him get that damned wolf out of here," Ananias whimpered. He despised the tawny eyes that had settled squarely on him.

Will laid a hand on Ananias' shoulder and spoke quietly but most authoritatively. "Shut up, Ananias. We have problems enough on our hands without your creating another one." He smiled grimly. "As long as you don't make a sudden movement, the wolf won't hurt you."

The discussion of the council members became even more heated, and Wise One kept pointing at the table. Without speaking, Lone Wolf looked at the weapons; then he looked at Ellen and Catherine. Finally he walked to the table and picked up a hatchet, his fingers easily gripping the shaft. He brandished it several times, the metal singing as it sliced the air, before he looked at the other chiefs, smiling and nodding his approval. That done, he laid the weapon down and rejoined the council.

Will moved closer to Manteo. "What do you think?" he asked under his breath, watching as the Indians made gestures and spoke at length.

"I am not sure, my friend," Manteo returned, his eyes never leaving the Scupperongac braves. "Lone Wolf is telling them that they need the weapons, but he's more interested in taking a captive." He listened for a moment. "Wise One is pointing out the reasons why weapons would be better for them." Manteo paused, straining to hear the undertones of the Scupperongacs. Eventually he said, "The old woman is agreeing with Wise One."

Satisfaction sighed through Will's lips, and he walked to the chair where Ananias still sat. Clapping his brother on the shoulder, he said, "I think all will be well, Ananias. Soon this will be over, and we shall be feasting with these wily devils." He smiled his praise of the Indian warriors. "God, but they are shrewd, my brother, and they are pushing a hard bargain."

The long conversation ended; the argument was over. Lone Wolf, walking to the center aisle where Will stood, folded his arms over his chest and rocked back on his heels.

Arrogantly he announced, "I have made my decision."

When Manteo's echo died away, all the settlers held thir breaths; anxiously they awaited the savage's next words.

His pleased smile revealed sparkling white teeth that contrasted with his copper skin. "I demand a captive—a woman who will be the life given for the one taken."

Like a black canopy of death, a heavy, oppressive quietness settled over the settlers. Though forewarned, they were not prepared for this decision. Will broke the silence. He lunged forward, and the wolf sprang to his feet, his hackles raised, his fangs bared. Cautiously Will stepped back.

"And what right do you have to demand?" he grated. "You're not the one who has the power to select or to make the decision."

As Manteo translated his reply, the Indian's eyes became slits, their obsidian depths smirking. "No one has a better right than I, paleface. The captive will belong to me. The maiden who was killed was to have been my wife. Because I had already given gifts of purchase to her parents, which they accepted and don't wish to return, the payment for her death belongs to me." Lone Wolf laughed as Manteo interpreted his words to Will. His gaze fastened on Ellen. "Now I shall choose the maiden."

Even before Manteo had completed the interpretation, Will's hand clamped on the hilt of his sword. Ellen, fearing for Will's life, lunged forward and screamed, "No, Will," at the same moment that Lone Wolf lifted his hand.

"I wouldn't if I were you," the chieftain advised, hardly waiting for Manteo's translation. "When I heard

99

about what you had done—destroying the village, needlessly killing my bride-to-be—I came prepared for the palefaces' treachery. My warriors surround your village, and your fort is completely cut off." His eyes were triumphant. "Your soldiers are being held captive, so you cannot expect any help from them." As if the subject were concluded, Lone Wolf insolently waited for Manteo to translate his words. The war chief smiled when Will's hand dropped, and the paleface warrior stepped back. "I would like to see that one," Lone Wolf repeated, walking to where the Graystone sisters sat.

Will's eyes darted to the bench where Ellen huddled fearfully against Catherine. He heard her gasp, and he saw her grip on Catherine's arm tighten. But Lone Wolf's eyes moved beyond the younger Graystone to rest on Catherine's face. They lingered on the defiant jut of her chin before they slowly crawled up the lacy veil that shielded her eyes, making him wonder at their coloring.

"You," he said in Scupperongac, his fingers banding around her upper arm as he jerked her to her feet, yanking her out of Ellen's grasp. "I want to see what you look like."

Catherine forced herself not to cower, not to tremble. Rather, she defiantly clamped her teeth together and jerked her arm from his grasp before she lifted her face, making herself stare into those sardonic eyes that stripped her bare. Catherine watched as Lone Wolf's line of vision leveled on her veil.

"Lift your face covering."

Before Manteo had interpreted the words, Catherine knew what they were. Without taking her eyes from Lone Wolf's, she lifted her hands and flipped the lace from her upper face. Proudly she stood, obeying his command, doing no more.

Pleasure winged through the bold warrior. The proud one, the defiant one was his autumn-haired beauty. Lone

100

Wolf wanted to reach out to touch the tiny splattering of freckles that teased the bridge of her nose, but he didn't. He would never show such a weakness in front of these werowances . . . or in front of these palefaces. He would never let Catherine know how much she appealed to him. He looked into her eyes, so full of life, so full of contempt and hatred. He smiled as he saw the defiance that sparkled within their frosty depths. He saw her fury.

He spoke softly, and Catherine could feel the tension that emanated from his huge frame. "Take the headdress off."

After she heard Manteo repeat the words, Catherine pulled the hood from her head, detemined she would give no more than Lone Wolf asked for—and that would be given grudgingly. What he got from her he would take!

Lone Wolf chuckled softly, speaking over her shoulder to the council. "She would strike me if she thought she could get away with it. I see all of autumn's fury in her eyes." All the council members except the old woman laughed with him.

Lone Wolf raised his hands, but when his fingers touched the ribbons that secured her coif beneath her neck, when the soft tips of his fingers touched Catherine's throat, a bolt of lightning zigzagged through her body. She jerked away from his hand. She wasn't about to let him touch her again.

Instantly Lone Wolf's fingers darted out and closed on the nape of her neck, hurting her as he dragged her to his large frame. Out of the corner of his eyes Lone Wolf saw Will clench his fists, jump to his feet, and start in his direction, but Manteo laid a hand on Will's shoulder and restrained him. Then the Croatoan chieftain walked to Ellen and caught her in his arms, pressing her cheek against the softness of his buckskin shirt.

Catherine could see nothing but Lone Wolf. His massive body blocked all else from her view, but she could hear the Indians' grunts of approval and their laughter. The war chief of the Scupperongacs jerked the piece of white linen off her head, and for a few motionless seconds, he looked at her russet mane before he turned her around. Her back to him, he pulled the styling form, the combs, and the pins out of her hair, dropping them on the floor at her feet.

When her hair tumbled down her back in wild abandon, it glistened copper in the early morning sunshine that streamed through the open windows. The members of the council started, unable to stifle their gasps of surprise. Wise One stared at Catherine's beauty, her autumn hair and green eyes, and the words of his vision returned to haunt him. His head moved and his eyes locked with the old woman's, their thoughts atuned. She nodded.

Catherine felt the savage's touch as his fingers splayed through the silken curtain of her hair. Again he spoke in low murmurs, but Manteo did not interpret. The voices of those on the council mingled in a chorus of undertones, and Catherine couldn't be sure who was speaking; yet she knew each member was voicing his opinion. Catherine wasn't sure how long she stood there; she wasn't sure what was happening.

"I will take this woman."

Manteo hadn't completed the translation before Catherine whispered, "No." Then she cried loudly, "No, I won't go with you. You've no right—"

"No," Ellen screamed, pushing out of Manteo's arms. Her fear was an impetus, giving her strength she would not have normally had. She raced across the floor. "No, Kate," she cried hysterically, throwing her arms around Catherine, "he's not going to take you."

The planters, almost in unison, jumped to their feet, and Will's face was gaunt with resolve.

"You'll not take her!"

102

Will's authoritative words reverberated through the small building with a clarion ring. Disregarding the growling of the wolf, he moved. His boots clicked off solid, determined steps, and in several long strides he stood fearlessly before Lone Wolf. He caught Ellen by the shoulders, and he gently pulled her away from Catherine. Then he motioned for Ananias, and pushed Ellen in his brother's direction.

"You have no right to make such a claim."

Lone Wolf's visage hardened, and his eyes narrowed. He heard a warrior's challenge, and he saw the paleface's hand grasp the hilt of his sword. He recognized the warrior's stance; he saw the muscled body which gave evidence of excellent physical training. Yet the Scupperongac warrior gave no outwardly evidence that he understood Will's declaration, nor did he unhand Catherine.

Manteo had not completed the interpretation before Will spoke again. "You will have to kill me first," he charged, his eyes dark and unreadable with anger.

Ellen balled her hands and pressed them against her mouth, smothering her cry. If Ananias had not been holding her securely at his side, she would have broken loose again.

"Whatever you prefer," Lone Wolf returned evenly. "I have killed for her before. I would not hesitate to do so again." He leveled his eyes on Will. "I will take her."

"She's not the one responsible for this death," Will thundered, trying to protect Catherine. "She's innocent of all wrong doing."

"My God!" Tom Small's voice shrilled through the room. He could just see William Dare demanding the savages take him because he was the one who had killed that wench. "Let him have her. Don't agitate 'em, Will. Dear God, you can git your self another wench. She ain't the onliest one in the world." He ran to where Will and

103

Manteo stood. "Besides it ain't really for you to decide. It's up to her."

"No," Will shouted, "it's not up to her." Turning to Lone Wolf, he said, "Take me. I'll be your prisoner. Torture me. I'll provide you with entertainment you'll never forget."

Manteo's interpretation died, and Lone Wolf spoke softly to Wolf Friend, calling him to his side. Though Lone Wolf admired the paleface warrior and knew that he was brave, Lone Wolf would not take him as prisoner. He had come to get Catherine. He would not leave without her.

"I don't doubt the truth of your words, my warrior brother. But you would not provide me with the kind of pleasure that I'm seeking."

Will was trembling with rage when Manteo's interpretation ended. "Then, by god, you savage, I'll fight you. You're not taking one of our women with you."

Had Lone Wolf not understood one word of English and had the words never been translated, the war werowance of the Scupperongacs would have understood their meaning. Will's tone and gesture were clear. Lone Wolf heard the threat; he saw the challenge in the depth of Will's eyes. Even more he admired and respected the courage of this paleface warrior.

Catherine saw Lone Wolf tense; she saw the indomitable thrust of his chin, the narrowing of his eyes. He had already killed one man for her, and he wouldn't hesitate to kill a second. She resolved that no more blood would be shed on her account. As Catherine searched his inscrutable face she knew her life was irrevocably bound to his people . . . and to this man in particular. Subconsciously she knew her destiny lay with Lone Wolf.

"For once, Will'am Dare," she said softly, breaking the tension, "Tom Small is right. The choice belonged to Lone Wolf, the decision to me."

104

"You can't go with this savage," Will thundered.

"I have no other choice." Catherine spoke to Will, but she looked at Lone Wolf. "I escaped him once. I shall do so again." To Manteo she said, "Tell Lone Wolf that I will go with him."

When Manteo repeated the words, Lone Wolf nodded. He had a defiant one on his hands—a woman full of spirit. And he had no doubt that she would be true to her promise. She would try to escape. But he wanted her— wanted her so much that he had paid a high price for her. Now that he had her, he wouldn't let her escape. He had found her, he had claimed her. She belonged to him. The Creator had smiled on him this day.

Running his fingers over the top of Wolf Friend's head, Lone Wolf murmured, "The easy task is over, my friend. I have found and claimed my paleface. Now the difficult one begins. I must teach her obedience."

Chapter VI

Catherine lagged farther and farther behind the small group of braves and the brindled wolf who maintained an even, swift pace through the forest. They had spent three days traveling by canoe, and four on land. Although they camped at night, they moved single-file through the forest during the day, allowing nothing to slow them down, not the canoes hoisted above their shoulders, not Catherine. Only for a drink of water did they occasionally stop. Catherine's trunk was so heavy that her arms ached from carrying it, and several times she tripped and fell, but Lone Wolf never looked in her direction; he kept his face set straight ahead, offering her no help.

Not whimpering or uttering one sound of frustration but silently cursing him, Catherine followed, alternately running, stumbling, and hobbling to keep up. Even though she hardly had the strength to pick her feet up, she didn't ask the savages to wait, nor did she ask them to rest. Finally, however, the Indians stopped of their own accord. They had reached the river on which they would canoe to Scupperong.

Dropping her chest to the ground, Catherine wearily trudged to the water's edge, washing her flushed face. Then she lifted her gown and dried her face on her linen petticoat. Taking off her hood and coif, she brushed damp wisps of hair from her temples and lifted her face, letting the wind cool her sweat-moistened skin. Finally she lowered her head and looked at the shredded lace. If she weren't so exhausted, she would have cried. Her fingers gently traced the remaining design, and she stared at the piece of material, wondering what purpose it had ever served.

After only seven days with these savages, she wondered why she had ever thought it was beautiful. As her fingers rounded the dome of the hood, she remembered making the hoop and the undercovering. She remembered the long hours spent on stitching the velvet in place and on weaving the lace. But all that belonged to the past, to her life as Catherine Graystone. Now she wasn't sure what her status was or would be. She was just like the name Lone Wolf had given her, Autumn Woman—here today and gone tomorrow like that illusive and ephemeral season.

Silently Lone Wolf stood, leaning against a tree, watching Catherine. He wondered what she was thinking. She looked bedraggled and tired, but she hadn't asked for any favors. She lagged behind, but she never complained. He had known it each time she had fallen, and he had wanted to go back to help her. But he couldn't. He would not allow his warriors to see how this woman—this slave—was affecting his heart. He didn't mind their knowing that she excited and pleasured his body, but he would never let them know that she occupied a tender spot in his heart as well.

Even now as he and the other braves munched on their parched corn, Catherine did not ask for food. Lone Wolf was concerned. She had eaten very little since they had left her village. Yesterday she had impassively watched them eat, but she had never asked for a bite. He had deliberately tempted her; he had waited, but she hadn't asked. Even now, he thought, she was defiant and proud, looking after her tattered paleface clothes and caring for

107

them as if they were new. She would die before she would ask him for help, Lone Wolf decided, pushing away from the tree and slowly walking to where Catherine sat. But he did not wish her dead, nor did he want her weak.

Crouching beside her, he took one of her hands in his and turned it over, pouring some parched corn into her cupped palm. Then he signed her to eat. Catherine leveled a frosty glare on him and looked in the fathomless depths of his eyes; then she lowered her head and looked at the meal. She was so hungry her mouth watered, but she could never give him the pleasure of seeing her eagerly gulp the food down. Knowing her stubbornness and understanding her thoughts, Lone Wolf gently pushed her palm upward.

"So you want me to eat, do you?" Catherine murmured, looking hungrily at the coarsely ground corn meal that glittered bright yellow in her palm. At the moment it glittered more precious than gold or costly jewels. Satisfaction written on her face for Lone Wolf to see, she looked up at him. "So I won this time, did I not, Lone Wolf?" She chuckled. Since he did not understand English, she could say anything she wished without incurring his wrath. "But it's not so difficult to explain." She spoke softly. "You see, I have no intention of dying or getting weak. I'm going to fight you every inch of the way, and I shall win."

She munched on the soft meal and swallowed. "I'll tell you another secret"—she lifted a hand to wipe the crumbs from the corner of her mouth—"I'm going to make your life so miserable, you'll wish you hadn't chosen a captive. Once I know my people are safe, I'm going to escape." Her laughter grew louder, but it wasn't laughter. It was a disguise for anger and humiliation and frustration. "Just like I did last time."

Lone Wolf stared impassively at Catherine, acting as if he couldn't understand a word she was saying. What she said didn't concern him; what he heard and what he saw

108

did. The lilting beauty of her voice had changed. Her tone was cynical and hard. Her eyes, circled with dark shadows of fatigue, were icy and cold. In them he no longer saw excitement or happiness; instead he saw emotions that troubled him.

When Catherine could no longer stand the penetrating gaze of his ebony eyes, she lowered her face, her eyes inadvertently lighting on the necklaces that hung about his neck in graduated sizes. They centered on the polished teeth—Lone Wolf's totem.

Lone Wolf, watching every expressiong that flitted across Catherine's face, now lowered his head, his eyes focusing on the center of her attention—the wolf fangs. His corn eaten, he dusted his hands on his leggings, and he reached up to his chest, his fingers closing around the necklace that he had given her once before. He lifted it over his head. When he went to loop it over Catherine's head, however, she dodged out of his way.

"I don't want your necklace," she stormed. "I don't want anything of yours. Remember, I'm just a slave."

Lone Wolf's mouth tightened in disapproval, but Catherine didn't care that her actions angered him. She wanted to anger and humiliate him, as he had her. She was elated when his immobile countenance distorted into a scowl. She knew she had penetrated that austere façade of the Indian warrior behind which he hid; he wasn't as indifferent to her reactions as he would like her to think.

Lone Wolf's hand tangled in her auburn hair, and he pulled Catherine close. Roughly he dropped the necklace over her head. "That's why you're wearing this," he snarled. "As my slave you will wear my mark so that everyone will know."

Tears threatened, and Catherine was dangerously close to losing her aplomb. "I hate what you're doing to me, Lone Wolf," she asserted. "But understand this. I'll fight you all the way. You can take me captive; you can forcibly take my body, but you can't take my love." Tears

109

of anger at her helplessness sparkled in her eyes, and her voice was thick with emotion. "You can have my body, but I promise I'll never give you my love or my respect."

She stood, her back erect, her shoulders squared. Haughtily, she tilted her face in the air, and she stalked away. But her haughty exit was thwarted. She hadn't taken two steps before her shoe caught on the hem of her gown, tripping her.

Flinging her arms behind her to break her fall, she landed on her buttocks, her straddled legs straight out in front of her. She looked so ridiculous sprawled at Lone Wolf's feet that he couldn't help but chuckle. Her headdress was crooked, its shreds of lace dangling on either side of her face. Her brocade shoes, worn through on the sole, peeped from beneath the tattered gown.

Fighting to hold back the tears that threatened to erupt, she began to brush her gown, then straightened her farthingale and her petticoats. Lone Wolf walked to stand in front of her. Realizing that he had pushed her too far, he extended a hand to help her to her feet. Squeezing back tears, she slapped his hand away.

"I'll get up by myself," she hissed. "I don't need your help."

Clumsily she stood and walked to the river's edge, where she knelt down and leaned over. Using the water as her looking glass, she adjusted her torn coif as best she could and set the hood over it. When she saw how pathetic and grubby she looked, a recalcitrant tear, defying her authority, rolled down her cheek. She shut her eyes, squeezing them tightly, and refused to cry; she refused to let this man know how he was affecting her. Then she heard his voice as she felt the soft thud of something landing in her lap.

Opening her eyes, she saw the moccasins. They were more beautiful and ornate than the ones Running Bear had given her, and they were the right size. As she thought about Running Bear, her tears could hardly be stayed. Swallowing them and pushing thoughts of Running Bear aside, she again looked at the moccasins. They would be so much more comfortable than the brocade slippers, she thought. She lifted them, pressing the softness to her cheeks. Then she sighed. She couldn't accept them.

Lowering her head again, she looked into the water. She didn't stare at her reflection, however. She stared at Lone Wolf's. He stared at hers, and seeing her fear and her fatigue, he felt a stirring of compassion.

He pointed to the soft leather shoes, his hands gesturing his words. "Put them on, Catherine. They will protect your feet."

Shaking her head, she handed them back to him. "Thank you," she said in a cold, stilted voice as if she were speaking to one of no consequence, "but I'll wear my own." When Lone Wolf didn't take the proffered shoes, Catherine flung them at him.

Lone Wolf's eyes narrowed to mere slits, and he barely controlled the anger that surged through him. Never had a woman treated him like this. Never had a woman defied him in front of his warriors. He reached for the moccasins with one hand; the other grasped Catherine, his hand banding around her arm. Roughly he yanked her to her feet.

"Then don't wear them, Catherine," he grated out, still refusing to speak in English, "but don't complain either. You'll be the one to suffer for your action this day."

Catherine twisted herself free and backed away. "I'll come with you. You don't have to beat me, nor do you have to treat me like this." Her green eyes glinted angrily. "If I were a man, you wouldn't treat me like this."

A slow, easy grin spread across Lone Wolf's face. He said something to his braves which Catherine didn't understand, and he motioned them to leave. One of the warriors, shaking his head and chuckling softly, handed Lone Wolf his knife; then the man turned and joined the group at the river's edge. Catherine watched them shove off and paddle away in the canoes without her and Lone Wolf.

Meanwhile Lone Wolf remained in front of her, his hands on hips in a leisurely stance, his powerful legs straddled. His eyes never left her face, and he continued to grin. Catherine was coming to dread that infuriating expression. His fierceness she could hate; his scowl she could detest. They made him a hated savage. But his smile was her undoing. It affirmed his masculinity; it defined him as a man. And it told her that she was a woman—a woman he would take.

When his braves were gone, he unsheathed his knife, handing it to her hilt first. The other blade he held in his hand. "You want me to treat you like a man, Catherine." He spoke in precise, fluent English. "Then I shall."

Catherine's jaw hung slack, and she glared at him. Finally she whispered, her voice no more than a croak, "You—you—speak English."

"I do," he replied with a calmness that further irritated Catherine. "As you learned from the Indians living among you, I learned from the palefaces who have lived among us for the past two winters."

The missing colonists, Catherine thought fleetingly.

"They were brave men who ran the gauntlet, taking refuge in my wigwam. After they became members of our tribe, they and I learned from one another. At present they live in a mountain village."

Suddenly the enormity of his confession hit Catherine, almost knocking the breath out of her body. "All this time," she murmured, her anger surfacing with all the fury of a coastal storm. "All this time you could understand every word that was said—that we said."

Still holding the knife out to her, Lone Wolf nodded his head. "I understood." His eyes mocked her.

112

"I hate you," Catherine screamed, reaching for the knife, her fingers closing around the hilt. "God, how you've humiliated me! I hate you, and I'll kill you. God help me, I'll kill you." Drawing her arm back, she flew at him, flailing, trying to stab him. "You're nothing but a . . . but a"—she groped for the worst term she could call him; then she remembered something Running Bear had once told her, the lowest name an Indian could be called—"you're nothing but a filthy dog."

Speaking softly to the wolf, telling him to sit, Lone Wolf easily fended Catherine off, but he hadn't reckoned on the added strength that resulted from her anger and humiliation. "This is the first and last time that you shall call me a dog," he grunted, his leg striking the backs of hers, buckling her knees and knocking her off balance. As they fell to the ground, he threw his weight on top of her, grabbing both her wrists in one strong hand. Holding her arms above her head and lying partially across her, he hissed in a dangerously soft voice, "I have allowed you your little tantrums but no more. We shall soon reach my town and my people. In front of them you will show me the respect due a war chief, the respect due a man."

"Respect," she spat, unwisely speaking without thinking. "What do you know about respect? You, the one who killed Running Bear, a peace man, by spearing him in the back."

Lone Wolf's eyes narrowed and his mouth thinned in anger. "No woman questions me," he barked. "I owe you no explanations for my behavior. But you—you will obey me. Do you understand?"

"I'll obey only if I wish," Catherine grated between clenched teeth, writhing beneath his weight. The warmth of his body fused through the layers of her clothing, reminding her that he was a man, she a woman. The nearness of his body made her forget their quarrel. "And I'll never respect you. I have sworn to fight you, Lone Wolf of the Scupperongacs, and I shall."

He laughed. "You'll obey me." Of that he had no doubt. "I promise that you will obey me."

"And if I don't," Catherine countered. "What are you going to do? Beat me?"

He smiled. "As you can see, Catherine, I don't need to beat you."

His eyes burned with a fire that Catherine had never seen before. The flames of anger and irritation, the flame of purpose and resolve she had seen. She even remembered the embers of passion glowing in the depths of those raven-black eyes. But this blaze was tempered with a new emotion that Catherine had never seen before.

"I would beat you if it were necessary," he affirmed without hesitation, "and I wouldn't give it a second thought. But I won't have to." He laughed, the sound, deep and quieting, touching and playing all the strings of Catherine's heart. "I shall love you into obedience," he breathed softly, the flames in his eyes warming her body. "I shall make you so passionately dependent on me that you will have no will but my will, no thought but mine, no body but mine."

Catherine laughed in his face, mocking him. "Your vanity is too great for you to carry any longer, Lone Wolf. I should think you would stumble beneath the heavy load."

"I speak only the truth as you will learn shortly. I do not have to force myself on any woman. Since we have been traveling in the company of my braves and you are exhausted, I had pity on you, letting you sleep." One hand went to the neck of her dress, and he began to unbutton it. "Now it is time for you to learn that I am your master." He pulled off her ruff and tossed it aside, his lips lowering to her neck and collarbone, his tongue gently licking the vulnerable place where her pulse throbbed. "Shall I prove that you are ready for me to have you?"

114

"No," she muttered, her mind tensing and rebelling against his intimate touches, her body half-heartedly following suit.

In response, with one hand Lone Wolf secured her arms above her head as he flung a leg over hers. She quivered, feeling every inch of his fiery length as he pinned her to the hard unyielding earth. She wanted to deny the effect of his touch, but she couldn't.

His firm lips whispered seductively over her virgin skin, pristine white in its innocence, even whiter when in contrast with the bronzed beauty of his masculine hand. He pulled the intrusive material of her dress open even more, and his lips continued their exploring.

"Have you lain with a man before?" Lone Wolf asked, remembering how easily she had surrendered to him in the bower.

"What if I have?" Catherine gasped.

His hand slipped under her petticoats. His fingers, brushing lightly against her flesh, moved up her ankles and then her calves; their touch a whisper behind her knees and on her thighs. Catherine's body was burning so, she could hardly speak. She turned her head and lifted her face as Lone Wolf lowered his lips to hers for a short warm kiss. Then his lips traveled over her face, sending tremors of delight through her body.

"I think I shall be the first man to lie with you," Lone Wolf mused, his lips toying with the throbbing pulse at the base of her throat. He chuckled, the sound rich and mellow, a sedative to Catherine's ragged nerves. "You may fight me," he granted, "and you may try to escape, but I promise you, Catherine, you will love me." His laughter didn't mock her; rather it warmed her soul. His warm, wet lips traveled seductively along her neck, her chin, the corner of her mouth.

"Don't . . ." Catherine mumbled, her lips opening enough so that his claimed hers with an intensity that drained her very life force. His hand cupped the back of

115

her head, forcing her mouth against his; his tongue demanded entrance, craving the sweetness which he remembered all too well.

When Lone Wolf finally broke the drugging kiss, he said, "I am glad that there has been no other man in your life."

Breathless from the emotion that blazed through her body but determined to keep him at bay, Catherine softly taunted him. "I have never said there was not another man in my life. I said no man has slept with me." She laughed, the sweet melody stirring Lone Wolf's senses as much as her words stirred his anger. "Perhaps you will be the first to know me, but perhaps there is another that I love. Perhaps that is why I gave myself to you, so that I could save the man whom I really love. Perhaps there is another whom I wish to bed, whom I really wish to marry."

As she spoke, Lone Wolf remembered the whinings of Tom Small. Perhaps she loved the paleface warrior, the one called Will. Lone Wolf caught her shoulders, and he scowled into her face. "Do you love another?"

"Do you?" Catherine countered, with a bravery she was far from feeling. Narrowing her eyes, she tried to see beyond his angry scowl; she wondered about the maiden who was to have been his wife. "Did you love the one whom Tom Small killed?"

For endless seconds Lone Wolf stared into Catherine's face, and he thought about her question. He thought about the Indian maiden whom he was to have married. Reluctantly he admitted, "No, I didn't love Wind Woman."

"Wind Woman," Catherine repeated softly.

"Aye," Lone Wolf concurred. "She was a gentle woman, named after a warm summer breeze."

"But you didn't love her," Catherine prodded.

Lone Wolf shook his head. "I chose to marry her because the council insisted it was time for me to have a

116

wife and children."

"Did she know this?" Catherine asked, and Lone Wolf nodded his head. "She was willing to marry you under these circumstances!" Catherine didn't bother to hide her incredulity.

Lone Wolf laughed in spite of his anger and irritation. "Many maidens want to marry me, paleface," he boasted. "They would be proud to have me for their husband. I am a good hunter. I will provide food for them and their children. I am a valiant warrior who will bring honor to them; my deeds will give them reason to sing and dance before the tribe."

"I don't know if you're a good hunter and warrior," Catherine dryly spat, "but I know for sure that you're an excellent braggart." Her words were too flippant and cocky for the Scupperongac war chief.

"What is a braggart?" His question was hissed through clenched teeth, and his clasp tightened, cutting into the soft flesh of her arms.

"One who—one who has no genuine substance. One who"—his fingers dug deeper into the tender skin—"who has a too high regard for himself and his abilities." Catherine's voice broke, and her arms hurt where his fingers bit into her flesh.

"Nay, Catherine Graystone," Lone Wolf whispered. "I am no braggart. You will soon learn. I speak the truth. And"—his voice lowered a husky octave—"you will soon learn why women are attracted to me." He loosened his grip, sliding his fingers down her arm. When his fingers curled around hers, he moved her hand to the most intimate part of his body. "You will soon learn that I am a man of genuine substance."

Catherine swallowed the lump that was lodged in her throat, and she forced herself to remain calm, but his voice was making her dizzy with its sensual softness. The touch of his burgeoning manhood was awakening a new sense of awareness in her. "You will soon learn,

117

Scupperongac war chief, that it takes more than hollow words to attract me to a man."

"Those are not hollow words which you are feeling, Catherine."

Lone Wolf shifted his weight, and Catherine felt his leg as it intertwined with hers, burrowing under and up the heavy weight of dress and petticoats. He was half lying on her, his dark eyes smoldering with naked desire.

"No man will know you but me. No man will have you but me."

His lips captured hers in a hard demanding kiss. Their very soul would be one if he had his desire; she would never escape him; she would never think of Will Dare again. Lone Wolf moved so that Catherine could feel the hardness of his body. His hands traveled tormentingly over her hips and up the side of her chest, causing her to writhe sinuously beneath his weight. Her stomach was tied in knots; her body clamored for him. She was starved for his love.

She lifted her lashes and gazed at Lone Wolf; her eyes were dark—intense—passion gleaming from their fevered depths. The reciprocal desire she saw smoldering in his eyes ignited feelings in her that she had never experienced before. Her breathing was shallow and labored, her breasts heaved against the straining confines of the bodice.

She wriggled, feeling pain as something pressed into her breasts. The wolf fangs. She remembered Lone Wolf's tenderess in the bower when they had first met, when he had circled the her neck with the gift. She remembered Wanchese standing in front of the assembly, holding the broken string of pearls in front of them. With all her heart she wanted to believe Lone Wolf was innocent . . . she did believe him to be innocent!

Her heart was in her eyes for Lone Wolf to read, but instead of taking her, he slowly disentangled himself. He

118

looked at her and smiled. "See, Catherine, already I have made you want me, and you would let me make love to you right now."

He spoke with a calmness he was far from feeling. He wanted to make love to her right now. But she was stopping him. An enigmatic flicker in her eyes—perhaps doubt or fear or both—stopped him. He lifted a hand and gently grazed his knuckles across her cheeks and the bridge of her nose. He would wait because he couldn't force himself on her. He wanted more out of their coming together. He pushed himself into a sitting position.

Catherine had thoroughly aroused his curiosity. He wondered about this man she loved. "Is this man whom you protect one of those who cower behind the skirts of a woman?" he asked, sprinting to his feet, brushing the twigs and leaves from his buckskin. "Is the one you would save yourself for cowering behind the palisades of your fort?"

With shaking fingers, Catherine buttoned her bodice, and she pushed wisps of hair off her cheek. Closing her eyes, she sought for a male image, one that bespoke courage, one that was young enough to be her lover. Her answer had to be convincing because this savage could read the very expressions on her face. Then she saw Will Dare's face.

"Nay," Catherine answered truthfully, "the man of whom I'm thinking is not one to hide behind a woman's skirttail nor does he cower behind the palisades of a fort." She opened her eyes. "This man is such that he would follow the woman he loves, and he would die fighting for her." She could speak the words with conviction because Catherine knew this would be the way Will loved. She could only hope that he would love Ellen.

Lone Wolf could not be privy to all Catherine's thoughts, but he could understand her words, her evasions; he could understand what she hadn't said.

"But this man would not follow you, my captive?"

"Nay, this man would not follow me." Using her palms, Catherine pushed to her knees then to her feet. After she dusted her gown, she walked to her chest. "He loves another." As she picked it up, she grunted, "So you need not think of murdering him." She heaved the chest up, staggering beneath the weight.

"Possibly your younger sister," Lone Wolf softly surmised.

"Aye," Catherine returned, "he loves Ellen."

"You are a noble woman," Lone Wolf said, true warmth infusing his praise. "More suited to be an Aa-da-mii than a paleface."

"What is an Aa-da-mii?" Catherine asked curiously as they began the last leg of their journey to the town of Scupperong.

"That is the name which the Grandfather gave to our people. It means 'the real people,'" Lone Wolf explained as he reached over and easily swung Catherine's chest onto his shoulder.

Startled by his taking her burden, Catherine stumbled and almost fell, but Lone Wolf's other hand darted out, and he caught her, holding her upright until she recovered her balance. She looked up at him in surprise, his gesture completely undoing her.

Wary of this change in his behavior, she said, "I thought you were the Scupperongacs."

"That is what others call us, but Manitou called us the Aa-da-mii, the real people."

"Manitou," Catherine murmured, the word disarming her, pushing away her anger and frustration, bringing to mind her dream.

"The Creator," Lone Wolf answered. "He is all wise and knowing, and he has many spirit helpers."

"That is the same with us," Catherine mused. "We, too, believe in the Creator and he has many spirit helpers whom we call angels."

"Why are your people called the English?"

Adjusting his gait to Catherine's and moving slower than he had previously, Lone Wolf walked beside her, encouraging her to talk about England and her life before she had come to America. Wanting to learn as much about the palefaces—about a possible enemy—as he could, Lone Wolf listened attentively as Catherine talked, and he asked questions, guiding the conversation. Unaccustomed to walking this slowly, Wolf Friend looked over his shoulder at Lone Wolf several times. Finally at Lone Wolf's soft command, the wolf bounded ahead of them.

The journey was altogether too short, and Catherine was unprepared for their arrival at Scupperong. The village, set on a hill, was surrounded by a strong palisade made of three rows of tall, upright pointed poles thrust close together and driven into the ground to form a strong barrier. Surrounding the palisade was a moat. Catherine and Lone Wolf walked up the broad highway to the entrance and crossed the drawbridge. Here, in single file, she followed him down the tree-lined corridor until the village lay spread before her. In the center, close to a huge tree, stood three large wigwams. One was the townhouse, the village meeting place; another, Wise One's home; the third, a guest house for important visitors. Many smaller wigwams were clustered about the townhouse, all connected by orderly and well-manicured streets bordered by low, reed fences.

When they reached the edge of the town, the inhabitants gathered. However, a group of women pressed forward, curiously peering at the paleface woman in her strange dress. Lone Wolf dropped Catherine's chest to the ground, and he and the women began to converse. Though Catherine couldn't understand the words, she knew they were asking him questions. She could hear the demands in their sharp words.

"We would torture her," Happy Woman declared,

121

peering curiously around Lone Wolf, trying to see the captive.

"I am going to keep her," Lone Wolf said to the young woman, crossing his arms over his chest. "She is to be my captive."

"You would deny us all our pleasure," she complained, her eyes derisively running the length of Catherine's dusty gown.

Lone Wolf laughed. "You would deny me my pleasure."

The other women chuckled softly, and Happy Woman bargained. "What will you give us in place of her?"

Lone Wolf looked over his shoulder at Catherine who had studied the group carefully; then he looked at her feet. He smiled. "You may have that." He pointed to Catherine's chest.

"I suppose we must accept that," the woman said, walking toward the object.

When she bent and picked it up, Catherine demanded, "What is she doing?"

Lone Wolf, walking off, replied offhandedly over his shoulder, "Happy Woman wanted to torture you. I told her that you were to be my captive, so she can have the chest instead."

"And I wish you were burning in hell, you dog," Catherine called to Lone Wolf as she ran after the Indian woman. Grabbing for the chest that held her most precious belongings, she screamed, "I have not carried this chest for so many miles to hand it over to a savage. This is mine, and I shall have it." To the Indian woman, she snarled, "And Happy Woman shall soon be Sad Woman, for I will get my chest back."

Happy Woman clutched the handle of her prize; then, shaking her head and swinging her hand, she slapped Catherine across the face. Catherine had taken all the abuse she intended to absorb. Against the Indian woman, she unleashed all the anger and frustration that had been

122

building up in her for the past seven days. She clawed and she scratched, returning blow for blow. When, finally, the furor died down, Catherine had her chest under her arm. Her breasts heaving, she drew painful gasps of air into her lungs.

With as much dignity as she could muster, she bent and picked up her ripped coif, defiantly capping it on her tangled hair. Then she clamped her hood over the coif. The throbbing in her head was so great, she could hardly stand on her feet, and her limbs ached so that she didn't think she could tolerate the pain; her integrity had been taxed to the limit. Tears were stinging her eyes, but she clutched her chest. She turned, seeing first the circle of people who stood around her, then Lone Wolf who had his arms folded across his chest, a pleased smile on his face. The wolf sat at his master's feet, panting—also grinning. Damned wolf! she fumed silently, her head lifting, her eyes correctly reading Lone Wolf's amusement. Damn both of you!

Catherine's face flamed with mortification, but her insides boiled with anger. How dare Lone Wolf do this to her! Instigate a fight and abandon her! Totally unaware that her bodice was ripped open, she moved to where Lone Wolf stood, ready to vent her anger on him. When her back was turned, however, Happy Woman lunged for her. Lone Wolf's sharp rebuke caused Catherine to spin about in time to see the Indian woman step back. Catherine turned to Lone Wolf, her words quiet but full of fury.

"Don't say another word to her, you filthy dog. You're the one who told her she could have my chest in the first place." Catherine's green eyes sparked her defiance. Her shoulders squared, her back straight, she purred, "This is mine, Lone Wolf, war werowance of the Scupperongacs. Don't ever make the mistake of giving it away again, or I shall kill you."

Lone Wolf chuckled, his ebony eyes glinting his

123

approval and admiration. Speaking to her in English, he said, "You should have killed me earlier today when I gave you the opportunity, my wild one. I fear that you are really soft when it comes to the savage who claims you as his own."

Again Lone Wolf chuckled, thinking Catherine had done well for herself. But she had also created an enemy. Happy Woman would never forget her whipping at the hands of the paleface captive. Still, he could hold his head up and walk through the camp proudly. His captive was worth having. Any of the braves would wish her in his wigwam and on his sleeping platform.

Remembering the paleface aversion to showing the body to strange men, Lone Wolf reached toward her bodice and would have lifted a piece of the torn fabric, but Catherine jumped out of his way.

"Don't touch me."

Lone Wolf laughed and shrugged. If she wanted her breast to show that was no concern of his. "Come with me, Catherine. I'll take you to our wigwam."

"To your wigwam," she spat out angrily. "I am an unwilling guest."

Lone Wolf paused, turning to level inscrutable eyes on her. "So be it."

Catherine saw the crowd step aside to let Lone Wolf walk through. In particular she noticed one young brave who stared at her, a smile in the deep recesses of his ebony eyes. Watching him more than her footing, Catherine took a deep breath and stepped forward, not knowing that she had knocked off her shoe heel during the fight. As her foot came down, she stumbled and fell against the brave who stood nearest her.

Automatically Kee-lee's arms surrounded Catherine, and he steadied her. She had fought bravely for her possessions; and even though her dress was ripped and she was dusty and disheveled, she was lovely. He had never seen a more beautiful woman. His eyes strayed to the gentle mound of creamy white flesh that innocently peeked through the ripped velvet. Never had he felt the wanting in his loins as much as he felt it at that moment.

Her hand on his chest, Catherine looked into Kee-lee's face and smiled. "Thank you," she whispered, seeing his compassion.

Before the warrior could utter a word, Lone Wolf's hand circled Catherine's arm, and he jerked her away, angrily snarling in his own language, "Never touch this woman again, my brave young fool. She is my property and until I'm through with her, keep your hands off. I would not hesitate to kill for her." Spinning around, Lone Wolf dragged Catherine through the village, ignoring the amused stares and the twittering laughter that echoed behind them.

Although Catherine hadn't understood what Lone Wolf had said, she'd understood his anger. She recognized jealousy when she saw it. "He was just helping me. You didn't have to make such a scene out of it."

"I saw the way he looked at you," Lone Wolf growled, spitting fire. "He would have you on his platform. He would like to touch your white skin; he would like to run his fingers through your hair."

Despite all her aches and pains, Catherine giggled. "You're jealous."

At the entrance of his spacious wigwam—secluded from the rest of the village, it attested to his wealth and position—Lone Wolf stopped. Looking at Catherine, he said, "Yes, I'm jealous. You're my property, and you will do well to remember that." He moved closer to her and lowered his voice until it was an ugly, sinister snarl, "You better than anyone should know that I will kill any man who touches that which is mine." He lifted his hand, grazing her cheek with his knuckles. "And you are mine, Catherine. Don't ever forget it."

Chapter VII

His words echoing in her ears, Catherine turned and stumbled through the opening into the small entry room of Lone Wolf's wigwam. Placing her chest at her feet, she slowly turned to look around. Neatly stacked against the wall of this narrow hallway were piles of firewood, and in one corner was a bundle of worked skins. She didn't have long to wonder what purpose they served. Following Lone Wolf into the wigwam, Wolf Friend bristled past Catherine to lie down and to glare disdainfully at the intruder. With as much dignity as she could summon Catherine straightened her aching shoulders and lifted her throbbing head to stare at the silent Indian who had followed her in and who now loomed over her, growing taller and more fierce by the second.

Dropping his hands to his hips in that easy stance that was so deceptive, Lone Wolf lazily looked at Catherine, his eyes slowly touching every inch of her bruised and battered body. She was so proud, he thought, looking at her dress that hung in tatters on her tall, slender body, her flesh peeking out in the most enchanting places.

When his eyes landed on her bodice, a slow smile surfaced, totally erasing his scowl and replacing it with a handsomeness that nearly decimated Catherine with the force of its sensuality. She recoiled from the intimacy, jerking her head up, haughtily defying him in gesture and pose; she wasn't going to let him arouse her again, she promised herself. That time by the river; then on the trail to Scupperong—these had been too devastating. She couldn't . . . she wouldn't. . . .

Lone Wolf's slow smile turned into beautiful warm laughter that was husky and resonant, it's vitality echoing through the wigwam. To Catherine, it seemed that he had not moved, but suddenly he was standing in front of her.

"I cannot resist touching you, Catherine. You're so different from any woman I've ever had before."

Bending his head, his mouth circled the breast that peeked so innocently out of the tear in her dress. He sucked it gently, and Catherine felt the excruciating pain of desire shoot through her body and then focus in the lower part of her stomach. She tried to resist the passion his caress generated, but her body ruled supreme at the moment, rendering her no more than a woman who desired a man's most complete, most possessive touch.

"Nay," she gasped. Closing her eyes, she unconsciously lifted her hands. She splayed her fingers in his thick black hair, massaging his scalp with the tips of her fingers, as he drew her nearer.

"Nay," Lone Wolf mocked, his tongue exploring the areola, his mouth moistily blazing a trail over the soft fullness around it. "Nay," he whispered, his breath oozing a warmth that fused through Catherine's entire being, "this is not the place. Come."

As suddenly as the caress began, it stopped. Lone Wolf caught her hand and guided her through the wigwam. When they reached the sleeping room, he left her standing near the cold, blackened fire pit, and he knelt beside the platform that circled the wall. While he made the bed, a bemused Catherine stared about. This was her first time in a wigwam, and she marveled at the spaciousness and functional practicality of the dwelling.

Oval in ground plan, the house was constructed on a framework of saplings which were set in the ground, bent over, and tied at the top to create a domelike frame. Over these rafters, Catherine noticed, braided reed mats were tied or pegged into place. The room through which they had just passed—the center room of the lodge and the only one that was directly connected with the hallway—was the largest. Built off from it were three smaller rooms, each of which had a doorway, a fire pit, and a smoke hole in the roof. Bark platforms, placed against the walls, were used as seats by day and beds by night.

"Now, Catherine Graystone," Lone Wolf softly intoned, halting her perusal of the wigwam, "it is time for you to rest."

By the time Catherine realized what was happening, Lone Wolf was lifting her into his arms and carrying her to the bed. Gently he laid her on soft bearskin blankets that covered the thick cornhusk mattress and then he leaned over, gazing at her, his dark eyes smoldering with tiny flames of passion that promised to burst into a blaze at any moment.

His hands, so big and strong, were also kind and gentle as they tenderly pulled the torn hood and veil from her hair, and stroked the tangled hair from around her face. He trailed his index finger over the delicate contour of her lips, brushing their fullness. When her mouth opened and she innocently glazed the tip with her tongue, Lone Wolf felt his manhood quicken.

Dirty and disheveled, torn and tattered she might be, but the Scupperongac warrior didn't care. She had never been more beautiful than when she had stood up to the women of Scupperong, valiantly fighting for her trunk. Even now, she is beautiful, he thought, moving his hand from her lips around her nose up to her eyebrows.

So as not to frighten her, his movements, though deliberate, were unhurried. He sat down on the platform beside her, and he worked the buttons through the openings of her dress. One . . . two . . . three. At first Catherine was content to lie in the euphoria his tender love foray provoked—the kissing and the fondling. But when he pulled her bodice aside, she realized his intent and suddenly came to life. She pressed against him and kicked.

"Get your hands off me, you dog!"

Only once did she scream; then his hand whipped out, catching her jaws, pinching into the tender flesh, and cutting off her protest. "Never again, Catherine!" he muttered hoarsely in his precise English, fighting her. "You will not scream in my wigwam, nor will you call me names. I am tired of all this fighting. I don't understand the ways of the palefaces, but you will soon learn the ways of the Indian. It is your duty to please me. You will warm my bed at night, and you will warm my body."

Shamed by her traitorous body, and again angered because he could speak English, because he owned her, Catherine cursed him, but only a muffled sound reached his ears. With one hand he held her mouth, the other her arm. As he had done earlier in the forest, he threw a heavy leg over hers, stilling their movement.

When she wilted, he laughed. "That's the way it should be. But you wouldn't please me nearly as much if you didn't fight." Again his laughter sounded through the lodge. "I shall tame you, Catherine. I promise you, I shall."

Catherine renewed her struggle, but Lone Wolf held her until she was spent and lay exhausted in his arms. He let his hand slip down over her mouth, not reckoning on another bout. Instantly, she opened her mouth, clamping her teeth into the thin stretch of skin between his thumb and index finger. Hissing his anger, Lone Wolf

129

jerked his hand away from her.

"No woman treats me like this!" he exclaimed, looking to see if she had drawn blood, but she hadn't.

When he drew back his hand to slap her, Catherine stared at him coldly. "Go ahead. Strike me. Sooth your wounded vanity with brutality. You let a woman fight me until I have no strength left. Perhaps now you can handle me." She glowered at him. "When you get through, perhaps you'll want to torture me somehow."

The anger drained out of Lone Wolf, the passion died. He stood and moved to the other side of the room. He couldn't understand this woman he had brought to his wigwam. He couldn't understand why he had insisted on her coming with him. Why hadn't he consented to the fine? His people could have used the paleface swords and knives more than they—than he—needed this woman. But he had been obsessed with her from the first time he had seen her walking out of the river, the water glowing on her beautiful skin. Because he had wanted her in his wigwam, to warm his bed and to gratify his sexual desires, he had defied the council, finally compromising when he had agreed to a political marriage in order to strengthen the ties between the Scupperongacs and the Lumbroans.

Catherine slid off the platform, pulling the shredded pieces of her dress over her breasts, and holding them up with her hands. Already exhausted from the long journey, she ached from her fight with the Indian woman. Having lost a shoe in the skirmish, she hobbled halfway across the room, stumbled, and fell; but she pushed herself to her feet. No matter how weary she was, no matter how hurt, she would never let this man see that she was defeated.

Taking off the other shoe, tossing it on the floor, she made her way to the entry room where her trunk was. She breathed deeply and bent over, the very movement, sending excruciating pain through her aching head.

130

Straining, every muscle in her body rebelling against the exertion, she lifted the chest. Then she tottered into the next room, her movements painfully slow. Lone Wolf looked up just as she stooped to come through the opening into the sleeping compartment. He didn't want to feel compassion for her, but he did. She was proud to the very last. Temporarily defeated but not destroyed. He walked across the room, took the chest out of her arms and heaved it under the platform where they were to sleep. Then he walked to where she slumped to the floor on her knees, and he scooped her into his arms.

"Don't fight me, Catherine," he murmured in his own language, not wanting her to hear his weakness. "It's time for you to bathe and rest."

Catherine heard the comforting sound of his words, but even if she hadn't, she wouldn't have fought. This time she had no fight left. She was aching all over; she was tired and hungry, so she just lay in the shelter of his towering strength, feeling his body as he moved. Her eyes were too weary to watch where she was going. Giving up, she closed them, unknowingly snuggling her face against the bronzed smoothness of his muscled chest.

Lone Wolf looked at the bundle of femininity he cradled in his arms, and he felt tenderness stir in his heart for this paleface maiden. Strangely enough this emotion was as strong as his passion had been earlier. Unseen by the villagers, he walked toward the river, not stopping until they were close to a small waterfall.

Laying her on a thick pallet of grass, he began to undress her, and she offered no resistance. She felt the overgown as he stripped it from her, the undergown, the farthingale, and the petticoats. When she lay naked and the evening breeze softly touched her battered body, she opened her eyes and stared at the man who stood above her.

She watched as he took off his moccasins, the leggings,

131

and finally the breechclout. Never having seen a man totally naked, she should have been embarrassed, she thought, but she couldn't take her eyes off him. He stood, august as a god, gazing down at her. His body, gleaming in the hue of the setting sun, looked as if it were sculpted bronze. Muscles rippled from his chest to his feet. Catherine's eyes touched every feature on his face, his chest, the thin hard line of his stomach. Her face stained red, she quickly dropped her eyes below his manhood to gaze at his muscular legs.

She couldn't bring her eyes up again. Large tears misted them and slowly ran down the sides of her face. "Please," she begged, "don't do this to me. Let me return to my people."

"I can't leave you alone, Catherine," he confessed in his own tongue.

He scooped her into his arms the third time, and he carried her into the river, slowly covering both of them in the clear, cool water. Then they were under the waterfall, and he was bathing her, massaging the soreness out of her arms and legs, cleaning her hair, combing the tangles with his spread fingers. Ironically, at the same time that the coolness of the water slowly rinsed Catherine's aches away it began to respark the fire of her attraction for Lone Wolf.

Letting her stand underneath the peppering spray, Lone Wolf walked to the shore, returning with a pouch. Thumping some herbs into his hands, he rubbed them together to create a fragrant lotion. Then he began to wash Catherine's face, careful to keep the suds out of her eyes, lightly touching her cheeks, her forehead, her chin. He brushed his hand over the arched column of her neck, and he cleaned her ears, feathering his fingers in every nook and around every curve.

Then Lone Wolf took a small piece of soft deerskin out

132

of the pouch, and using it as a washing cloth, he swept his covered palm over her collarbone, the ends of the skin tantalizing her breasts. His palm slowly inched down over the wet smoothness of her breasts, every stroke starting a new fire of excitement in her body until she was ablaze.

He deliberately dropped the cloth, leaned over, and picked up the pouch, filling his hands with more herbs. Taking his time, he rubbed his hands together. Then he lotioned her breasts as he massaged, his touch a silky caress that Catherine could hardly stand. His fingers rolled the nipples; his hands slid under and over.

"Now to rinse you," Lone Wolf husked, his voice thick and guttural.

He moved aside, exposing Catherine to the full spray of the waterfall, and he watched as the clear, cool water cascaded over her body. When her skin glistened, clean in the muted glow of the setting sun, and she looked at him with passion-glazed eyes, his tongue gently lapped the water droplets from each breast. Catherine's soft moan turned to a husky groan; she was unable to suppress the love sound. Then his mouth closed around one of the hardened tips, and he gently sucked.

The final attack came. Catherine felt his hand, stroking her inner thighs; she felt those fingers as they went higher, tantalizing her, whetting her desires. She shuddered, and her fingers clenched in Lone Wolf's hair. She couldn't stand any more of the sweet torment.

Finally Lone Wolf picked her up in his arms and carried her out of the water. Not stopping for their clothes, he walked to the wigwam, stooping, easily carrying her through the house to the sleeping platform. When he stood her on the floor, he pulled a large deerskin from the shelf above the bed, and he began to dry her, each touch as evocative as her bath.

At last Lone Wolf handed her the deerskin, and he stood, waiting for her to reciprocate his caresses. Wide-eyed, Catherine shook her head. She couldn't—she wouldn't—dry him. Shrinking away from him, she stumbled backward.

"Touch me," he commanded.

His fingers closed around her wrist and tightened, biting into her tender flesh. He dragged her closer to his lean hardness, and he pressed the deerskin into her hands.

"Dry me off."

Catherine's face was ashen with fear, not fear of Lone Wolf but fear of her own treacherous emotions. She nodded her head, clutching the skin in both hands. Closing her eyes, she began to touch his arms, rubbing them . . . feeling them . . . finally caressing them. Her breathing was labored and shallow; her chest hurt, and her heart beat frantically.

"Open your eyes, Catherine, and look at me." When Catherine shook her head, his hand rose and fisted. He tapped her chin, lifting her face. "I'm not asking. I'm telling."

His fingers bit into her soft flesh, and she slowly opened her eyes, the thick lashes evocatively sweeping up. Drawing a ragged breath and dropping her vision from his dark, somber eyes, she rubbed the soft skin over his sun-bronzed body. Gently she patted the moisture off the tender scar tissue on his chest; gently she raked the soft skin down his stomach. She knelt, and she dried his legs, her hands running down the powerful muscles from thigh to ankle.

In doing so, Catherine experienced a new and exhilarating feeling when she sensed the massive brave tremble beneath her touch. From her kneeling position, she looked up to those eyes that were glazed and drugged with passion. "Do you like this, Lone Wolf?" She feathered her fingernails around the back of his legs.

Lone Wolf, with effortless grace, stooped, picked her

134

up, and carried her to the bed. "I like that, Catherine, but I also like more."

As he laid her down, he straightened his lean body along the length of hers, the bronzed beauty of his masculinity complimenting the ivory whiteness of her femininity. His lips closed over hers, and his desperation made him less than gentle, frightening Catherine. She balled her hands and crammed them between their bodies, pushing against him, fighting. She would never willingly give in to him. She wriggled beneath him, but Lone Wolf was not to be stopped. For days he had wanted this woman, and he had killed for her. Now he would take what was his.

His long leg covered both of hers, and he stopped her movements; then he heaved his body up and over, his chest touching her breasts. He pulled her hands above her head, clamping her wrists together in an iron-banded fist, and instantly he brushed his lips down her throat, across the collarbone, back and forth in whisper-soft motions that teased and tormented.

His mouth, hot and moist, reclaimed the creamy whiteness of her breasts. His tongue sought the pink tip that was now hard with desire. When he felt her quiver beneath his caresses, he murmured in his own language, too caught up in his passion to think in English. His other hand brushed over her breasts, down her stomach, around her navel. Then his fingers touched her downy soft triangle.

Sensing her surrender, Lone Wolf loosened his grasp, and Catherine slipped her hands down, raking them through his hair. She arched until she felt him flatten his body against hers, the smoothness of his chest rubbing her nipples. She automatically began to move her hips as she felt the hardness of his arousal. His fingers touched her, preparing her. They slipped in and out the moist portal, rubbing against the point of highest sensitivity.

Catherine unconsciously whimpered her pleasure, lifting her body to his when he removed his hand. She cried out to him, begging for his touch. Then he lowered the weight of his body over hers, his knee spreading her legs apart, his hand stroking the inner line of her thigh. She felt his hardness as it touched the gate of her maidenhood, and she tensed. But his hands reassured her before he gently sheathed his masculinity in the warm folds of her femininity. He felt the tightness, the moist warmth. He sighed his joy, glad that he had waited for the coming together.

Catherine gasped as she felt his bigness in her, the strangeness of him, and she began to cry. But Lone Wolf would have no tears. He caught her chin and pulled her face up, his lips touching hers, tasting the salt of her tears. He kissed her at the same time that he gently moved in her, at the same time that his hand gently kneaded her breast.

Catherine moved, trying to jerk her body from his touch, but instead she found that the movement brought her pleasure that could not be denied. Her arms closed around his body, and her fingers dug into his back. Locked in combative oneness, she clung to him, and he began to move faster and deeper, murmuring sweetly to her.

Lone Wolf brought her to the realm of womanhood, gently, caringly. He was in no hurry; time had ceased to exist. His hands, his lips—they spoke to her of his needs and his wants. They told her of his pleasure in touching her and in loving her. Unselfishly he gave—a new experience for him. His lovemaking was different from that which he had shared with Morning Star, or with the other women since Morning Star. He made love to Catherine more softly, more gently; his every gesture filled with meaning. Always before he had taken, not really given. Now his utmost thought was to give—of

136

himself—as he had never done before.

At last Catherine tore her lips from his, and her head rolled to the side; her body drew taut as she reached the pinnacle of fulfillment. In that moment of explosive joy, the moment when lovers become one, she gasped with pleasure, then moaned softly. Her body shuddered, and her arms tightened around him. She turned her face to his shoulder, her teeth softly biting into his burning flesh, her fingers digging into him. She felt the small beads of moisture that had formed on Lone Wolf's hot skin, and she rubbed her cheek against the dampness of his smooth chest.

"Oh, Lone Wolf," she cried, "what have you done to me?"

Not sure of Catherine's emotions, not sure if her cry were one of pleasure or pain, Lone Wolf didn't immediately answer. Finally, however, he rolled to his side, holding her tightly. "I have made a woman out of you." He pushed the thick auburn mane from her face, and his lips covered her eyes, her cheeks, her lips with soft, quick caresses. "I have made you mine."

"Just a woman or your woman," Catherine whispered. In the warmth of their love, she wanted to confess her feelings; she wanted him to confess his. "Am I to share your bed as your slave or your wife?"

Lone Wolf turned on his back, twining his fingers together and pillowing his head on them. "For now as my captive. Perhaps in time I shall make you my wife." Then he promised, "But even if you should never become my wife, I will always take care of you."

Although the words weren't those Catherine wanted to hear, they were the ones she should have expected. She shouldn't have been surprised, but she was. "Will you take care of my babies too?"

He turned and propped himself on one elbow, stretching his hand on her flat stomach. The idea of her carrying his child made him happy; it filled him with pride. They would have beautiful children. A strong son. A beautiful daughter. But he didn't like her asking these questions; they stirred up feelings he wasn't ready to deal with.

"I said as long as you please me you will have a place in my lodge," he snarled.

"But the day will come, Lone Wolf, when you no longer desire me. Then, what will happen to me and my babies?"

Lone Wolf leaped to his feet and stood in the center of the room, his nakedness gilded silver by the moonlight that streamed in the opened smoke hole.

"I will love our sons and our daughters," he softly admitted, his back turned to her, his arms crossed over his chest. "And our children shall have a respected place in our village."

Familiar only with the narrow restrictions of European custom, Catherine said, "And what kind of position can a bastard expect?"

Lone Wolf turned to peer down at her curiously. "A bastard?" he questioned. "I'm unfamiliar with the word."

"In our land a child born out of wedlock is disgraced. Such a child has no name and no place in society," Catherine explained bitterly. "It is an outcast."

Lone Wolf's eyes narrowed. "Thinking it is the same with our people, you wish marriage to me only to protect your children from this disgrace?" Her desiring to become his wife for this reason angered him.

Allowing him to believe his misconception, Catherine said, "I am concerned about my children."

"Our being unmarried will not effect any children we may have," Lone Wolf explained. "I am their father no matter what the status of our relationship, and as long as they belong to one of our clans, they can be whatever

138

they wish to be in our society. All they must do is prove themselves." He smiled reassuringly. "I will allow my favorite wife to adopt them, and they will become members of her clan."

Catherine bolted into a sitting position. "Your favorite wife!" she shrieked, forgetting all about the children. "How many wives will you take?"

This was something new to her; something she hadn't counted on. Being a slave was one thing. His having several wives was something else. She was appalled at the idea of someone else adopting her children.

Pleased by her jealous outburst, Lone Wolf would have laughed, but he was vexed by Catherine's behavior. No woman ever questioned a chief as she was doing. He was also angered because this discussion brought the unpleasant thought of his arranged marriage to mind.

"As many as it pleases me," he returned with infuriating calmness. Catherine looked so shocked that Lone Wolf could no longer contain his laughter, and he wondered if she knew how beautiful she was, her anger and astonishment draped silver by the moon. "It will be up to you, Catherine, to see that it doesn't please me." He returned to the sleeping platform and lay down beside her. His voice was soft, and his fingers sent pleasurable tingles through Catherine's body as he ran them lightly up and down her thighs. "Perhaps you ought to try persuading me right now."

"Never," Catherine hissed, giving vent to her hurt and her anger. "Anything you want from me, you savage, you'll have to take it."

He pulled her down beside him, and his lips began to sweep softly back and forth across her collarbone. "I think I've already proven to you, Catherine, that I'm quite capable of doing just that."

"You beast," she cried, pushing against his chest with her fisted hands, "haven't you had enough?"

139

Laughing softly, Lone Wolf raised his head, and he looked into her face. "Never."

When Lone Wolf's deep, even breathing told Catherine that he was asleep, she slipped off the platform. Not bothering to stop for her clothes, not turning to look back, she slipped out of the wigwam and headed for the river. The water was cold, but she didn't mind; she wanted to wash the savage's touch from her body. She lifted her face to the peppering spray of the waterfall, letting her hot tears merge with nature's cleansing flow.

How different her life was going to be, she thought dismally. So different from what she had planned when she'd joined John White's venture in England. She had sailed away from her home secure in her reputation as a skilled needlewoman. Now she was a slave, less than a captive, less than a concubine.

Catherine stood beneath the shower of water so long her teeth were chattering when she walked ashore. Having felt Lone Wolf's presence, she wasn't surprised when the soft bearskin blanket fell across her shoulders. She welcomed the warmth. Neither spoke a word when he swept her into his arms, carried her into the wigwam and laid her on the platform.

Sleepy now, Catherine turned on her side. Lying beside her, curving his large frame around her smaller one, Lone Wolf draped an arm over her, locking her in his embrace, leaving her in no doubt of his ownership.

Chained to him for the rest of my life, Catherine thought. Or until I escape. Catherine consoled herself with the thought of running away. But no matter how far you run, Catherine Graystone, a small voice assured, you will never run far enough to escape. Lone Wolf has branded you his.

Chapter VIII

Disoriented by her dreaming, Catherine awakened the next morning thinking she was at the cabin with Ellen. A winsome smile playing upon her full lips, she leisurely stretched and yawned. Then, in that split second when she heard the strange noises of the village coming to life around her, the dull thud of recognition came. She was in Scupperong—a slave of Lone Wolf. She ran her hand down the side of the bed, but she knew without feeling for the long, lean body that Lone Wolf was gone. She looked about the wigwam, but it, too, was empty. Relieved that she wouldn't have to face him in daylight, she turned on her back and looked through the smoke hole at the blue sky, watching the thin, wispy clouds drift by.

She had lain awake until the early hours of morning, reliving the events of the past few days and rethinking her situation. Quiet resignation had finally replaced self-pity and sorrow. A born optimist, she determined to make the best of her circumstances. As she had been taught by her father, she would fight for what she wanted. She would stay with Lone Wolf long enough for the supply ships to arrive from England and for the settlers to remove themselves to Chesapeake Bay. Perhaps by that time the colonists would have made an alliance with other tribes, and they wouldn't need the protection of the Scupperongacs.

Pleased with her decision, Catherine was at peace with herself. Her smile deepened and a satisfied chuckle whispered through her lips. Before this captivity was over, it would be she who had seduced the mighty war chief of the Scupperongacs. He would be her slave. She would make him love her with an intensity that far outmeasured the lust he felt for her now. She would strip his integrity from him layer by layer just as he had done with her. When he was naked and vulnerable, she would leave him.

As only the desperate do, Catherine savored her plan for retribution, and she drew momentary strength from it. The bittersweet taste of revenge helped her retain a tenuous grasp on her integrity and her sanity. As the morning sun warmed her face, she breathed deeply, and her eyelids slowly drooped. Giving in to the peaceful languidness that settled over her, she dozed again.

When Lone Wolf walked in later, she was sleeping soundly, her lips gently curved into an enigmatic smile. Dropping her tattered clothes on the floor, he moved to the platform to gaze at her sleep-softened countenance. He wondered what she was dreaming.

His hands rested lazily on his lean hips, and a roguish grin played across his face. "Is there a reason why you are not yet up, Catherine Graystone?"

Immediately, Catherine's eyes opened, and she bolted up, tightly clutching the bearskin blanket under her chin. She blinked in confusion, licked her lips, and shook her head.

Lone Wolf chuckled. He found Catherine full of delightful surprises. She was lovely in her innocence. "Perhaps like me"—his fingers touched the knot of the wide buckskin belt that held his knife and war club—"you are wanting more of the pleasure that we shared last night." Although the timbre of his voice was flavored with amusement, his eyes were warm and suggestive. He was serious. "Perhaps that is what you are waiting for?"

Catherine's eyes rounded even more. "In—in the daytime?" she stammered.

"In the daytime, yes."

Nodding his head, Lone Wolf laughed; but his fingers stilled their movement. He was fascinated by the way embarrassment quickly colored her neck and face a rosy hue. But he saw more than her confusion. He saw the glowing embers of passion, the same passion that flamed through his body, ever burning but never consuming—the same passion they had shared last night. At the moment there was nothing he desired more than to make wild, passionate love to Catherine, to slake the hunger in his body, but he couldn't.

There was an emotion flickering in the depth of those enigmatic green eyes that stopped him. Unknowingly she elicited a response from him that angered and perplexed him. He cared for her; he cared too much. He found himself thinking about her and her needs more than his own. Curbing his amorous desires, he hid them behind gentle banter.

"Can the English make love during the night only?"

Catherine's eyes were locked to the strong, lean fingers which, though not moving, rested on the knot of his belt. She opened her mouth to speak, but no words would come. Taking advantage of her state of bemusement, Lone Wolf sat down on the platform beside her. Reaching out, he tenderly traced the outline of her face, finally letting his finger rest on the freckles sprinkled across her nose and cheeks. They never ceased to fascinate him.

"I don't think you have enough knowledge of such matters, Catherine Graystone, to give me an answer," he said quietly. "So I shall tell you. A man and a woman can make love at any hour of the day or night."

143

His soft, intimate touch jolted Catherine out of her bemusement.

"And we shall. I promise."

She jerked her face away and moved away from him, squirming into the corner of the platform. Defensively she clutched the blanket with shaking hands, holding it under her chin. Despite the trembling that threatened to render her a victim to his passion, she countered calmly, "I may not have had the experience, but I do have that knowledge. No one reaches spinsterhood without having heard about such going's-on."

"Spinsterhood?" Lone Wolf repeated the unfamiliar term absently, his eyes moving over her face, settling on her hair. Clearly his attention was elsewhere.

"In England a . . . a woman who . . ." Catherine began a stammering explanation, fully aware that Lone Wolf wasn't listening.

His hand strayed to the mass of auburn tangles that rioted around her face and shoulders. Like all woodland Indians he considered a woman's hair to be her crowning glory, and he took pride in Catherine's. In the early morning sun that streaked through the open smoke hole and the door, her hair gleamed a fiery autumn color, vibrant and rich. Lone Wolf admired the color because red was a favorable omen for the Scupperongacs—one which symbolized victory. Also he was glad that Catherine's hair was thick and healthy. It would look beautiful hanging in shiny, long braids. He would be the envy of the entire tribe for having such a slave as Catherine.

". . . and a spinster is one who— Ooowww!" Catherine's explanation ended in a shriek as Lone Wolf's hands settled on her shoulders. In one unexpected and quick motion he had turned her around so that her back was to him. "What are you doing?" she screeched indignantly, frantically clawing for her cover.

144

"I'm going to comb your hair."

His calm matter-of-factness infuriated Catherine. His presumption that she would accept his ministrations with docility galled her. When Lone Wolf stood, reaching for the comb on the shelf above the sleeping platform, Catherine grabbed the bearskin robe, awkwardly wrapping it around herself as she flounced off the bed. Defiantly she stood in the middle of the wigwam. Surprised, he turned to look at her.

"You're not going to comb my hair," she retorted. "When I want my hair combed, I'll do it myself, thank you."

Holding the comb in one hand, Lone Wolf continued to gaze at her. Irritation flickered in the depths of his dark eyes. "I think you have forgotten your place," he reprimanded, his quietness covering the brewing storm of anger. He motioned her to him, but she shook her head. Lone Wolf's eyes narrowed to a slit, his mouth thinned. "If there is one thing you will learn, Catherine Graystone," he said tightly, "you will learn to obey me."

His quietness, like the illuminating brilliance of lightning that splits the darkness, was a prelude to the ominous clap of his thunderous anger. Still she didn't move. Again she shook her head. "When it pertains to my duties, I shall obey you," she told him, "but not when it comes to your pleasuring yourself with my body."

Lone Wolf took a step toward her. "As my slave your primary duty is to please me, whether it be pleasuring me with your body or not, and the sooner you learn this the better it will be for you." His fingers tightly circled her upper arm, and he dragged her to the platform. Unceremoniously he pushed her down, and she sank onto the softness of the rabbit furs that lay upon a thick cushion of pine needles and reed mats. Lone Wolf sat on the platform and penned the wriggling, uncooperative woman in place with his legs. "Right now it will give me

145

great pleasure to comb your hair."

"Well, that doesn't pleasure me," Catherine grunted, jerking her head from his grasp at the same time that he pressed the quills of the porcupine tail hairbrush into her auburn tangles. "Ouch," she cried, "that hurts."

"It wouldn't hurt if you'd be still," Lone Wolf responded. "You'll learn in due time, Catherine Graystone, that your defiance will gain you nothing but pain and misery." He ran his palm over the crown of her head. "If you'll just relax, I can give you much pleasure."

Lone Wolf caught the length of her hair and began to pull the brush through the ends, gently easing the tangles out, moving higher with each stroke. Finally when Catherine had ceased to fight him, he relaxed his legs.

"Your hair is beautiful, Catherine, and I take great pride in it. I'll ask No-am-ee to give you a pouch of herbs for your hair and face." Lone Wolf's words ceased as he concentrated on pulling the comb through Catherine's thick, vibrant waves, capping her skull with his palm and running the comb down the auburn lengths.

Catherine sat quietly, her mind totally consumed with curiosity. Finally she ventured, "Who . . . who is No-am-ee?"

Unable to resist teasing his captive, Lone Wolf chuckled. "She is the person whom I love most."

"Is she the one whom you would wed?"

"Aye," Lone Wolf answered, his chuckle burgeoning into deep, quiet laughter as Catherine wilted into silence. "I would wed her, Catherine, but she has chosen to live by herself." Laying the comb on the platform, he gently massaged her scalp. Moving his fingers from the crown of her head to the nape of her neck, he kneaded into her flesh, releasing, digging in again. "Why do you ask?"

"Just curious."

"Perhaps a little jealous?"

"Nay. In order to be jealous I would have to love you."

146

"I think not," Lone Wolf countered. "I am jealous of anything I possess."

As his hands massaged Catherine's tense shoulder muscles, he willed her to relax beneath his touch. Closing her eyes, she slipped into a euphoric state. Nothing existed but her body and Lone Wolf and his touch. Penetrating the languid haze of contentment that surrounded her, she heard his voice.

"Every morning you must wash your hair with the herbs No-am-ee will give you. When you get through washing it," he told her, picking up the comb and parting her hair in a straight line down the middle, "rinse it with sunflower-seed oil. That will keep it shiny and healthy." Nudging her around with his knee, he dropped the comb and pulled her hair to one side. "It is the custom in our village for the married women to wear their hair in one braid, unmarried in two." His fingers deftly wove the thick strands in and out. "And so shall you."

"Only if I choose to do— Oh-oooo . . ." Her defiant retort ended in a howl of pain when Lone Wolf yanked on her hair.

"I choose for you to do so, and you will."

Although she didn't intend to comply with his command merely because it was his wish, Catherine knew arguing would get her nowhere. After Lone Wolf finished the braiding, he wrapped a decorated thong around the end of each plait and dropped them over her shoulders. When Catherine lifted a hand and touched the curl that hung below the band, she touched something hard. Lifting the braid up, her eyes widened in disapproval.

"A wolf fang," she gasped.

"My totem," he explained matter-of-factly as if she didn't already know. Again he declared his ownership of her. "Always wear it so everyone will know that you belong to me."

147

"Branded with a wolf fang so that everyone will know that I am your slave," Catherine murmured bitterly. "Branded by two braids so everyone will know I share your mat but not your life as your wife."

"Branded?" Lone Wolf asked, trailing his index finger over the splattering of freckles on her exposed shoulders.

"Wearing your marks," Catherine explained, shrugging away from his touch and turning so that she was looking at him.

"Why do you dislike wearing my totem?" Lone Wolf's face was impassive, but Catherine could see the puzzlement in his eyes.

"Being a slave is one thing," she said, "but having to make a public display of it is something else."

"I am not making a public display of you," Lone Wolf denied softly. "I am protecting you."

"Protecting me?" Catherine's words were whisper soft, and her eyes questioningly ran over his face.

"As long as the people know you are mine, they will not hurt you. They must answer to me for anything they do to you."

"I . . . I don't understand you," Catherine said, getting to her feet and awkwardly pulling the blanket around her nakedness in an effort to keep the enticing beauty of her slim body hidden. When she saw the rakish grin split Lone Wolf's face, she knew she had not succeeded. "One minute you can be so hard and cold. You brand me a slave and make me your concubine. Yet the next minute you can be warm and caring. Bathing me and combing my hair."

Lone Wolf smiled. The more he was around Catherine, the more she delighted him.

"Perhaps you could understand me, Catherine Graystone, if you thought of me as a man rather than a savage." His lips curved, and friendly lines splintered from the corners of his eyes.

"How can I think of you as anything but a savage?" Catherine countered. "You have abducted me, have taken my virginity, and have made me a whore."

As the full impact of her accusations hit her, Catherine lowered her head. In a few short weeks Lone Wolf had done to her what no other man had been able to do. He had completely divested her of her integrity and her freedom; he had taken the honor of her maidenhood away from her. No honorable man would want to marry her now. She was an outcast in both societies.

As suddenly as the wave of depression prompted by that realization had swept over Catherine, it receded, and she whipped her head up. "And how can I think of you as anything but a savage when your totem"—she caught one of the braids in her hand and held it out, dangling the polished teeth in front of Lone Wolf—"was found on the murdered body of Running Bear, Peace Chief of the Roanoacs." She laughed at her insinuation, the sound a bitter snort. "You seem to enjoy hanging your sign on all your handiwork—the bad as well as the good—and on all your possessions."

The friendliness on Lone Wolf's face quickly vanished. His visage set in uncompromising lines, his chin lifted an arrogant jot, and his eyes glittered like polished ebony. "An Indian is always proud of his work and of his possessions," he told her in flinty tones. "And he would be a fool not to mark what is his. Otherwise, he is giving someone permission to take it from him." His voice was the lowest Catherine had ever heard it; yet it was as hard as a finely tempered sword, as sharp and cutting, as deadly.

"You are mine, and I care about what's mine. But I will not tolerate your questioning me. I have already told you that I answer to no one but our tribal council for my actions." His eyes swept contemptuously over her bearskin-draped figure. "Remember this and remember

149

it well, Catherine Graystone, I care for you and I shall protect you as long as you are mine. But that is exactly what you are. You are mine. My slave. My possession. As my chattel you owe me an explanation for your actions."

Catherine willed herself to stare unwaveringly at the man across the room who seemed to be as immovable as a stone statue. He would have locked her gaze to his; he would have captured her proud spirit, but Catherine would not allow him to. Even in the face of such great odds, she challenged him; she defied him, proudly letting him read the defiance in her eyes.

"If you'll get out," she said quietly, "I'll put on my clothes."

"These will be more suitable." Moving to the edge of the platform, he picked up a buff-colored buckskin dress and moccasins, and held them out to Catherine.

As many times as she had commented to Ellen that she would like the freedom of movement which Indian garments provided, Catherine balked now that the opportunity to wear them presented itself. She was determined to challenge Lone Wolf's every wish and command. Looking at the dress and moccasins with disdain, she walked to where her clothes lay. Holding the blanket with one hand, she stooped and picked up her farthingale.

"I prefer to wear my own clothes." She straightened and glared at him.

Her continued defiance and obstinance irritated Lone Wolf, but he said nothing. He had known from the beginning that she was spirited and stubborn. As much as he wanted to tame her, he didn't want to break her spirit. She was one who would learn only through experience. He smiled inwardly as he thought about one of the first lessons his grandfather had taught him: experience is the teacher we remember longest because it can be the most arduous and the most humiliating. Finally Lone Wolf dropped the dress and moccasins onto the platform.

Shrugging, he conceded, "Wear whatever you wish."

"If you'll just step out . . ." Smugly Catherine motioned him out of the wigwam.

Sitting on the platform, Lone Wolf shook his head. "Nay, Catherine Graystone. I shall let you wear what you wish, but I shall not be ordered out of my wigwam. When and if you dress in the wigwam, it shall be in front of me." He laughed when he saw the rich color that stained her cheeks. "Is there more for me to see than what I saw last night?"

Although the tanned hide was slipping off her shoulders and drooping so low on the floor that she was tripping as she walked, Catherine marched across the room with as much dignity as she could muster. Stooping at her chest, she unfastened the lock and lifted the lid. Rather than taking out her linen house gown, however, she chose one of her best dresses, the golden velvet. She looked at the dress, then glanced over her shoulder at Lone Wolf. There was only one problem. She couldn't dress without undressing.

Lone Wolf's rakish grin and position announced that he was not moving. Taking a deep breath, Catherine stood and dropped the blanket, her body gleaming gold in the sunlight. Although she tried to avert her gaze from the man who lounged on the platform, she couldn't. Like a magnet he compelled her to look at him.

When she saw the fire that smoldered in his eyes, her entire body burned with remembered pleasure. She could feel every touch and sensation. She felt the liquid heat of desire turn her blood to fire and rage through her body, reducing her resistance to nothing, reaffirming that she was passionately enslaved to this man.

Marshaling her errant emotions and placing them under the tight rein of feigned indifference, Catherine put on her undergarments one by one. Despite Lone

151

Wolf's low chuckles of amusement at her clumsy movements and the ridiculous-looking clothes, she maintained her aplomb, managing to keep her motions slow and deliberate. When she had finished dressing, she ironed the wrinkles out of her dress with her hands.

"If you'll tell me what my duties are, I'll begin working." Her voice was filled with disdain. Not waiting for his reply, she immediately said, "I suppose we'll begin with the meals first . . . breakfast, noon—"

With an indolence that belied his reed strength and agility, Lone Wolf uncurled his body and stood. "We eat two meals a day," he informed her. "For the morning meal we warm over the food left from the meal we've had the night before." Bruskly he added, "But it is not for me to inform you of a woman's duties. Come I'll take you to No-am-ee. She will teach you."

Is this an added punishment? Catherine wondered, thinking she was to be tutored by the woman whom he wished to wed.

Immediately, when they walked out of the wigwam, Wolf Friend materialized, quietly moving to one side of Lone Wolf, Catherine on the other. As they walked through the village, Catherine quickly learned the folly of her decision to wear the velvet overgown and the brocade slippers with high heels. Although it was early morning, perspiration glistened on her forehead and rivuleted down her back, staining her garment. Added to the discomfort of her sweat-damp clothes, her feet, still tired from the four-day overland trek, were hurting. When she reached up to wipe the sheen of moisture from her face, Lone Wolf looked at her and grinned. Noticing that she pampered her aching feet with a slight limp, he chuckled aloud.

He lifted his face to the sun and said conversationally, "It's going to get warmer. Elder Brother shares his heat with us through Big Chestnut. Next moon, however, we'll begin to have cool weather."

Catherine wanted to smack the pompous grin off his face, but she knew she had no one to blame for her predicament but herself. "What is Big Chestnut?" she asked instead.

"Like you we divide our year into twelve moons," he quietly explained.

"Then October is Big Chestnut," Catherine interposed excitedly. "What is November called?" she asked. When Lone Wolf looked at her questioningly, she said, "Next moon. What is it called?"

"Change in Weather," he answered. "That's when Grandfather of the North begins his journey through the land, bringing the cold, ice, and snow."

They lapsed into a comfortable silence and walked a way before Lone Wolf asked, "Why did you want to know what we call the coming moon?"

"My—my birthday is next month," Catherine answered. "I was born on the twelfth of November, and I just wondered what it would be called in your language."

Her face glowing with fond memories of past birthdays, days spent with her father and Ellen, she looked at Lone Wolf and smiled, the gesture causing him to catch his breath at her beauty. Excitedly she told him about the parties and the presents. "My father gave me a freedom that only men have in our country," she said reminiscently. Then her voice lifting excitedly, she revealed, "I'm reckoned quite a bowman. Father had a special bow and arrows made for me by the finest bowman and fletcher in all England." Before she knew it, she was singing a ditty her father had written for her twelfth birthday—the last one she had shared with him. As the last note died, she lapsed into a moment of saddened silence.

"What's wrong?"

Softly she said, "All I have left are a few momentoes

and many memories."

"What are momentoes?" Lone Wolf questioned.

"Possessions," Catherine explained. She unbuttoned the small purse that was attached to the waist of her gown. Pulling out a small gold band, she held it up for Lone Wolf to see. "Like this—a ring that belonged to my father."

Interested, Lone Wolf stopped walking and turned to face Catherine. He reached for the piece of jewelry, turning it in his hand.

"Just before she died, my mother gave that to Father," Catherine said. "It was a wedding gift to express her love for him."

With his fingertip Lone Wolf brushed the inscription on the inside of the ring. "Is this his mark?"

Catherine looked at the words, her tears causing them to swim in front of her eyes. But she didn't have to read them; she had committed them to memory many years ago. "To my darling, with all my love."

"Yes," she whispered, too choked up to say the words. "It is my father's mark."

"It is a beautiful totem, Catherine." He paused. "You will give it to the man whom you love? This will be your mark of love to him?"

"To the man whom I marry," she averred softly, adding with a teary catch in her voice, "I—I just wish Father could have lived longer. My life would have been so different."

"Grandfather Time is far wiser than we are," Lone Wolf told her, handing her the ring. "He knows when to cut the string of life for each individual." He smiled, again exposing that vulnerable, tender side of his personality. "I'm sure your father is happier in the spirit world."

"Aye," Catherine whispered, dropping the jewelry into her purse and buttoning the flap, "he would still be suffering." She smiled through her tears, her eyes sparkling like gems.

"And once you've accepted your fate," Lone Wolf nonchalantly stated, "you'll be far happier."

Catherine's smile faded, and her eyes hooded. "Could you be happy in slavery?"

"I am a man," he answered. "For me it is different."

Catherine nodded. She'd heard that answer so many times before. Truly there was a greater chasm between a man's and a woman's world than there was between life and death. "Tell me something about your parents," she said.

"A family does not discuss its dead," he returned with quiet reverence. "To talk about them or mention their names would cause them unrest in the world of Manitou and his spirits. Others may speak of them and their valiant deeds, but they are always careful not to call them by name until they have been dead a year and have had time to make their journey to the land of Manitou."

"But I thought—" Catherine was clearly puzzled. "I mean, Will said according to your law one of us could be adopted to take the dead maiden's place."

"It is the family's right to replace their daughter, but Manitou allows the adopted one to choose her own name according to her deeds and the path which she walks. At birth we are named by our grandmother. Later after we have proven ourselves warriors we can choose our own names. Sometimes a girl changes her name when she reaches womanhood but most frequently she does not."

"You chose to be called Lone Wolf?"

The words, like a knife, twisted into Lone Wolf; they echoed through his head, refusing to be silenced. The question jarred memories he had tried to forget— memories of a young warrior called Growling Wolf and of his beautiful bride Morning Star.

155

After marriage, as was the custom of his people, Growling Wolf had moved to his bride's wigwam and had lived with her family. He had hunted, fished, and fought beside his father-in-law and his brothers-in-law. Two winters later, Morning Star had given birth to their first child—a boy.

There had been cause for celebration, and the dedication ceremony had been one of the finest their village had ever seen. The great tribal chief, the Wise One, had traveled from Scupperong to hold the baby up to Manitou; he had spoken words of wisdom over him. Wise One's wife, Sunflower Woman, chieftain for all who belonged to the Bear clan, had spoken over the babe too. At the end of the ritual, Herb Woman, Morning Star's mother, had picked the infant up. She had walked to the center of the ceremonial hall, and standing close to the sacred fire that burned always, she had lifted the baby to the heavens, and had prayed for them to watch over the child forever.

Then had come the day in late autumn, two years later, when Growling Wolf was returning to the village after several days of hunting. He smelled the smoke before he saw it, a banner of death spiraling its message through the air. Dropping his deer, he ran the next several miles, arriving too late to save his family. The Iroquois, always harboring enmity for the Cherokee whose lands bordered the Scupperongacs, violated a trading truce, warring with their ancient enemies, marauding and looting other villages as they passed by. Hurrying to reach their homes in the North Land before the winter snows came and fearing immediate reprisal, the Iroquois had taken no captives. They had spared no one. In the rubble of ashes and bodies, the young warrior searched for his family. He found them.

Pride filled his heart when he saw that Morning Star, a war club in her tiny hand, had died fighting, but anguish

156

seared his soul when he took her lifeless body in his arms, when he thought about his unborn child. And he could hardly endure his pain when he found Little Eagle's body lying beneath the protective frame of his mother. Tenderly Growling Wolf scooped Morning Star into his arms, and he prepared her for burial; then he returned for his son.

He held the tiny form in his arms. Little Eagle they had all called him. Clumsy Eagle they had said teasingly as he'd toddled behind his mother and his grandmother, Chattering Eagle when he had asked so many questions. But they had all known that one day he would preen his feathers and soar like the mighty eagle. Disciplined from birth not to cry but to accept life stoically, the brave held the lifeless bundle, his son, in his arms. Dropping his face, he laid his forehead against the boy's ash-smudged cheek. Too little to fight but not too little to die. Truly he was a Brave Eagle. Unashamedly the lone brave let the tears stream down his cheeks as he placed a farewell kiss on his son's head. Then, lifting his sun-colored face to Manitou, he chanted the sorrow of his heart.

After he had buried his family, Growling Wolf buried the others. Not much more alive himself, in a waking stupor, he walked through the smoldering waste of the village one more time. He almost didn't hear the low moans. Someone was alive! Frantically he searched through the underbrush. There he found the old one, Laughing Brook, badly wounded but not dead. In the coming days he tended her wounds, promising that he would take care of her as long as she lived. When she was strong enough to be moved, he carried her to Scupperong; the two of them had lived here ever since—each alone. Both had taken new names. Laughing Brook had become No-am-ee or The Woman Who is Alone, and Growling Wolf had become Lone Wolf.

Lone Wolf's withdrawal and his preoccupation

157

bothered Catherine. She wondered why he was ignoring her question. More curious than before, she repeated it. "Can you not tell me why you are called Lone Wolf?"

Jarred out of the painful past, he said, "At one time I was called Growling Wolf. After a trading party broke the autumn truce and attacked our village, killing everyone but No-am-ee and me, I called myself the Lone Wolf."

"Did you tame the wolf because of your name?" she asked.

Lone Wolf smiled, shaking his head and looking at the animal who walked so proudly beside him. "No. I found him when he was a pup." Lone Wolf's voice never betrayed his emotion, but his eyes were softer than usual and his smile deepened as he remembered that cold winter day. "Though a tiny pup, he was lying beside the cold, stiff body of his mother, protecting her. If I hadn't come along, he would have died because he was too small to make it by himself. I brought him to No-am-ee, and we nursed him back to health. He's been with me ever since."

At a small one-room wigwam on the outskirt of the town, Lone Wolf stopped talking, and Wolf Friend, accustomed to coming here, lay down, his golden brown eyes following Lone Wolf's movements. Before Lone Wolf ducked through the open door, he cautioned, "You must stand behind me until I sit; then sit behind me. But say nothing until No-am-ee addresses you directly and never call her by name."

Catherine gazed at him, her eyes narrowing with inquiry. "What do I call her?" she asked.

"She will let you know," he answered, stooping to enter the wigwam.

"Aren't you going to knock?" Catherine asked, placing a detaining hand on his arm.

"She welcomes visitors," he replied, pointing to a large, squared piece of bark that leaned against the

158

wigwam. "When the bark is removed from the opening, people may walk in unannounced." Through the door, he straightened up.

Curiously, Catherine peered around him at the white-haired woman who knelt on her knees in front of the fire burning in the center of the room. Catherine's eyes widened with recognition. No-am-ee was one of the council members who had been with Wise One at the settlement. No-am-ee, however, did not acknowledge Catherine's presence.

With a wooden spoon, she stirred fresh corn mush in a tall clay pot. Venison, potatoes, and wild onions, impaled on a long stick, roasted on the fire. In order to brown the meat evenly, No-am-ee turned the stick constantly. The odor that permeated the wigwam tantalized Catherine's taste buds, reminding her that she had eaten nothing but parched corn since she had left the settlement.

"Good morning, Grandmother," Lone Wolf said, moving farther into the room. "How are you today?"

"I am fine, my son," the old woman returned, evincing no curiosity about Catherine, ignoring her presence altogether. "Grandfather East has touched my wigwam with his goodness. He has brought the cooling winds from the Great Water and warm rains for our cornfields and gardens." Her voice softened as she praised the East Wind for his blessings. "I awakened this morning to the sunlight that streamed in my door and thanked Grandfather East for waking me to a new day." She pushed the logs into the fire. "And how are you?"

"I'm fine, Grandmother."

"Are you hungry?" No-am-ee asked, rising with easy grace. Her wrinkled face lifted, and she peered at the standing brave.

"I am."

"Then be seated, my son. I have prepared your food. We will eat." Not by word, gesture, or glance did the old woman acknowledge Catherine. Nor did she offer her anything to eat.

Cross-legged, Lone Wolf sat before the fire. He held both hands out. From one dangled a tobacco pouch, from the other a wampum belt. "I have come to ask a favor," he said, "and I bring you gifts. An embroidered pouch from the Cherokee filled with fine tobacco, and a string of white wampum from the Lenapi to ensure you happiness and health. A string of white wampum for the continuation of our peace."

No-am-ee looked at both gifts, but she made no move to take them. Instead, she spoke in the quiet melodious tones that Catherine was coming to associate with the older woman. "The legend goes, my son, that wampum is like the very heart of our people. Anything we say with wampum will live forever and never be forgotten by our people. Manitou has said that anyone who accepts a string of wampum must fulfill the promise made when the gift is received, and an Aa-da-mii always keeps his word because of this sacred wampum."

Although Lone Wolf had heard the legend told and retold many times, he listened as if this were the first time, and he answered respectfully. "That is so, my grandmother."

No-am-ee reached across the fire, taking both the gifts. "What would you have me do, my son?"

"I would like you to teach my slave," he said.

"That is the paleface you have brought to our town?" No-am-ee asked, her gaze never flickering from Lone Wolf's face.

"That is so, Grandmother. I have brought her for you to meet."

For the first time since they had entered the wigwam, Catherine's presence was acknowledged. Lone Wolf turned and motioned for her to sit down behind him. Seconds of silence stretched into minutes as No-am-ee stared impassively across the flames at the English

160

woman. Her black eyes accented by thick gray eyelashes seemed to penetrate Catherine's soul.

"This is a hard task you ask of me, my son."

"But you, my grandmother, are the one whom I would have do it."

Catherine knew they were talking about her, but she didn't understand their dialect well enough to interpret what they were saying. Forgetting Lone Wolf's admonition, Catherine slowly signed a greeting to No-am-ee.

Lone Wolf spun around and opened his mouth to reprimand her; however, before the words came out, No-am-ee spoke.

"Leave her alone, my son. I would have her speak to me."

"I am the one called Catherine," Catherine signed, trying to remember all that Running Bear had taught her.

"I am the Woman Who Is Alone," the Indian woman replied. "How did you learn our silent words?"

"From Running Bear, Peace Chief of the Roanoacs," Catherine explained falteringly with a mixture of signs and utterances. "He was my friend. He taught me to speak his language."

"You wish to learn the ways of the Aa-da-mii?" No-am-ee asked.

"Not really," Catherine replied without hesitation, "but I have no choice. I must learn your ways because I am Lone Wolf's slave."

Catherine thought she saw a twinkle of amusement in the depths of those flinty eyes, but she couldn't be sure.

"You forever speak words of truth?"

"Aye," Catherine signed. "I speak words of truth."

"It is good," No-am-ee said. "Have you eaten?"

When Catherine shook her head, the old woman reached under the platform and pulled out three reed mats. She placed one in front of each of them. Then she filled a wooden bowl with warmed-over corn mush, seasoned with tasty bear fat and berries, and set it

161

between them.

Because Lone Wolf was the guest of honor, No-am-ee handed him an ornate buffalo horn spoon that she had bartered for. She handed Catherine a wooden one, signing, "A woman must wait until the brave has taken the first bite of his meat before she begins to eat. If there are no men present for the meal, she must wait until the oldest woman present has taken the first bite of meat."

Catherine nodded her head, her mouth watering as the aroma of the sweet corn and the broiling venison tempted her nostrils. Her stomach growled. But No-am-ee was not to be hurried. True, the girl was only a slave, but it had been a long time since No-am-ee had had the responsibility of a family, and she rather liked the idea of teaching the paleface. She would enjoy having someone to work with and to talk to . . . and she would like to learn more of this paleface.

. . . *with the hair the color of the sunset and eyes like the green leaves of the forest. The one who came to them in the autumn. Was she the one?*

Lifting her head, No-am-ee prayed over their meal. "Our father, hear us, and our grandfather," she began, chanting a haunting melody of thanksgiving, which she concluded with, "Listen to us, Father, Grandfather. We ask thought, heart, love, and happiness. We are going to eat." She nodded to Lone Wolf.

He dipped into the bowl. Taking his first bite of the mush, he smacked his lips appreciatively, complimenting the cook. When he reached for the stick of impaled venison chunks, potatoes, and wild onions, the aroma renewed its attack on Catherine's taste buds. Laying his spoon down on his mat, he pulled off the first chunk of meat and tossed it into the blaze as an offering to Grandfather Fire, but he bit into the second piece, making sounds to indicate his pleasure as he ate. No-am-ee nodded to Catherine, and both women dipped their spoons in at the same time. Never had Catherine tasted a

162

meal to equal this one. When she thought she couldn't eat another bite, she laid her spoon on the reed mat as Lone Wolf and No-am-ee had done.

No-am-ee quietly walked across the wigwam, reaching into one of the larders buried under the earth to pull out some large, succulent grapes and a melon that she had been cooling in some spring water. To Lone Wolf and to Catherine she gave a liberal helping. While they ate the fruit, No-am-ee wiped the bowls and spoons with dried grass and returned them to their basket beneath the platform.

Then she stood, stretched her hands to a rafter, and took down a long buckskin pouch. Pulling the string, she extracted a beautiful, hand-carved pipe. She crumbled some tobacco from the gift pouch Lone Wolf had brought her and, raking a live coal on a small piece of bark, lit the pipe.

No-am-ee took a few puffs. "Thank you for the *kinni-kinnik,* my son," she said, referring to the mixture of tobacco, sumac leave, and dogwood bark. She handed the pipe to Lone Wolf. "It is as you wish. I will teach your slave the ways of the Aa-da-mii."

Lone Wolf inclined his head in gratitude and lifted the pipe to his lips, taking two puffs like No-am-ee. "Thank you, Grandmother, for your consideration." He handed the pipe to Catherine, saying in English, "Take two puffs; then thank No-am-ee for her generosity in sharing her food and her knowledge with you."

Catherine took the pipe, wishing the women of the court could see her now. They would be green with envy, she thought, a small smile tugging her lips. Smoking was all the rage in England, but what little tobacco the English received came from Spain so it was scarce. No one did much smoking. There the finely made pipes were empty, and here hers was full.

Following the example set by No-am-ee, Catherine took two puffs of the tobacco, coughing and sputtering as she swallowed the smoke. Chuckling softly, Lone Wolf took the pipe from her and returned it to the smiling No-am-ee as Catherine wiped the tears from her eyes.

The wampum accepted, the promise made, the ritual over, No-am-ee said, "How was your journey to the North Land, my son?"

"Conditions are far worse than we feared, my grandmother. Although the Scupperongac are strong, we must form alliances if we are to keep the Iroquois from taking our lands, and now we have another confederation to consider. A few of the small, scattered tribes of the Chesapeake are uniting into a confederacy. I fear the palefaces will soon join one faction or the other."

Her eyes closed, No-am-ee asked, "How long will our people accept war as the answer? How long will you walk the trail of revenge?"

"I will not rest, Grandmother, until I have revenged the death of my family." Lone Wolf growled low in his throat. "I would see all Iroquois dead."

"All Iroquois would see you dead, my son," No-am-ee replied. "You have become their most dangerous enemy, and to the Lumbroans you are but little better." She thumped her pipe and reinserted it in the long slender pouch, hanging it on the rafter. "Though I tire of being confined to the wigwam, I look forward to the winter, my son. Then the forest is naked and offers a warrior no protection. I welcome the peace that it brings to our villages."

Lone Wolf chuckled. "Old woman, it is not peace you are looking forward to. You are looking forward to the ball games and the harvest festival when you can make large wagers."

No-am-ee laughed. "If I do not get out to the fields and help the women gather the corn, we may not have feasting this year. Certainly no gaming and no betting." Her eyes swept over the ornate gown that Catherine wore; her gaze lingering on the ever-growing stains across the shoulders and under the arms. "Did you not give her the dress?"

"I did," Lone Wolf answered, "but she is a spirited one, my grandmother. She refused to put it on, preferring her paleface clothes."

No-am-ee said, "So be it."

A young girl about seventeen years old ducked through the opening of the wigwam and walked to the center of the room. Because it was not considered good manners for an unmarried woman to look directly into the face of a man until given permission by her father or her husband, the maiden never looked in Lone Wolf's direction. However, she cast her somber eyes in Catherine's direction, curiously running them over the rich velvet material of her gown, her gaze lingering on the exquisitely embroidered designs and on the delicate ruffs at the neck and the wrists.

"I am glad that you are here Re-bekk-ana," No-am-ee said. "You will watch the fire while I teach the one called Catherine how to care for Lone Wolf."

When Catherine heard No-am-ee say the young woman's name, she smiled, but Re-bekk-ana, again bowing to custom, did not return the gesture. Until she knew Catherine better and accepted her as a friend, Re-bekk-ana's expression would remain closed, her eyes would be hooded, her words guarded. But already she liked the paleface woman. Catherine was pretty, and her smile was warm. It came from her soul.

"Re-bekk-ana," No-am-ee said to Catherine, pointing at the young girl. She signed for Catherine to repeat the name.

"Re—Re-bekk-ana," Catherine stammered, mimicking the sounds of the older woman.

"Cath-er-ine," No-am-ee said to Re-bekk-ana, waiting for the maiden to repeat the name.

Slowly Re-bekk-ana repeated Catherine's name,

stammering over the strange sounds as Catherine had done. Then the young women looked at each other and smiled, instantly warming to one another.

"Watch the fire." No-am-ee repeated her instruction to Re-bekk-ana.

Smiling at No-am-ee, Re-bekk-ana laid her basket of mending on the floor. "I shall be careful, Grandmother."

Re-bekk-ana understood No-am-ee's fears, and she didn't resent the old woman's repetition of her instruction. Fire was the tragedy all Indians feared most. It destroyed wigwams, household possessions, and clothes. More, it destroyed all the underground stores of food. Since the household goods, piled neatly along the walls, were made of wood, grass, or skins, they burned easily; therefore, one spark might set the entire village on fire. A girl or older woman always stayed inside the house to tend the small cooking fire, getting coals ready for roasting meat and watching the water that was being heated in the large clay pot.

No-am-ee walked across the wigwam and picked up a wide-mouthed burden basket which had a narrow flat bottom and curving sides. Motioning Catherine closer to her, she adjusted the braided buckskin rope so that it fit under the curve of the basket and over Catherine's chest and shoulders. "While you are training for the first game, my son, I will train your slave." A smile touched her wrinkled face as No-am-ee slipped the flat braided band over Catherine's forehead. "When you return to your wigwam tonight, we will have a fire and a hot meal waiting."

Turning, No-am-ee ducked through the doorway, stepping into the brilliance of the new day. Without a backward glance, she marched through the village. Catherine followed several steps behind her, the burden basket and her position announcing her servility to the villagers.

166

Chapter IX

The sun relentlessly beat down on Catherine, and for the hundredth time she wished she could vent her fury on Lone Wolf. When he had so easily conceded to let her wear her best gown, he had known she would be working in the cornfield! And he had been laughing at her. If only she hadn't been so obstinate! . . . If only she had taken Lone Wolf's suggestion about wearing the buckskins! . . .

What a pathetic sight she was! She bowed her head and looked at herself. Gone was the fashionable gown of brocade and velvet. Her skirt, having dragged against the rough cornstalks and the charred tree stumps that dotted the cornfield, was dirty and snagged. Her bodice was drenched with perspiration, and her shoes were ruined. She had broken both heels before she had filled and emptied her basket the third time. Her face, already baked a bright red, was streaked with dirt where she had wiped the perspiration from it. Her fingernails were broken, her hands blistered.

Catherine's morale was at its lowest level since she had arrived in America. No-am-ee had taken her to the cornfield and had shown her what to do, but the old woman, in order to get a fire started in Lone Wolf's wigwam so she could prepare the evening meal, had left Catherine to harvest alone. In addition to battling the elements and learning the antiquated farming methods of the Scupperongacs, Catherine had to cope with the festering resentment of the women. Being something of a linguist and a quick learner and already knowing Running Bear's dialect, Catherine quickly recognized words and phrases in the Scupperongac language, and she knew Happy Woman was ridiculing her to the other women. But Catherine continued to work, ignoring the Indian woman.

Her row finished, her burden basket filled, Catherine straightened. Passing a dirty hand over her forehead and running her finger under the tumpline to ease the pressure, she sighed, wondering how much longer she was going to have to work today. She lifted her hand to her forehead and shielded her eyes, scanning the horizon. How many acres of corn did they have to pick? She couldn't guess, but she reckoned the cornfield stretched into eternity. If they must pick all the corn today, she knew she wouldn't make it. Not only corn, she thought grimly, her gaze sweeping the field, but sunflowers, beans, pumpkins, squash, gourds, and tobacco. She could foresee many long hours of work before the harvest was gathered.

Hearing laughter and good-humored yelling from a nearby field, she looked at the ballplayers who were practicing for their first game of the season. One of the braves who was laughing and boasting the loudest was Lone Wolf—the man responsible for the mess she was in right now. At this moment Catherine hated him more than she had ever hated anyone in her entire life. She was working like a beast of burden in the cornfield, and he was running around, frolicking like a carefree child on a game field. He was having a wonderful time, swinging his rackets in the air, chasing a stupid ball, while she was the focus of ridicule and malicious jokes as she hauled baskets of corn back and forth from the cornfield to the village square. He, the prince; she, the pauper. Tears of anger and frustration filled her eyes.

At about that time she heard the whine of a switch, and she felt a stinging blow on her arm. Spinning around as quickly as she could while burdened with the filled basket, she saw Happy Woman standing by her, a smug, what-are-you-going-to-do-about-it grin on her face. Verbal abuse was one thing; physical abuse was something else. Catherine didn't care that Happy Woman was the cornfield supervisor; she'd taken quite enough from this woman. Catherine's eyes glinted with fury, and she glared at the Indian woman.

"Don't you ever use that switch on me again," she barked, too angry to sign. Though her aching body rebelled at every movement, Catherine took a step, almost hobbling because of the heavy weight of the corn on her back and her precarious balance on the heel-less shoes.

Happy Woman didn't understand what Catherine said, but she understood her actions. Automatically the Indian shrank away as Catherine stepped closer. Reaching out, Catherine jerked the switch out of Happy Woman's hand, breaking it. When she threw the broken splinters at the Indian's feet and started untying the tumpline on the burden basket, one of the women sent her child racing to Lone Wolf's wigwam to get No-am-ee. Before Catherine and Happy Woman had freed themselves of their baskets, No-am-ee had come running. She stood between the two women, breathing deeply, both hands planted on her hips.

Turning to Happy Woman, No-am-ee charged between ragged breaths, "The paleface doesn't know any better, but you, my daughter, have shamed me by your action."

"She was not doing her work, my grandmother,"

Happy Woman said defensively, pointing a finger at Catherine. "She was loafing, watching the men as they practice."

No-am-ee looked from Happy Woman to Catherine, but she spared neither one any compassion or understanding. She was clearly irritated that she had been called from her task to settle a dispute between quarrelsome women.

"We do not have to like the paleface, but we must not harm her." She held up the end of one of Catherine's braids. "She is the property of Lone Wolf, our war chief, and she bears his mark. He will be most displeased with you if anything happens to her."

"She is nothing but a slave," Happy Woman spat out. "She should be punished for not doing her work."

"If she is lazy, she will be punished," No-am-ee declared, "but her punishment is for Lone Wolf to decide not you." No-am-ee waved her hand, motioning Catherine toward the crib. "Back to your work, Happy Woman. I'll take care of the paleface."

Happy Woman glared resentfully at their retreating figures, promising herself revenge. Twice the paleface woman had ridiculed her in public. She would not do so again.

Turning to the women and children who still flocked around her, Happy Woman snapped, "Get back to work. If we're going to have food ready for the ball game, we must work. It doesn't look as though Lone Wolf's captive will be doing her share."

She tossed one last venomous glance over her shoulder, at Catherine. Taught patience from childhood, the Indian did not hurry retribution. When the opportunity for it came, Happy Woman would be prepared.

Meanwhile, angry because she had been disturbed over such a trivial matter, No-am-ee walked to the crib with

Catherine and waited for her to dump her basket. Then the old woman motioned the younger to follow, again indicating Catherine was to lag several steps behind her. When Catherine stumbled into Lone Wolf's wigwam, she saw the child from the cornfield sitting by the fire playing with a doll.

When Catherine breathed deeply, her nostrils were filled with the odor of the cooking food. Never in her life had she smelled anything so tempting. The savory aroma of the food made her realize just how hungry she was, and the number of pots in the fire indicated a much larger meal tonight. Her basket still on her back, she crawled to the fire pit and looked into one of the cooking pots, her mouth watering when she saw chunks of meat bubbling in a thick broth rich with potatoes and onions and garlic.

No-am-ee walked to the platform and pulled out a basket. Taking off the lid, she returned to the fire. "Thank you, Little Flower, for coming to get me and thank you for tending my fire and my meal." She held the basket toward the child.

Her brown face impassive, Little Flower surveyed the big red berries. They looked delicious, and she wanted one. Rather than reaching for them, however, she crossed her hands behind her back. "Thank you, my grandmother, for remembering me so kindly. But you don't have to give me your berries. You will need these when Old Man Winter comes. I tended your fires because I respect and love you."

No-am-ee smiled and lifted a gnarled hand to pat the child's thick black hair. "You are indeed a fine young girl to worry about me, Little Flower. But I have Lone Wolf to take care of me this winter. He will fill my wigwam with fresh meat, and his slave will share her food with me." She reached behind Little Flower, unlocked her hands, and put one in the basket. "Take as many as you like."

171

"Thank you, Grandmother," the child cried jubilantly, glad the choice had been taken from her. She closed her hand over three of the succulent berries. "I will share them with my little brother and Sunshine Girl."

No-am-ee looked at the berries that Little Flower had picked up. Shaking her head, she said, "If you're going to share, you will need more. Take three for each of you." When the child opened her mouth to protest, No-am-ee said, "You must remember, you never question an elder and you never refuse a love gift."

The smile that split the girl's tiny round face was a glorious sunbeam piercing heavy, black rain clouds. "Yes, Grandmother, I will remember." Skipping out of the wigwam, she looked over her shoulder, her glance full of warmth and love. "Thank you, Grandmother."

Having understood a little of the exchange between the child and old woman, Catherine smiled. The little girl was very young to act so prudently. But Catherine had noticed that day, as she'd worked with the women, that the children were unusually well behaved and were constantly at the beck and call of their elders who sent them on errands. She marveled at the way the villagers had their children take care of the older people.

Every inch of Catherine's body hurt as she disengaged the tumpline that ran across her chest and pulled the strap from her forehead. Levering herself to a standing position, she dropped the empty burden basket on the floor and hobbled to the platform. Gently easing her sore body down, she crossed one leg over the other, taking off her shoes. For the longest time she sat, grimly surveying their tattered remains; then, sighing deeply, she dropped them onto the mat carpet.

Looking up, she saw No-am-ee sitting in front of the fire, tending the meal. Catherine knelt on the floor and scooted closer to the pit. Looking into the pots, she signed, "What are you cooking?"

Spooning for a piece of the meat, No-am-ee held it up. "Bear," she said in Scupperongac, repeating it several times to Catherine.

So, Catherine thought, her mind as bruised and tattered as her body and clothes, the weary are not to rest. On with the studies. "Bear," she finally mumbled, too tired to really care.

The lesson continued: No-am-ee ladled out a spoonful of each food, holding it up for Catherine to see, to taste, and to smell. Squash. Succotash. Roasting ears. Corn-flour bread. The names of the dishes No-am-ee patiently repeated time after time, not satisfied until Catherine labeled them correctly. Finally No-am-ee pinched a tiny piece of bread from the corn-flour patty, and she dipped it into a bowl of thick syrup.

"We traded for this," she said, holding both the dish and the morsel up to Catherine's lips. "It comes from the trees that grow in the North Forest."

The crisp corn-bread patty, soaked in maple syrup, melted in Catherine's mouth. She thrummed her appreciation but had no time to say more. No-am-ee, returning the bowl to one of the smooth rocks that rounded the firepit, rose and walked across the room, gesturing for Catherine to follow. The old woman removed several mats, uncovering the underground larder, a pit lined with skins and interfaced with bark. Stored here were bell-shaped baskets covered tightly with lids. Lifting the lid from a basket lined with cornhusks, No-am-ee pointed and spoke.

Never had Catherine seen such a variety of food. Baskets of dried fish and of different kinds of meat. Baskets of corn—white, black, yellow, and red. Hulled, bleached corn for hominy, some already ground into flour and mixed with ground chestnut meat for added flavor. Sunflower oil for baby food and flavoring.

173

Hickory-nut oil for flavoring succotash and bread. Wild onions and garlic—these flavored meat. Countless berries.

Impressed by the Indian pantry but too exhausted to evince much enthusiasm, Catherine repeated every word No-am-ee said. On and on the grueling lesson went; No-am-ee pointing, Catherine identifying and explaining in her faltering but ever-growing Scupperongac vocabulary. No-am-ee didn't move until she was satisfied with Catherine's progress.

Eventually the old woman bobbed her head and said in her own language, "That is good." Shuffling back to the fire, she pointed to the platform and told Catherine to bring her one of the storage baskets. Although her muscles cried aloud at the exertion, Catherine got the basket. Opening it at No-am-ee's direction, she lifted out the eating mats, the spoons and the wooden serving bowls.

Gesturing for Catherine to remain seated by the fire, No-am-ee then walked out of the wigwam, returning in a few minutes with several pouches dangling from one hand and Little Flower in tow on the other. Walking into the sleeping room, No-am-ee called, "I will return quickly, Little Flower. I must show Catherine how to prepare for Lone Wolf's coming." She knelt by the sleeping platform and pulled out a drying skin. Draping it over her arm, she returned to the main room, crooked her finger at Catherine and ducked through the doorway.

Catherine levered to her blistered and swollen feet and slowly limped out of the wigwam, following the old woman. Each step proved to be more agonizing than the one before; the twigs pricked Catherine's sore feet and sent excruciating pain through her body.

When they stood on the bank of the river, No-am-ee directed Catherine, by gesture, to take off her clothes and to walk into the water. The old woman opened one of the pouches, and taking Catherine's hand, she turned it palm up and dumped some herbs into it. Stating the names of the herbs in Scupperongac, No-am-ee lifted her hand to her face and body and pantomimed bathing.

Taking the herbs, Catherine wet them and liberally rubbed them over herself, pampering her body with the herbal lotion. In no hurry to conclude her bathing, Catherine stood under the peppering spray of the waterfall, welcoming the chill that blocked out her pain. She enjoyed the pricking of the icy water on her aching muscles and joints.

Eventually No-am-ee motioned for her to come ashore. By the time Catherine reached her, the old woman had opened another pouch. She poured more herbs into Catherine's hands. This time No-am-ee pantomimed washing her hair. Returning to the waterfall, Catherine lathered her hair with the herbal preparation. When she had finished doing this, No-am-ee put a daub of oil in her hair and gently massaged it through the thick auburn waves. After Catherine rinsed her tresses, No-am-ee beckoned her to the shore.

Teeth chattering, the young woman quickly dried herself. Then, wrapping the bearskin around her, she trudged behind No-am-ee on their return journey to the wigwam. Dropping some plants and berries by the fire, No-am-ee dismissed Little Flower and sent her scurrying to her wigwam to help Re-bekk-ana with the evening meal. Then the old woman motioned Catherine to drop the bearskin and to lie down on her stomach on the platform. Catherine didn't hesitate, nor did she mind No-am-ee ordering her about. She willingly succumbed to a state of insensibility in which she didn't have to think. Taking a bunch of sweet-smelling herbs, No-am-ee dipped them in water, then lightly rubbed them over Catherine's body, their odor a perfume, their juice a soothing lotion to her work-abused limbs.

With firm, practiced movements, No-am-ee kneaded the young woman's aching shoulders and upper arms before she ran her fisted hand down Catherine's spine, splaying her fingers into the tensed muscles across her charge's lower back. She rubbed the sore muscles in Catherine's thighs, the knots in her calves, and then she lifted Catherine's leg, bending it at the knee and slowly rotating her foot at the ankle. First one foot then the other.

Letting Catherine lie there, relaxed and hovering close to sleep, No-am-ee returned to the fire pit. She dropped several roots and some dried berries into a pot of hot water and stirred the mixture until it boiled and turned a deep amber color. Pouring some of the root tea into a cup, she returned to the bed and tapped Catherine on the shoulder. Handing her the cup, she motioned her to drink. Thirsty, Catherine needed no inducement. She lifted the cup to her lips and slowly drank its contents, savoring the hot, sweet liquid. It burned her throat as she swallowed, but it filled her with a warm glow and she liked the spicy aftertaste.

Later, feeling refreshed and slightly light headed, she handed No-am-ee the cup. "You're welcome, Catherine," she repeated several times. Giggling softly, she indicated that she wanted the older woman to say the words in English.

Not a smile, not a flicker of emotion passed over the old woman's countenance. She took the cup, and she listened as Catherine repeated the words over and over. Finally she said, "You're welcome, Cath-er-ine." Without further preamble, No-am-ee picked up the buckskin dress and the moccasins that lay on the end of the platform. Handing them to Catherine, she gestured for her to put them on.

This time Catherine did not argue; she wasn't sure what the evening held, but this time she was going to be prepared. The touch of the yellow, tanned, and worked doeskin was like that of velvet. It whispered over her body in a soft caress. The dress was one piece, fringe hanging from the neckline, the shoulders, and the hem. It was embroidered with colored porcupine quills and dyed moose hair which No-am-ee proudly explained that she had obtained through barter during the last trading season.

By the time Catherine finished twirling around and admiring herself, No-am-ee was sitting on the platform, holding the hairbrush. She motioned Catherine to sit on the floor in front of her. Opening her cosmetic pouch, No-am-ee extracted more herbs which she rubbed in her hands before hand-combing them through Catherine's long, auburn waves to make her hair silkier and more manageable. Quickly No-am-ee brushed Catherine's hair, murmuring her praise of its beauty. Then she plaited and banded it with Lone Wolf's thongs.

Picking up a small, narrow strip of deerskin that was also embroidered in colored quills and moose hair, No-am-ee held it out for Catherine to look it.

"It's exquisite," Catherine declared with feeling, as she admired the delicate embroidery work. Looking into the old woman's weathered face, she smiled, softly saying, "Thank you, No-am-ee."

"You're welcome, Cath-er-ine," No-am-ee repeated, pressing the band to Catherine's forehead and tying it at the back. When Catherine turned around, No-am-ee sighed and stated slowly in Scupperongac, "I am giving you the headband as a gift from me. It looks pretty with your dress and your hair."

"Thank you," Catherine whispered again, truly touched by the kindness of the woman.

No-am-ee reached into her pouch again, pulling out a small packet of eagle fat. Dipping two of her fingers in the mixture, she began to massage it into Catherine's face

177

and neck. That done, she moved to the fire and began to mix several concoctions in small bowls. As she worked, No-am-ee softly talked, repeating the names of the herbs, the roots, the bark, and the animal fat she was using. Spellbound, Catherine watched her dip a small, slender feather into one of the bowls. Returning, No-am-ee pointed to Catherine's eyes, signing that she wanted to outline them with the black mixture. At first Catherine shook her head, but the Indian insisted.

"It will make your eyes more beautiful," she argued. "They will be much larger. Lone Wolf will like them much better."

The outlining wasn't all that No-am-ee did. Using pulverized bark, she shaded Catherine's eyelids gray, not putting the feather and bowl aside until she was satisfied. Picking up her flint knife, she sliced a big red berry and rubbed it against Catherine's cheeks, using her index finger to brush the soft color toward her hairline. With another berry she colored Catherine's mouth. Then, her work almost completed, No-am-ee took a soft, fluffy cattail, and using it as a puff, she dipped it into the powder she had made from the dry-rotted inner part of the pine tree. Lightly she tapped the perfumed mixture on Catherine's face.

"Pretty," she signed to Catherine, leaning back to inspect her handiwork.

Quickly No-am-ee cleaned up the clutter before returning to the fire to check on the meal. "I must go to my wigwam," she said as she gestured. "Lone Wolf will be coming shortly. Do you know how to serve him?"

Catherine nodded, her hands moving in graceful motions as she used the silent language and spoke falteringly in Scupperongac. "Will you not eat with us?"

No-am-ee shook her head, tying her pouch to her belt. "No, Re-bekk-ana and her sister, Little Flower, will be staying with me this winter, and they are cooking the

178

evening meal." As she talked, Catherine sat cross-legged in front of the fire. Noticing the younger woman's position, No-am-ee said, "A woman does not sit with her legs crossed. A man sits like that. You must sit like this." In one fluid motion, she sat down, bending her legs and curling them to one side.

After No-am-ee left, Catherine walked into the sleeping room and opened her chest. She carefully extracted a small mirror. Moving so she stood beneath the smoke hole, she gazed at her reflection. Amazed at the transformation in her appearance, she stared at herself. Her eyes, subtly shaded with the blue-gray shadow, looked bigger and greener. She ran her fingers down her softly colored cheek and traced her full lips that were tinted rose by the berry juice. Opening her mouth, she ran her tongue over them.

"Good afternoon, Catherine."

Startled, Catherine spun around, almost dropping her mirror. She hadn't heard Lone Wolf enter the wigwam, and she had been too caught up in studying her own image to be aware of his presence. Running the tip of her tongue over her lips again, she glazed them with the moisture of her mouth.

The late afternoon sunbeams surrounded Catherine in a soft, golden nimbus. Her hair shone like polished copper, and her eyes, wide and luminous as No-am-ee had promised, sparkled.

"I—I didn't hear you come in," she said, surprise lowering her voice to a whisper and giving it a seductive huskiness.

She had always thought Lone Wolf handsome, but he looked different today. The rugged primitiveness which she admired so much was tempered somehow. His harsher angles seemed to have been touched by the gifted hands of a potter, brushed and stroked until they were softer, lending him thereby a vulnerable, tender beauty

179

that smote her heart. Admiring his lean strength, Catherine's eyes roamed his body. His hair, almost dry, was hanging loose, and he was wearing only his breechclout and moccasins. His bronze body gleamed in the late afternoon sunlight that generously spilled into the wigwam, and his hair was burnished to a blue-black luster.

"You have already bathed," she murmured, swallowing the emotion that threatened to clog her throat.

Lone Wolf nodded, not trusting himself to speak. Absently dropping his rackets and leggings on the platform, he walked nearer to her. He lifted one hand, tenderly mapping the outline of her face with his fingers.

"You grow more beautiful each day, Catherine."

He cupped her chin with both hands, and he held her, looking into her eyes. As a moth drawn to a flame, Catherine was drawn to Lone Wolf. She had no thought of the consequences. Her anger and her grievances were temporarily forgotten. Her body, swaying toward his, begged for his touch; her lips pouted for his kiss. He lowered his head, his firm mouth touching hers and lightly brushing back and forth before it settled into a warm kiss.

Her arms encircled his waist, and her hands slowly climbed his smooth, muscular back. Intuitively she opened her mouth to him and pressed her breasts against his chest. Lone Wolf's grip tightened, and their kiss deepened. Trembling her need, Catherine dug her fingers into his shoulders.

Slowly he lifted his mouth from hers, breathing deeply. "You smell good, woman. No-am-ee has done her job well."

Snuggling her head against his shoulder, Catherine giggled. "No-am-ee has bathed, rubbed, and painted me. And she has filled me with herbs." Taking a deep breath, her nostrils drew in his pine-scented fragrance. "You

180

smell good too."

He laid his cheek on the crown of her head. "I have missed you today, Catherine. For the first time in many moons I was glad to return to my wigwam." His arms tightened around her, and his hands leisurely moved up and down her small back.

Lifting her face, her lips tremulous, Catherine said, "I'm glad you're home. I, too, have missed you."

"I would like more than kisses," Lone Wolf said, strewing quick kisses over her face, "but I think we're going to have to wait until later. The Wise One has asked me to attend the boys' games this evening." Clasping a hand on each of her shoulders, he moved her. "There's much to do before I go."

Disappointed, Catherine watched him walk to the platform, pick up the hairbrush, and run it through his coarse black hair. Silently moving to where he stood, Catherine took the brush from his hand.

"Let me," she said when he looked at her in surprise. Remembering the drink No-am-ee had served her, she returned to the fire. She lifted the pot of root tea and poured Lone Wolf a cup. When she had handed it to him, she scooted behind him on the platform.

Surprised but pleased with her ministrations, Lone Wolf took the cup of tea and lowered his large frame to the floor, turning his back to her. As he sipped the hot liquid, he smiled, recognizing it for the love potion it was. No-am-ee was a cunning old woman who had prepared his slave for him. When Catherine laid the brush down and began to massage his scalp with the tips of her fingers, Lone Wolf totally relaxed. Letting the empty cup roll on the floor beside him, he closed his eyes and sighed his contentment while Catherine's hands kneaded the muscles of his neck and shoulders.

In a state of euphoric abandonment, Lone Wolf untied his breechclout and reached under the platform, pulling out his bearskin blanket. Spreading it on the floor, he caught Catherine, pulling her down to him. Stretching out beside her, the movement leaving him naked, he said in a voice that was husky with desire. "I had thought to wait, but I can't Catherine." His hand touched her legs below the hem of her dress, slowly moving from her kneecaps to her thighs. "I am like a man possessed. I must have you. Not food, not drink, but you." Turning on his side, he gently pushed Catherine onto her back.

"Have you placed the bark across the door?" Catherine asked, her lips curving in a sensuous smile.

"Aye," he replied, his hand pulling her dress up, his fingers sliding between her legs.

Catherine gasped with pleasure as his hand moved higher and higher, tracing designs on her sensitive skin. His lips nipped at hers while his fingers teased her maidenhood, wisping between her parted thighs, brushing lightly against the point of highest sensitivity. Every so often he deserted that tender, throbbing area to stroke her inner thighs.

Catherine's hips began to move to the rhythm of his hand, and she opened her mouth, capturing his lips with hers and tentatively trailing her tongue along the line of his mouth. Groaning out of mounting desire, Lone Wolf's lips firmed. His tongue slipped into Catherine's mouth as his fingers slipped into the moist cavity of her body. The faster he moved them within her, the more Catherine undulated her hips, and the more intense their kiss became.

Moving her head from side to side, Catherine's body tensed, and she arched closer to the gaunt strength of the warrior. She pressed her breasts into his chest; she lifted her buttocks, straining against his moving hands. Feverishly she climbed the peak of fulfillment. Just as she bit her lips in ecstasy, just as she shattered into tiny pieces, Lone Wolf shifted above her.

His fingers stilled their movement, his palm rested on the soft, crisp hair of her mound. Kneeling he posed, his manhood erect and throbbing, her lower body moving spasmodically against his hand. Breathing in small gasps, Catherine opened her eyes and beheld his protuberance. She lifted her hand and lightly touched the sensitive head with the tips of her fingers, then nimbly ran them the length of the shaft. Her tongue spread the glistening nectar of her mouth over her lips as her fingers gently cupped his masculine sacks. Again and again she caressed him, her hand gently closing around his masculinity, softly brushing its length, and then unclosing, until she felt him shudder as passion racked his body.

Sliding between her legs, he touched the mouth of her maidenhood with his erection. Slowly he rubbed it back and forth, reacquainting her with his most intimate self, touching that tiny spot of sensitive flesh and bringing it to life. He rubbed until Catherine was breathing hard, until her hands were alternately gripping then releasing the solid, flexed muscles of his buttocks. Still he didn't encase himself in her moist warmth. He teased and whetted her until she was almost out of her mind with wanting.

"Please, Lone Wolf," she cried. "Please love me now."

He lowered his body, his powerful hardness slipping into the delicate portal of heated desire. Now he began to move with bold strokes in and out, the same passion consuming both of them. A tender mating he had given Catherine last night; tonight he was taking her with the desperate urgency of a man in need; she felt the same desperation, the same urgency. Intuitively she lifted her legs, circling his body, locking her ankles around him. Time and again she drove against him, seeking a deeper penetration.

Following her injunction, his strokes became deeper

183

and more powerful. He gasped as her hands stroked his buttocks, tracing the shape of each, her fingers always returning to the tender flesh between them, feathering designs in the sensitive line. When he thought he could stand no more, when he thought his pleasure was surely killing him, he tensed and plunged his manhood deeply into the moist velvet encasement. Catherine's body shuddered, and she clawed his back. Then spasms of pleasure overtook Lone Wolf. At last he gasped and collapsed on her, relaxing totally before he rolled to her side.

Later—much later—after they had cleansed themselves Lone Wolf stirred in Catherine's arms. "I fear, my paleface enchantress, that I need physical sustenance."

Smiling contentedly, Catherine purred, "Am I not enough for you?"

Lone Wolf smiled, and his chuckle slowly burgeoned into rich laughter that filled the wigwam. "Perhaps I should fear that you will be too much for me, Catherine. Now that I've awakened the desire in you, you are indeed a passionate woman." His hand touched a silky braid. "Your nature is fiery like the color of your hair, my Autumn Woman."

Slowly Catherine moved, hating to break the beautiful moment. Never had she been so content in all her life; never had she loved so much or been so loved. Sitting on the platform, she motioned Lone Wolf between her legs. Quickly she brushed his hair and plaited it for him. While he put on new leggings and moccasins, she folded the bearskin and pushed it under the platform.

Returning to the main room, she remembered No-am-ee's instructions. She sat in front of the fire, bending her legs to the side. Then she dipped stew into one bowl. The next one she filled with soft, yellow squash, and yet another with succotash. In the fourth bowl she laid two ears of steaming, roasted corn, a sharp stick jutting from one end of each. On the flat round stone that lined the fire pit were two flat corn cakes.

His dressing completed, Lone Wolf entered the room and sat across from Catherine. Picking up his spoon, he dipped it into the bowl of squash. He tasted it and murmured his approval. Then he sampled the succotash. Finally, lifting the ear of corn to his mouth, he sank his teeth into the tender, juicy kernels. He dipped his bread in the stew, the aroma of the garlic, onion, and bear meat filling the wigwam. Finally he spooned out two pieces of bear meat. One he threw into the fire, the other he ate. After he had swallowed his bite, he laid his spoon down and said the prayer for the evening meal.

When his chant died, he again lifted his spoon; then he smiled and nodded to Catherine. Smiling back, she dipped her spoon into the bowl of stew at the same time he did. Eyes locked, they raised the food to their lips, sipped the broth, and ate the meat. Never uttering a word, Lone Wolf took her spoon and laid it down. He fed her from his. When she had eaten her fill, she took the spoon from him and fed him. Never in her life had Catherine been this attuned to another person. No longer were they master and slave; they were man and woman. She and Lone Wolf were one life with two bodies. Without him she wouldn't—she couldn't—be complete.

When the meal was over, Lone Wolf reached for his pipe. As he smoked, he watched Catherine clean the dishes and return them and the eating mats to the basket.

"I heard the women talking about the harvest festival today," Catherine commented. "What is it like?"

"It is our autumn festival," he answered. "A time for thanksgiving. We celebrate and honor Manitou and his many helpers, the Manitouwuk, who have been generous to us."

"Good evening, my brother," Wise One's deep, mellow voice interrupted Lone Wolf. "May I come in? I would speak with you on a matter of importance."

"Remove the bark and enter, Great Chief. You are

always welcome in my wigwam," Lone Wolf replied. When Wise One had done so, Lone Wolf said, "Come sit with me and smoke the pipe of friendship." He waved a hand toward Catherine. "My slave you know."

Wise One inclined his head in acknowledgment before he sat down in the cross-legged fashion. He stared at the paleface woman, and he, like No-am-ee, wondered. He watched the light dance over her hair making it like the golden fire of the sunset.

Sensing the importance of this visit, Catherine silently slipped into the sleeping room. Opening her chest, she took out her sewing basket, and while the two men talked quietly around the fire, she worked. Smiling to herself, she measured the white linen against one of Lone Wolf's buckskin shirts.

Meanwhile, marshaling his thoughts, Wise One said to Lone Wolf, "While you were gone, the trading truce was declared." His solemn eyes, fixed on Lone Wolf, were watchful and alert.

"You know that I make no truces with the enemy," Lone Wolf declared. "It was during such a truce that my village was destroyed." The younger warrior handed his pipe to Wise One. "Destroyed by an Iroquois trading party," he reminded the peace chief.

"You have had your revenge, my son," Wise One sagely pointed out. "Old grievances must be forgotten. We must work for a better understanding with our neighboring tribes."

"I respect your opinion and your thoughts, my chief," Lone Wolf admitted. "I respect your age and wisdom, but I disagree with you. I do not trust the Iroquois. I have seen too many of our trading expeditions end in a pitched battle. The goods were scattered and destroyed; the warriors killed. Because we have trusted the Iroquois in the past, the scalps of many Scupperongac braves hang in their long houses."

Wise One took several long drags from the pipe, and he

186

listened to all Lone Wolf said. Then he sat in silence for a long time, eventually saying, "I am asking you to lead the next trading expedition. Meeting together will be representatives from the Cherokee Nation, the Five Nations, the Lumbroans, and the Falling Water Confederacy. We are having a bountiful harvest this year, my son, and this will be an opportunity for us to get new goods for our women and children, better seeds for planting next summer, maple syrup from the North Land."

Lone Wolf's visage never changed. His obsidian eyes were squarely leveled on the face of his chief. No matter how much he disagreed with the tribal chief, to refuse his command never crossed his mind. "I will do as you ask, my chief. When are we to leave?"

Wise One took a last drag from the pipe, and he handed it to Lone Wolf. "After the harvest festival. We will have a council meeting in the morning to decide the day of trading. I will send an official runner with a gift of peace and our answer."

"That is good," Lone Wolf replied.

"We also have a much graver matter to discuss at the Big House, my son. Two messengers arrived this afternoon with disturbing news." Lone Wolf didn't prod the Wise One to speak. Discipline and training had taught him to wait patiently. "You have been charged with the death of two braves—a Roanoac peace man and a Lumbroan warrior."

Catherine understood the word for the Big House. She had heard the women using the term today when they had talked about the harvest festival. But she knew Wise One and Lone Wolf were not talking about the coming festival. Their conversation wasn't light and animated as the women's had been. Instead, the atmosphere was heavy.

"Of one I am guilty, my chief," Lone Wolf replied. "The other I know nothing about. I will speak to the council tomorrow."

Wise One nodded his head. "The great chief of the Lumbroans has sent us a special message which shall be spoken tomorrow at the council meeting."

Although Lone Wolf wondered what demands the Lumbroans would make because of the death of Red Fox, he evinced no curiosity. Again he waited.

"I am glad that Old Man Winter is coming." Wise One broke the silence, his words almost identical to those of No-am-ee. "The naked forests affords the warrior no hiding place; the snow, the rains, and Grandfather North Wind keep him in his lodge. But what will the spring bring, my son? I fear"—he sighed—"if things have not changed there will be many painted warriors walking the warpath."

"Our tribe is large, Great Chief, and we are many. We have mighty warriors."

"That is so," the older man agreed, "but we are going to be caught between two leagues which are greater than we, my son. The Iroquois and their league of seventeen winters and the Lumbroans have been our enemies since the beginning of time. Both have sworn to destroy the Aa-da-mii."

"I will speak to the council tomorrow," Lone Wolf replied. "I will tell them that you are right, my chief. If the Iroquois can band many tribes together in one nation, so can we. The Cherokee are also longtime enemies of the Iroquois, and they are a large powerful tribe. If we can band together with them, we will have strong allies. There are other tribes in the Great Forest who will join us."

Quietly the two men continued to talk, their conversation moving from the disturbing to the exciting, from the concerns of the impending council meeting to the coming ball game. Catherine was able to discern the change of topic by the difference in their expressions and voice quality. The two men laughed with one another, recalling

188

other great games, reciting the names of the villages with the better players.

Wise One finally stood. "Thank you for your hospitality, Lone Wolf. I will see you later?"

Lone Wolf accompanied Wise One out of the wigwam, and Catherine set her sewing aside, thinking he would return soon, but he didn't. Half-heartedly she continued to sew, but her mind wasn't on her needlework; she was wondering where Lone Wolf was, what he was doing.

As the afternoon sun disappeared in the western sky, shadows stealthily crept into the wigwam. Hearing the activity of the village, Catherine curbed her curiosity no longer. She stepped outside the wigwam and walked to the big fire that burned in the center of the compound. Women sat in groups around the fire, laughing and gossiping and husking the corn they had gathered. With much laughter and joking, some of the younger men pitched in just to show the women how fast they could work. But the older men sat in small groups, some of them smoking, some carving. One played a small water drum. Another shook rattles and sang.

Stopping at the fringe of activity, Catherine gazed longingly at the happy scene. Some of the younger boys twisted cornhusks into clubs and started a battle. Yet another gang with cornhusk spears attacked them, yelling war whoops. The battle became so noisy that an older woman, who was sitting next to the fire, stopped her work and told the boys to quiet down.

Kee-lee, the brave who had befriended Catherine when she'd first arrived, and Happy Woman jumped to their feet and formed two lines, stamping out a dance as they moved in two small circles around the blaze. Older boys and girls who knew the steps trailed along after them, imitating every movement of their leaders.

Catherine lifted her eyes, and on the far side of the blaze, she saw Lone Wolf, standing by himself. The orange glow of the fire accented his strength and muscularity, erasing the softness she had seen earlier. His features were sharp and indomitable; he was the Scupperongac war chief. The polished wolf fangs gleamed about his neck, and the eyes of the brindled wolf at his side glistened in the firelight.

Mesmerized by the haunting rhythm of the dance, Catherine watched as Happy Woman danced in front of Lone Wolf, swinging her buxom body, chanting her song. Lifting her arms and crooking her fingers, the Indian woman invited Lone Wolf to join the dance circle. When Happy Woman pivoted, Catherine saw her face, and it was radiantly beautiful. Makeup enhanced the beauty of her dark features, and a soft smile curved her lips. Again Happy Woman motioned Lone Wolf to join them.

When Lone Wolf threw back his head and laughed with abandon, jealousy wrapped its ugly tentacles around Catherine's heart. When he caught Happy Woman's hand and circled about the fire to the rhythm of the buckskin drum and the low chanting of the men, who were not dancing, Catherine could hardly choke back her tears.

Without anyone knowing that she had ventured so close to the big fire, Catherine returned to the wigwam, but she didn't enter. Instead she walked to the river. She sat on a large boulder and watched the moon cast its silvery net across the rippling water. She thought about her strange dream, and Running Bear's promise that God would send her a warrior. Catherine wasn't sure how long she had been sitting by herself when she heard Lone Wolf approach.

"Why are you sitting by yourself?"

She shrugged, saying nothing. She was still too near tears, and she didn't trust herself to speak.

"Come, let's go. You will enjoy the storytelling which is about to begin."

"I don't care to," Catherine declared, keeping her eyes on the river.

190

"I didn't ask you, Catherine," Lone Wolf softly retaliated. "I am telling you."

"Wouldn't you rather be with Happy Woman?" Catherine spat out the words, unable to contain her jealousy any longer.

A smile touched Lone Wolf's lips. "You were at the fire?"

"I was."

Lone Wolf's hands settled over her shoulders, and his fingers gently bit into the tender flesh. "Ah, Catherine, you are jealous."

Jerking out of his grasp, Catherine bounded off the rock and turned to face him. "No," she said, giving credence to her evasion, "I am not jealous. I am humiliated. As a slave I don't know where I can or cannot go. I do not know what I can or cannot say or do. I don't like trailing behind people to announce my servility to the world. I don't like having a man order me about."

Drawing in deep breaths after her angry tirade and straightening her shoulders, Catherine thrust her breasts forward, the movement causing the soft doeskin to rub across them, stimulating the nipples. Only when Lone Wolf's eyes lowered and lingered on the gentle swells was she aware of her provocative pose. Quickly she crossed her arms across her breasts.

"I'll admit I don't like seeing the man I'm forced to live with, forced to sleep with, and forced to wait on flirting with another woman. And if I'm jealous, Lone Wolf, I'm jealous because I'm not free like Happy Woman is. It is not because of your dancing with her." The man and the woman glared at each other across the moonlit clearing, neither giving an inch. "Go back to your fire and leave me alone."

"I'm going back to the fire, Catherine, but you're coming with me." His hand shot out, his fingers gripping her upperarm, biting into the work-sore muscles. Catherine winced with pain, but Lone Wolf didn't turn

191

her loose. "I may have made a bad bargain when I demanded you rather than the weapons, but now that I've got you, I'm going to keep you, and I'm going to tame you."

"You'll never tame me," Catherine said angrily, trying to yank her arm from his clasp. "You may eventually break me, but you'll never tame me."

"No," he softly declared. "I have no desire to break you, Catherine. I mean only to tame you and make you love me."

Catherine shook her head, denying herself the luxury of tears. "You'll never force me to love you." When a smile curved his lips, Catherine said, "You've proved that you can awaken passion in my body and that you can stimulate passion. It's true I desire you and respond to your passion, but I don't love you. I never will because I love another."

Lone Wolf's fingers tightened, causing Catherine to whimper, and his other hand banded around her other arm. Jerking her toward him until their noses almost touched, he gritted, "You are mine. You will belong to no other."

"You own my body," she cried, "but you cannot own my heart or my soul, Lone Wolf. Only I possess that, and in order for you to get it, I must love you enough to give it to you. Love is giving, not owning or taking."

Lone Wolf recognized the truth of Catherine's words, and he sensed her anguished cry for an admission of his love for her. But love was an emotion the warrior would not entertain. He would make an arranged marriage because he wanted sons and daughters and because he wanted a strong alliance with the Lumbroans, but love he shunned. He had loved once, and his love had made him vulnerable. When his wife and son had been stripped from him, a part of him had died. Now it lived only in recurring dreams and in memory. Vulnerability was not a virtue; it made a warrior weak and ineffective.

Releasing his grip, he backed away from Catherine. "Come," he said, "I would have you hear the stories of our people." Emotionally spent, Catherine argued no longer. She nodded her head. "Walk by my side," Lone Wolf said in a rather subdued tone, his stride slackening to accommodate her smaller step.

They were welcomed as they joined the circle around the fire, and several of the women cast tentative smiles at Catherine, showing her how to husk the corn. Small children were already seeking the comfort of their mothers' and grandmothers' laps. Young girls continually husked the corn, while others took up some of the husks and quickly made dolls for the sleepy children.

Little Flower, smiling shyly, slid down beside Catherine. Picking up several cornhusks, she twisted and folded, making a doll for Catherine, a figure with a head, a body, arms and legs. When she had finished, Little Flower held it up for Catherine to see.

"How pretty," Catherine said in Scupperongac, holding the doll up so she could see it better.

When she handed the doll back to Little Flower, the girl shook her head. "If you like it, you may keep it," she signed. "Tomorrow I will show you how to make clothes for it."

Catherine smiled and before she thought, she draped an arm around the child, hugging her. "Thank you," she whispered, her words husky with unshed tears. She signed, "I shall treasure this doll very much." Already Catherine's thoughts were speeding ahead, planning a gift to show her appreciation to the child.

An old warrior, chanting softly, laid his pipe aside and stood. Activity ceased, and everyone fell silent. They knew the storytelling was about to begin. Before the tale ended, Little Flower had snuggled close, laid her head on Catherine's lap, and fallen asleep. Smiling, Catherine stroked the girl's face.

When Catherine looked up, she encountered Lone

Wolf's pensive gaze. Their eyes locked, but Catherine couldn't tell what he was thinking. He had drawn an invisible shutter over his face, blocking out his thoughts and emotions.

When the story ended, Lone Wolf stood, scooping Little Flower into his arms. "Come Catherine, we have a full day ahead of us. We must rest."

Holding her doll, Catherine nodded. "Are we taking Little Flower home?"

Lone Wolf smiled. "No, she will be staying with us. I had No-am-ee speak to her mother earlier."

Surprised Catherine asked, "You mean her mother won't mind?"

"Her wigwam is close to ours so she will see her family every day, and you will soon learn that someone must always attend the wigwam. While you are away from the house, Little Flower will tend the fire for you. When you are home, she will help you."

"Where will she sleep?" Catherine asked, ducking through the door of the wigwam.

"In the small compartment next to our sleeping room," he replied.

Running ahead of him into the small room, Catherine knelt to pull one of the soft cornhusk mattresses from storage. She flipped it onto the platform and covered it with skins and furs. After Lone Wolf laid the child down, Catherine tucked a rabbit-fur blanket over her. Sleepily, Little Flower opened her eyes and smiled at Catherine and Lone Wolf.

Long after Lone Wolf had gone to sleep, the pine-rosined torch flickered in the main room, and Catherine worked by the fire. She snipped the material with her shears; she whipped the needle and thread in and out. She added the lace; she embroidered; she made a small set of ruffs. When the cornhusk doll was fully clothed in European garb, she laid it beside the sleeping child.

"This is my gift to you."

Chapter X

In rapturous silence Little Flower sat on the platform, holding the cornhusk doll in her hands, gently touching the delicate lace and embroidery with the tips of her fingers.

"Do you like it?" Catherine asked slowly in Scupperongac. She was speaking more, signing less, as she became familiar and comfortable with the language.

Little Flower lifted her small, round face, ebony eyes shining, lips curving into a sweet smile. "She is the most beautiful doll I have ever seen."

"You may keep her to play with," Catherine said; then she signed. "Be careful. I shouldn't like anything to happen to her. She is my second gift since I arrived in Scupperong, and I like her very much."

Little Flower's smile expanded from ear to ear. Jumping off the platform, she laid the doll down so she could sign to ask, "Do you mind if I show your doll to my brothers and sisters? I will be very careful."

Smiling at the child's excitement, Catherine shook her head.

"Has Lone Wolf seen it yet?" Little Flower asked.

Catherine shook her head and gestured. "Not yet. He had to leave very early this morning to meet with Wise

195

One and the tribal council. Are you going to show it to your family before or after we eat our morning meal?"

Little Flower stood, her puckered brow and pursed lip revealing deep thought. "I will go before the meal," she finally decided. "I would like them to see it before the council meets. Sometimes the meetings last from the time Elder Brother rises in the east until he has moved to the west."

"Are you going to eat with us or in your wigwam?"

Ducking out the open door and forgetting to sign, Little Flower called. "Here."

With both Lone Wolf and Little Flower gone, the wigwam was unusually quiet and lonely. Kneeling beside the fire, Catherine stirred the mush before she walked into the sleeping room to comb her hair. Despite having sat up so late to sew the doll clothes, she was rested, and much to her surprise she wasn't as sore from her field work as she had expected to be. With quick movements she brushed and rebraided her hair. Then she used the sweet-gum twig as Little Flower had shown her earlier, and she cleaned her teeth.

That done, she straightened the beds, quickly rolling the blankets and furs and storing them under the platform with the cornhusk mattress. She untied the remains of the torchlight and threw them in a large basket that sat at the opening of the wigwam. Later she would carry them to the square in front of the Big House where they would be thrown on the village fire around which the people gathered in the evening to visit and to work.

As she reentered the main room, Catherine wondered if Lone Wolf would return in time to eat before the council meeting. He had assured her he would, but Catherine had seen meetings and conferences make innocent liars out of the most honest of people. She pushed the logs into the center of the fire with a smile.

196

Considering she had been at Scupperongac for only a day, she wasn't doing badly. She had built her own fire the way No-am-ee had taught her, unaided she was preparing her first morning meal, and she was communicating quite effectively.

Smiling, Catherine picked up the burden basket that was filled with cornhusks. Until yesterday she had not known the importance of corn. Sitting cross-legged because it was more comfortable and no men were present, Catherine picked several husks which she folded and twisted into thin, tight lamplighters as she had seen the women doing last night. Then she laid them in a bark box which she stored under the platform.

Finished with that, Catherine stood and moved the burden basket to the far side of the room. Preparing for the coming evening, she hung fresh torchlights. Then she took bunches of the sweet grass that Little Flower had picked earlier, dampened them, and hung them from the rafters throughout the wigwam. It wasn't long before the clean, sweet fragrance of the grass filled the rooms, deodorizing the house.

When Lone Wolf came home half an hour later, Catherine was sitting in front of the fire braiding cornhusks for clotheslines which she would string in the sleeping room. Looking up, her glance taking in his total appearance, she smiled. Her breath caught at the sight of him, and her heartbeat accelerated. In full dress he was more handsome than any man she had ever seen, Catherine decided, admiring the white buckskin garments—jacket, breechclout, leggings, and moccasins.

Their soft tone, showing to advantage the intricate designs and colors of his beaded necklaces and embroidery, contrasted with his dark complexion, as did the soft material with his craggy features. He smiled at Catherine and murmured a greeting, but she could tell he was preoccupied. Cross-legged, he sat in front of the fire. Placing a wrist on each knee, he stared pensively into the flames, lost in thought.

"Are you ready to eat?" Catherine asked, laying her work aside.

Lone Wolf, looking at the cornhusk string, slowly raised his head and gazed at her. He lifted a hand and opened his mouth. Thinking better of it, he closed his mouth, dropped his hand, and nodded.

Concerned about his preoccupation but saying nothing, Catherine filled the bowls and set them before him. She watched as he dipped his spoon into the bowls, tasted the food, and made the meat sacrifice. She listened to the prayer he mouthed, and she watched as he absently stirred the stew with his spoon. She knew his mind wasn't on food.

Engrossed in his own problems, Lone Wolf was unaware of Catherine's scrutiny. He had received some disturbing news. First, he'd learned that the tribal council as well as the village council was meeting today. Already he had met with the tribal council and had heard their words in private. This group of men, representatives chosen by the Scupperongac people to make important decisions for the entire tribe, informed Lone Wolf that it was time for him to remarry. The injunction wasn't a surprise to Lone Wolf; he had agreed to an arranged marriage in order to get Catherine. The surprise was the sudden immediacy of it. The council had insisted that he marry Little Doe at the harvest festival, but he had refused, postponing the ceremony until the strawberry festival in the spring.

Then, as if the demands of the tribal council were not enough, Lone Wolf was to answer two accusers at the council. The accusation of the Lumbroans he was prepared for; the other he wasn't. He had killed Red Fox honorably and had brought no shame on his name or his village. But the Lumbroans were using the incident to pressure the Scupperongacs to allow them to stipulate all the conditions of the treaty between the two tribes, and Lone Wolf suspected they were the pressure behind the tribal council's request that he marry the Lumbroan princess immediately. He was sure that was why the tribal council had convened today in order to hear the words of the Lumbroan runner.

Lone Wolf knew nothing of the peace man's death. He had met Running Bear only once in the forest, the day he was returning from his journey to the village of Lumbroa. Why was the Roanoac Confederacy questioning him? he wondered. This was a mystery he couldn't solve.

The heavy silence would have continued if Little Flower had not bounded into the wigwam. "Did you see what Catherine made me, my uncle?" Little Flower addressed Lone Wolf with a title of respect and held the doll out for him to see.

His brows lifting in surprise, Lone Wolf laid his spoon down and took the doll. After careful scrutiny, he said, "She is beautiful. I didn't know you were so skilled."

Catherine nodded. "I had intended to earn my living by sewing."

"Earn your living?" Lone Wolf asked, raising his thick brows.

"Uh-huh," Catherine thrummed as she handed Little Flower her spoon. "People would pay me to embroider and make lace for them." Seeing the quizzical expression on his face, she could tell that he didn't understand. "They would give me money in exchange for my services."

After a long discussion in which Catherine explained the concept and importance of money, comparing it to the system of barter used by the Indians, the meal was eaten, and the dishes were cleaned and replaced in the storage basket under the platform. Little Flower sat quietly in a corner playing with her doll, and Lone Wolf, again preoccupied, smoked his pipe.

"What's wrong, Lone Wolf?" Catherine ventured, wishing she could penetrate the shell into which he had retreated.

He raised pensive eyes from the fire and gazed at her. "I am being questioned today at the council meeting," he said dismissively, gently tapping the bowl of his pipe on one of the rocks that rounded the fire. "I am thinking of the most honorable way to explain the death of Red Fox to his people." Again he lapsed into silence.

When the messenger called, "It's time for the council meeting," Lone Wolf beckoned to Catherine. "Come. You will go with me. Little Flower will watch the fire while we are gone."

As they walked out of the wigwam, Wolf Friend, panting and wagging his tail in greeting, stood and padded to Lone Wolf's side; Catherine walked on his other side. At the Big House, the animal lay down at the entrance, his eyes following Lone Wolf as he and Catherine walked in.

"The village and tribal councils and guests sit on the raised platforms," Lone Wolf told her, pointing to the north side of the building, "and the rest of the townspeople sit by clans." He pointed to seven stumps that were spaced around the room. "A village clan chief sits on each; his clan behind him. Since you belong to no clan, you will sit on the floor over here." His hand moved to an area in front of the raised platform. "You must promise to be quiet, not to speak unless you ask and are given permission."

Gazing into Catherine's eyes, he smiled and placed his hands on her shoulders, drawing her closer to him. "This time hear me, Catherine. Do not be stubborn and go against my words."

The pensive sadness in his eyes touched Catherine, eliciting her promise: "I'll obey this time."

"I wish I could believe you, Catherine, but I don't." He chuckled. "You're too fiery, and if something is said you don't like, you'll probably jump up and voice your opinion."

Though he teased, Catherine knew his words were an ominous forewarning, and they frightened her. "What's wrong, Lone Wolf?" she begged in a half-whisper. "Tell me what's happened?"

"Council meetings are very important," he explained gravely, ignoring her question, his ebony eyes locked on hers. Almost as if he had no control over his actions, he lifted his hands and cupped her face. "They must not get out of order. If someone creates a disturbance, the chief throws that person out, and there is nothing any of us can do about it. The offender and his family are publicly humiliated by the entire town." His voice lowered, and the brave almost begged, "Please, Catherine, obey me this time." He looked at her a second longer before he turned and took his place on the platform.

Sitting on the dry grass that covered the townhouse floor, Catherine watched the men, women, and children as they gathered, grouped according to their clans. Much to her surprise several of the clan chieftains were women; two of the village council members were women, and one of the tribal council members was the distinguished No-am-ee. The Lumbroan messenger Catherine didn't know; the other she did. She rose onto her knees, smiling and waving, but Manteo never looked in her direction. That Wanchese's face remained immobile and his gaze straight ahead didn't surprise her.

Her greatest surprise came when someone sat down beside her. Because she was busy studying the gathering crowd and wondering about Manteo's strange behavior, she noticed only the fringed leggings and moccasins at first. But when her face lifted, she saw thick blond hair and a golden beard; she saw laughing gray eyes.

201

"Who are you?" she cried jubilantly.

The man laughed at her excitement. "Around here I'm called the Yellow Hair Face," he answered. "Back in England I was known as Henry Flint. In addition to being Lone Wolf's paleface slave, just who might you be?"

Laughing happily, she said, "I'm Catherine Graystone."

Holding out his hand, Henry took Catherine's in his. He bent his head and lightly grazed the top of her hand with his lips. "Pleased to make your acquaintance, Mistress Graystone."

Lone Wolf jealously watched the interchange between the two palefaces. He could hardly remain seated as he heard the tinkle of Catherine's soft laughter and saw the happiness radiating from her countenance. When Henry lowered his head and touched Catherine's hand with his lips, Lone Wolf almost leaped from the platform. Anger boiled through his veins, burning away years of discipline and custom; jealousy reduced him to a mere mortal.

Unaware of the fevered gaze directed her way, Catherine asked, "What are you doing here, Mr. Flint?"

"At first I was a prisoner like you," Henry replied. "I was one of the caretakers left by Sir Grenville in 1585. Not long after the ship set sail, and we were left to ourselves, hostile Indians attacked us." As memories of that experience flooded back, he ran his hand down the thick growth of hair on his face. "Only four of us escaped that I know of—John Fletcher, Timothy Wainwright, Matthew Miller, and me. I don't know what happened to Fletcher. Matthew, Wainwright, and I managed to get as far as Scupperong where we were given shelter. Wise One listened to us, and the people voted to let us live if we ran the gauntlet bravely." He laughed grimly. "I still have the marks to show for that licking."

"What happened to the other two men?"

"Matthew made it through the gauntlet, same as me, but Wainwright was too weak. He was beaten to death."

Catherine closed her eyes and shuddered at the horrible thought. The people with whom she was living, perhaps even the man with whom she was cohabitating, were responsible for the senseless murder of a white man. Eventually she asked, "What are you doing here at this particular council meeting?"

"On my way to barter with the settlement," he answered. "Because my village is so far inland we just heard about 'em and their need for food." He grinned. "Thought we could do a little trading. Don't want them to burn our villages and kill our women and children."

"Are you going to stay at the settlement?" Catherine asked, a sudden wave of homesickness washing over her.

"I doubt it," Flint drawled. "The Scupperongacs have been good to me. They adopted me into their tribe, and now I've got me a fine wife and son."

"If they have adopted you, why are you sitting down here with me?" Catherine asked.

Henry chuckled at her curiosity. "I wanted a chance to visit with one of my countrymen, so I asked Lone Wolf if I could sit by you." The chuckle swelled into laughter. "He refused, but Wise One convinced him that it would be all right. Said I could interpret for you."

Shifting her eyes, Catherine glanced over her shoulder at the scowling Lone Wolf. She favored him with a smile and then returned her attention to Henry Flint. It would do her master some good to simmer awhile in his own stew, she thought, remembering his seductive dancing with Happy Woman.

"When are you leaving for the settlement?" Catherine asked Henry, her thoughts again on her people.

"Day after tomorrow. I want to spend some time with my friends here."

There was time for no more conversation. Wise One

walked to the center of the room, and talking ceased. Moving to the fire, the chief threw some tobacco leaves into the blaze, the sweet aroma permeating the lodge. He lit his pipe, taking several puffs and blowing the smoke in the direction of each village clan chief. Then, holding his pipe with both hands and extending his arms above his head, Wise One began to pray, the soft chant sounding throughout the room. The prayer over, he laid his pipe on one of the seven large smooth stones which circled the fire.

"We have many questions to discuss today, my brothers, and we cannot arrive at an answer until we have heard all sides. Each village clan chief one by one will rise and tell us his grievances. We will hear all who wish to speak."

Whispering in Catherine's ear, Henry said, "We're in for a long time here, missy. The Indians let everybody but the young'uns have their say. And they listen to what everybody says and weigh it."

With Henry to interpret, the time passed swiftly for Catherine. She enjoyed listening to both sides of the issues, and it amazed her that the women were allowed to participate in their government. She was more surprised to see that the men held the women's opinion in high regard. A younger woman usually had an older brother or a husband speak for her, but widows and older women spoke for themselves. Children were quiet and attentive.

Local business finally attended to, Wise One said, "Now we will hear what the Lumbroans have to say to us." He picked up his pipe, refilled it with tobacco and, scooping up a live coal on a small piece of bark, he lit it again.

One of the visitors, a lean, muscular Indian, stood and walked to the center of the building. After Wise One had taken a puff on the pipe, he handed it to Snapping Turtle who took a drag. Handing it back, the Lumbroan began to

204

speak in his own language and to sign.

Leaning his head closer to Catherine, Henry mumbled under his breath, "He's telling the village that Lone Wolf killed Red Fox, one of the Lumbroan's most valiant warriors."

Her eyes never leaving the Lumbroan who stood in the center of the building, Catherine listened as Snapping Turtle described the events that had led to Red Fox's death. For a man who had never witnessed the combat, his story was detailed and accurate.

"My brothers, you have heard the report we received concerning Red Fox's death. Now my great chief, Flying Eagle, would hear what Lone Wolf, war werowance of the Scupperongacs, has to say."

Lone Wolf stood and walked to the center of the lodge. He took the pipe from Wise One and smoked it. Then he began to speak and to sign his story. His gestures were beautiful and fluid as was his deep, mellow voice. When he had concluded, he said, "That is the way it was, my brother, Snapping Turtle. I tell the truth."

"So be it," Snapping Turtle said. "I will tell my people. My chief sends word that we, the Lumbroans of the Great Forest to the North, would live in peace with our Indian brothers, the Scupperongacs, and would join ourselves to you in a pact of brotherhood. However, he and our tribal council must have time to consider all you have said. We will give you our answer by the strawberry festival."

"We will eagerly await your answer," Wise One said. "We extend your tribe an invitation to celebrate the harvest and the strawberry festivals with us. We invite you to participate in our songs, dances, and games."

"I will take the invitation back to my chief," Snapping Turtle replied. "We will send an official messenger to give you our answer before Little Winter."

"How will he remember all of this?" Catherine asked

skeptically. "So much has been said I doubt I could repeat it accurately."

"Don't you fret your pretty little head none," Henry told her. "The Indians remember very well. Without a written language, they have no way to record their songs and stories but through the ear and the tongue. They've been taught since birth to listen, and they learn to memorize by repeating their stories and songs over and over again. They're also taught that it's important for a story to be told or a song sung exactly as they hear it. Now this is nigh impossible for you and me, Mistress Graystone, since we're used to reading from books. But the Indians listen so carefully and have such good memories, they can repeat a long story, a chant, or message without a mistake. If something is repeated incorrectly," he said, running his hand down his beard, "you can bet it isn't by accident. It's a deliberate mistake on somebody's part."

By the time Henry had finished talking, Wanchese, ready for his discourse, was standing in the middle of the townhouse, handing the pipe back to Wise One. Speaking his language and signing, the war chief of the Roanoacs said, "The Roanoac Confederacy, made up of small coastal tribes, including the Roanoac and Croatoan Indians is no more. In two winters the treacherous palefaces have reduced our numbers and scattered our people throughout the Great Forest. Added to our grief is the death of my friend and our peace man."

Without a show of outward emotion Wanchese described the events leading up to Running Bear's death and his discovery of the body. His dramatic summation was climaxed when he held the fang necklace for everyone to see.

"I found Lone Wolf's totem in Running Bear's clenched fist." He paused, walking around the semicircle of people and dangling the necklace in front of them. "I,

Wanchese, werowance of the Roanoacs, have come to ask your war werowance for an explanation. Before we judge, before we paint ourselves for war, we listen to all sides of the issue."

Wise One nodded. "So be it," he said, stooping to pick up the pipe.

After he had gone through the tobacco ritual the second time, Lone Wolf again was the center of attention. He took the broken necklace from Wanchese and looked at it. He fingered the softly colored shells, the pearls, the bone beads, and the wolf fangs.

"This is my necklace, my brother the Roanoac," he admitted, his voice loud and strong for everyone to hear, "but I would not bring dishonor on my name, my relatives, or my tribe by killing a peace man."

"How did your necklace come to be in his death grip?" Wanchese asked.

"I know not, Roanoac War Chief. I only know how he came to have my necklace in the first place. That I will tell you."

His head near her ear, Henry interpreted Lone Wolf's words for Catherine, who never took her eyes off his hands which eloquently signed his story.

"Returning from Lumbroan territory after having delivered a message for the Wise One, my braves and I met the peace man in our forest. I offered to travel with him—I offered him my protection—but he said he could not. He was waiting for another to join him, but he promised he would be along shortly. Knowing the unrest in the Great Forest," Lone Wolf continued, "I was afraid for the peace man, so I gave him my mark. As long as he was wearing it in Scupperongac territory, I knew he would be safe from one of ours."

Lone Wolf paused, letting his words sink in. As he had been taught to do from infancy, he impassively looked his interrogator in the face, never flinching from the

207

accusing eyes or wavering in his resolve.

"My brother, I would never stoop to kill any man without giving him an opportunity to defend himself. I am Lone Wolf, war werowance of the Scupperongacs, a warrior of honor and valor who boasts many features for his war lock. I am not the Sneaking Wolf, killer of innocents."

Lone Wolf's words rang true, and Catherine believed every word. Her heart was suddenly lighter, and her love for him swelled until she thought surely she would burst with happiness. She was so caught up in her elation, she didn't really hear anything else that Wanchese or Wise One said. She wasn't jostled back to reality until Henry Flint groaned, "Oh, my God!"

"What's wrong?" she cried, looking from him to Wise One to Wanchese, and finally to Lone Wolf.

"Since there is no proof of Lone Wolf's innocence other than his word, the Roanoacs are demanding that he subject himself to a test of truth."

"But he's told them the truth," Catherine whispered. "What more does Wanchese want?"

"They want him to run the gauntlet."

Catherine saw the shadow of pain in Henry's eyes, and she heard his hesitancy. "What—what exactly is the gauntlet?" she asked.

"Two parallel lines of braves or women whichever the case may be," he said. "They stand a few feet apart and form an aisle down which the man proving his innocence is to run. As he runs, the braves beat him with their war clubs."

Henry almost winced with pain. As he described the ordeal, he was remembering the excruciating pain and agony associated with the vicious blows that pounded him from all directions. He would never forget that agonizing torture or the screams of his friend who had eventually been beaten to death.

208

"No," Catherine cried, love erasing the memory of her promise to Lone Wolf, "he can't do that." She pushed away from the platform and balanced on her knees, gritting out, "I won't let them do this to him. I won't let him do this to himself."

Before she could stand, Henry reached out and caught her, dragging her down beside him. Clenching his fingers tightly around her arm, he grated in a hoarse whisper. "Mistress Graystone, I don't mean to hurt you, but you just sit right here and keep your mouth shut. This is a matter for the Indians to work out using their own system of justice."

"A system of justice," she scoffed disdainfully. "You call it justice when a man has to prove he's telling the truth by going through a hell like that."

"They're not so different from us," Henry said out of the corner of his mouth. "'Twasn't so long ago that we proved our innocence by ordeal, and still do in some parts of the country."

Lone Wolf heard the scuffle and the whispering, and he knew it was Catherine. He wanted to go to her, but he couldn't. Custom demanded that he give his full attention to the proceedings of the trial. Because he was thinking about Catherine, because he was worried about her, he didn't hear Wise One speak.

Wise One's troubled eyes followed those of his beloved warrior, and he, too, looked at the frightened, wide-eyed paleface. A slave she might be, the peace chief thought, but Lone Wolf was enslaved to her.

"What is your answer, my son?" Wise One asked the second time.

"I will do it, my father chief," Lone Wolf answered, not a flicker of emotion in his words or expression. "At what time and place?"

"No." Icy fear chilled Catherine's heart, and the whispered cry escaped her lips before she thought. "Why

209

doesn't he tell them no?" she wanted to know. "His people know he's telling the truth."

"To refuse is an admission of guilt," Henry told her. "It is also cowardly and would dishonor Lone Wolf's name, his relatives, and his tribe."

Wise One spoke to Wanchese. "Let the ordeal occur here in our village. Bring your warriors and your council chiefs. As is the law, your warriors will form the gauntlet, and the council chiefs will act as mediators." Wanchese acknowledged Wise One's statements with a curt nod of his head. Crouching, Wise One measured two stacks of twigs, seven in each. Handing one pile to Wanchese, he said, "When this many suns have risen, my son, the war chief of the Scupperongacs, will run the Roanoac gauntlet." Wise One then handed Wanchese a pouch, beautifully embroidered and filled with tobacco. "Accept my gift and return to your people. Tell them all that you have heard this day. The Scupperongacs will act honorably. We expect the same behavior from the Roanoacs who will be our guests during the Ceremony of the Ordeal."

Henry's strong fingers bit into Catherine's flesh, holding her close to him as the closing ritual was performed by Wise One. After the old warrior chanted the benediction and the people began stirring, Henry said under his breath, "Don't make a scene, missy. Your man has got a powerful weight on his shoulders right now without your adding to his burden. If you know what's good for you, don't humiliate him in front of his people or his accusers." Henry's gray eyes pierced into Catherine.

She nodded and whispered, "All right."

"Hold your head up and smile. Your man has reacted like a mighty warrior today. You can be proud of him."

Tears sparkled in Catherine's eyes. "I'm proud of him already. I know he didn't kill Running Bear. He doesn't

210

have to run the gauntlet to prove it to me."

"Nonetheless, madam," Henry said, reaching up a hand to flick the lone tear off her cheek, "one of the first lessons an Indian learns is to hide his emotions in front of strangers."

"I'm not an Indian," Catherine sniffed.

"Lone Wolf is, and your tears will bring shame to him."

"It doesn't matter that his death will bring sorrow to me?"

Henry shook his head. "I'm sorry, Mistress Graystone, but Indians don't view things as we do. It'll be easier for you if you'll just accept their way."

Blinking her eyes and holding back her tears, Catherine stood, nodding her head. Rubbing the back of her hands across her eyes, she straightened her back and squared her shoulders, tilting her head. Across the milling crowd, she saw Lone Wolf, still standing by the sacred fire in the center of the building. Pensively he gazed at her. Green eyes, sparkling with love, caught and held black ones. Slowly Catherine smiled, and she moved across the room, her carriage regal and commanding.

When she stood in front of Lone Wolf, she said in her faltering Scupperongac, "Although you have grieved me this day, you have also made me proud. It is an honor to be the woman of such a brave warrior."

Lone Wolf saw the traces of tears in her eyes. He saw the shadows of worry and concern. He wanted to take his paleface in his arms, to hug her and to reassure her, but decorum demanded otherwise. He lifted a hand, his finger gently touching the line of freckles across her nose.

"Thank you, Catherine. You have brought me much honor today. You are behaving like a Scupperongac woman rather than a paleface slave."

Manteo and Wise One approached Lone Wolf and

Catherine, the chief of the Scupperongacs saying to Lone Wolf, "Manteo would like permission to talk with Catherine. The white settlement would have news of their daughter; they would hear her message to them."

Lone Wolf glared at the Indian who had befriended the palefaces, the one who lived in the village with them. He had already shared Catherine with Yellow Hair Face. Now Lone Wolf wanted her to himself. So little time was left. When Lone Wolf didn't immediately give his consent, Catherine turned pleading eyes to him, but she didn't beg. Her voice was soft and firm.

"I would consider it a gesture worthy of a warrior if you would let me speak to him," she said. "I would learn about my sister and Will'am Dare." She spoke Will's name without thinking.

Lone Wolf's eyes shadowed. He looked long and hard at Catherine, Will'am Dare's name echoing through his head. Would he never wipe the image and the memory of the paleface warrior from Catherine's mind?

Curtly he nodded his head. "You may talk with him, Catherine. I will wait for you at the door. Come when you are finished." Jealous because Catherine wanted to speak with Manteo, Lone Wolf adhered strictly to custom. He beckoned No-am-ee and said, "I have given Catherine permission to talk with Manteo. Would you please stand with them?"

"I will," No-am-ee returned.

"Hello, Catherine." Manteo spoke English, his pleasure at seeing her again obvious in his eyes. "How are you doing?"

Catherine smiled at her old friend. "I am doing well," she answered, but she had no time for conversational protocol. Curious, she asked, "What are you doing here?"

"I am a Croatoan tribal chief and was a Roanoac Confederacy chieftain. Because Running Bear was the

Roanoac peace man and my closest friend, I will help Wanchese avenge his death."

"Even if it means that Lone Wolf must run the gauntlet?"

Sensing her unspoken confession of love for the Scupperongac warrior, Manteo wished he could give Catherine another answer. "That's Indian justice, Catherine. Neither you nor I can change that."

Catherine lowered her head, saying, "How is Ellen?"

"She has grown up," he said gently, "but she wants to see you. She sent a letter." He reached into his pouch and extracted the small square of paper.

Catherine and Manteo stood in the center of the building in the morning sunlight that streamed through the smoke hole. Quickly they spoke, first one asking questions, then the other. Catherine laughed as Manteo repeated all the settlement gossip; he smiled as she gave him messages to take back. Lone Wolf's eyes followed her every movement, and when her hand reached out and touched Manteo's arm, the war chief of the Scupperongac started. Catching No-am-ee's eye, he motioned impatiently from the door that he was ready to go. No-am-ee cupped Catherine's elbow with her hand.

"It is time to go, Cath-er-ine," she said, gently tugging. "Lone Wolf beckons."

"Tell Ellen that I love her," Catherine said to Manteo. Over her shoulder she looked at Lone Wolf who scowled and motioned for her to leave.

"And you?" Manteo asked. "What shall I tell her about you?" His eyes ran the length of the pale yellow buckskin, then returned to her shining auburn braids.

"Tell her that I am fine. Although I am a slave, they are treating me well. As long as I belong to Lone Wolf no one will harm me. I will send her a letter," Catherine cried hurriedly, "and tell her all these things. When are you leaving?"

"We must leave before the sun sets today," Wanchese said, materializing from the shadows and smiling at Catherine. "We have much to do." He had always admired and liked her, but this new Catherine pleased him greatly. "I am glad that you have accepted the Indian way of life, Catherine," he said. "It is good, and you will be safe."

Catherine had no time to ponder his words. Lone Wolf strode across the room, and his hand banded around her elbow now.

"Come, Catherine," he gruffly commanded. "There are many things we must do in preparation for the Ceremony of the Ordeal."

Over her shoulder, as Lone Wolf all but dragged her out of the wigwam, Catherine called out, "Tell Ellen I love her."

Lone Wolf was silent as he and Catherine walked through the village. Covertly he watched her fondle the small piece of paper, and he jealously wondered what it was. When they entered the wigwam, he said to Little Flower, "You may go outside and play."

After the child had gone, he turned to Catherine. "What did Manteo give you?"

Catherine smiled, mildly amused by his jealousy. "A letter from my sister."

"A letter?" Lone Wolf asked.

"Like you we have our silent language," Catherine explained, holding the letter out, letting him look at the sprawling characters that comprised her name. "Rather than signing them with our hands, we make marks on paper. The person who receives the paper can then read the marks." She handed him the letter, and he turned it over in his hands several times, running his fingers over the glob of wax that sealed it.

"If that is broken," Catherine explained, "we know that someone has opened and maybe read our message."

214

Taking the letter, she used her thumb to break the seal. She unfolded the paper and handed it to him again. As Lone Wolf gazed at the writing, he said, "We also use talking marks."

"There is a difference," Catherine said, explaining the difference in hieroglyphic and alphabetic writing. "You use a picture to represent a word or sounds whereas we use a letter to represent a certain sound. In our language we have twenty-six letters, called an alphabet, from which all words are composed, and each letter has its own sound. In order to read the marks you must learn to say the letters and you must learn to recognize them. Then you must learn the combine the letters into words."

"Leaves that talk," Lone Wolf exclaimed wonderingly. He lifted a surprised face to Catherine. "You must teach me this, Catherine. I would learn to talk on paper like you do."

Catherine smiled shyly, nodding her head. "Would you like me to read Ellen's letter aloud?"

Lone Wolf wanted Catherine to read the message to him, but he shook his head. Because she respected his privacy, he would respect hers. Folding the letter, he said, "This is a message to you from your sister. After you have read it yourself, if you still wish, you may read it to me." He handed it to Catherine, saying, "The marks in your father's ring, what do they mean?"

Walking across the room to her chest, Catherine lifted the lid. Placing her letter in her writing box, she reached for her purse. Unbuttoning the flap, she extracted the ring. She crooked her finger, beckoning him to her. When he squatted beside her, she pointed to the inscription, reading aloud: "To my darling, with all my love." She waited for a second, then said, "My mother gave it to my father as a token of her love for him, and he gave her one also. That one I let Ellen have; this one I kept." She smiled as she remembered. "The rings were

215

symbols of their love and commitment to one another."

Folding his big hand around hers, Lone Wolf said in a soft apologetic tone, "You miss your people very much, do you not?"

"Yes," Catherine murmured, lowering her face, looking at the ring. "Very much. Especially my sister."

"Would you like to have her come live with us?" Lone Wolf asked. "I can send for her, and she can live in our wigwam and work with you."

"Oh, no," Catherine quickly replied, returning the ring and purse to the chest. She didn't look at Lone Wolf because she wasn't quite comfortable with this show of consideration from him. "Ellen wouldn't be happy living here."

"Are you happy living here, Catherine?"

Still Catherine didn't look at him, nor did she answer. Instead she closed the chest and ran her hands over the designs on the lid.

"Look at me," Lone Wolf barked, "and answer me." As a piece of metal is pulled by a magnet, Catherine slowly turned, her face locked to his. The obsidian eyes looked directly into hers; they demanded an honest answer from the heart as well as the lips. "Are you happy living here, Catherine?"

Catherine returned his gaze for a long time before she reluctantly admitted, "Yes, I'm happy. In England I always envied men their freedom. Here in your village I see freedom and equality for all people. The women not only have your children and manage the homes, but they help to run the government of your village and tribe." She rose, moving to the center of the wigwam. "Under other circumstances, I could be quite content with my life here."

Lone Wolf's eyes studied hers. Carefully he formed his question. "Would other circumstances refer to marriage, Catherine?"

An enigmatic smile tugged at her lips. Quite adept at sparring herself, she countered, "Are you considering marriage to me?"

"Yes," he replied, surprising Catherine with the quick admission. He waited a second before he added, "I'm also considering telling you that I love you." His expression remained serious, but his eyes were twinkling.

His confession momentarily took Catherine aback. Her eyes danced her joy, and her heartbeat accelerated.

"Will you marry me, Catherine Graystone?"

Squealing her delight, Catherine ran to him and threw herself into his arms. "Oh, Lone Wolf," she mumbled, burying her face in the soft buckskin jacket, "I didn't think I'd ever hear you say those words to me." She lifted her tearstained face. "I love you, my darling, and yes. Yes, I'll marry you." Again she nestled her cheek against the steady, rhythmic beating of his heart. Lone Wolf's arms tightened around her, and he held her close, resting his cheek on the crown of her head, rubbing his face against the silky texture of her hair. Finally Catherine pulled her shoulders back and looked up at him. "You really want to marry me?"

He smiled, that special smile that singled her out of all the people in the world—the smile that was hers alone. "Yes"—he chuckled indulgently—"I want to marry you." He kissed the tip of her nose. "Perhaps the question is do you really want to marry me?"

"You know I do," she declared, sniffing and laughing at the same time.

"Will you still desire it after I reveal some of the secrets of my heart?" His husky tone touched Catherine, sending a thousand erotic splinters prickling through her body.

"Aye." Catherine's reply was light. Her desire was blocking coherent thought, blinding her to the cultural differences between her and Lone Wolf. "Nothing will make me change my mind."

"I wish that were true," Lone Wolf said, sadness tinging his words. He hugged her more tightly, relishing this moment when she freely gave herself to him, freely came to him. "No matter what happens, Catherine, no matter what the coming suns may bring, I want you to know that I love you; I want you to know how much you mean to me."

"Everything's going to be all right," Catherine assured him, a catch in her throat. "You'll run the gauntlet, and you'll make it, my darling." She lifted her arms and locked her hands at the nape of his neck. Pressing her lips to his, she murmured into his mouth, "I know you will."

The kiss, soft and warm, was the first caress Catherine had ever given Lone Wolf as an expression of her willing love. Lone Wolf was content to let Catherine's mouth explore his. Her discovery was gentle and tentative. As her mouth moved on his, his hands slid down over her buttocks, holding her slight frame to his, but he made no effort to change the content of the kiss.

Then her tongue ceased tracing the line of his lips and gently slipped into his mouth, touching all the sensitive hollows, inundating Lone Wolf with heated desire. He moaned and pulled Catherine's hips closer to the growing hardness of his lower body. Her fingers locked at the nape of his neck, binding their lips together. The kiss was no longer gentle and warm and inquiring. Now it was a hot, urgent demand. Bursting into fiery passion, it threatened to consume both of them.

Lone Wolf, grinding his lips into Catherine's, his tongue dueling with hers, took the initiative from her as she pressed closer to him, wanting to become a part of him. Their breaths mingled, their vapor becoming one. Finally, Lone Wolf lifted his face from hers, and breathing heavily, his chest heaving, he spoke.

"The gauntlet I don't fear." He paused. "I fear losing

your love."

"Never," she promised.

"More than life, Catherine, I want you, and I want to marry you, but I must also think of my people." His hands cupped her chin, and he looked into her expectant green eyes. "We are desperately seeking a way to protect ourselves from our enemies. We are but one tribe among many, and we have foes. The most menacing and the most powerful at the moment are the Iroquois. Like them we must make an alliance with other strong tribes, if we are to survive."

Tiptoeing, Catherine placed her lips against Lone Wolf's. "I don't understand all your customs and politics, my darling," she whispered, her tongue tracing the firm line of his lips, "but I'm sure you'll do whatever you think is best for you and your people. Now," she murmured, "let's not waste any more time discussing the tribe's policies."

Lone Wolf was tempted to follow Catherine's injunction. To keep his silence and to make love to her would be so easy for him—so wonderful. This promised to be the most precious mating she and he would experience. This time she was coming to him willingly; she wanted him as much as he wanted her. No. She loved him as much as he loved her.

But his love demanded he tell her the truth.

"The tribal council demands that I marry a Lumbroan princess in order to bring about an alliance between our two tribes."

Chapter XI

Slowly Catherine dropped her hands from his face, and she stared at him. Shock rendered her insensible and speechless. She wasn't sure how long she remained in Lone Wolf's arms, staring into his immobile face.

"What about me?" she finally asked, her voice so calm she marveled that it could be hers. She hadn't left his arms, yet Catherine had removed herself from Lone Wolf.

"I can marry both of you," he replied simply. "According to our customs, a man of my position in the tribe and village may have more than one wife as long as he cares for each and takes care of the children. If I consent to marry the Lumbroan princess, it will bring peace between our tribes. As such it will be only a political marriage. Our son, a future chief, will unite our nations into one." He smiled. "You and I will marry for love."

She backed out of his arms, wildly shaking her head from side to side. When he took a step toward her, she flung out her arms, warding him off. "No." She shook her head more vigorously and spoke again in that deathly quiet voice that contrasted with her nervous movements. "Tell me," she begged, "tell me this isn't happening to me. You're not really going to marry her, are you?"

"I am."

As Lone Wolf pronounced the words, he looked at Catherine's haunted face. If she were an Indian and understood our customs, he thought, she would accept this other marriage without question. Perhaps in time she would even welcome it.

"I will not be your second wife." Catherine's hoarse cry sandpapered through the wigwam. "Nor will I be one wife of many." She tossed her head defiantly, her braids swirling over her shoulders to land on her back, her eyes sparkling.

Although Lone Wolf appreciated her spirit, Catherine's rebelliousness angered him. More, her attitude saddened and disappointed him. He had explained why the marriage was necessary, and it seemed to him that Catherine was being deliberately obstinate.

"You have forgotten your place, Catherine," he replied. He didn't move a muscle, but his words jarred her like a slap. "You are my slave, and you will do whatever I tell you. Whether I have one wife or many, you and I will be married."

Having known Lone Wolf for only a short period of time, Catherine already recognized the stubborn jut of his chin, the indomitable gleam in his obsidian eyes. She saw his nostrils flare in anger, and she heard the unyielding promise in his words.

"Lone Wolf," she whispered, appealing to the man beneath the façade of a hard, disciplined warrior, "if you love me, please don't do this to me. Don't punish me this way." Tears, misting her eyes with sparkling brilliance, gently rolled down her cheeks. "If you must marry another"—her voice was so low, Lone Wolf could hardly hear her—"set me free. Let me go."

The warrior was touched, as was the man, but he would not grant her appeal. That sacrifice was too great for

221

either of them to make. In one flowing movement he covered the space that separated them, and he took her into his arms. Offering no resistance, Catherine lifted her face, placing her hands on his chest.

"I cannot free you," he murmured, his lips tasting the sweetness of her flesh, the saltiness of her tears. "I love you, Catherine, and I will do whatever I must to keep you by my side." His lips settled on hers, sealing his promise, stopping her protest.

"If you don't wish to be disturbed, you should have the bark over your opening," No-am-ee said as she walked into the wigwam, not one whit disconcerted by her untimely interruption.

Hurt by Lone Wolf's confession and his decision, and embarrassed that No-am-ee had walked in on such an intimate scene, Catherine jerked her head away from Lone Wolf, breaking the kiss. She would have pulled out of his arms altogether, but he held her tightly. Chuckling, he capped her skull with his hand and pressed her face into his shoulder.

"I never wish to be disturbed when I am with Catherine, Old Woman, but there is much that has to be done before I leave for purification."

No-am-ee nodded, looking at and speaking to Catherine. "You were brave today, Cath-er-ine, and you behaved honorably. I was pleased with you."

"Thank you," Catherine mumbled, pushing herself out of Lone Wolf's arms.

"I would find great pleasure in your calling me grandmother," No-am-ee said, the gesture simultaneously surprising and pleasing Catherine.

After the way No-am-ee had reacted to her little scene with Happy Woman, Catherine couldn't believe this offer of friendship. Hesitantly she said, "Thank you, Grandmother."

No-am-ee gave a curt nod of her head in acknowledgment, and she again had that visionary awareness, that disturbing stir in her heart that made her wonder about the paleface and about the Wise One's vision.

The paleface had come to them during the autumn, and her hair was the color of the sunset.

But also coming with the harvest was Little Doe, the Lumbroan princess, No-am-ee thought. When she and Lone Wolf married, she would become an instrument for peace, giving birth to a son. No closer to an interpretation than she had been the night Wise One had shared his vision with her, No-am-ee sighed. Long and hard, she pondered the words she had hidden in her heart. Many times she had chanted them as she prayed for the interpretation.

Finally, pushing her troubled thoughts aside, No-am-ee turned her attention to Lone Wolf. "I am inviting you and Catherine to my wigwam tonight, my son. I am preparing the evening meal, and there will be no need for a fire in both your wigwam and mine while you are gone. I know you would not want Cath-er-ine to be alone, so I am offering her shelter and food during your absence." Her eyes became shadowed with a meaning neither Catherine nor Lone Wolf understood. "I have much to teach her and much to learn."

"Thank you, Grandmother, for your generosity and hospitality," Lone Wolf said. "We will bring our mattress and blankets when we come for the evening meal."

"I will stop by the wigwam of Little Flower and will tell her mother of your decision," No-am-ee said, stooping to go out.

After No-am-ee left, Catherine heard the whooping and hollering from the ball field. Looking at Lone Wolf, she said, "Are you not practicing today for the ball game?"

"No," Lone Wolf answered. "When Elder Brother

ends his journey in the west, we begin the ceremony of purification. I leave you tonight, not to see you again until after the ordeal. This afternoon I spend with you." He smiled. "Come. The sun is shining. Let's walk through the woods."

Out of habit, Lone Wolf draped his folded bearskin over his arm, and they walked out of the village into a forest aflame with it's autumn vesture. Yellow, red, and brown leave vibrantly fluttered through the air and crackled beneath their feet as they strolled the familiar paths.

Lone Wolf laughed at the playful antics of the wolf as he dashed here and there, chasing the falling leaves; Catherine, heavy-hearted, only smiled. When Lone Wolf circled her shoulder with his arm and drew her closer, she stiffened and would have pulled away, but his fingers bit into her flesh and his arm held her like a vise. Her response to his caresses were perfunctory; her answers to his questions, her comments, were indifferent. Glancing up, Catherine saw the irritation that flickered in his eyes. Her nominal surrender displeased him.

Both were glad when they finally reached the waterfall. Dropping his arm from her shoulder, Lone Wolf spread the blanket on the ground. He looked at Catherine, his expression a gesture—a command—for her to sit. When she didn't immediately obey, his face tightened, but he said nothing. For a timeless moment, he looked into her green eyes, and he read Catherine's hurt, her disapproval. Unable to stand this censure, he spun on his heels and moved closer to the river, sitting on one of the large boulders, his back to Catherine.

For a long time Catherine stared at the broad expanse of his back, thinking it was as hard and unrelenting as the boulder on which he sat. Eventually she lay on the bearskin. Caught up in their personal problems at the moment, neither appreciated the lazy beauty of the day that was reminiscent of summer. Catherine gazed abstractedly at the blue sky dotted white with small puffy clouds, and Lone Wolf sat pensively, staring into the forest.

"Why did you agree to the ordeal?" she finally asked.

"It is our custom," he explained flatly. "I have no evidence to prove my innocence, and the Roanoacs would like to be reassured. So I must prove my innocence." He breathed deeply. "I can understand their thoughts. Running Bear was a peace man."

"You could die. What then?"

"When I successfully run the gauntlet, my innocence will be proved." Still he didn't turn his head to look at her.

"I have a feeling that more than proving your innocence is involved. I wonder what else Wanchese has in mind," Catherine remarked, voicing her premonition. She closed her eyes. "No one believes you are guilty of killing Running Bear." Her voice, though soft and far-away, was resolute in its assertion.

Lone Wolf turned, and he gazed at the slender woman who lay on the blanket. His heart seemed to melt within him, and he wanted to deny her nothing. He moved, his trained feet stepping so softly that Catherine wasn't aware of his nearness until he knelt beside her and leaned over. She opened her eyes to his warm smile, to the laughter in the depth of his eyes. His hand brushed tendrils of hair from her forehead and cheeks.

"After all that anger and those accusations, you're saying you believe me, Catherine."

"Aye," she replied, lifting her hand to touch his face. "I think I knew from the beginning that you could never murder someone." Her fingers touched the prominent cheeks, the thick black eyebrows, the aquiline nose. "I was angry at myself," she admitted. "I was afraid that I would fall in love with you." Her hands stilled their

225

movement, the palms resting on his cheeks, the fingertips resting at his temples. "Now I'm afraid that you might die."

"Why do you fear for my life, Catherine?" His warm breath splayed across her face.

"You are a great warrior," she answered, looking at her image in his eyes, "and an honorable one. You will not lead your people on the path to war until you have exhausted all means to keep peace."

Lone Wolf chuckled. "It has nothing to do with your loving me?"

For a fraction of a moment Catherine hesitated. "Nay," she teased, "nothing to do with my loving you."

Lone Wolf had no fear of death, but he dreaded the thought of being separated from Catherine. He would not admit this, however, especially not to Catherine. "Surely Manitou will watch over one who tells the truth and acts honorably."

Catherine rolled her head from side to side, tears misting her eyes. "Sometimes it seems to me, my darling—" The endearment, an unconscious admission of her love for Lone Wolf, slipped from her lips.

"My darling," he repeated softly, thinking of the inscription on the ring. "What do the words mean?"

"It means my favorite one," Catherine whispered, her fingers gently brushing his thick black hair.

"Am I your favorite one?" he questioned. When Catherine nodded her head, he said, "Thank you, my darling." He turned his face, pressing a warm kiss into the palm of her hand.

His gentleness and love made Catherine tremble; she forgot their previous disagreement. She forgot Little Doe and the coming marriage. She remembered only that in seven days he must run the gauntlet; in seven days he could be dead.

"What does it sometimes seem to you, my darling?"

Lone Wolf asked, picking up the forgotten thread of conversation. His cheek nuzzled her hand, his lips and tongue nibbling at the sensitive skin of her inner wrist.

Catherine looked at him blankly. Then she recalled. "That God . . . that God," she said softly, "is far away when we need him most. It seems that he doesn't hear our cries."

Catherine remembered the tears she had shed for her father, the prayers for his healing. Instead death had come. She thought about being taken captive, made the slave and mistress of a man whom she and her people had considered a savage. She thought about the injustice of her loving a man who was marrying another, one who would force her into a plural marriage.

"No matter how things may look, Catherine, we must never give up hope," Lone Wolf told her, his hand closing around her small waist, his lips nipping her palm and wrist. "We don't always understand the ways of God, but we must believe that he directs our path."

Catherine guided his face to hers, and his lips softly touched her cheek, her forehead, her mouth, the gestures infinitely tender and reassuring. Then his arms fully encircled her, and she pressed her face against the soft buckskin shirt, deeply inhaling the clean, forest scent of his bathing herbs. His warm, strong hand stroked the length of her slender frame, from the back to the hip, stroking again and again.

Lone Wolf's lips were warm and tender against Catherine's. Gently they opened and his tongue caressed her lips. Answering him, she opened her mouth and allowed him access. When they drew apart, both were shaking from the intensity of the emotion they felt and transmitted to the other.

"You are mine, Catherine," he whispered triumphantly. A beautiful smile—that special smile—split his face, breaking the sorrowful mood that threatened to enshroud them. "You are my darling."

Looking into his face, Catherine could not help but respond with a timid smile of her own. "Yes," she acquiesced sadly, "I am yours."

"And I am yours." Catherine saw the tiny reflection of her image in Lone Wolf's glowing eyes as he made this declaration. "I love you."

"I love you," Catherine whispered. She swallowed her tears, and she smiled. "I thought love would bring me great happiness and joy." She laughed scornfully at those words. "How wrong could I have been. I love you with all my heart, and there's nothing in the world I want more than to marry you. But I'm miserable. My heart feels as though it's been broken into a million pieces."

Hearing the sadness in her confession of love, Lone Wolf gathered her into his arms and held her, consoling her. "Catherine, I love you; nothing will ever change that." He pressed kisses over her face, her eyes, and the tip of her nose.

"Don't marry Little Doe," Catherine begged. "Don't force me into such a situation."

"I am a Scupperongac war chief," Lone Wolf muttered harshly. "I am a warrior and a man of my word. Can you not understand that I wanted you so much that I agreed to this marriage so I could have you? Can you not understand that this marriage is important for the welfare of my people?"

His lips touched hers, brushing back and forth softly. "We have only this afternoon to spend together, Catherine," he murmured. "Let us be happy and enjoy it. Let's not think of what may or may not be. Let's just enjoy the moment which Manitou has given us—you and me."

Fearing that she might not again have the opportunity to show her love, Catherine pushed her dissatisfaction aside. Desperation silenced her questions and doubts,

228

and deferring to Lone Wolf's sweet persuasion, Catherine showered him with the abundance of her love. They laughed, and they talked. They touched. But they went no farther than the most innocent caresses, postponing the moment of ultimate surrender, drawing as much pleasure from the foreplay as possible.

Sitting up, Catherine unbraided Lone Wolf's hair. When it was free, she splayed her fingers through the shining black strands. "So long and so beautiful," she cried, then added, "but everything about you is beautiful." She laughed aloud, sharing her joy with him. "Perhaps now, my darling, you can change your name. No longer will you be the Lone Wolf."

Smiling his thanks, Lone Wolf touched her forehead with his lips; then he sighed. "Catherine, you asked me a question yesterday and I did not answer you . . . because I couldn't." He pushed himself up, twisting his head, swinging his hair so that it hung down his back, the ends softly dancing in the morning breeze, strands of it wisping across his face. He, too, knew that trial by ordeal was not necessarily just or merciful, and he knew time was limited. He wanted nothing to stand between him and Catherine, no misunderstandings, no disagreements, no person dead or alive. Though Scupperongac custom deemed it inappropriate for him to tell the story of his dead, Lone Wolf felt no guilt as he said, "Today, I would like to tell you about the young warrior who was called Growling Wolf."

His back to her, his voice faraway, Lone Wolf began to talk, pouring out the sorrow of his soul. He didn't spare himself one ounce of anguish as he recounted the finding of the bodies of Morning Star and the Little Eagle. He didn't hold back the tears that flowed down his cheeks as he spoke of his dead unborn child.

Seeing his pain, Catherine circled his body with her arms, wrapping him in the warmth of her love and caring.

She said nothing; words were an unnecessary encumbrance at a moment like this. Now was a time for caring, a time for sharing. Burying her head in his back, letting the wind tangle his black hair around her face, she cried with him, hot tears running down her cheeks.

With a groan, Lone Wolf turned, taking Catherine in his arms, his mouth finding hers, their tears mingling together; their sorrow becoming one. But Catherine would not leave Lone Wolf tied in the bonds of grief forever. She would replace his anguish with her love. Though she would not willingly marry him, she would love him as no other woman ever had or ever would. She would give to him as no other woman could.

A woman with a purpose, she slowly pulled her mouth from his. Gently she laved the tears from his cheeks with the tip of her tongue, and one by one she lifted the necklaces over his head and laid them on the blanket. Smiling seductively and stopping his hands, she unfastened the thong that secured his jacket. Taking that garment's fringed hem in hand, she pulled it over his head and tossed it aside. Then she placed both palms on his smooth chest and gently shoved him against the blanket.

Leaning over him, her lips touched his face, brushing kisses over his forehead, his eyes, his nose, and his cheeks. They blazed a fiery path down his throat and across his shoulders, to the pulsing point at the base of his neck. She opened her mouth and, with her tongue, drew ever-growing circles on the throbbing spot, her fingers leisurely traveling the length of his lean torso and lightly tickling his sensitive flesh.

One hand slipped beneath the belt of his breechclout as her mouth slid down his chest, her lips stopping when they reached a nipple. She laved, she nipped, she kissed until the tiny points were strutted, until Lone Wolf moaned his pleasure. Then she turned her face, her cheek grazing Lone Wolf's chest as the tip of her tongue traced the length of his scar. Inhaling raggedly, Lone Wolf circled Catherine with his arms and would have pulled her beneath him, but she resisted that loving injunction. This time she was the giver, and she was giving the gift of love. She was giving what he could never force from her.

Catherine stared at him with passion-glazed eyes, smiling enigmatically as her fingers roved from his waistband to his chest back to his waist. She untied his belt, threw it aside, and pulled the soft deerskin flap down. Blatantly she looked at his swollen manhood. Then she feathered her fingers the length of his body, from his collarbone to the end of his distended shaft, touching it, loving it, fondling the delicate sacks beneath, glorying in her ability to stimulate such trembling responses in this forest creature, in seeing the man as well as a warrior.

Rocking back on her knees and toes, Catherine whipped the wolf-fang necklace over her head. Both their eyes on it, she held it for just a second before she dropped it to the side on the blanket. She tipped her smiling lips with her tongue, and she laughed. It sounded like the morning breeze that danced through the trees. With flowing movements, she took the hem of her dress in both hands and pulled it over her head, throwing it to the side.

Proudly she sat on bended knees, staring at him, marveling at the desire she saw blazing in his eyes. He raised his hands and cupped her breasts, and Catherine breathed deeply, almost convulsively, as desire leaped through her body. She luxuriated in his caressing touch, her blood soaring through her body as he gently thumbed her crests to throbbing life. Then, supporting himself on an elbow, Lone Wolf leaned closer to the fleshy morsels, his mouth closing over a bud, the tip of his tongue circling, licking, finally sucking.

Pained pleasure winged through Catherine, and selfishly she wanted to lower herself, to give herself up to Lone Wolf's expertise and guidance. She wanted to let him take the lead, to whet her passions to the keening point. But this time she would not. This must be her gift of love to him.

"Just a little more, my darling," she promised in a thick, husky voice, and lifting her hands to her head, she untied the headband and threw it toward the growing mound of discarded clothing.

She smiled wantonly as she performed her last act of undressing. Untying the thongs that bound her braids, she unwove the silken strands until their auburn length hung in coppery beauty over her breasts and down her back. The wind danced through it, picking up the ends, caressing her face and Lone Wolf's with its feather-soft tendrils.

Catherine stretched her slender frame beside his, her hands and her mouth moving over his body, eloquently bespeaking her passion and her desire. But today Catherine would have him know even more. She would have him know her love. As her lips caressed his navel, she gently raked her nails up and down his legs, around the sensitive arches of his inner thighs. She touched the head of his masculinity, and she found him moist and waiting.

Again Lone Wolf caught her, intending to tug her body beneath his for the natural culmination of their passion, but Catherine shook her head and whispered, "This is my day to love you."

Smiling at the puzzled look in his desire-glazed eyes, Catherine straddled Lone Wolf, slowly lowering her body over his. Her purpose revealed, Lone Wolf arched his buttocks as Catherine carefully and gently encased his manhood in the warm, moist sheath of her inner flesh.

When she suddenly lunged down on his expectant body, taking his bigness and length within herself, Lone Wolf's moan of excitement turned into a growl of pleasure.

Their groans and sighs, their cries of anguish mingled in the language of love. Catherine felt him inside her, moving as he filled her, as he completed her. His hands cupped her buttocks; he squeezed; he released. He guided her movements. In the primeval throes of passion, Catherine lowered her body, then withdrew, only to plunge again and again. Urgency subjugated gentleness, giving rise to a fierceness in their lovemaking. With each stroke Catherine lifted him higher and higher, carrying him with her as she climbed the pinnacle of love. Her body grasped his swollen manhood; she flexed her buttocks, holding him tightly within her.

A joyous prisoner of her pulsating tightness, Lone Wolf groaned his pleasure. "I love you, my darling slave."

Catherine, pleased with her ministrations, leaned back and gasped for breath, her hands splaying across his moisture-sheened chest.

"Don't stop, Catherine," Lone Wolf rasped. "Don't stop now."

Exultant in her prowess to bring this warrior to the apex of desire, Catherine laughed softly. "I am not about to stop, my darling. This moment of love has just begun for you."

Her lips, red from their lovemaking, curved into a beautiful smile. Lifting her hands in flowing gestures, Catherine gently rotated her lower body, and she began to sign.

"I love you, my dear one, my favorite one, and slave or not, my heart will always belong to you."

Lone Wolf, unable to discipline the ripple of desire that raced through his body, raised his shoulders, his arms closing around Catherine's small body, and he

233

pulled her down on him. Cupping her buttocks with his hands, he began to rear, pressing, shoving his muscle higher and higher into her. They moved together, gasping, letting the waves of sensation wash over them.

Finally there came the wave that inundated both of them, sweeping them into its torrential fury. Catherine's teeth bit into Lone Wolf's shoulder, and his hands grasped her buttocks. She tensed, she cried out, her lower body shuddering. Then she sighed, exhaled the air she had been holding in, and wilted. His eyes closed, Lone Wolf's hands flexed into her buttocks, and he moved that last time, penetrating Catherine more deeply than she had thought possible. His eyes closed, he shuddered and gasped, his cries of release and pleasure muffled by Catherine's shoulder.

Later they bathed in the river, not returning to No-am-ee's wigwam until the sun was sinking low in the west. After they ate, No-am-ee, knowing the two of them wanted to be together, insisted they let her clear up the dishes. Grateful for the old woman's thoughtfulness, the two lovers moved to the platform, not even noticing when No-am-ee quietly slipped out of the wigwam.

Holding Catherine close, Lone Wolf sat, his back against the wall that was covered in soft rabbit fur. He ran his hand over her head, his palm resting on the smooth part of her auburn hair, his fingertips on her soft cheek. Catherine nuzzled her face into his warmth and listened to the rhythmic thumping of Lone Wolf's heart.

"What's going to happen?" Catherine whispered, fearing the unknown as much as she dreaded the ordeal itself.

"I will not see you again until the trial, and I cannot speak to you until after the ordeal," Lone Wolf explained. "I go now to meet with Wise One and the tribal council, and we will begin the purification ceremony. The next six days I will spend by myself, praying, fasting, and seeking a vision from my spirit guide. One the seventh day I return, physically and spiritually cleansed, ready for the ordeal."

He caught Catherine's head between his hands and pulled it away from his chest so he could look into her face. He smiled tenderly, running his eyes over the lovely sprinkle of freckles that never ceased to fascinate him.

"No-am-ee will take care of you and will explain all the woman's work that you must do." His lips touched hers in gentle farewell. "Be brave, my darling." The European endearment, a part of his vocabulary now, slipped easily from his tongue. "The punishment will soon be over, and we'll be together again."

"What—what—if—" Catherine couldn't put her thoughts into words.

"I will instruct the tribal council." His voice was low and constrained. "I will ask the Wise One to free you from your captivity and to take you back to your village and to your people."

"Oh, Lone Wolf," Catherine sobbed, unable to stop the rush of tears, "please let me come with you."

"I wish you could." He chuckled softly. "But I wouldn't get any praying done, sweet one, nor would I be waiting for my spirit guide to speak to me. You would occupy all my time and thoughts. I would hear only what you were saying to me. I would feel only your touches." Catherine's teary laughter joined his. "But if you wish, you may give me something of yours to carry with me. Something that will bring me good magic."

"Wait right here," she cried, pushing herself off the platform. "I'll be right back."

She ducked through the door and raced across the village to their wigwam. With fumbling fingers she eagerly opened her trunk and searched for a special gift. She found the handkerchief, the last one her mother had sewn for her. She spread out the small fluff of material, the tips of her fingers gently tracing the monogrammed initials in the corner. As she lowered the trunk lid, she spied her purse.

She hesitated; then she pulled the lid up again. She reached for the purse and unfastened the flap, tossing the ring into her palm. She held it for seconds in the waning light, looking at the inscription. She wanted to give it to Lone Wolf, but she couldn't. Her love she could admit, but she couldn't part with the ring—not yet. Reluctantly she returned the ring to the purse and closed the trunk.

She was breathless when she reached Lone Wolf. "Here," she said, pressing the handkerchief into his hand. Unable to meet his gaze, she lowered her head, saying, "My . . . my mother made this for me just before she died." She pointed to her initials that were monogrammed in the corner. "This is my mark."

"It's beautiful," he said, disappointment hollowing the sincerity of the statement. He took the delicate piece of lace and linen, and he drew the softness through his hand, allowing the silence to grow more pronounced with each stroke of his fingers.

Finally Catherine looked up into the face that tenderly gazed at her. When she saw his sadness, she couldn't hide her tears. She had wanted to give him the ring, but she couldn't. His arranged marriage still stood between them.

He took her into his arms, crushing the piece of linen cloth between them. "Don't cry," he enjoined softly, kissing the droplets from her cheeks. "It only makes it worse for both of us."

"I know," she sniffed, smiling in spite of her grief. "Thank you for the handkerchief."

"Lone Wolf, I—"

He laid a finger over her lips. "You don't have to explain, Catherine. I understand." He smiled, his lips brushing hers in a final kiss. "I must go."

236

Chapter XII

Caught in the conflicting throes of love, wanting to cry to ease her own hurt but wanting not to in order to ease Lone Wolf's pain, Catherine stood, dry-eyed, outside the wigwam. Stoically she watched the brave bestow last-minute affection on his animal. She watched him rub the wolf's head and ruffle the hair around its neck. She heard Lone Wolf croon softly to Wolf Friend.

When Lone Wolf rose, he held his arms out, and Catherine moved to him, their hands clasping that one last time. Each, knowing time was precious, memorized the other's features, locking an image safely and securely in the coffer's of the heart. They shared that last, lingering look, a last lingering kiss. Then they parted.

Lone Wolf took a step, stopped and turned. He smiled and raised his hand in a gesture of farewell. Catherine waved and smiled in return, her lips tremulous as she valiantly struggled to keep recalcitrant tears from flowing. Lone Wolf, nonetheless, saw the shimmer of a tear on her cheek before he turned and walked toward the Big House. Silently the woman and the wolf stared at his retreating figure.

When Lone Wolf disappeared into the ceremonial house, Catherine turned and walked inside the wigwam, her heart heavier than it had been since her father's death. Bereft and lonely, she paced around the large room, wondering when No-am-ee would return. Then she remembered the letter Ellen had written to her.

Sending one of the children after Little Flower, Catherine waited impatiently for the child to come watch the fire while she was away. Then she raced across the village, down the well-manicured paths to Lone Wolf's wigwam. Kneeling in front of the chest, she quickly unfastened the lock, lifted the lid, and took out the letter. Sitting down and leaning back against the chest, Catherine unfolded the sheet of paper and pressed out the wrinkles.

Dearest Kate,

After you left, I moved in with Eleanor and Ananias. I am quite content considering the circumstances, but I really do miss you. Will said he would bring me to Scupperong to visit you as soon as Lone Wolf grants us permission. At the same time that I am writing you this letter, Will is sending a message to Lone Wolf.

Also, I wanted to tell you that Will and Manteo have been meeting with a delegation of Indians from many small tribes in the area. A treaty and alliance with them looks favorable. I will let you know more about this later.

Now let me tell you about life in the great city of Raleigh. . . .

Catherine chuckled as she continued to read Ellen's humorous account of the goings-on at the settlement.

Rising to her knees, Catherine dug through her trunk again. She then took her writing case to the platform, where she composed a long, newsy letter to Ellen, grinning as she described Indian life to the younger Graystone. Once the letter was folded, Catherine tucked it into the belt at her waist.

Long after she had repacked her writing case, Catherine sat on the floor, thinking about her future. If the colonists made an alliance with the coastal tribes, there would be no political advantage in her remaining in Scupperong. And if that were the case, she would not have to subject herself to living through Lone Wolf's taking a bride.

If she hadn't fallen in love with him, it would have been so simple, she thought. Now there was no answer to her dilemma—simple or otherwise. Whatever she did, she would be hurt. Standing, she walked through the wigwam, stopping in the sleeping compartment. Her eyes swept around the room, and she looked at Lone Wolf's bow which lay on the platform above the bed. His quiver of arrows hung from the rafters. She glanced at his clothes basket. She smelled the pine-scented herbs he used when he bathed.

Retracing her steps, she walked from the main room into the porchlike entry area. Then she pulled the bark over the door and slowly made her way through the village to Wise One's wigwam. Although the door was open, Catherine was reluctant to walk in unannounced. Balling her hand, she gently tapped on the frame.

Wise One's wife, Sunflower Woman, responded. She was surprised to see Lone Wolf's slave, but she didn't show it. "Come in, Cath-er-ine." Catherine wiped her feet on the cornhusk mat outside the door and stepped into the entry room, following Sunflower Woman to the platform. "What may I do for you?" the Indian woman asked, speaking slowly and signing.

Sitting down, Catherine gestured, "I would like to ask a favor please." Tugging the letter from her belt, she handed it to Sunflower Woman and signed. "Mr. Flint,

239

the one called Yellow Hair Face, said he was going to visit the settlement. I would like to ask him to deliver this to my sister."

Sunflower Woman took the letter, and she looked at the strange marks. "I will be happy to give it to him for you, Cath-er-ine. I would let you speak with him yourself, but he has gone hunting with some of his friends." A gracious hostess, she asked, "May I serve you some berries or melon?"

"No, thank you," Catherine replied, instantly liking Sunflower Woman. "I'd better get back to the wigwam. I have work to do, and I promised Little Flower that I would return soon. She must help her mother tonight."

Waving goodbye to Sunflower Woman, Catherine turned and slowly walked to No-am-ee's wigwam. After Little Flower left, Catherine stood in the center of the room, the emptiness and solitude closing in on her. Needing something to do to occupy herself, she pulled a basket of cornhusks from the upper shelf and sat down by the fire. Imitating the women she had seen working last night, she braided cornhusk doormats until a slight shadow fell over her.

Dropping the mat she was braiding and looking up, Catherine cried happily, "Re-bekk-ana!"

"I came to visit you," Re-bekk-ana said, a sweet, timid smile hovering at the corners of her mouth.

"You didn't come to see No-am-ee?" Catherine asked in surprise.

Re-bekk-ana shook her head and spoke softly. "When Sunflower Woman brought my mother some extra porcupine quills earlier, she mentioned you. She thought perhaps you were lonely. Knowing it will be a long time before No-am-ee returns from the council hall, I came over, hoping perhaps you would want my company."

"I do," Catherine confessed.

The girl's simple gesture of friendship touched

240

Catherine so deeply that tears threatened. Irritated with herself because she was so emotional and weepy, Catherine rubbed the back of her hand over her eyes.

"I don't know how to thank you," she murmured.

"You don't have to," Re-bekk-ana answered. "You have been good to my family already, talking with Little Flower, my sister, and making her the doll clothes."

Catherine's sniff was lost in a chuckle. "That was nothing." She dismissed it with a wave of her hand. "Just a few scraps of material and some odd lace and ruffs."

"Don't discount any good that you do, Cath-er-ine. Perhaps the clothes themselves were not much, but you sat up late into the night sewing by a torchlight. You gave Little Flower the greatest gift one can give: yourself. And when you gave to Little Flower you gave to all her family."

Humbled by the wisdom that flowed from the seventeen-year-old, Catherine lowered her head and resumed her weaving. Eventually she said in faltering Scupperongac, "I have not been here long, Re-bekk-ana, but already I have learned so much." She lifted her face and gazed at the girl who knelt across from her. "All of you give so unselfishly to one another."

"We have to," Re-bekk-ana replied simply, bending forward to push the logs into the fire. "Our survival depends on our taking care of one another."

"How long have you been taking care of No-am-ee?" Catherine asked curiously.

"Ever since she came to Scupperong three winters ago," Re-bekk-ana returned.

"Lone Wolf told me that she lost her entire family in an Indian raid."

"She lost her immediate family, but as long as one member of the Turtle Clan lives, No-am-ee has family." Reaching into the basket, Re-bekk-ana picked up a handful of cornhusks and began to weave them. "I have been helping her ever since Lone Wolf brought her to our village. When all my mending is done and I must work outside, Little Flower comes to watch the fire and cook for Grandmother. In turn, Grandmother teaches us. Right now, she is teaching Little Flower to embroider." Her round face lifted and her smile widened. "You embroider well, Cath-er-ine. The clothes you made Little Flower's doll are beautiful."

Catherine felt the warmth and sincerity in the compliment. "Thank you," she replied.

"Little Flower was very proud. After she showed it to everyone in her wigwam, she came rushing over here to show it to Grandmother and me." Re-bekk-ana chuckled indulgently. "Then she showed it to all her friends."

Time passed quickly as the two women laughed and talked. Finally when the shadows began to lengthen and No-am-ee hadn't returned, Catherine asked, "What's the purification ceremony like?"

"For men I'm not sure," Re-bekk-ana answered. "I have never been to one, and it's not talked about. I only know the great chief, the tribal council, and the village council are meeting with Lone Wolf now. They will give him instructions tonight. Afterward the medicine man will lead him deep into the forest. There Lone Wolf will stay alone for six days and nights, seeking his spirit guide who will give him the magic to run the gauntlet bravely if he is telling the truth and who will forgive him if he has lied."

"Will he see no one during this time?" Catherine asked, her voice lifting in incredulity.

Re-bekk-ana reached into the basket for more husks. "Only the medicine man who will pray for him."

"Will he sleep in the open?"

Re-bekk-ana shook her head. "The elders selected the spot for his purification this afternoon, and they constructed a teepee for him. It is not as comfortable as his wigwam, but it will protect him from the worst of the elements."

Worried about him, Catherine continued to prod Re-bekk-ana with questions. "Will he eat nothing during the fast?"

"A little." Re-bekk-ana smiled, patiently answering Catherine's questions. "Someone will take him a small portion of food and water each morning and leave it by the clearing."

Catherine's face lit up. She knew she couldn't speak to Lone Wolf, but if she carried his food to him, she might be able to see him. "I will do that," she cried.

"I don't know if they will let you." Re-bekk-ana shrugged. "Generally it is done by one of the grand-parents or one of the parents, but since Lone Wolf has neither—" She stopped when she looked up and saw the disappointment on Catherine's face. "But I know what you can do." Before Catherine could ask, Re-bekk-ana hurried on, "Lone Wolf will need new clothes for the celebration and games after the trial. You can ask Grandmother if you can make them. She might let you."

After Re-bekk-ana discussed the clothes Lone Wolf would wear, she described her new dress, but Catherine listened with only half an ear. Her mind was already designing a garment for Lone Wolf and embroidering it with colored beads.

When it was too dark to see, Catherine picked up one of the husks. She folded and twisted it into a lamplighter. Inserting one of the spindly ends into the flame, she held it there until it caught on fire. Gracefully, she stood and lit the torchlights that were suspended from the ceiling, the scent of burning pine-rosin filling the house as the flame spit and sputtered to life.

When No-am-ee returned later, she was unusually quiet. She sat in front of the fire a long time before she picked up some cornhusks and absently braided mats with Catherine and Re-bekk-ana. Although Catherine was agog with curiosity, she did not ask No-am-ee any questions. Bowing to Scupperongac custom, she waited for the elder to speak first.

Finally, without lifting her head or taking her eyes off her work, No-am-ee spoke slowly and distinctly. She explained the ceremony, then added, "After tonight we will not mention it again. It is not our custom to talk about the coming ordeal since we do not wish any evil spirit to hear us and to cause Lone Wolf harm. Nor do we worry about it. If Lone Wolf is honest, all will be well. Manitou will take care of him."

No-am-ee stood, moved to the sleeping platform, and tugged on a large storage basket that was beneath it. "We have plenty of work to keep us busy and our minds occupied. The Roanoacs will be arriving soon, so we must have plenty of food to serve them. The braves will leave tomorrow for the hunt, and we will join some of the women in the nut gathering while the others tend to the corn. Also we have new clothes to embroider for Lone Wolf." When No-am-ee took the lid off the basket, she pulled out several pieces of buckskin. The leggings and moccasins she dropped to the floor. The jacket she held up, slapping it through the air. "He will need these for the celebration," she announced.

Taking the soft tan-colored skin in her hands, Catherine asked, "May I create my own designs for Lone Wolf and embroider them, Grandmother?"

Mulling the question and the answer, No-am-ee stared at Catherine for a moment before she nodded. "The embroidering we will do at night. During the day we must get things ready for the harvest festival. Now," she said, lifting a dark tan buckskin dress out of the basket, "we must hang our new clothes so the wrinkles will fall out." She whipped the dress through the air a time or two; then she laid it over the line that was strung from one side of the wigwam to the other. "Since you are not much larger than I," No-am-ee continued, "and you have not had time to sew a new dress, I will give you another of mine." She held the pale green dress up, lifting her face to look at Catherine. "Do you like it?"

Rising, Catherine crossed the wigwam and took the dress from No-am-ee's extended arms. She gently fingered the soft skin, admiring the color. She had never seen such a delicate shade of green before. "I think it is beautiful, Grandmother." Holding the dress up to her face, Catherine raised her head. "Are you sure you want to give it to me?"

No-am-ee smiled. "I am sure. It deepens the beauty of your eyes."

Laughing her thanks, Catherine grabbed No-am-ee in a bear hug and danced around the room with her. All three of the women then released their anxiety and tension through laughter.

Pleased by Catherine's exuberance, No-am-ee teased, "If this continues, we won't be ready for the ordeal or the harvest festival. Now you must get to work."

After Catherine hung her dress, she and Re-bekk-ana scampered to Lone Wolf's wigwam, giggling as they carried the sputtering lamplighter, shielding it with cupped hands so the wind wouldn't blow the flame out. When the torch was lit, Catherine knelt before her chest. Lifting the lid, she sorted through her material, laying it in neat stacks to the side.

"Oh, Cath-er-ine," Re-bekk-ana exclaimed, falling to her knees beside Catherine, "this is truly the most beautiful buckskin I have ever seen." She gently ran her hands over the soft brocades and satins.

Laughing as she searched for the glass beads, Catherine explained the difference between the material and buckskin. She picked up her shears and handed them to Re-bekk-ana, naming them and explaining their use.

The needles. The thread. The thimble. The sack of colored beads.

After Catherine repacked her chest, she handed Re-bekk-ana her sewing basket, and she doused the torch lamp, making sure all the embers were out. Then she walked outside the wigwam and dropped it. As she and Re-bekk-ana sped back to No-am-ee's wigwam, they were unaware of the figure who lurked in the darkness, watching their movements.

Under the flickering glow of the torch lamp Catherine and Re-bekk-ana worked. Re-bekk-ana sorted the beads into small baskets by color, and Catherine began to decorate. When she had finished with one cuff, she held it out for the Indian woman to see.

"This is beautiful," Re-bekk-ana exclaimed, looking at the exquisite needlework, "Lone Wolf is going to be proud to wear this jacket." She ran her fingers over the brightly colored glass beads. "All the warriors are going to envy him, and they'll be wanting him to wager you at the games."

Re-bekk-ana's remark startled Catherine so that she poked herself with the needle. "Wager me?" she exclaimed disbelievingly.

Laughing and nodding her head, Re-bekk-ana said, "All of them are going to want you for their slave when they see how well you embroider."

Stunned, Catherine repeated, "Wager a person?"

Re-bekk-ana nodded, the occurrence so commonplace she didn't look up from her sorting. "After the harvest festival we will play our first game of the season." Her eyes glowed. "The games are more exciting than the festivals, and anyone who can afford to bet on a team puts up his most valued possessions: strings of wampum, embroidered belts, pouches, pipes, and tobacco. And you, Cath-er-ine, would be Lone Wolf's most valuable possession. All the players will be trying to persuade

246

Lone Wolf to bet you."

"But I'm a person," Catherine howled indignantly, turning her head to look at No-am-ee. "Surely Lone Wolf couldn't wager me!"

"The child speaks the truth, Cath-er-ine," No-am-ee confirmed. "Only the most valued possessions are considered for a wager. And you must never forget that you belong to Lone Wolf. You are his property."

Catherine stared at the old woman for a long time, No-am-ee's words poignantly reminding her of her status. She wasn't a person; she was a slave. Dryly, she said, "I better not prove myself too valuable."

Re-bekk-ana laughed softly and, lifting a handful of beads, let them flow through her splayed fingers. "I don't think Lone Wolf would be so foolish."

Catherine continued to work, stopping only when No-am-ee insisted that she and Re-bekk-ana go to bed. "We have much work to do tomorrow," the old woman scolded lightly. "And whether you need your rest or not, I need mine. With so much talking going on, I can't sleep."

Laughing, Catherine rolled the shirt up, and Re-bekk-ana closed the basket of beads. When all the sewing paraphernalia had been tucked away beneath the platform and the women were snugged under their bearskin blankets, No-am-ee said softly, "May Manitou bless each of you with pleasant dreams."

It seemed that Catherine had hardly closed her eyes, before she heard the cry.

"*Fire!*"

On cue the village came to life. Partially clad, people, water jugs in hand, raced toward the flames. Some held torchlights high above their heads. Not taking the time to put on her moccasins, Catherine raced behind No-am-ee and Re-bekk-ana. By the time the three of them arrived, the fire was out, and the villagers were standing outside

Lone Wolf's wigwam.

No-am-ee pushed through the circling crowd. She looked at the smoking remains of the fire; then she turned to look at Catherine and Re-bekk-ana. Before she had time to say anything, Wise One spoke.

"No great damage has been done." He moved closer to the smoking area, scuffing the toe of his moccasin against the charred basket of used torchlights. "Who discovered the fire?"

"I did," the medicine man replied. "I was returning from the forest when I saw the blaze."

"Who is responsible?" Wise One asked, his eyes scanning the shadowed faces that circled him.

"I am the one who used the torchlight," Catherine admitted, stepping forward, "but I doused it before I threw it away."

Happy Woman, standing with the crowd, smiled maliciously, and her eyes glowed menacingly. She hated the paleface, and she was glad she was getting into trouble. Wise One would punish her for having been so careless with the torch. Starting a fire was the second most serious crime in the village, murder being the first.

The old chief sighed. Today he felt the full weight of his responsibility, and his aging shoulders were sagging beneath the heavy load. The man he loved like a son was preparing to run the gauntlet; now the village had been threatened by fire, and Lone Wolf's slave was responsible.

"One who is careless with fire is seriously punished," Wise One said.

Catherine nodded, her eyes meeting and locking with the old man's. "I understand. Although I know my words will not erase the gravity of the deed, Great Chief, I am . . . I am sorry for my carelessness."

Wise One admired Catherine's courage and her strength. She offered no excuses. "You will receive fifteen lashes on your uncovered back, Catherine."

All color drained from Catherine's face. She had never received a beating in her entire life. Not a lick had her father given her. "That seems to be a most severe punishment for a first offense," she said, striving to keep her emotions under control.

"The crime is severe."

"My chief," No-am-ee said, "I would like to speak in Catherine's behalf."

A murmur went up through the crowd, and Happy Woman's jaw went slack. Catherine deserved punishment not leniency.

"I am guilty. I am the one who sent her to Lone Wolf's wigwam to get the beads so that she might make him new clothes for the trial." No-am-ee's voice softened as she interceded for Lone Wolf's slave.

Using her arms to propel her through the crowd, Little Flower raced to Wise One. Cradling her doll close to her small frame, she said, "Great Chief, according to our law I would like to take Catherine's place. I will receive the lashes for her."

"No!" Catherine cried, touched by the generosity of the child.

Simultaneously Wise One knelt, and he took Little Flower in his arms. Running his palm down the smooth crown of black hair, he said, "Why would you do this for the paleface slave, little one?"

Little Flower held the doll for Wise One to see. "Catherine can make clothes that have great magic, my chief," the child explained simply. "And if you were to beat her, she would not be able to make Lone Wolf new clothes for the trial." Her small round face looked earnestly into the wrinkled visage of the chief as she appealed to the wisdom of his years. "Also, my chief, Catherine is new among us and doesn't understand our customs. She is very soft and is unaccustomed to pain.

The beating might kill her."

Amazed at the child's wisdom, Catherine was dumfounded, unlike the Indians around her who expected mature behavior from their children.

No-am-ee said, "I must agree with Little Flower, my chief."

Wise One took the doll and motioned a torchbearer to come closer. He inspected the delicate needlework. "You sew well, Catherine."

"Thank you," she murmured respectfully, wishing he would pronounce judgment and be done with it.

"Little Flower," Wise One said, handing her doll back to her, "you have spoken well. May your family be proud of you today, and may you tell your story of valor before the big fire for all to hear. I hear you, and I will grant mercy to the paleface." He looked at Catherine. "Because you are new to our way of life and ignorant of our customs and laws, we will not whip you this time. In the future, though, we ask you to be more careful. Next time do not expect leniency."

Happy Woman's face contorted with anger. Again she had been denied the sweetness of revenge. But the day would come, she promised herself.

"I'll be careful," Catherine answered, her gaze shifting to her stalwart champion who still stood beside the chief, cradling her doll.

"Now let us go to sleep," Wise One said. "We have much work to do in order to have our harvest ceremony."

Kneeling beside Little Flower, Catherine hugged the child, tears of gratitude moistening her eyes. "Thank you, my friend. I shall never forget this brave act of yours."

The child wrapped her arms around Catherine, returning the hug. "May I come stay with you?" she asked.

250

Surprised, Catherine hesitated momentarily before she asked, "Will your mother mind?"

It was Re-bekk-ana who answered. "An Indian is taught to make decisions from childhood, Ca-ther-ine. Our parents listen and they point out the consequences, but they do not make the choices for us. Once we have chosen, we must walk the path, taking the bad with the good and never complaining." She smiled at her sister. "If Little Flower has finished all her chores, Mother won't mind."

Rising, Catherine said, "It is all right with me, but since it's No-am-ee's wigwam, you must ask her."

Within moments, permission asked and received, No-am-ee, Catherine, Re-bekk-ana, and Little Flower slowly returned to the wigwam.

"Grandmother," Catherine said, "I would like to tell you that I was most careful in putting out my torchlight. I followed your instructions very carefully."

"I hear you," No-am-ee replied softly, thinking about all she had seen and heard, "and I believe you. The past is behind you, so put thoughts of it out of your head. It will hinder you from doing what must be done today."

Smiling, Catherine took the empty jug from Re-bekk-ana. "I'll go to the river and get us some more water. We'll need it before morning."

As if nothing untoward had happened or was going to happen, No-am-ee awakened the girls early the next morning, sending them to the river for their bath. Teeth chattering, the two young women and the child quickly bathed, giggling and talking to one another. When they returned to the wigwam, No-am-ee was dishing up the savory corn mush and pouring them a cup of hot herb tea.

"Today will be a good day for you to take Catherine nut

251

gathering," No-am-ee announced to Re-bekk-ana as they ate.

"Me, Grandmother!" Re-bekk-ana was so excited she almost spilled her tea. Next to the games and festivals, nut gathering was her favorite time of the year.

No-am-ee chuckled. "You have finished your mending, haven't you?"

"I have," Re-bekk-ana replied eagerly. Then she quieted. "But who will watch your fire and your cooking, Grandmother?"

No-am-ee looked at Little Flower and winked. "Little Flower has consented to tend our fire and watch our evening meal. She has some mending to do. Also I promised her she could bring several friends over when she finished her chores."

No-am-ee stood, moving toward the platform above her bed. Tossing Catherine a set of baskets that were braided together with two wide thongs, she said, "Throw these over your shoulder so that one basket hangs in front and one in back. And this one," she said, dropping a handbasket into Catherine's lap, "carry in your hand. When you have filled one of the shoulder baskets, reverse it and fill the other. Fill the hand basket last. If the spirits are with us, we shall come home this afternoon with all our baskets filled."

After the morning meal the three women walked out of the wigwam and joined the stream of women and children headed for the forest. Laughing and talking, the group disappeared into the woods, sharing family news and gathering nuts. Hickory nuts and chestnuts were the favorites, but they also gathered acorns, black walnuts, butternuts, and hazelnuts. In late afternoon the women returned from the woods.

When they set their baskets down in the village square, No-am-ee motioned Catherine and Re-bekk-ana behind a large, flat boulder. "Show Catherine what to do," she said, moving in the direction of the fire where many jugs of water were boiling.

Sitting down behind the natural table, Re-bekk-ana laid one of the hickory nuts in a small hollow in the boulder. "You're going to enjoy this," she bubbled, clutching a smooth, round stone in her right hand. "At the rate we're gathering nuts, we will be able to serve nut bread at the feast." She cracked and then picked the nut, dropping the fresh meat into a bowl. "Do the hickory nuts first," she said.

Following her example, Catherine sat down beside her and found another hollow. Laughing and talking, the two of them spent the remainder of the afternoon cracking and shelling nuts. When the bowl was full of fresh nutmeat, a child picked it up and dumped it into one of the log mortars to be ground into fine meal by one of the women. No-am-ee boiled the ground meal in water, the oil coming to the surface. Sometimes using a wooden ladel, at others a clam shell, she skimmed the oil off, just as cream is skimmed from milk, and stored it in clay jugs.

"The hickory nut oil," Re-bekk-ana explained, pounding away at their dwindling supply of nuts, "is used for flavoring succotash and in making bread. Mixed with butternut oil, it is fed to babies."

And so the days passed quickly. No-am-ee, Re-bekk-ana and Little Flower instructing Catherine in the ways of Indian life. In addition to nuts, they gathered the roots used for medicines and dyes. They picked and cooked edible mushrooms and puffballs, wild onions and garlic, blending them with nut oil and sunflower oil, and using the mixture to season meat.

On the sixth morning, however, No-am-ee didn't lead the girls to the forest to gather nuts or to the field to harvest corn. As soon as they had eaten, she left Little Flower in the wigwam to tend the evening meal and instructed Catherine and Re-bekk-ana to follow her to the river.

"We have much to do today," she announced as they walked single file. "According to the runners, the Roanoacs will arrive this afternoon."

"Will any be staying in the guesthouse, Grandmother?" Re-bekk-ana asked.

"No," No-am-ee returned. "Since Wanchese and Manteo are not married and have no one to prepare for them, they will be staying with Wise One. We will prepare shelters for the others who come."

"You mean"—Catherine suddenly injected herself into the conversation—"we're going to build houses for the people who have condemned Lone Wolf to the gauntlet!"

No-am-ee spun around and glowered disapprovingly at Catherine, but her voice, when she spoke, though heavy with reproof, was soft and kind. "My heart hurts for the pain Lone Wolf must suffer, Cath-er-ine, but I do not punish innocent people. The Roanoacs have done nothing to merit my hatred. Their peace man was killed, and they are asking for justice. Our tribe would have demanded the same justice had one of our braves been killed. One thing you must understand: The Roanoacs have not condemned Lone Wolf; he will be condemned only if he is lying, and the ordeal will prove whether he is or not."

"I'm sorry, Grandmother," Catherine murmured.

No-am-ee smiled, and for the first time since she had known Catherine she reached out, caught one of her hands, and patted it between hers. "Don't fret, my child, and don't let my words condemn you for emotions which are as natural to you as the running of the brook and the rising of the sun each morning."

The old woman's obsidian eyes were made gentle by love and understanding. Suddenly her gnarled hands moved, tugging the bereaved white woman to her bosom. "I sometimes speak more bravely than I feel. I speak words that are hard for me also. I can understand your feelings which grow from your love for Lone Wolf. I can understand your hatred and your bitterness."

As if Catherine were a child rather than a grown woman, No-am-ee held her close, soothing and consoling her. As if No-am-ee were strength itself, Catherine clung to the Indian woman's frail form for a long time, listening to and taking courage from the prayer No-am-ee chanted in a low monotone. Finally Catherine pushed away and smiled.

"I'm sorry," she whispered, embarrassed over her moment of weakness. "I know you don't believe in showing emotion—"

"That's where you're wrong," No-am-ee corrected her. "We believe in showing emotion—love, anger, bitterness, hatred. Perhaps differently, but we give them expression." No-am-ee's voice seemed faraway and dreamy. "Every phase of our life—our joys, our sorrows, and our aspirations—is expressed in our words and our music." Sadly she added, "Sometimes our laughter and our songs are all we have." She lapsed into silence, but she didn't lose herself in memories. Her black eyes twinkling, she said, "We just don't display our feelings publicly for outsiders to see."

It took a few seconds for No-am-ee's words to penetrate the hurt and anguish that dulled Catherine's thinking. Eventually, however, her embarrassed smile vanished to be replaced by a genuine one, a heartfelt gesture of appreciation. No-am-ee no longer considered her an outsider.

When No-am-ee saw happiness radiate on Catherine's face, she said, "Now the two of you start gathering pine branches while the men and boys erect the poles."

By late afternoon many overnight shelters had been constructed, and a temporary village lined the river.

255

Stopping and leaning against the trunk of a large oak tree, Catherine dropped the boughs she was dragging, and she surveyed the visitors camp. Like the Scupperongac wigwams, she noticed, the shelters all faced east, their doors welcoming the east wind and the morning sunshine. Unlike the wigwams, the overnight shelters were conical, or teepee shaped, and were set upon tepee poles which interlocked at the top. From floor to peak, the shelter measured between six and ten feet; the floor diameter ranged from twelve to sixteen feet.

"If it were warm weather," No-am-ee had told Catherine earlier, "we would cover the frame with a thick layer of pine branches, but since the nights are cold we'll cover the boughs with reed mats and stuff moss into the cracks to keep out the wind."

The women dug a fire pit in each shelter, and children ran back and forth, delivering basket after basket of fallen pine needles which were thickly layered over the ground to insulate and cushion the reed and cornhusk floor mats. Once the floors were carpeted with the pine straw, the children gathered firewood which they stacked at the opening of each shelter. Meanwhile, the older women tied and pegged the mats into place around the frame.

In the late afternoon the Roanoacs began crowding into the temporary wigwams. If Catherine had not known better, she would have thought they were gathering for a festive occasion. They laughed and talked in their own dialect, their hands flowing with sign language. They had brought goods and food to barter; they were laying wagers on the ordeal. Would Lone Wolf make it? Or would he die during or after the ordeal? If he lived, how long would it take him to run the gauntlet? How many times would he fall? Could the Roanoac warriors make him cry out? Could they make him hush his death chant?

These questions were spinning around in Catherine's head, making her dizzy. Her work finished, she ap-

256

proached No-am-ee who was talking and gesticulating with one of the Roanoac women. Waiting until she had completed her bartering, Catherine asked, "May I return to the wigwam? I would like to work on Lone Wolf's clothes."

"I too, Grandmother?" Re-bekk-ana asked, choosing to return with Catherine.

No-am-ee smiled brightly and nodded, her attention quickly returning to the visitors and the news and goods which they brought.

"Is it always like this?" Catherine asked Re-bekk-ana as they moved away from the noisy din.

"Like what?"

"The laughing and the jesting—the wagers."

Re-bekk-ana smiled and nodded her head. "Always."

Lapsing into an introspective silence, Catherine walked through the town. Already the village boasted a bountiful hunt. Men and boys carefully plucked and dressed turkeys and geese; the deer they butchered. They had fish in abundance and squirrel for a succulent stew. At that moment a group of hunters returned to the village, a deer suspended from a pole which they carried between them.

"We are going to have plenty of food for the feasts," Re-bekk-ana said.

"Feasts?" Catherine asked, her eyebrows rising. "How many are we going to have?"

"The first one is tonight." Re-bekk-ana's eyes twinkled, and her face glowed with excitement and anticipation. "In the morning when Younger Sister, the Dawn, comes we have the purification ceremony. When Elder Brother, the Sun, is directly overhead the ordeal will begin. And tomorrow night we will have another feast."

"Will Lone Wolf be at the feast tonight?" Catherine asked.

"No, we won't see him until the purification ceremony

in the morning. He won't join the feasting until after he has run the gauntlet."

Re-bekk-ana continued to talk, but Catherine wasn't really listening. Her eyes strayed to Lone Wolf's wigwam, and she saw the wolf who lay outside. Since his master had retired to the forest, the animal had denied himself food and water. Separated from his master, Wolf Friend had no desire to live.

"After the ordeal we have games," Catherine heard Re-bekk-ana say. "You will enjoy them."

"No matter what the outcome of the ordeal is, you will continue with the feasting and the games?" Catherine questioned, incredulity in her voice.

Re-bekk-ana nodded her head. "We never dwell on what could be, Ca-ther-ine. Worrying about whether Lone Wolf will make it or not will not help him at all. We believe if we are happy, we show the spirits and our warrior that we have confidence in him." Her eyes mirrored the same belief. "We know he told the truth, so we have nothing to fear."

Re-bekk-ana did not accompany Catherine to No-am-ee's wigwam. Seeing a group of her friends, she joined them, ohing and ahing over their new clothes for the ordeal celebration. Shaking her head in puzzlement, Catherine ducked into the wigwam.

"You may go outside and play if you wish," Catherine said to Little Flower. "I'm going to embroider Lone Wolf's clothes, so I'll watch the fire."

Chapter XIII

"Come," No-am-ee said as she entered the wigwam. "Tonight we feast with the Roanoacs."

"I'm not hungry," Catherine replied, loathe to attend the celebration. Festivities were not the way she chose to approach the gruesome punishment awaiting Lone Wolf. "I would prefer to stay here and work on Lone Wolf's clothes."

"How much do you have left to do?" No-am-ee asked, walking across the room to look at Lone Wolf's garments that hung, finished on the clothesline.

"A part of a moccasin," Catherine admitted sheepishly.

No-am-ee clucked her disapproval. Moving closer to the line, she peered at her dress. She lifted a gnarled hand and touched the tanned and worked deerskin, smoothing out the creases. Doing the same to Catherine's dress, she said, "You must go. It will not look well for Lone Wolf if you are absent."

Weary of everyone considering Lone Wolf's feelings but not hers, Catherine asked, "Who will tend the fire?" She sought any excuse to remain home.

"No one tonight," No-am-ee replied. "The weather is not so cold that we cannot put the fire out for a little while.

We will relight it when we come in." Brooking no more argument, accepting no excuses, the old woman said, "Everyone attends the feast."

Reluctantly Catherine dropped the moccasin and slid her sewing basket under the platform. By the time she and No-am-ee left the wigwam, the sun was setting low in the west, and the air had the briskness of an autumn evening. Men and women, working together, prepared the feast. While some cooked, others lined the streets with reed runners that were to be used as eating mats. Down the center of the mats, the Indian women set the large, flat serving bowls and the newly carved spoons.

In the town square at the head of the runner the three chiefs—Wise One, Manteo, and Wanchese—sat; to the right and left of them the tribal chiefs sat. Sitting across from each other in family groups, Scupperongacs faced Roanoacs. Following No-am-ee's instructions, Catherine sat beside her, but she didn't join in the talking. She preferred to watch the people and to listen.

Finally when she tired of watching those who sat around her, she lifted her gaze, looking at the three chiefs. Whereas Manteo was laughing and talking with Wise One, Wanchese was withdrawn and pensive. Catherine hoped she would get an opportunity to speak with Manteo later. Perhaps he had brought her another letter from Ellen. She hoped Ellen and Will would soon be coming for a visit. Then it struck her that perhaps she would soon be returning to the settlement. The realization, which should have brought her great joy, brought only sorrow.

Sunflower Woman set a bowl on the eating mat in front of Catherine, and the aroma of the food filled Catherine's nostrils, briefly taking her mind off her perturbing thoughts. Her mouth watered when she saw the variety of dishes. Impaled on sticks and basted with a rich oil made from nuts and berries were alternate chunks of venison and bear, wild onions, mushrooms, and potatoes. Roasted to a golden brown, their aroma filled the air. Various sorts of wild fowl were being turned on spits, while cornmeal dumplings, simmering in large clay pots, floated in squirrel and rabbit stew that was seasoned with garlic and wild onions.

Broiling on smooth, heated stones at the fire's edge were filleted flounder, and more kinds of bread than Catherine could name were baking. Huge sturgeon were laid out on an elevated grill made of reeds, the grill supported and kept away from the flames by four large stakes driven into the ground. One of the braves, a large forked stick in hand, turned the fish periodically. From large pots that held several gallons of vegetables—succotash, pumpkin, beans, peas, squash—women continued to refill the serving bowls. Buried in the glowing coals of the fire, ears of corn, protected by their husks, roasted to golden brown.

Hungrily everyone ate, washing the food down with a sweetened, berry drink Catherine had never tasted before. After the feasting, the women cleaned the bowls and spoons, and stacked them near the fire; the musicians migrated to the huge fire in the center of the square. An older man beat the drum; another chanted. War clubs in hand, twenty-four of the Roanoac warriors, led by Wanchese, gracefully unfolded, rose and moved into the dance circle, stamping their feet. Catherine watched as they formed two lines, facing each other, yelling their war cries and brandishing the horrible war clubs in the air.

With a start, she realized they were enacting the ordeal. They stamped, they yelled, and they beat the imaginary warrior who ran the aisle between them. The audience roared their pleasure, cheering them on. The chanting became shriller, the drumming more intense. A frenzied excitement filled the air. In horror Catherine watched, unable to take her eyes off the actors. The flames of the huge fire leaped higher and higher as the tenders threw on more wood, and the light danced menacingly over the warriors' visages. Their painted faces were distorted by their cries; their backs, coated with dried clay, were etched in designs.

"If your war chief is speaking with a forked tongue," the Roanoacs chanted, "he will surely die. Hah! Hah!"

The Scupperongacs answered in kind. "Our war chief is brave and honest. He speaks straight. We have nothing to fear."

Unable to stand the emotional furor any longer, Catherine jumped to her feet and ran into the forest. The others were so caught up in the song and dance that no one noticed her disappearance. Tears streaming down her face, hands clamped against her ears, she ran until she was staggering and her breath was coming in deep ragged gulps. Falling against a tree, she paused, but she couldn't stop. The drums chased her, mocking her, taunting her. The beats sounded louder and more ominous, the tempo accelerated feverishly, the chanting and yowling rose accordingly. Catherine ran deeper into the forest. Finally in a moonlit clearing she collapsed, unable to go farther, unable to escape the sound of the drums. Lying there on the bed of soft pine needles, she cried her heart out.

Foremost in her mind was the scene she had left behind. Although Catherine had seen some of the most sophisticated European weapons, none compared to the war clubs the Roanoac warriors had brandished through the air. Their crudeness, their primitiveness lent them a menacing aura. Even the most simple tomahawk, a huge round or pointed stone tied to a handle with deer sinews, was a powerful and effective weapon, she decided, shivering with fear.

If Lone Wolf survived the ordeal, Catherine thought,

visions of the menacing tomahawks swimming in her mind, the Roanoac warriors would beat him senseless. No mercy would be granted! She lay there until her tears were spent, and her deep, soul-felt sobs became small sniffs. She had thought she was strong enough to endure anything—she remembered having told Ellen as much time after time—but her love for the Indian war chief had rendered her a vulnerable woman, a selfish woman who wanted to keep him alive and well. She wanted to love him forever . . . and ever.

"Our war chief is brave and honest," she chanted, her mimicry near hysteria. "He is telling the truth. We have nothing to fear." She sobbed. "He is brave and honest, but he's dead . . . dead . . . dead. . . ."

She lifted her head, and she cried softly, "Lone Wolf. Please hear me. Please answer me."

Leaning his shoulder against the trunk of the huge oak tree, Lone Wolf, clad only in breechclout and moccasins, stood at the edge of the clearing. Six days he had gone with little food and drink. Six days he was supposed to have fasted and prayed, beseeching Manitou to send a spirit guide to help him. But he had done little praying, and his only vision had been one of a green-eyed, auburn-haired woman.

Tomorrow was the seventh day—the day he ran the gauntlet. Even now, even this deep in the forest, he could hear the drums and the death chants. *Soon comes the appointed time!* they mocked. He could visualize the Roanoac warriors as they danced. He wasn't afraid, yet he shivered with apprehension and he wished for Catherine more than he wished for his spirit guide. Pushing himself away from the tree, he moved to the shelter of the teepee which was hidden by the trees. He ducked and entered, lying on the bearskin blanket and

263

pulling another over his chilled skin.

Soon comes the appointed time! the drums continued to taunt. *Soon comes the appointed time!*

Finally he dropped into an uneasy sleep, disturbed by a nightmare. He was running the gauntlet, running for his life, but the blows kept knocking him down. The pain was excruciating, yet he sang his death chant. Falling to the ground in a state of insensibility, he heard a soft voice. Forcing his eyes open, he looked through the forest of legs. His vision was blurred; he couldn't focus on anything. Again he heard the voice calling his name; he blinked his eyes several times. He squinted, trying to focus. The haze cleared, and he saw Catherine's face; then he looked up. The death blow! The root-spiked war club was coming toward his face. . . .

Lone Wolf suddenly bolted up, his body drenched with perspiration. Unable to sleep anymore, he threw the robe over his shoulders and walked out of the teepee, moving into the silver-streaked forest. Welcoming the autumn coolness, he walked toward the river. As he cautiously moved to the edge of the clearing, he saw the slight form lying on the carpet of pine needles, cloaked in the soft glow of Elder Sister, the Moon. From where he stood, Catherine looked as if she were asleep.

As if in a trance, Lone Wolf stood, gazing. He knew he should turn from her and return to his shelter, but he couldn't. He wouldn't awaken her, nor would he go to her. Yet he would look at her and remember: her tinkling laughter, the sparkle in her green eyes, the copper color of her hair in the sunshine, the taste of her lips, the feel of her soft curves beneath his hands, her soft moans of pleasure.

Attuned to the changing sounds of the night, Catherine knew she was no longer alone. Yet she wasn't afraid. She sat up and looked around, her eyes already accustomed to the moonlight. When she moved, Lone

Wolf unconsciously took a step forward. She saw him, standing tall and proud at the edge of the clearing.

"My love." The endearment escaped her lips as she held her arms out to him.

Mesmerized, they stared across the clearing at one another, neither moving, neither saying a word. Finally Lone Wolf walked to where Catherine sat. He stooped and lifted her into his arms. Catherine looped her arms over his head, twined her fingers together, and locked them behind his neck. Then she pressed her face into the soft bear fur that covered his chest, snuggling into his warmth and strength.

She felt the pull of his muscles as he carried her effortlessly through the forest to his shelter, and she luxuriated in his strength. As he stooped to go through the opening of the teepee, she lifted her face and touched his smooth cheek with her lips. When he laid her down, she didn't unlock her hands; instead, she pulled his face down to hers and pressed his lips onto hers.

There was no urgency to their lovemaking. No desperation. It was flowing softness, almost a mystical coming together. Their endearments were gentle, their sighs tender, their touches warm. With movements which didn't interrupt their rhythmic caresses, Lone Wolf divested Catherine of her clothes; and while she moved sinuously on the bearskin blanket, he loosened his breechclout.

His hands touched her breasts, each swelling mound crested with a pink nipple. His lips whispered over their fullness, closing around a tip, nipping it to a throbbing awareness. His hands flowed over her body, touching her in all the remembered places, kindling the fire of passion inside her. At the same time Catherine touched his male organ, and his sudden intake of breath escalated her excitement. She caressed him tenderly, moving her hand in gentle, stroking motions, their passions soaring as the muscle firmed within her clasp.

Lone Wolf's lips touched Catherine's, nibbling their fullness before settling into a timeless passionate kiss. His mouth sank deeper and deeper into hers, his tongue dipping into the sweet moistness of her mouth. Then the weight of his body settled on Catherine's, the tips of her breasts brushing tantalizingly against the smooth wall of his chest. And as his distended male organ slipped into the warmth of her maidenhood, she lifted her arms, splaying her hands through his hair, grinding her lips into his.

His strokes were deep and slow, carrying Catherine to a pinnacle of joy she had not reached before in their lovemaking. His kisses were not only a physical expression of love, but a spiritual one as well. Two souls touched, united. Unable to bear her anticipation any longer, Catherine met Lone Wolf's heated thrusts, and their movements accelerated until they matched the frenzied pounding of the village drums. Her hands clinging to his shoulders, Catherine welcomed the penetrating lunges, rising to meet him and holding him tightly in her warm sheath before she released him. Again and again they rose and fell, finally reaching that catalytic moment when Catherine felt as if she had burst into tiny particles. When Lone Wolf heard Catherine's cries of culmination, he made a final, deep lunge, then shuddered and groaned as he collapsed on top of her, his pleasure complete.

Slowly he rolled to the side, but he didn't relinquish his hold on Catherine. Tenaciously he clung to her, cradling her next to him, and without saying a word they drifted into a peaceful sleep. When the tempo of the drumbeats changed, Catherine awakened, but she didn't move immediately. She listened to Lone Wolf's even breathing, and she pulled the blanket tighter around them, snuggling closer to his warm, hard body. Eventually she eased out from under his arm, and propped herself on an elbow to look at him. Her breathing stopped momentarily as she gazed at his mascline beauty.

Lightly she feathered her fingers over the scars on his chest and abdomen. "Even with these, my darling, you are indeed a handsome man," she murmured.

Taking advantage of his sleeping moments, Catherine allowed herself the indulgence of studying this Indian warrior to whom she was so mysteriously attracted and with whom she had fallen so deeply and irrevocably in love. She gazed leisurely at his huge, strong body, committing every line and muscle to memory as Lone Wolf's chest rose and fell in slow, even rhythm.

His face was relaxed, and his lips were curved in a secret smile. Fleetingly Catherine wondered if he were dreaming about her. She reached out a tentative hand and touched his silken black hair that was securely bound in thick braids. When he didn't stir, she touched the thick eyebrows that arched above those obsidian jewels now closed in sleep. Then her glance fell on the thick crescent fringe of blue-black lashes that gently fanned against his cinnamon cheeks, almost touching his high, prominent cheekbones. When her eyes found his lips, unable to stop herself, she leaned over him, softly touching her lips to his in a breath of a kiss, just a whisper of a caress. But that whisper-soft touch was her undoing; the sleeping giant opened his eyes. A deep husky laugh rolled from his inner being, and his strong arms gently closed around Catherine.

"Surely you can do better than that, Catherine," he teased, his voice husky with renewed desire.

He was starved for her. For six days he had been haunted by the vision of her loveliness. Now he was holding her, seeing her again; and in reality, she was much more lovely, much more satisfying than hollow dreams.

Catherine, eager to comply, wrapped her arms around him and moaned low as he maneuvered their bodies so that she was lying beneath him. He was half-leaning over her, his hand rubbing her waist and stomach, his lips moving across the sensitive skin of her face. He kissed her eyes, her cheeks, her mouth. He nibbled her chin, her throat.

Desire flowed through Catherine's body, and she caught Lone Wolf's head in her hands. She guided his face to hers, and hungrily, as if she had never made love to him before, she sought his mouth; sought his kisses. His mouth slanted over hers, moving gently, his lips molding themselves to hers, his hands smoothly running over her hip and her thigh. As their kiss deepened, Catherine's mouth welcoming the love swirls of his tongue, she whimpered her need. Arching her body, her hand caught his and guided it to her throbbing breast.

Lone Wolf's mouth pressed and gently tugged; it teased, it gave, it took. His hand cupped the fullness of her breast; her fingers gently exciting the sensitive tip. He was delighted when she cried out as he lifted his lips from her, exhilarated when her hands moved to the back of his head, forcing it down to her. She became the aggressor, her tongue exploring the musky warmth of his mouth, her lips nibbling his.

When she finally ended the kiss, letting her head rest on the bearskin, totally drained of emotional energy, Lone Wolf rained light kisses from her mouth to her cheek, then down the slender column of her throat and back up to her ears. His tongue explored each tender curve and hollow, while his fingers blazed a hot trail down her back, stopping only when they cupped the round firmness of her buttocks. Just a little pressure from his hands, a slight movement of his hips, and Catherine began to arch toward him, an intense, aching need rekindled in the lower part of her body.

"I never knew that I could want anyone so much," he

breathed raggedly in Catherine's ear. "I cannot put you out of my mind. For days I have thought of nothing else but holding you in my arms and making love to you." Though the words were a declaration of love, they were also a cry of despair, wrenched from his heart. "You shouldn't have come, my love."

"I had to," Catherine murmured, kissing him between words. "You should see the Roanoac warriors," she cried. "They were dancing and—"

"Shh," he thrummed, his breathing mingling with hers. "Do not think of that," he murmured. "Think on pleasant subjects, my love." Then his kiss swallowed her words and her fears.

When the kiss ended, Catherine nestled closer to him, hiding her face on his chest, lying for a long time in the security of his arms. Finally she asked, "Are you going to let Ellen and Will come visit us?"

Lone Wolf hesitated before he spoke. "You wish for this?"

"I do."

"I will let them come to the strawberry festival."

Disappointed, Catherine murmured, "Not sooner?"

"No sooner." His answer final, he resituated Catherine's head on his chest, and they lay quietly for a while longer. This time he broke the silence with a sigh of regret. "I've got to get you back to the village."

"Let me stay with you," she whispered. "Let's spend the rest of the night together."

"I wish we could, but we can't. My people would never understand."

Sliding her hands between their bodies, Catherine flattened her palms on his chest, careful not to press against his recent wound. She rolled out of his arms. "Your people will always come first, won't they?" she asked accusingly. "You marry for them; you die for them."

Lone Wolf sat up, the blanket falling and covering only

269

his lower body. "I am a war chief, Catherine, a leader of my people, and I do not take my position lightly. Their welfare and safety are my first concern."

"And what am I?"

"You are my love," he replied, "and I'm desperately trying to stay alive for you." He turned, running his fingers over the smooth part in her hair. "If the tribe should learn that we had been together, both you and I would be punished. We have defied the purification ritual."

Remorseful, Catherine turned onto her back and gazed into his face. "I didn't mean this to happen," she confessed. "I just—"

Lone Wolf laid a finger across her mouth, silencing her. "I know. It's not your fault." He smiled. "It's mine; I couldn't leave you alone."

He stood and then lowered his hands, catching hers. Gently he tugged her to her feet. They were beautiful in their youth, their naked bodies gilded silver by the moonlight. His eyes moved down her body, visually touching her breasts, her stomach, the downy triangle. Dropping one of her hands, freeing one of his, he flattened his palm against her stomach.

"Our child, even now, may be growing in your belly," he said, the thought bringing a smile of happiness to his face.

"Aye," Catherine whispered.

"I would marry you tonight," he told her, grief tearing his heart and soul asunder, "but I cannot, my love. The Lumbroan Princess must be my first wife. But you will be the next, always my favored and my beloved." His lips touched hers softly, and he said, "Before Manitou, this night, I vow to take care of you, my slave, and our children." Remembering her concern, he promised, "Only you shall rear your children, and they will never be taken from you, no matter what your status within or without our tribe."

Catherine's mind could understand the logistics of Lone Wolf's political marriage, yet her heart could not accept it. That night, however, she would not discuss it. Silently they both dressed. Then Lone Wolf draped his blanket around Catherine's shoulders and held her close to him as they walked back to the clearing. At the forest's edge, silhouetted by the night's soft glow, he kissed her a last time.

"No matter what happens"—he spoke softly—"I am innocent of Running Bear's death . . . and I love you."

Before Catherine could respond, Lone Wolf turned and quietly retreated into the darkness of night. She drew the robe closely around herself and stared after him for a long time. Finally she turned and slowly retraced her steps to the village. She hadn't walked far when she met No-am-ee.

"I've been looking for you," the older woman said. "I was worried."

In a dull tone Catherine stated, "The dance and the weapons . . . they frightened me. I had to go away by myself to think."

"I understand," No-am-ee said. "You can return now. The ceremonial dancing is over; the festivities have begun."

The two women lapsed into silence as they walked toward No-am-ee's wigwam, each preoccupied with her own thoughts. Ironically both women were thinking about Lone Wolf. As they moved through the village square where the people had grouped, Catherine glanced about. The chiefs were still together, talking. Young couples danced around the fire. Mothers acted as chaperones. Others talked.

Catherine and No-am-ee hadn't progressed far when Happy Woman, rising to her feet, left her group and moved toward them. "How did you enjoy the festival?" she asked Catherine, a sly smile hovering on her lips. She had seen the paleface cower when the Roanoacs had begun their dance; she had seen her run into the forest.

Catherine looked squarely into the other woman's eyes. Thinking about her evening with Lone Wolf, Catherine smiled. The enigmatical quality of the gesture intimidated Happy Woman.

"I'm enjoying the festival very much," Catherine answered, laughing softly.

Happy Woman's eyes narrowed. "Do you think you'll be able to watch the ordeal tomorrow?"

"Yes," Catherine replied quietly. "I'll be watching."

"What makes you think she wouldn't?" No-am-ee snapped, irritated by Happy Woman's rudeness.

Immediately apologetic, Happy Woman said, "I didn't mean to anger you, Grandmother. I was thinking only of Lone Wolf."

No-am-ee sighed. "I know, my child."

Happy Woman's eyes darted to Catherine, raking over her wrap. Suddenly conscious that she had Lone Wolf's bearskin over her shoulders, Catherine tensed, but Happy Woman didn't recognize it.

"I don't want anyone to bring evil magic to him," Happy Woman said, adding. "Lone Wolf needs a strong woman, Grandmother, not a weak one."

"That is not for us to question," No-am-ee responded sharply, turning away. "Lone Wolf has made his choice. Now, return to the dance. Catherine and I must complete Lone Wolf's clothes for the games."

No-am-ee did not utter another word as they walked to the wigwam, and her silence persisted as the women busied themselves with lighting the torch and the fire.

"Before the harvest festival," No-am-ee said, kneeling in front of the fire pit, "we must put two more layers of mats and bark on the wigwam and stuff moss between them to make our house warm for the coming winter. And if we have enough furs, we will line the walls." She watched the small flame flicker into life, and she nursed it tenderly, slowly building it into a comfortable blaze.

"Soon the weather will be too cold to let our fire go out. Then we must keep the bark covering over the outside of the door at all times and a bearskin lining over the inside."

Catherine listened, hearing more than the instructions No-am-ee spoke. The younger woman knew the words were prompted by her deeper concern.

Catherine spread several rabbit blankets over the floor near the fire. "Sit here, Grandmother," she enjoined. "It will be much warmer."

After the old woman had moved her stiff, aching body, Catherine draped a robe over No-am-ee's shoulders. Then she unlaced her leggings, knelt, and slipped No-am-ee's moccasins off to massage her feet. Gently Catherine moved the feet and ankles, easing the arthritic pain. Afterward she tucked another blanket around No-am-ee's legs and feet.

For a moment they sat, letting the warmth of the blaze slowly chase the chill out of their bodies, before Catherine reached for her sewing basket. Picking up the moccasin and her threaded needle, she began to string the beads.

"Are Re-bekk-ana and Little Flower going to stay with us tonight?"

"Not tonight," No-am-ee answered absently, reaching for her pipe. "They wanted to stay until the dancing was over, so I told them to sleep in their parents' wigwam."

She crumbled the tobacco into the clay bowl, then scooped a glowing coal onto a piece of bark and lifted it to her face. Her tobacco lit, she returned the ember to the fire. For a long time neither she nor Catherine spoke. She smoked and Catherine sewed, the only noises in the wigwam the merrymaking from the square.

No-am-ee closed her eyes, the dim light flickering over her wrinkled face. Finally she gave voice to her worry. "You saw him tonight." The words were soft, carrying no accusation or reprimand.

273

"Aye." It never occurred to Catherine to lie.

"You knew he was not supposed to see or speak with anyone while he was in purification."

Catherine knotted off the bead and looked across the fire at No-am-ee. "Aye."

"It was wrong of you to seek him out. He has enough on his mind without emotion blinding him."

"I didn't seek him out," Catherine declared. "The music and the dancing frightened me." She lowered her head, securing another bead to the buckskin. "But I'm glad I found him."

"An Indian woman wouldn't have behaved as you did. She would not want to bring evil magic to her warrior."

"But then I'm not an Indian, am I?" Catherine quietly responded, stung to retaliation. "I'm a paleface who thinks and acts like a paleface, and although you don't credit me with much intelligence, I didn't want to bring him evil magic." With angry jerks, she knotted another bead. "You've never approved of me have you?"

No-am-ee's eyelids slowly lifted, and she returned Catherine's gaze. The old woman was as dedicated to telling the truth as was Catherine. "I do approve of you," she said, "even though you have shamed me this night."

"I didn't bring evil magic to him," Catherine cried out defensively. "I brought him love, which is good magic, my grandmother."

"We'll see in the morning," No-am-ee thrummed.

"His making it through the gauntlet has nothing to do with my seeing him tonight," Catherine contended. "His living or dying will not prove his innocence or his guilt. Surely you understand that? You, of all people, know that Lone Wolf is not lying."

No-am-ee made no comment. Unperturbed by Catherine's tirade, she continued to smoke.

Remembering the council meeting at the settlement, Catherine asked accusingly, "You didn't want Lone Wolf to select me, did you?"

274

"No."

"Why?"

The old woman sighed. "I knew from the beginning that he would fall in love with you."

"Is that so wrong?"

"For the Lone Wolf, yes," No-am-ee replied. "There is so much he has to do, and it would have been so much easier for him if he were not in love with you."

"Why Lone Wolf?" Catherine demanded. "Why not another warrior?"

"Lone Wolf's name and prowess are known throughout the Indian kingdoms," No-am-ee explained. "They strike fear and dread into the best of warriors. Flying Eagle, the great chief of the Lumbroans, has no son, only a daughter. Flying Eagle wants her to marry Lone Wolf, and we want it also. The marriage would strengthen the bond between our people. A child would be the sinew to tie two warring nations together into one confederacy of peace."

"What Lone Wolf wants doesn't matter?" Catherine asked, surprised at the calm way she was discussing her future.

"Lone Wolf has been disciplined to be a warrior," No-am-ee replied, her words carefully chosen. "Doing what is best for his people is what is best for Lone Wolf. If he were to sacrifice his people for your love, the two of you would gain nothing," the old woman said. "You will have lost the man you love because he will hate himself; he will have lost his integrity."

Catherine made no reply. She dipped her needle into one of the baskets and speared more beads. Then she plunged the needle into the soft leather, and she sewed.

"At one time, Cath-er-ine," No-am-ee continued softly, "the Scupperongacs were the most powerful tribe in this area. But no longer is that true. We are still strong, but warfare has taken its toll, steadily reducing our numbers. The Lumbroans and the Five Nations to the

North are continuously enlarging their kingdoms at the expense of the smaller tribes. To the south and west of us are the Cherokee."

No-am-ee drew on the pipe before she said, "If we are to survive as a tribe, we must do as the Iroquois have done. We must unite with other tribes. Already Wise One has spoken to Wanchese, and he has agreed to join in with us. Other smaller tribes have become part of the confederation, but we need the power and number of a large tribe."

"The Lumbroans," Catherine said. No-am-ee nodded her head. Catherine took several stitches, jabbing her needle in and out the buckskin. "You have nothing to worry about," she announced, tying knots between the beads and dropping the finished moccasin into the basket. She didn't attempt to hide her bitterness. "Lone Wolf has already explained to me that the welfare of his people is his primary concern. He will marry the Lumbroan princess first."

"He has chosen to do the honorable thing," No-am-ee murmured. "That is good." Her worries expunged, the old woman leaned forward to thump the ashes out of her pipe. "I will go to sleep now and rest."

Sleep and rest were far from Catherine. Long after No-am-ee had gone to bed, she sat in front of the fire, the immediacy of the ordeal weighing heavily on her. She loved Lone Wolf. Despite the differences in their cultures, she loved him. No matter what decisions he must make because of his people, she loved him. If he died without her having a chance to tell him . . .

Suddenly a person obsessed, Catherine began to scurry about the wigwam. Getting a lamplighter and setting it aflame, she slipped out and rushed across the village which was still abuzz with activity. In Lone Wolf's wigwam she lit a torch in the sleeping room; then opened her chest, quickly sorting through it and pulling out what she would need. When she was through, she closed and locked the chest. Then she stood, moving to the platform above their bed. She opened the basket that held Lone Wolf's prized possessions and extracted a small bark box full of his favorite tobacco mix and a string of white wampum. Returning the basket to the platform, she picked up her material, unfastened the torch, and took it with her. When she hurried past the village square, she tossed it into the fire.

Ablaze with purpose herself, Catherine lit a new torch and hung it from the rafters of the wigwam. She put more logs on the fire, and she rethreaded her needle. Ignoring the set of curious eyes on her, she worked into the night. She snipped and she sewed. She strung the colored beads. At last she slipped out of the wigwam and raced to the shaman's lodge. In her hurry she forgot to grab her cape or robe.

A fire burned low, and the door was open, but Catherine had not yet learned to enter without announcing herself. Clenching her hand, she pulled her arm back to knock. Before she could move, a voice spoke.

"Enter, paleface. The bark is not covering the door." Shivering, she moved close to the fire, waiting for Ho-sa-eeth to motion her to be seated. He puffed on his pipe several times before he asked, "Why are you here?"

Because Ho-sa-eeth was looking at the flames rather than her, Catherine spoke slowly, using the Scupperon-gac dialect. Remembering the ritual she had witnessed between Lone Wolf and No-am-ee her first morning in Scupperong, she said, "I have brought a gift for you, my father the shaman." She knelt across the fire from him, extending both hands over the flame. In one she held a small brocade tobacco pouch, which she had sewn and embroidered herself and had filled with Lone Wolf's prized *uppowoc*. From the other, the string of white wampum dangled.

Surprised and interested, Ho-sa-eeth laid his pipe on the smooth rock that bordered the fire pit, and lifted his weathered face. He stared at Catherine, finally reaching out to run a gentle finger down the shell chain.

"Do you understand the significance of giving such a gift as wampum, paleface woman?" he asked.

Catherine countered, "Do you understand the significance of accepting such a gift as wampum, my father?"

Ho-sa-eeth was clearly taken aback by Catherine's straightforwardness, but he gave no indication of his surprise. He pulled his hand back, and he watched the shadows leap golden red over the shiny shells.

Softly Catherine repeated the words she had heard No-am-ee say to Lone Wolf. "Manitou has said that anyone who receives a string of wampum has to fulfill the promises made when the gift is accepted, and an Aa-da-mii always keeps his word because of this sacred wampum."

"That is so," Ho-sa-eeth said.

"I give this pouch of *uppowoc* to you, my father, as a gift from me. I will hold the wampum until I have asked my favor."

Ho-sa-eeth took the bag of tobacco, and he held it over the fire looking at the delicate embroidery. As custom demanded, he turned the bowl of his pipe, thumped it empty, and pulled the string of the new pouch. He poured the new mixture into his pipe, and he lit it with a burning coal.

When he placed the pipe into his mouth, Catherine said, "I would have you deliver a gift to Lone Wolf for me before he runs the gauntlet."

Ho-sa-eeth, ignoring Catherine, closed his eyes and continued to smoke. The seconds slowly stretched into minutes. When Catherine had almost despaired of an answer, he spoke.

"Why did you not give it to him earlier when you were with him in the forest?"

"I hadn't sewn it," Catherine responded, wisely

offering no excuse for her action and, at the same time, wondering if the entire village knew of her visit. "I made it after I returned."

"Let me see it."

Catherine held up another bag of white buckskin. As it spun on the ends of the drawstring, she said, "On one side, great shaman, I have embroidered Lone Wolf's clan totem and his mark. On the other, I have put my totem."

Ho-sa-eeth opened his eyes, and he looked at the beautiful stitching in colored thread and European beads. Still he made no effort to take it or the wampum.

"Is your medicine strong?"

Looking at the small pouch—the bag that symbolized all she had become, that symbolized the enormity of her love for Lone Wolf, Catherine nodded. "It's the strongest medicine I have, my father. It contains what I have treasured most in this world." She thought of the lock of hair, and she smiled. "It contains something that Lone Wolf treasures very much."

"Will it protect him from evil spirits which wish to harm him?"

"Yes, my father," Catherine answered, never taking her eyes from the symbol of her love, "it will protect him."

Ho-sa-eeth laid his pipe down, and he stretched his hands across the fire, taking the wampum in his right hand, the pouch in his left. Laying both of them on the skin rug beside him, he took a puff on the pipe.

"Thank you for the *uppowoc*," Ho-sa-eeth said. "It is as you wish. I will deliver your medicine bag to Lone Wolf."

Catherine tilted her head in gratitude, and she accepted the pipe which he handed her. After taking several puffs, she said, "Thank you, my father, for your consideration."

"Go now and sleep," Ho-sa-eeth ordered.

Chapter XIV

When Lone Wolf awakened quite late the next morning, sunshine streamed into the teepee, its warmth quickly chasing away the nightly chill. Lifting his arms, he stretched and yawned, locking his hands behind his head. Then he lay in the stillness for a few minutes, smiling as he reveled in sweet memories of the previous night. Having Catherine with him, though for only a little while, had been restful and refreshing. Although their being together had violated all the tribal taboos for the purification, he felt no regrets. Hearing the soft coo of the shaman, Lone Wolf stood, rising fluidly and gracefully. As if he had all the time in the world, he folded his bearskin and draped it over his arm. Then he walked to the river to meet Ho-sa-eeth.

When Lone Wolf arrived, the medicine man was kneeling in front of a fire, tending several pots of smelly concoctions. His face, upper body, and legs were smeared with vermilion—the color of victory; his eyes were ringed in white for happiness. On the deerskin spread beside him, lay a bundle of clothes, a seven-pronged comb—each prong a sharp-pointed turkey quill—and a medicine bag.

Without looking up, Ho-sa-eeth said, "As soon as you have cleansed your body and put on your new breechclout and moccasins, I will burn your old ones. Then I will anoint you and pray for you."

Walking to the water's edge, Lone Wolf dropped his breechclout and slipped out of his moccasins. By the time he had waded waist-deep in the water, the shaman had disappeared into the forest, chanting as he searched for more roots, berries, herbs, and leaves. Lone Wolf bathed and dried off, quickly dressing and putting on the new clothes which Ho-sa-eeth had brought for him. He was braiding his hair when the shaman emerged from the woods, his pouch bulging with his gathering.

Squatting before the fire, Ho-sa-eeth carefully sorted his findings, cleaning, cutting, and dropping them into the pots of bubbling liquids. His chore finished, he laid his knife down and picked up his rattles, one in each hand. Then he rose, a low chant on his lips. Slowly he circled the fire, the shuffling of his feet becoming faster and faster as the volume of his chant grew into a piercing wail. When he was through dancing, Ho-sa-eeth returned to the deerskin.

"Paleface woman has sent you a gift of her magic," he said, stooping and picking up the small medicine bag. He handed the soft, white buckskin pouch to Lone Wolf. "Let us hope her medicine is as strong in the day as it is in the night, my son."

Lone Wolf and Ho-sa-eeth leveled a long, measuring look at one another, but neither said more on the subject. Dropping his gaze, Lone Wolf took the bag, a soft perfume wafting to his nostrils and reminding him of the way Catherine had smelled when he'd met her at the paleface settlement. He turned the bag over in his palm and looked at the design.

"On the one side is your totem and your clan totem,"

281

Ho-sa-eeth said. "On the other are the marks of the paleface woman who calls herself the Forest Woman. She said you would understand what that meant."

Lone Wolf looked at the design, and he read the picture writing. She was Forest Woman—her eyes the color of the green leaves in the spring time, her hair the color of the leaves in the autumn. With a reverential softness, Lone Wolf traced the outline of the bright green and russet leaves. Unfastening the drawstring, he thumped the opened pouch into his hand.

The lock of auburn hair fell out, glinting red as it picked up the sunlight. When the lone gold ring rolled across his palm, Lone Wolf's smile turned to an expression of surprise. Her father's ring. Picking it up, he ran his fingers over the smooth band; he touched the inscription: *To my darling with all my love.* Knowing the importance of the ring to Catherine, he understood the importance of her giving it to him today.

Lone Wolf held the golden circlet for Ho-sa-eeth to see. "This belonged to Catherine's father," he explained, pointing to the engraving on the inside of the ring. "These marks are his totem." He paused momentarily before he added, "His wife gave it to him as a token of her love."

"As the paleface gives it to you now," Ho-sa-eeth said, taking the ring, turning it in his fingers. "It is strong medicine, my son." He handed it back to Lone Wolf. "Never take it off, and keep the pouch to remember your Forest Woman by."

Lone Wolf slipped the band onto his fourth finger, and he held his hand out, admiring the ring. The handkerchief he pulled out of his belt, folding it and tucking it into the pouch. Ho-sa-eeth smiled to himself and motioned Lone Wolf closer to him.

"Come. It is time to begin. We shall see how strong the paleface's medicine is, my son."

He crumbled some tobacco leaves over the fire and lifted his hands in the prayer.

"Ca-ther-ine!"

A gentle tugging on her shoulder and No-am-ee's soft call awakened Catherine. Blinking her eyes, growing accustomed to the brightness of the morning sunlight that spilled through the opened doorway, Catherine stared into the old woman's face.

"While I tend the fire and get the morning meal, you take your bath," No-am-ee instructed, signing very little and speaking rather briskly. "Then I will go." She returned to the fire pit. "We must hurry so we'll be ready for the ceremony of purification."

Catherine's feet hardly hit the floor before she was rolling up the bearskin blankets and the mattress, and slipping them under the platform. Today was special; she didn't want to dress at the river. She wanted to look her best, and she wanted to take her time. So she reached into one of the large clothes baskets and picked out a wraparound skirt and a cape which she would wear after she had bathed. Then she slipped down to the river.

Autumn is quickly racing by, she thought, admiring the colorful splendor of the forest. Soon the weather would be changing even more, the days becoming as chilly as the nights already were. She undressed, gasping as she dipped her foot into the cold water. The sun hadn't yet warmed the river. Quickly bathing and drying off, Catherine dressed and hurried back to the warmth of No-am-ee's wigwam. Shivering, she huddled over the fire.

No-am-ee poured her a large cup full of hot, root tea. "Here," she said. "Drink this. It will take the chill out of your bones. By the time I return, our morning meal should be ready."

Leisurely drinking her tea, Catherine sat around the

fire, watching the flames as they leaped into the air. Warming herself until her legs and feet were toasted a bright red, she finally stood, shedding the skirt and cape. She walked across the wigwam, hanging them over the clothesline. Returning to the platform but sitting on the soft furs that lined the floor, she pulled her cosmetic box from beneath the shelf. She opened the small containers and rubbed herbal lotions, oils, and perfumes over her body.

Then, her toilet completed, she dropped the pale green dress over her head, loving the feel of the soft buckskin next to her tingling skin. She slipped her feet into her new fur-lined moccasins and leggings, lacing them from the ankle to the knee, and finally she brushed her hair until it glimmered. By the time No-am-ee returned to the wigwam, Catherine was banding her braids with the thongs Lone Wolf had given her.

While the old woman put on her new dress and combed her hair, Catherine laid out the eating mats and spooned out the food. She dipped the corn-flour cakes out of the boiling water and laid one in each bowl. Her dressing completed, No-am-ee moved closer to the fire, sitting across from Catherine. She lifted her head and prayed over the morning meal.

The prayer over, Ho-sa-eeth walked to Lone Wolf's discarded clothing, picked it up, and dropped it into the fire. As he slowly circled the flames, shaking his rattles, Wise One, his face striped red and white with the marks of victory and peace, led the villagers, single file, to the secret place by the river for the purification ceremony. After they spread their blankets on the ground, they sat down, the crowd orderly despite the large numbers that had gathered. Wise One and the village chiefs sat off by themselves. Others sat in family groups.

Catherine draped a fur-lined cape around No-am-ee's shoulders and tucked one around her legs and feet. Sitting beside the old woman, Catherine craned her neck as she searched.

"Where's Lone Wolf?" she whispered anxiously.

"He's in the forest," No-am-ee said. "He'll be out later."

She turned her head and looked at Catherine. Anxiety was evident on the younger woman's face, and No-am-ee felt the tension that emanated from her. Admiring the paleface, loving her and Lone Wolf, No-am-ee wished things could be different. But both of them were stubborn; each accustomed to having his or her own way.

Also, No-am-ee was aware—more than Lone Wolf and Catherine—of the moral differences between the two lovers. Catherine would never be happy with the kind of life Lone Wolf would give her. She was too high-spirited to accept second place to the Lumbroan princess who must be Lone Wolf's first wife. On the other hand, Lone Wolf could never sacrifice his duty for his love. To do so would make him less than a warrior and a man. Unable to reconcile the dilemma, No-am-ee sighed and returned her attention to the ceremonial field.

Agog with curiosity Catherine contemplated everything she saw or heard. She watched as the singers and musicians, the last to file onto the field, isolated themselves in one corner opposite the crowd. The few old men who knew the sacred songs for the ritual sat side by side, the musicians together at one end. Softly one man began to beat the water drum, the others shook their gourd rattles that were filled with pebbles.

When Wise One walked to the center of the field, the crowd quieted and the squirming ceased. Wearing several heavy necklaces of teeth and shells over his richly embroidered buckskin shirt, the chief of the Scupperon-gacs stood before the villagers, opening the ceremonies

285

with a long speech. He mentioned by name all the brave warriors of the Scupperongacs, going back many years and explaining their acts of valor. The chief did not hesitate to boast of his own bravery although the details were known to everyone. The audience, acting as if this were his first repetition of these exploits, exclaimed, "Hear! Hear!" and clicked their tongues at every pause.

Wise One's last words still hovered over the field when the musicians shook their rattles and beat the drum. Seven girls and seven boys, one from each of the seven clans slowly filed in. They were dressed in white buckskin robes embroidered with brightly colored porcupine quills. The two groups stopped between the musicians and the audience, forming two parallel lines, the girls facing the boys. The drummer, who knew all the songs, began to chant the ordeal song. The girls and boys joined him, singing softly as they danced in rhythm— heel and toe—rocking back and forth.

Suddenly with a loud "Hey! Hey!" that startled the entire crowd, Lone Wolf, wearing only breechclout and moccasins, his body painted with red and white stripes, trotted in from the forest where he had been hiding. He stopped by the musicians, and Catherine saw her pouch secured to his belt, her totem displayed not his. As she wore his mark, he wore hers.

As desperately as she had sought him, Lone Wolf now sought her. His eyes raced over the assembled crowd, looking only for the copper braids. When he singled her out, his eyes lovingly lingered on the sweet features of her face: the sprinkle of freckles across her nose; the arched eyelashes; the green eyes, their color intensified by the dress which she wore.

Drawn by the magnetism of his visual touch, Catherine slowly lifted her face from the medicine bag. Locking her gaze to his, Lone Wolf silently talked with her. When he lifted his hand to his chest, spreading his

286

fingers over the wolf-fang necklace, Catherine caught her breath. The sunlight reflected off her father's ring. Then Lone Wolf lowered his hand, touching the pouch that dangled from his waist. Catherine's gaze followed the movement. Fascinated, she watched him unfasten the drawstring and pull out the whiff of white lace. Her lips trembled when he waved it through the air.

Smiling tremulously and defying custom, Catherine raised her hand. Touching it to her lips, she blew Lone Wolf a kiss. At that moment they were the only two people in the world. Lone Wolf's expression didn't change, but Catherine knew he smiled; she felt the warmth of his love as tangibly as if he had pulled her into the circle of his arms.

That tender moment, one of the most delicate of their lives, was suddenly shattered. A musician with a rattle jumped up, shouting, "Hi!" The sound pierced the silence. But the love Lone Wolf and Catherine felt, the love they communicated endured, defying death itself. Dragging his eyes from Catherine and returning his concentration to the ceremony, Lone Wolf replaced the handkerchief, and he drew the strings on the pouch.

The war werowance of the Scupperongacs looked at the old man and answered, "Hi! Hi!" Crouching, he slowly and cautiously approached the dancers, coming down on his toes, then his heels. He looked neither to right nor left; his eyes never left the gauntlet line. Ho-sa-eeth, slinging his rattle through the air, kept chanting, and Lone Wolf echoed his call, their voices growing louder and louder, harmonizing with the crescendo of the drums.

The two rows of dancers waved their arms as if brandishing weapons, and Lone Wolf moved closer to them. Keeping beat with the drums, he slowly stamped his way through the dancing gauntlet, dodging the flailing arms. After he had run the gauntlet, he leaped into the air several times. Then he stamped in a circle around the dancers, ending with his own dance and song commemorating his victory. Now that he had shown the spirits what he wanted to do, the people were sure the spirits would help him prove his innocence by successfully running the gauntlet.

Finally with a rush Lone Wolf danced over to the women, not stopping until he stood in front of Catherine. "Hu! Uh!" shouted the audience. Lone Wolf answered the villagers, and he shouted victory for them, but he was looking at and speaking love to Catherine.

Excited to a frenzied pitch, the villagers watched him run to the river for the final dip; he dived into the cold water four times while the shaman said the ordeal prayer. Then he returned to the ceremonial fire.

Stooping, Ho-sa-eeth picked up the comb and motioned Lone Wolf to stand in front of him. Ready for the scratching which was part of the preparation and purification, the shaman handed Lone Wolf a root and instructed him to chew on it. Spellbound, Catherine watched Ho-sa-eeth wave the slender seven-toothed comb in the air. She gasped and flinched when the shaman scratched Lone Wolf's arms from shoulders to wrists with the split turkey quills and the sharp slivers of turkey-leg bones. As Ho-sa-eeth drew the comb down, it made seven white streaks which soon turned red; Lone Wolf chewed the root of the herb and looked into space without seeming to mind the pain of the scratches.

"What is he doing?" Catherine cried to No-am-ee, agonizing because Lone Wolf was having to undergo an ordeal before the ordeal.

As Ho-sa-eeth scratched Lone Wolf's thighs and legs, No-am-ee quietly explained, "Everyone will see Lone Wolf is a brave man, unafraid of pain. The spirits that watch over the ordeal will now surely pity this brave man and the pain he is made to undergo."

Ho-sa-eeth finally scraped the comb across Lone Wolf's chest. Then the war chief, his face still impassive, spit the juice from the roots he had been chewing into his hand and rubbed it over the scratches.

The crowd dispersed now, heading for the ceremony ring on the outskirt of the village where the visitors had already begun to congregate. Wise One joined Manteo who sat on the sidelines in front of a small ceremonial fire. Then he lifted the sacred pipe and filled it with the tobacco mixture.

Catherine, carrying the blankets and robes, followed No-am-ee. When the old woman chose the spot where she wanted to sit, Catherine spread the bearskin. After No-am-ee sat down, Catherine again tucked the other robes around her frail form. Preferring to stand herself, Catherine studied the people who were gathering together, both the Roanoacs and the Scupperongacs. Hundreds of Indians streamed in from all directions. Laughing and talking loudly, men and women met, some for the first time, others renewing old friendships. Her gaze shifted and she looked at Manteo, who stared straight ahead at the ceremonial field. Wanchese she couldn't find.

Like the ball field, Catherine absently noted, the ceremonial field was a large square piece of ground near the river. Several days ago the men had carefully scraped and leveled it. Outside the field they had piled the extra topsoil they had scraped off. With this and with extra soil they had brought, the men had made a small mound at each end of the field for the audience. Standing on these earth mounds, even small children were able to see everything.

At the same time that the Roanoac shaman lifted his voice in prayer and shook his rattle, the Scupperongac shaman stood on the riverbank, holding red beads in one hand. These stood for victory and were meant for Lone

289

Wolf. In the other hand, he held black beads. These were for defeat and were meant to ward off the evil spirits that would hinder Lone Wolf's victory.

Holding the red beads toward the river, Ho-sa-eeth prayed, first to the river for purification, then to the deer to make Lone Wolf swift, to the hawk to make him keen of sight, and to the bear to make him strong enough to endure the beating of the Roanoac warriors.

Sitting on the huge mound of dirt, the crowd eagerly awaited the ordeal. They tensed slightly when, suddenly, twenty-four painted Roanoac warriors emerged from the forest, led by Wanchese. They trotted straight to the field, and drew up in two lines of twelve each. Their faces and their upper bodies colored, they chanted, brandishing their war clubs and weapons in the air. Much to Catherine's horror, the crowd jumped up and cheered the Roanoacs.

Before the ordeal began, however, Catherine discovered the Indians had one more ritual—the final round of wagers. People in the crowd called to one another, waving the buckskins, necklaces, embroidered headbands, arm bands, shells, war clubs, pipes, and blankets that they wanted to bet on their favorite team. Many valuable belongings were wagered. Finally, when the betting ceased, the crowd settled down, awaiting the outcome.

Looking at the Roanoac warriors and their weapons, Catherine asked No-am-ee who now stood beside her, "Will Lone Wolf wear his new clothes when he runs the gauntlet?"

"No, he will wear the clothes the shaman has provided for him. The new ones he will put on after he cleanses himself." Talking more freely about the ordeal now, No-am-ee added, "Until he is ready for his victory dance he will stay with the shaman who will tend his wounds." She smiled, and her eyes twinkled. "Then he will wear the clothes you have sewn for him."

Wise One walked to the center of the field. Lifting his hands, he prayed. Then he motioned for Lone Wolf to join him. "Your refuge will be Ho-sa-eeth's lodge, my son the Lone Wolf."

"My father, wise chief of the Scupperongacs, I place Catherine in your hands. You will do as I asked."

"I will. If you should die, Catherine will be returned to the palefaces." Wise One clasped Lone Wolf's hands in his. "I love you, my son."

"I love you, my father." Lone Wolf's eyes clouded, and his voice was thicker than usual, lower, more husky. "Catherine could be with child, my father. If so, I would consider it an honor if you would extend your love and guidance to my unborn child. No matter where Catherine may live, my chief, I wish you to tell my child the stories of the Scupperongacs. Remind the child of his heritage."

Lone Wolf's hands tightened, and Wise One understood the young war chief's anguish. "Not only to your child, my son, but to your slave I will give love. I will see that the child hears and learns the ways of the Scupperongacs." The ring cut into Wise One's flesh, and he looked down at their entwined hands.

Without Wise One asking about the gold band, Lone Wolf said, "Catherine gave it to me."

"I hope her magic is as strong as her love, my son," Wise One stated. He led Lone Wolf to the starting line. Then he said, "Brave warriors of the Roanoacs we ask for no mercy on Lone Wolf, war chief of the Scupperongacs. He is a valiant brave who speaks straight."

As Wise One spoke, Lone Wolf glanced at the Roanoac warriors, some of whom had a weapon in each hand. They lifted their arms into the air and flourished their war clubs menacingly. Lone Wolf had seen the gauntlet run many times during his life, but this was the first time that he would do it. He lifted his hand, rubbing the thin sheen

291

of moisture from his upper lip. The tension was thick, the excitement high as everyone waited for the signal to begin. When Wise One withdrew to the edge of the field and yelled, "Run to victory, my son," the quietness exploded into sound. The Scupperongacs cheered Lone Wolf to victory; the Roanoac warriors taunted him.

Lone Wolf darted a swift glance at the cheering spectators, openly smiling at Catherine, waving the ringed hand at her. Then he turned to his taunters, concentrating on the task at hand. His voice lifted as he sang his death chant, a song which appealed to his protecting gods to save him and to give him more courage to stand the pain. He crouched, bending his legs several times, giving himself leverage and force as he bounded down the aisle of ordeal.

The crowd rose with him, their voices elevated in praise. Catherine also jumped to her feet and screamed, but her cries were not a part of the cheers. She screamed her fears as the war clubs slammed against Lone Wolf's body. Some hit his head, others his chest and back; a sharp flint war club dug into the old wound on his chest.

Happy Woman moved closer to Catherine. She glared disapprovingly at the paleface. "It would be better if you were not here, paleface. By showing your fear, you bring shame on Lone Wolf. You bring much evil magic."

Ramming her fisted hand over her mouth, Catherine stifled her cries and glowered at Happy Woman. Finally she returned her attention to the gauntlet, stoically watching Lone Wolf slowly battle his way through it. Her heart lurched when he fell to his knees, his head drooping, his torso awash with blood. Each time he pushed himself up, another blow knocked him to his knees.

"Get up, Lone Wolf," Catherine screamed, desperation and anxiety making her forget the pressing throng of Scupperongacs.

Lone Wolf didn't hear her; he couldn't distinguish one cry from the other. The war whoops above him drowned out the cheering of his people, and his head spun from the blows that racked his body. His eyes stung from the blood and sweat that ran into them. He lifted his hand, brushing the back of it across his forehead. He felt the metal as it grazed his skin. He focused his spinning vision on the small, gold band. Catherine's words spun around in his mind: "To my darling with all my love." *To my favorite one!*

Flattening his palms on the ground, he drew on his last reserve of energy, pushed to his feet and rammed through the flailing war clubs. His death chant grew louder and bolder, his steps surer. Throwing back his head, pressing on with all his strength, he lunged past the last two braves.

Catherine threw her arms into the air, screaming her delight as she danced around. When she started to run onto the ceremony field, however, No-am-ee caught her arm and pulled her back. At the same moment, Catherine's exuberance died. Lone Wolf was still running. Close on his heels were the twenty-four Roanoac warriors.

Turning to No-am-ee she demanded hoarsely, "What's happening?"

"He is spared only if he reaches Ho-sa-eeth's wigwam."

"Oh, my God!" The agonizing cry was wrenched from Catherine's soul. Paralyzed with fear, she stood, a fist pressed against each cheek, her breath caught in her throat.

Lone Wolf slipped, breaking his fall with a badly bruised knee. Unable to regain his balance, he stretched out his arms, balancing his weight on the heels of his palms. Renewed spasms of pain racked his body as he landed; he wanted to scream. He had pulled the cut across his chest open and blood rushed from it. Looking over his shoulder, he saw the Roanoacs gaining on him. Seconds before Wanchese fell on him, Lone Wolf rolled over and slowly pushed to his elbows. Closing his eyes, breathing deeply, raggedly, he stood, and he staggered, almost falling again. He felt the blow of a tomahawk on his shoulder. The impact hurled him forward, and he stumbled the last few feet, dragging himself into Ho-sa-eeth's wigwam before he passed out.

The crowd went wild with enthusiasm and happiness. The first round of bets were collected. The racket—people laughing loudly and jesting with one another—was more than Catherine could tolerate. Her stomach was churning so, she retched. Stumbling away from the crowd, she drew in deep, refreshing gulps of air. When her nausea had passed, she moved in the direction of Ho-sa-eeth's wigwam.

"We cannot go to him, Ca-ther-ine," No-am-ee's call landed softly on Catherine's ears. "We must wait." She pointed at the young boy who stood outside the shaman's wigwam. "Swift Deer is Ho-sa-eeth's runner. When Ho-sa-eeth has news, he will send Swift Deer."

"He . . . he could be dead," Catherine whispered.

"I doubt it," No-am-ee negated calmly. "Even so, we must wait. And if he is alive, we cannot see him until he has washed the evil magic from his body and has danced his victory." That announcement made, the old woman turned her attention to gathering her wagers.

The minutes dragged by for Catherine. She squirmed restlessly on the blanket, nervously running a hand through the fur. Unable to tear her gaze from the shaman's wigwam, she held her other hand over her eyes to shield them from the blinding brilliance of the midday sun. Anxiously she awaited news of Lone Wolf. When the bark before Ho-sa-eeth's wigwam was finally pushed aside, Catherine jumped to her feet. She could hardly wait for Swift Deer to bring the message.

Cupping his mouth with his hands, Swift Deer cried as he neared the field, "Lone Wolf lives! Lone Wolf lives!" Closer he came, walking through the crowd, stopping in front of Catherine. "Ho-sa-eeth sent me to fetch you, Forest Woman. Your magic is strong. Lone Wolf has washed away the evil magic, but he is badly wounded."

Happy Woman, sitting not far from No-am-ee and Catherine, overheard the runner. Her face remained expressionless, but anger boiled through her veins. Her hatred for the paleface grew each day. Catherine had escaped torture; she had escaped punishment for her laziness and for having started the fire. Now the shaman was summoning Catherine because her paleface magic was strong. Happy Woman's jealousy flared, and she became a woman obsessed with destructive revenge.

Catherine looked down at No-am-ee. "May I go?"

Hardly had the "Yes" slipped through No-am-ee's lips before Catherine was racing to Ho-sa-eeth's wigwam. Entering, she stopped inside the door, blinking as her eyes grew accustomed to the dim interior light. Naked, Lone Wolf lay on the platform on his back. Washed clean of paint and blood, his battered body was now coated with a smelly ointment. Bending over Lone Wolf, the old man sprinkled crushed leaves over the reopened chest wound to stop the bleeding.

Lone Wolf, sensing Catherine's presence, turned his head, smiled, and held his arm out. Catherine, allowing her tears to flow, rushed across the room, kneeling beside the platform. Disregarding Ho-sa-eeth's presence, she cradled Lone Wolf's face in her hands, planting kisses all over it.

"You made it," she cried over and over again. "You made it, my darling."

Lone Wolf chuckled weakly, lifting his hand and running it down the back of her head. "Of course I did," he said as if he had never had a doubt in his mind. "Didn't I tell you I would?" The smile trembled on his lips as pain speared through his chest. "Besides you gave me your magic."

"I'm sure that both of you are glad to see one another," Ho-sa-eeth interjected dryly. "But if his wounds are not tended, he will be unable to do his victory dance."

Laughing and wiping away her tears, Catherine looked at the medicine man. "What do you want me to do?"

Ho-sa-eeth didn't answer immediately. Rather, he cleaned the abrasions and dressed the minor cuts with clean, dry cornhusks. Eventually he pointed to the gash on Lone Wolf's chest. "This one will pull apart if he moves, and the bleeding will start again." He replaced the blood-soaked cornhusks with new ones, dropping the soiled husks into a basket. "The more blood he loses, the weaker he gets."

"The wound must be sewn together," Catherine replied, her fingers tenderly probing the skin around the small, deep cut. Lone Wolf never moved, his expression never changed, but Catherine could see the pain that clouded his eyes. Leaning over him, grazing her lips down his cheek, she whispered, "It will be painful, my darling, but I have to sew it together."

Lone Wolf nodded. "Do what you must."

Standing, Catherine said to Ho-sa-eeth, "I'll return shortly. I need to get my sewing basket."

When she returned, Ho-sa-eeth didn't acknowledge her entry. In a trancelike state, he sat in front of the fire, mumbling and throwing tobacco into the flames. Needing help and not wanting to disturb Ho-sa-eeth, Catherine called for Swift Deer's assistance. She knelt beside the bed and explained to the young Indian what she planned to do. Then she pointed to the wall.

"I'm going to need light. Remove some of the upper

mats, please."

After the young boy quickly unpegged three mats, creating windows on the side of the wigwam, he stood beside Catherine, awaiting her command. His meditation over, Ho-sa-eeth rose and joined Catherine at the platform.

"Chew on this," he told Lone Wolf, handing him a root. "The juice will make the pain more bearable." Weakly Lone Wolf nodded and opened his mouth for the proffered medicine. Then Ho-sa-eeth laid a stick across his stomach, telling him to grasp it with both hands.

Catherine brushed her hands down the side of her dress, wiping the perspiration from her palms. Her movements were methodical, as if she were somewhere outside her body, watching all that was going on. She threaded the largest and sharpest needle she had, and she pushed the small metal thimble over the tip of her third finger. Refusing to think about the pain she would be inflicting on Lone Wolf, focusing her attention on the task to be performed, she rose to her knees.

When she looked into his black eyes, she saw his suffering, the gray pain at the corners of his mouth. "This will hurt," she said, her voice husky as she valiantly fought back tears.

Lone Wolf's eyes flickered open for a moment, and he nodded his head. His lips twitched into a smile, then his eyes closed under the pressure of renewed agony. "I prefer the length of life over the shortness of pain," he murmured, tensing as he felt the needle pierce his inflamed flesh.

In and out, in and out, Catherine wove the thread, drawing the severed skin together. Lone Wolf, lying still throughout the operation, slowly chewed the root and swallowed the juice. He never groaned or grimaced. Only once did he tense. After she tied off the thread and cut it, she laid her cheek next to Lone Wolf's.

"I'm sorry, my darling," she whispered, her tears falling onto his face. But the brave didn't hear her. He was unconscious.

Catching Catherine by the shoulders, Ho-sa-eeth gently removed her. He knelt over Lone Wolf and looked at the stitching, lightly running his finger over the tiny, pink pucker. "You have done well, Ca-ther-ine," he praised. "Truly you have strong magic."

Dropping a powder made from crushed leaves over the wound, he covered it with clean, dry cornhusks. Then he moved back to the fire. Calling Catherine to him, he pointed to the stinking gelatin that was melting in the clay bowl.

"If you rub this on these cornhusks, we can use them to hold his bandage in place and to keep the dirt out of his wound," he instructed.

Catherine dipped the stick into the gluelike mixture and smeared it over the cornhusks as the medicine man had directed. One at a time she handed the husks to Ho-sa-eeth, watching as he crisscrossed them over the wound, tightly binding the incision. Then the shaman and the woman cleaned, doctored, and bandaged Lone Wolf's other wounds.

That done, Ho-sa-eeth returned to the fire and pointed to a clay pot. "When he awakens, give him a cup of this," he said. "He will feel the pain and the stiffness but little." Picking up his buckskin satchels and pouches, he slung them over his shoulder and moved toward the door. "I will go to the river and pray. You stay here and help Lone Wolf. When he is ready to dance, send Swift Deer to fetch me."

Ho-sa-eeth and Swift Deer disappeared through the opening, the boy closing the door with the bark as Ho-sa-eeth walked away. Sitting beside the platform, Catherine laid her head on the mattress. She would rest while she waited for Lone Wolf to awaken.

When she felt the light touch of his fingers on her cheek, she roused. Lifting her face, she blinked her lashes in mild surprise. Not fully awake, she innocently peered at Lone Wolf. He smiled, his hand cupping her chin.

"You went to sleep."

She grinned. "I had little sleep last night."

"If I were not so battered and bruised," he told her, "you would get little sleep tonight." He chuckled when he saw the color rush up her throat into her face.

Remembering Ho-sa-eeth's instructions, Catherine scooted to the fire and poured Lone Wolf a cup of the tea. As he propped up on one elbow, she handed him the drink. "Ho-sa-eeth said you would feel your aches and soreness much less after drinking this."

She sat on the platform beside him, her eyes tracing the thin comb marks that striped his arm. She looked at the bruises that darkened his body, the cuts and abrasions, and her gaze lingered on the bandages for a moment before she lifted her face and chuckled.

"I never knew the importance of corn, my darling warrior, until I came to live with the Scupperongacs. It's the center of our existence. We eat it and we drink it. We use it for food, fuel, and medicine. For mats, for clotheslines, for fire starters, and even for bandages." Her chuckle ripened into rich, mellow laughter. "And now I find another use for cornhusks."

"And what is that?" Lone Wolf asked, tender amusement twinkling in his eyes.

"Clothing," she whispered. "I see absolutely no need for your new buckskins. You are already covered from head to foot in cornhusks. You could attend the feast in these tonight."

Giving no evidence of his pain, Lone Wolf laughed with her. He picked up her hand and moved it lower on his body. "Nay, woman, I'm not completely covered in cornhusks."

Catherine's face flamed brighter as her eyes followed the movement of his hand. Following the loving injunction, however, her fingers circled his manhood, and she lowered her mouth to his, careful not to press her weight against his body. Their kiss blazed with deep desire that bespoke their love. It stirred both of them, eliciting a commitment from each.

When he freed his lips, Lone Wolf said, "There is another use for cornhusks which you did not mention."

"What's that?" Catherine murmured, her mouth nipping at his.

"A braided hammock for the baby."

The whispered words mingled into a kiss as Lone Wolf capped the back of Catherine's head, pulling it down on his mouth. Like the petals of a flower in the spring sunshine, her lips opened to the warmth of his caress. She welcomed the gentle thrust of his tongue; she hungered for the possessive touch of this man.

Eventually Catherine murmured, "You had better get dressed, my darling. The people are waiting to see if you live or die. A few more wagers are to be collected, and the people can't eat until you've been pronounced dead and guilty or until you have performed your victory dance."

Smiling at the grim truth, Lone Wolf slowly levered himself into a sitting position. He rested for a moment, taking a few deep breaths. He took the fawn-colored breechclout Catherine handed him, but he didn't immediately bind it around his body. He held it in the afternoon sunlight that filtered through the smoke hole, and he looked at the beautiful embroidery work, its predominent colors a vivid green and a burnt orange. Catherine, kneeling in front of him, watched his expression. He looked at her strangely.

"I embroidered them for you," she quietly explained. "I used beads from England rather than porcupine quills." She handed Lone Wolf the jacket, the leggings,

300

the moccasins. "I wanted you to be the most envied man at the feast tonight."

"I will truly be envied," he admitted, reaching for her and drawing her between his legs. He pressed his cheek against her breasts. "But not solely because of your skill with the needle. I am envied because men want my beautiful woman, my woman with the strong magic."

Catherine lifted her hands, running them down the smooth confines of his hair. "Right now, my darling, your woman has a strong desire for the man she loves." Catherine stood, Lone Wolf following. His hands sliding from her shoulders down the line of her back, his fingers gripped the firm roundness of her buttocks. "But the people have a stronger desire to see you do your victory dance," she added quickly.

Lone Wolf laughed quietly. The medicine had dulled his aches and pains. "Will you always find reasons not to make love to me, woman?"

"Nay," Catherine whispered, her face glowing a delicious pink, "there's nothing I wish more."

Lone Wolf threw back his head and guffawed, the gusty sound echoing through the wigwam. Raising his voice, he called to Swift Deer. "Go get Ho-sa-eeth, my young brother. I am ready for my victory dance." To Catherine he murmured, "In order to initiate the ceremony of love, my darling, I must end the ceremony of ordeal."

With Catherine's assistance, he slowly dressed. When Ho-sa-eeth arrived, the three of them walked to the ceremonial ground where the villagers patiently awaited news of their war chief. At the edge of the field Catherine and Lone Wolf parted. She returned to No-am-ee, while Lone Wolf, the champion, held his arms up and trotted to the center of the field.

At first the cheering voices of the joyous Scupperongacs drowned out the music, but soon the loud, slow beat of the drum silenced the crowd. The Scupperongac dancers filed to the field, the girls facing the boys. They flayed their hands through the air, stamping heel and toe, as Lone Wolf danced around them. The onlookers, partaking of the victory and the vindication of their war chief, clapped their hands to the beat of the drums, louder and louder, faster and faster. When the dance was over, the people thronged around Lone Wolf.

The ordeal ceremony ended, the contests began. Excited young boys raced to their wigwams to get their equipment, and the captains in charge of the entertainment headed to the ball field to organize the afternoon competition. The spectators, as excited as the contestants, gathered their robes and hurried to the game field, leaving Catherine and No-am-ee far behind.

Catherine, carrying No-am-ee's robes and blankets, adjusted her steps to fit the old woman's shuffle. Over her shoulder she glanced fondly at Lone Wolf who walked between Manteo and Wise One, the withdrawn Wanchese following a few steps behind. Catherine was puzzled by the Roanoac's strange behavior, but she didn't take time to ponder it.

Today she joined the merrymaking. She was delighted when the women complimented the clothes she had embroidered for Lone Wolf, and she gladly showed them how to draw her designs. She laughed and talked with them, exchanging patterns, recipes, and remedies, and by the time they spread their robes and sat down, the games were about to begin. Leaving Manteo and Wanchese with Wise One, Lone Wolf came to sit with Catherine and No-am-ee.

Looking at him, Catherine knew the ordeal was taking it's toll. Neither his face nor his posture betrayed his suffering, but Catherine had learned to read his eyes. In them she saw fatigue and agony. Leaning closer to him, she whispered, "Shall we go home?"

Shaking his head, Lone Wolf smiled wanly, his face ashen with pain. "I'll be all right," he replied. "I'll rest while we're watching the games."

Kee-lee, captain of the contests, stood in the center of the game field announcing the different events. After each announcement he gave the people time to place their bets. Caught up in the celebration spirit, Catherine beamed her happiness and leaned over to whisper to Lone Wolf; then she made a wager or two herself. Manteo, sitting with Wise One and Sunflower Woman, joined in the merriment, but Wanchese, still preoccupied, sat apart from the crowd.

"Now for the races," Kee-lee shouted, addressing the audience.

The cheers were deafening as the young runners took their places behind the line, but Catherine didn't notice or mind. She clapped her hands, jumped up and down, and shouted as loudly as anyone. The afternoon passed quickly as they moved from one game to the next—darts, marksmanship, blowgun matches, spear throwing, and hoop-and-pole—laying their bets and collecting, cheering the contestants on to victory, jeering the losers.

At sunset the games ended. When the crowd dispersed, most of the people returned to their wigwams and shelters to rest before the evening meal. Sunflower Woman and the wives of the village council members hurried to the town square to check on preparations for the banquet. Catherine and Lone Wolf walked to their wigwam.

When Wolf Friend saw his master, he jumped to his feet, wagged his tail, and growled low in his throat. Bending stiffly, Lone Wolf spoke to the wolf and patted his head. Then the wolf turned, and for the first time in seven days, he trotted through the opening to his bed in the entrance room.

Once they were inside, Catherine quickly made their

bed, throwing several blankets over the thick, cornhusk mattress. Thankful for the softness, Lone Wolf needed no encouragement to lie down. Carefully he stretched his stiff, bruised body out on the platform, and holding a hand out, he gestured for Catherine to join him. Exhausted from the ordeal herself, she lay down, letting him curve his body around hers.

"You feel so good in my arms, Catherine," he murmured, drifting off to sleep. "I just need to hold you."

Later the chilled darkness awakened Catherine. Moving carefully so as not to disturb Lone Wolf, she reached for the blanket at the foot of the platform. Pulling it over them, she lay back down, listening to the hustle and bustle outside the wigwam. Looking through the open door, she could see the glow of the huge fire that burned in the center of the square.

"Is it time for the banquet?" Lone Wolf murmured.

"Aye," Catherine replied.

"Then we should be going."

"Aye."

Neither moved immediately; rather they lay for those extra seconds, enjoying a last doze. Eventually Lone Wolf stirred. He pushed the blanket down and tapped Catherine on the buttocks.

"Come, woman," he commanded lightly. "It's time for us to go."

Catherine quickly straightened the wigwam, and soon they were walking toward the center of town. Although Lone Wolf was still stiff and sore, he was rested. When he and Catherine reached the townhouse, the eating mats had been rolled down the streets to form a large square, in the center of which a large ceremonial fire burned. Catherine smiled and waved at No-am-ee who sat with the Roanoac women. But she didn't join the old woman. She sat with Lone Wolf.

Wise One set the feast in motion with his prayer and food sacrifice to Grandfather Fire, but Lone Wolf concluded the festivities. After the dancing ended, Wise One called upon Lone Wolf to tell his story. Although the audience had heard Lone Wolf speak on more than one occasion, they were attentive tonight. Eloquently the war chief filled in the details of his ordeal, carrying the listener through all his experiences, his joys, his sorrows, his pain, to his ultimate triumph.

"My paleface slave has given me much good magic," he said, holding up his hand so they could see the gold band. "She has given me this totem which I wear always on my hand; she had given me a handkerchief, and this medicine bag." He pointed to the pouch. "Today when I was losing much blood through the wound in my chest, Ho-sa-eeth sent for her because her magic and her skill is great. She came and sewed me together."

As Lone Wolf spoke, Manteo leaned over to Catherine. "Your warrior loves you, Catherine."

"Aye," Catherine agreed, "he loves me."

"Perhaps when I return with Will and Ellen in the spring, we'll be attending a wedding."

Catherine shook her head, a sadness in her eyes. "You may be attending a wedding," she conceded, "but it won't be mine. He loves me, but he must marry another."

Manteo was curious, but he didn't trouble Catherine with questions. Knowing the ways of politics, he understood arranged marriages.

Later that night after Lone Wolf and Catherine had bid their guests good night, they returned to their wigwam. Because the night was chilly, Catherine built a fire to warm the sleeping room before they undressed and snuggled under the bearskin, side by side, spoon fashion.

They lay there quietly for a long time before Lone Wolf sighed deeply and said, "After the harvest festival, I'll be leaving."

Catherine waited.

"I'll be gone the winter."

"The trading expedition?" Catherine watched the flames of the fire as they leaped into the air, piercing the blackness with their glowing light and warmth.

"That, and I promised Wise One that I would travel to the Cherokee Nation." Again he lapsed into a silence that was difficult for him to break. "I wish I didn't have to go, but I do."

"I know," Catherine murmured. "I would like you to stay with me, but I understand that you must do this for your people."

"My people demand much of me," he said impassively. "Flying Eagle and his family are celebrating the harvest festival with us."

"The"—her heartbeat accelerated, and she could hardly breathe—"the Lumbroan princess is coming here for the harvest festival?" Lone Wolf didn't speak; he just nodded his head. Catherine felt the movement against her back.

"She is going to live with us awhile in order to learn our ways."

"What of me, Lone Wolf?" she asked. "What am I to do while you're gone? Where am I to live?"

"You will live with No-am-ee. She will teach you our ways."

"Where is Little Doe to live?"

"With Wise One and Sunflower Woman."

"When will you wed her?" Catherine could hardly utter the question, she was so choked up.

"At the strawberry festival."

Knowing how badly it hurt Catherine for him to discuss his coming marriage, Lone Wolf hated to mention it, but he wanted her to know. He felt that it was better to face it than to hide from it.

"I don't want Will and Ellen to come then," Catherine

306

said, her voice small and tight.

Lone Wolf's hand capped her shoulder, and he tugged her gently, trying to get her to turn over. But she wouldn't.

"I don't want Ellen to see you marrying someone else. She would never understand."

"You don't either, do you?" Lone Wolf asked, exasperated with her . . . exasperated with himself. The more he tried to make her understand why it was necessary for him to marry Little Doe, the less he understood why it was himself.

"As I said before," she whispered, tears scalding her cheeks, "I understand but I don't accept it."

He ran his fingers lightly down her arm. "Catherine . . ."

Catherine jerked her shoulder away from him, refusing to turn over. She didn't want him to see her tears. "Don't!" Her cry was born of anguish not anger. "When you love someone, you don't hurt them as you're hurting me."

Lone Wolf lay on his back, staring into the sky through the open smoke hole, Catherine on her side. Neither slept, but neither spoke. Both pondered the situation.

Chapter XV

Catherine and Lone Wolf didn't resolve their disagreement, but it was pushed into abeyance during the coming weeks because they saw little of each other. In the mornings Lone Wolf practiced for the first ball game of the season, and during the afternoon and evenings he organized the trading expedition: he amassed the products to be bartered, he listed the goods which the villagers wanted in exchange, and he met with the traders who had begun gathering items from the surrounding villages.

Likewise, Catherine's days were busy ones. From sunrise to sundown she worked. As the hunters brought in the game for the winter months and for the harvest festival, the meat had to be stripped and dried, and the skins processed—a long, tedious procedure that required them to be soaked in water, stretched on the frame, oiled and dried, worked until they were soft and smooth, then smoked. These tasks Catherine did before and after her day in the field. At night around the large fire, she shucked corn, and later with the help of No-am-ee, Rebekk-ana, and Little Flower she sewed, making Lone Wolf new clothes and extra pairs of moccasins to take on his trip with him. She made shirts and breechclouts, fur-lined jackets, leggings, moccasins, and robes. She monogrammed his initials on a new buckskin blanket, and she filled his pouch with his favorite tobacco mixture.

Most evenings by the time Lone Wolf returned to the wigwam, Catherine was already asleep. Many evenings she was so exhausted, his coming to bed didn't even arouse her. But when she did awaken, their nights were filled with passion and blazing desire. Though Catherine staunchly fought against wanting him and though she never initiated the lovemaking, she always capitulated, eventually crying out in pleasure and begging for his touch.

"Cath-er-ine," Re-bekk-ana called one morning as she rushed to the river where Catherine was bending over a water trough brimming with deerskins. "Sunflower Woman has just announced that the women are going to compete in the festival contests for the Lumbroans."

Grabbing a water-logged skin in both fists, Catherine heaved it out of the water. "Am I supposed to find that news exciting?" she grunted dryly, conversing fluently enough in Scupperongac that she no longer needed to sign.

"Oh, yes," Re-bekk-ana squealed. "To play for our guests is one of the greatest honors we can have. But that's not all." The young girl clapped her hands together, dancing around. She paused a moment to let suspense build. "Sunflower Woman is going to ask you to play in the ball game."

"What!" Catherine cried, so surprised she dropped the heavy skin into the trough, water splashing on her skirt and moccasins. She spun around, staring wide-eyed at the Indian woman. Then, lifting her hands to her lips, she blew warm air on her cold, chaffed fingers.

When Re-bekk-ana opened her mouth to repeat what she had said, Catherine muttered, "That's all right. I heard you the first time."

"Will you?"

"Not me," Catherine declared hotly, shaking her head. She had seen the beating Lone Wolf took at practice, and she had spent several evenings applying cornstalk lotion to his bruised body and massaging his aching muscles. She could easily imagine what the result of one game would be for her, much less an entire contest. She had no desire to submit herself to such torture . . . or to the humiliation she would suffer if she lost.

"Maybe one of the other contests," Re-bekk-ana suggested tentatively, blinking in surprise at Catherine's vehement outburst. Re-bekk-ana couldn't understand anyone not wanting to compete in the games. "Please, Catherine. Your magic is good." Catherine opened her mouth, but Re-bekk-ana raced on, refusing Catherine the opportunity to speak. "The Turtle Clan wants you to play for us in the festival contests.

Catherine's protest gave way to complete bafflement. "The festival contests!" she exclaimed. "Not only the ball game. But the contests!" When Re-bekk-ana nodded, Catherine asked, "What kind of contests?"

Re-bekk-ana allowed herself a small smile of hope. "Same as the ones after the ordeal. Hoop-and-pole, racing, spear, knife, and tomahawk throwing, and the bow and arrow."

An enigmatic smile curled Catherine's lips. Nothing would please her more than to challenge Happy Woman and to win, she thought. After all she had been an avid sportswoman and an excellent marksman with the bow and arrow. Her smile widened. Her knowledge of weaponry would stand in good stead. Thanks to her father, she was familiar with the pike and the battle hatchet, both of which were similar to the spear and the tomahawk, and during Running Bear's stay in England, she had become quite skilled at playing hoop-and-pole.

"Do the women compete in all these games?"

"A few do," Re-bekk-ana replied guardedly.

"And Happy Woman is one of the few?"

Re-bekk-ana nodded, her hope rising. "But the most important contest for the women is the ball game."

"Is it like the game Lone Wolf had been practicing for?"

"Similar," Re-bekk-ana answered.

Catherine shook her head. She might be a worthy adversary in the archery contest; possibly she could hold her own in canoeing, tomahawk throwing, or hoop-and-pole; but as for the ball game—she shrugged—she didn't stand a chance against Happy Woman. She sighed.

"I don't think so, Re-bekk-ana."

"You must, Catherine," the young girl insisted.

"Why must I?" Catherine asked, dropping her head so she couldn't see the disappointment in Re-bekk-ana's eyes. She plunged her arm into the trough and, using her hand as an agitator, swished the skins around in the water.

Re-bekk-ana moved closer. "The Beaver Clan has had the best player in Scupperong for many winters now. Your magic is strong. You could be the champion for the Turtle Clan."

Catherine laughed. "You're forgetting, Re-bekk-ana, I'm a slave and a paleface. I belong to no clan."

"But that's all been taken care of," Re-bekk-ana announced gleefully. "Since No-am-ee is teaching you and you will be staying with her when Lone Wolf is gone, she said that you could represent the Turtle Clan. The captains of the contest and the players on all seven teams have agreed with her."

"I don't know the games," Catherine protested stoutly, knowing she was losing the argument. She shrugged her shoulders. "No amount of magic is going to help me win, Re-bekk-ana. You win a game with skill not magic."

Re-bekk-ana didn't hear Catherine. She was too engrossed in what she was going to say next. "Happy Woman also thinks you have strong magic, Catherine, but she doesn't think it's strong enough. She and several of the women have volunteered to teach you how to play, but they don't think you will accept their offer. They"— Re-bekk-ana paused—"they think you're a coward."

Re-bekk-ana's eyes lowered to the trough. She knew she had Catherine's attention when she saw her fists open and turn the deerskins loose.

"Just think, Catherine, when you play ball, you don't have to work. Sunflower Woman will assign someone to all your duties. And if you win, you may be named the best player in all Scupperong. That is a great honor for you." When Catherine didn't respond, Re-bekk-ana added, "And for Lone Wolf and the Turtle Clan." Still Catherined didn't speak. The silence seemed to crackle between them. Finally Re-bekk-ana slipped in a little more persuasion. "If you don't accept the challenge, Catherine, Happy Woman will ridicule you in front of the entire village."

Either way, Catherine thought irritably, Happy Woman will make a fool of me. Venting her irritation on the skins, she gave them one last jerk and dropped them with a splat. She watched them as they slowly sank, gurgling, beneath the water. Spinning about, she wiped her hands down the sides of her dress and headed back to Lone Wolf's wigwam. Re-bekk-ana, smiling to herself, fell into step with Catherine, regaling her with story after story about Happy Woman's victories. When Catherine darted a suspicious glance at the young Indian woman to see if she were rubbing salt into an open wound, Re-bekk-ana bestowed an innocent smile on her. No mischief was apparent on her face, but her eyes glowed with embers of

312

sheer devilment.

Interrupting Re-bekk-ana's continuous flow of conversation when they reached the wigwam, Catherine asked, "Will you join us for the morning meal?"

Re-bekk-ana nodded and followed Catherine through the door. "I was hoping you would ask. When Sunflower Woman gave me permission to tell you of the coaches' decision to let you play, I was so excited that I missed the morning meal at home."

Catherine, being sincerely fond of the girl, couldn't stay irritated long. She chuckled softly and walked into the main room where Little Flower was dishing out the food. As she did so, the child looked up from the fire.

"Catherine," she cried, waving the serving bowl through the air with one hand, with the other dropping the ladle into the pot. "Did you hear the good news?" Her excitement was as great as her sister's.

"Be careful." Catherine eyed the tilting bowl. "You're about to spill the mush." She added dryly: "Yes, I heard the news, but I'm not sure how good it is." Sitting down beside the child, Catherine took the bowl from her hands.

"It is good," Little Flower solemnly assured Catherine, bobbing her head up and down. "You'll get to play with Re-bekk-ana, and you'll be the village champion."

More than likely I'll be slaughtered by Happy Woman, Catherine thought, dipping her spoon into the thick, creamy broth. As they ate, Little Flower and Re-bekk-ana continued to talk about the coming festival, and what enthusiasm Catherine lacked, Little Flower and Re-bekk-ana more than made up for. Any detail one missed, the other added with a grand flourish.

The meal over, Little Flower began to clean the dishes. Re-bekk-ana walked into the entry room and picked up her racket, a long, crooked stick that resembled a shepherd's staff, and Catherine walked to the platform, reaching for her burden basket.

"Cath-er-ine!" Re-bekk-ana shrieked, her eyes rounding with disbelief. She raced across the room, fanning the racket in the air as if it were a club. Then she lightly tapped the basket. "You can't go to the field today. You've got to play with us!"

Catherine shook her head and smiled placatingly. "If I were more experienced, Re-bekk-ana, I would gladly represent the Turtle Clan. I would challenge Happy Woman for you, but—"

"Good morning."

The silent-footed woman moved through the doorway, her greeting interrupting Catherine in midsentence. Tumpline in hand, basket perched precariously on one shoulder, Catherine spun around to look at Sunflower Woman.

"I would like to speak with you, please."

Catherine shrugged her shoulders, and the basket slid to the floor. "Please come on," she invited politely, leading the way into the main room. She pointed to the fire. "Will you sit down?"

As Sunflower Woman knelt, Re-bekk-ana called from the doorway, "I must go, Catherine. I will visit with you later."

"You don't need to leave because of me," Sunflower Woman said. "I have a feeling that both of us are here for the same reason." Her eyes twinkling, she added, "You may as well hear what I have to say now as later."

Re-bekk-ana grinned and nodded her head. These were the words she had wanted to hear! Quickly she leaned her racket against the platform and returned to the main room. Both of the younger women stood until Sunflower Woman sat down; then they sat beside her. Again deferring to convention, they allowed her to address them first.

314

As Sunflower Woman talked, Little Flower quietly cleaned the dishes, making as little noise as possible so she could hear the conversation. She stacked the bowls, spoons, and eating mats in their basket under the platform. Then she retreated to her corner of the room, holding her doll, pretending to play but keeping an ear on the discussion. Re-bekk-ana, her eyes dancing with excitement, kept swinging her gaze back and forth from Sunflower Woman to Catherine, listening to the older women but watching the reaction of the younger one.

"Our chief has asked that the women play a game in honor of Flying Eagle and his family who will be celebrating the harvest festival with us." Totally guileless, Sunflower Woman continued, "My husband wishes the best of the Scupperongac teams to play. He wants to impress the one whom Lone Wolf is to wed."

Though Catherine inwardly started at Sunflower Woman's confession she gave no outward show of emotion. She sat decorously as No-am-ee had taught her, guarding her expression as carefully as did the Indians. Without a twitch of a muscle, without a blink of surprise, she quietly waited.

Sunflower Woman smiled; she was pleased with the paleface's progress. No longer could one look at her white face and read Catherine's thoughts; no longer could one look into her mind through those expressive green eyes. An invisible mask now shielded the eyes as well as the face.

"All of us have seen how strong your magic is, and the Turtle Clan has requested that you represent them in the contests," Sunflower Woman said.

"Thank you for asking," Catherine replied courteously, "but I don't know your games." Out of the corner of her eye, she caught Re-bekk-ana's start of dismay, but the young woman's disappointment didn't deter Catherine. "Because I have no knowledge or skill of the games, I would not be a valuable player."

"Happy Woman, our best player," Sunflower Woman announced proudly, "is willing to teach you." She glanced in Little Flower's direction when she added, "Because our village honors a ballplayer so greatly, someone will volunteer to do all your duties."

Little Flower nodded her head with such vigor all three women laughed. Scooting out of her corner, she cried, "What I cannot do, Catherine, my mother and younger sisters will help me do. That way we will be blessed by your magic."

Catherine shook her head and opened her mouth to decline, but Sunflower Woman spoke again.

"I can understand your hesitancy," she conceded softly, "but Happy Woman has let it be known throughout the village that the Turtle Clan is asking you to represent them, and she wants to compete against you." The woman's voice lowered. "She has boasted that her magic is much greater than yours." She paused, watching the impact of the words on Catherine; then she continued. "Also she has suggested that you are afraid of her magic." Sunflower Woman shrugged as if Catherine's decision didn't matter to her. "The villagers saw me coming here to see you today, so if you refuse . . ."

Catherine didn't need to know the rest of the sentence to understand what Sunflower Woman was implying. She understood perfectly. She drew in a deep breath, exhaled, and smiled grimly.

"When do we start?"

"Today."

Re-bekk-ana could hardly suppress her enthusiasm; Little Flower didn't. Bubbling with excitement and joy, she clutched her doll under her arm and ran from the wigwam. She called over her shoulder. "I'm going to get my mother. I'll be right back."

Smiling at the exuberant child, Sunflower Woman stood. "I'll be leaving also." At the exit she turned. "The two of you must get to the ball ground as soon as you can."

Shortly Little Flower returned with her mother, Cor-an-a-me. After Catherine explained all that she was doing, Cor-an-a-me bobbed her head.

"I will take care of your work, Cath-er-ine," the tiny woman assured her. "Do not worry. And I will let Little Flower tend your fire and wigwam. Re-bekk-ana will show you what to do."

As Catherine picked up her burden basket and reshelved it, a grim sigh escaped her lips. Cor-an-a-me felt Catherine's dismay. She walked to where Catherine stood and laid her hand on the paleface's shoulder.

"Playing for the Turtle Clan is an honorable thing, Catherine. Thank you."

Catherine nodded and smiled tightly. She felt guilty. Honor had had little to do with her decision. She had agreed only to avoid humiliation. Ironically, because she had done so, she was now heaping ridicule upon herself. Feeling a soft tug on her hand, she looked into the shining, upturned face of the child.

"You'll play well, Catherine; I know you will! And you'll be much better than Happy Woman." Little Flower grinned. "To make you feel better I will give you a love gift." The child held her doll out. "She has great magic, and she will help you win."

Catherine felt the sting of tears. She didn't know what she would do without her little ministering angel. Unconsciously she again sighed. She didn't dread playing ball; she dreaded fighting Happy Woman. The Indian had experience and knew all the rules; Catherine knew nothing.

Knowing she could not refuse the gift, Catherine's hand closed around the doll. Clutching it close to

317

her breast, she said, "Thank you, Little Flower. I shall treasure this more than any other gift I ever receive." She lifted her head and looked across the wigwam at Little Flower's mother. "And thank you, Cor-an-a-me." Catherine moved to her chest, unlocked it, and opened the lid. "After the festival," she said to Little Flower, "I will return the doll. Until then I will place her here for safekeeping."

Chattering happily, her racket in hand, Re-bekk-ana led Catherine to the ball ground where the women were practicing. The two of them stood at the sidelines for a long time watching. With the slow majestic sweep of a pendulum, Catherine's gaze swung from right to left. Goal posts, made of three saplings—two forked ones standing upright, one resting horizontally in the fork— were at each end of the field. One was designated for the Beaver Clan, the other for the Wolf Clan. Six women stood on the sidelines, and forty young women battled from one end of the field to the other.

Pointing to the sidelines, Re-bekk-ana said, "Those are our coaches and managers. We have seven, one from each clan. When they were younger they were the best players in the town."

Seeing only six women, Catherine asked, "Where's the seventh?"

Again Re-bekk-ana lifted her hand and pointed, this time at the players who were racing toward the Beaver goal posts. "The umpire," she said. "Sunflower Woman. In the red cape." Re-bekk-ana's words came out in unattached phrases, her attention captured by the game. Grabbing Catherine by the shoulder, she shook her and squealed, "Look at the way Happy Woman is receiving the ball, Catherine. The way she's holding her racket. See how she's moving only her upper body." Re-bekk-ana lifted her right arm, swinging her racket through the air. Unconsciously she rocked to her toes and swayed,

318

emulating the graceful sweep of Happy Woman's execution. "She plays well, but someday I shall play better." Re-bekk-ana's words ceased as she lost herself in the swift action on the field.

When the game ended, the two teams—the Beavers shouting their victory, the Wolves bemoaning their fate—ran to the mound and flopped down, huffing and panting. Over their good-natured laughter and banter, the team coaches congratulated the winners and chastised the losers. Point by point, the coaches discussed strengths and weaknesses with their respective teams.

Finally Sunflower Woman yelled, "It's time for game two. The Beavers and the Turtles."

"Come," Re-bekk-ana said, "it is time for us to play."

"To play," Catherine whispered, the sound so hollow she wasn't sure Re-bekk-ana could hear her. "Don't you mean to battle!"

Re-bekk-ana chuckled softly and nodded her head. "That's the only way to learn."

And a sure way to die, Catherine thought, wiping her sweat-moistened hand down the side of her dress as she followed Re-bekk-ana to the center of the field. Ma-wa-ska, the coach for the Turtles, quickly introduced Catherine to the other team members. Nervously she smiled and looked at the twenty faces that circled her. As if their impassive countenances were not forbidding enough, she glanced at the Beaver huddle. Groaning inwardly, she wished her first practice was not against Happy Woman's team.

"Here is a racket you may use today," Ma-wa-ska said, tossing one to Catherine. "Tomorrow you should have your own."

Her eyes still fixed on the other team, Catherine was unprepared for the coach's sudden move. She didn't throw her hand up in time to catch the racket, and it fell at her feet, slithering in the soft dirt. The Turtle players looked dismayed, and several of the Beaver players snickered. As Catherine bent to pick it up, out the corner of her eyes she saw Happy Woman watching her and smiling maliciously.

Kneeling beside her, Re-bekk-ana whispered, "Don't worry, Cath-er-ine. They're trying to make you nervous."

And they're succeeding, Catherine thought, her fingers gripping the smooth handle of the racket. Straightening up, she moved into the tight ring around Ma-wa-ska, and she listened as the older woman gave them last-minute instructions. Taking her racket in her right hand, the coach showed them different ways to catch a ball. She lifted her arms and leaped into the air, stretching her arm and gracefully maneuvering the racket. She pirouetted from heel to toe and back again, teaching them tricks in throwing the ball.

Then, lowering her voice and drawing the huddle into a tight circle, Ma-wa-ska laughingly demonstrated the art of tripping an opponent so she would lose the ball. With even greater relish and with agility unusual in a woman of her age, Ma-wa-ska demonstrated the tactic for disqualifying a player. Throwing the stick aside in one swift motion, she grabbed one of the unsuspecting players with both hands, lifted her up, and dropped her to the ground.

"The game is hard and fast," Ma-wa-ska said, her gaze aimed at Catherine.

To emphasize her point, she pitched the double ball. Catherine watched the two small deerskin balls connected by a short, heavy thong sail upward through the air, then down, looping around the end of Ma-wa-ska's extended racket.

"To win and to be the best ball player requires much magic. To be the champion of the contests is a great honor."

320

Before Catherine knew what had happened the instructions had ended, and she was no longer a spectator; she was a participant. The teams trotted to the center of the field and stood facing each other, Sunflower Woman standing between the two lines. Catherine found herself face to face with Happy Woman.

"Playing is the best way to learn," the chuckling coach said.

If not the best, certainly the most painful, Catherine thought dismally, trying to concentrate on Ma-wa-ska's instructions as she battled swinging rackets, flying balls, running weapons. No matter how fervently Catherine wished to be disqualified, she would not utter the thought aloud.

After the Beavers made the twelfth point, the teams regrouped. A bedraggled Catherine sprawled on one end of the field. Using her bleeding hands, she wearily pushed herself to her skinned knees, then to her feet. Bracing herself with her racket, she brushed the dirt off her dress and limped to the tight cluster of women. Lifting her aching arm, she wiped the sweat and grime from her forehead. She looked across the neutral zone at Happy Woman, and she glared at the gloating Beaver champion.

Without lowering her gaze, Catherine spit the blood and dirt out of her mouth, and she gingerly touched her cut lip. She was tired of eating dirt; she was tired of being a doormat for the players to run over. She was furious, ready to do battle. Determinedly she trudged to the center line.

This time, when Sunflower Woman threw the ball into the air, Catherine jumped higher and swung harder than anyone else. She ran, she elbowed, she pushed, and she tugged. A point scored! The teams lined up again; Sunflower Woman tossed the ball. Forty sticks clashed as they shot into the air, straining for the ball. By chance the thong caught on Catherine's stick and balanced.

Dazed but cheered on by her teammates, she raced down the field. Happy Woman darted in front of her, lowered her racket and tripped Catherine. Catherine lost her footing, she stumbled, but she didn't fall or lose her racket. Another Beaver player, taking advantage of the situation, deftly twitched the thong off the end of Catherine's stick.

Catherine spun around, leading nineteen women in a mad scramble. They pushed, elbowed, rolled, and tumbled. In the shuffle, the Beaver player tossed the ball, a teammate picked it. Catherine, in hot pursuit, closed in on the woman. Seeing the maneuver, Happy Woman dropped her stick and caught Catherine from behind. But this time, Catherine wasn't that easily thrown. Bringing her stick down, ready for battle, Catherine jerked out of the vise and gave Happy Woman blow for blow. In the struggle both fell to the ground.

When Happy Woman realized that one of Catherine's teammates had the ball and was racing for the goal, she suddenly remembered the game. Pushing her personal feud aside, she bounded to her feet, grabbed her stick, and gave chase. Since she was the fastest female runner in the village, Happy Woman easily overtook the Turtle players. With effortless grace, she spun around at the same time that she swung her racket and flicked the thong from her opponent's stick. Then she sped down the field and, leading the pack of howling players, hurled the ball through the goal posts, scoring a point.

As the women regrouped, Catherine's eyes swept the sidelines. Her disinterest suddenly changed to surprise. Many of the men had gathered to watch the game, Lone Wolf and Kee-lee included. Caught up in her observation, Catherine failed to see the leg that darted out, and before she knew it, she again lay in the dirt, flat on her face, her arms and legs outstretched.

She sat up to loud guffaws of laughter from the men.

Swallowing the tears that threatened, she cast a furtive glance at Lone Wolf who was enjoying her embarrassment as much as the others. Anger quickly blazed up within her, completely incinerating her humiliation. Laugh at her would he! She jumped to her feet and joined her team.

The score was tied, and a single goal would decide the winner. The players, facing each other, lined up for the last time. Catherine lifted a hand, running her fingers under her headband and pushing strands of hair out of her eyes. She gave Lone Wolf one last defiant glare, but he wasn't looking at her. He was looking at Kee-lee's rackets. As Kee-lee spoke, Lone Wolf held each one up, running his fingers over the handle and the net. Then Lone Wolf held out his hand and nodded as the young warrior touched the gold band. After more conversation Lone Wolf reached up and fingered the pearl necklaces that hung around his neck.

What are they talking about? Catherine wondered.

"Cath-er-ine"—Re-bekk-ana dug her elbow in Catherine's ribs—"pay attention. We've got to make this goal if we're going to win."

Reluctantly Catherine returned her attention to the game. Sunflower Woman threw the double ball into the air between the teams, and at once there was a mad scramble of women with sticks. Catherine skillfully caught the thong between the balls on her stick. Dodging right and left, she managed to get past the women of Happy Woman's team. When she had gained a lead, she stopped short and with sure aim, drew her arm back to make the game point. But Catherine was too slow. Happy Woman reached her, catching her from behind and hurling her to the ground. Catherine and the thong sailed through the air in different directions.

The jeering guffaws of the men bombarded Catherine, and she bit her lips and clenched her teeth, blinking back the tears that threatened. One of Happy Woman's teammates caught the ball and sent it flying toward the goal. The thong caught neatly on the crossbar of the goal posts, twining about it in victory for Happy Woman's team. The game was over.

The men clapped their hands and cheered the winners. They laughed at Catherine who slowly crawled into a sitting position, her face twisted with pain as she nursed a twisted ankle.

"Her medicine is not so strong now," one of the Beaver women taunted.

Happy Woman beamed. "Perhaps we shall have to ask Little Doe to take the paleface's place when game time comes."

Catherine boiled. Not content that Little Doe was taking her place in marriage with Lone Wolf, Happy Woman wanted the Lumbroan to take her place in the contest. Catherine hobbled to her feet and glared at Happy Woman, saying between clenched teeth, "I have been invited to participate in this contest against the Lumbroans, Happy Woman, and I shall. No one will take my place."

"If you survive . . ." Happy Woman purred.

"I shall," Catherine promised.

"Shall we make a wager?" Happy Woman gurgled gleefully.

"Wager!" Catherine sputtered indignantly, her eyes grazing over Lone Wolf who nonchalantly leaned against a tree, his arms folded across his chest. An infernal grin twitched his lips, and his eyes danced with laughter. Dragging her gaze from him, Catherine asked Happy Woman, "Is that all you can think of, betting?"

"Are you afraid to do so?" Happy Woman jeered.

Catherine did not answer. She continued to stare.

"The chest," Happy Woman suggested, thinking she was well in command of the situation. "If I am the better player, I get the chest and all that's in it."

Overhearing Happy Woman's baiting and taunting, the players hushed and crowded closer. Expectantly they looked from one woman to the other. Catherine slowly turned her head, her eyes sweeping the circle of faces. Fury whipped through her body; again Scupperongac custom dictated her actions. If she refused to wager, the villagers would jeer her. If she lost the wager, she lost her most prized possessions.

"If you win," Happy Woman goaded, one hand rising to touch a large copper medallion that rested on her breast, "you will keep your chest, and I will give you my victor's necklace."

A gasp of astonishment rippled through the crowd. Happy Woman was staking her most valuable item. No champion parted easily with a medal of honor. All eyes swung back to Catherine, and with bated breath everyone awaited her response.

"I have no desire for your champion's medallion," Catherine replied. "I have plenty of necklaces of my own." Excitement quivered through the crowd. "Since you have such a love for betting," Catherine said calculatingly, "why not extend the wager?"

Lone Wolf jolted to attention. He pushed away from the tree and took a step forward. His hands fell to his sides, and his jaw went slack. Happy Woman and Catherine were carrying their personal feud a little too far. Catherine would be no match for the Scupperongac warrior woman. Lone Wolf's first inclination was to run to Catherine's rescue, but Catherine happened to turn her head as he took a step. She speared him to the tree with her eyes. Silently he questioned her; silently he offered her his support. With a haughty flounce of her head, Catherine refused it and twirled her attention back to Happy Woman.

The warrior suddenly relaxed, an amused grin

325

spreading across his face, silent laughter shaking his thick chest. He refolded his arms and leaned against the tree to watch. He would let his beautiful slave work this one out for herself. What Catherine lacked in skills, he had found, she more than compensated for in audacity.

Lone Wolf wasn't the only one whom Catherine caught off guard with her question. She had disconcerted Happy Woman. The Indian woman's eyes narrowed, and she shifted her racket from her right hand to her left and back again. She was nervous. What is the paleface doing? she wondered. What kind of game is she playing?

"I said," Catherine declared loudly and a little more boldly, "how many contests are you going to enter?"

"Why?" Happy Woman asked suspiciously.

"I would like to suggest that we consider more than the ball game in the wager."

Catherine's voice carried so that the entire group heard. She smiled when the crowd murmured their approval. Then she darted a furtive glance at Lone Wolf, suppressing a giggle when she saw his dumbstruck expression.

"If you are the winner of a certain number of contests—"

"The contests?" Happy Woman said, her voice escalating to a squeal of surprise. "All of the contests?"

"How many are there?" Catherine countered coolly.

"I will enter the ball game," Happy Woman began, holding out a finger for each competition she listed, "shooting the bow and arrow, canoeing, racing, the tomahawk and knife throwing, and the hoop-and-pole."

Quickly Catherine counted, stooping as she did so. She picked up seven twigs and broke them, seven for her, seven for Happy Woman. "One for each game," she said to Happy Woman. Holding up four, she said, "Whoever wins four out of seven shall be the champion."

Happy Woman took the seven twigs, and she separated them. Four in one hand, three in the other. She stared at them for a long time before she lifted her head and laughed in Catherine's face.

"You are challenging me, paleface!" she exclaimed. "Me—the village champion."

"I am."

Catherine's confidence was nerve-shattering. Happy Woman looked at the twigs; she looked at the paleface. She wondered. "Four out of seven games, paleface! You think you can win four out of seven games?"

Catherine's fingers tightened around the staff she held, but her facial expression never changed. Her eyes never wavered from their target. "If you win four of the games, Happy Woman, you shall be the champion, and you shall have my chest and all that is in it. But . . ."

Catherine looked at the crowd, her gaze slowly moving from one face to the other. Finally she stared at Lone Wolf, but she read nothing in his guarded face. His amusement was wiped away, and he was tense. So were the onlookers. A twitter of tension rippled through the crowd.

". . . if I am the champion of the contests, if I win four out of seven, you Happy Woman will become slave to the slave."

Happy Woman's visage sobered immediately, and she locked gazes with Catherine. They looked at each other; they measured. Worthy adversaries, neither quailed. Although each wished the other would renege, both knew that was impossible. The silence stretched, long and taut. When Happy Woman inhaled, the soft sound was like the mighty rush of stormy winds. The onlookers gaped, waiting for her answer.

"If you win four of the games," Happy Woman agreed in an odd voice, "I will become slave to the slave." She turned to the people who thronged around them. "Mark my words this day. I, Happy Woman, have spoken."

Excited people rushed from the ball field into town, spreading word of the wager—the greatest one in many

327

winters. Happy Woman, thinking to push Catherine into a corner, had wagered for the chest, but the shrewd paleface had driven the harder bargain. Who would have thought—a slave to a slave! Individual wagers were laid. People of both clans, the Turtles and the Beavers, each group supporting its champion, scurried about, collecting talismans of good magic, brewing potions, and making medicine bags.

When the crowd had dispersed, Catherine looked around for Lone Wolf, but he and Kee-lee were walking off together. Swallowing her disappointment, she smiled at Re-bekk-ana. She used her racket like a staff and hobbled off the field. Re-bekk-ana slackened her gait to walk beside Catherine.

"Cath-er-ine!"

Catherine recognized Ma-wa-ska's voice. She stopped and waited for the spry woman to join her, but she didn't turn around.

"You cannot win without the proper equipment and training," the Turtle Coach said briskly. "Follow me."

Re-bekk-ana sidled up to Catherine, her eyes almost bulging out of her face. When the dumfounded Catherine made no effort to move, the young woman jabbed her elbow into Catherine's ribs. "Follow her," she whispered. "She's going to help you."

Catherine could hardly lift her feet to place one in front of the other. Her muscles were so tight, they screamed every time she flexed them. Her ankle throbbed, and her bruised shoulders ached from the heavy blows of the racket. Suddenly her head swam, and her vision blurred. She lifted a hand, looking at the abrasions on her palm before she ran soft fingers over her face—over her swollen, bleeding lip; the purple knot on her forehead; the cut above her eyes.

She was so exhausted she was almost at the point of hysteria. On one hand she could easily give in to tears; on the other, she wanted to laugh. Here she was at death's door, and nobody cared. Lone Wolf had laughed at her throughout the game, and even now he had deserted her, walking away with Kee-lee. Happy Woman's teammates had hoisted her onto their shoulders and were carrying her through the village, shouting her praise and adulation. Catherine's teammates had scoffed at her, and Ma-wa-ska's main concern was having a Turtle champion.

Bracing her weight on the staff, using it as a walking cane, Catherine limped behind the straight-shouldered Indian woman. Ma-wa-ska's braids were slightly streaked with white, but her back was straight, her steps crisp. Quickly Ma-wa-ska strode down the streets to her wigwam; Re-bekk-ana and Catherine followed. Inside, the Turtle coach stopped in front of the shelf above her sleeping platform.

"This is my racket," she said, holding out a beautifully carved staff. Her voice was soft, filled with happy memories.

Taking the proffered staff, Catherine brought it closer, looking at the intricate and flowing designs. "It's beautiful," she whispered.

Ma-wa-ska cleared her throat and stated, "You may have it. It has much good magic."

"I—I couldn't take your racket," Catherine refused softly. "It means so much to you."

"It means more to me that the Turtle Clan wins," the older woman returned laconically and dismissively. "I will see that you get all you need. The Turtle Clan will give you weapons that have powerful magic." The older woman's eyes settled on Catherine. "You must provide the magic to use them."

Hoping to assuage the old woman's doubts and reservations, Catherine laid a tentative hand on Ma-wa-ska's arm and said, "I will do my very best for the Turtle Clan."

Ma-wa-ska looked down at the white hand that

329

contrasted with her copper-toned skin. Slowly she pulled her arm away. Lifting her head, she stared impassively into the green eyes. "To defeat Happy Woman, Cath-er-ine, you must do better than that."

Later as Catherine and Re-bekk-ana walked to Lone Wolf's wigwam, Re-bekk-ana said, "I'm sorry this has happened, Catherine. I didn't think Happy Woman would push you into a wager such as this."

One arm hoisted in the air, Catherine balanced her racket over one shoulder. She lifted her free arm and dropped it around Re-bekk-ana's shoulders. Then she pulled the younger woman closer to her in a warm hug. "Don't worry about it, my friend. I've handled worse situations before."

"In your land perhaps, but not here, Catherine." Re-bekk-ana smiled sadly, shaking her head. "Happy Woman is a warrior."

"Happy Woman is a warrior!" Catherine's emotions finally erupted in laughter. "And I, my sister, am nothing but a paleface needlewoman. Is that what you are thinking?"

Re-bekk-ana nodded, crying, "What are we going to do?"

"You, my friend, are going to do nothing." Catherine chortled with glee. "I shall act." Her smile was cunning, but she kept her silence. She would let no one know that her father had taught her to be the son he never had. All she had to do was gain some familiarity with the Indian weapons and then practice. "I have challenged Happy Woman and I shall compete with her. She may win but not without a fight. Now," she said, "let's go take a bath."

The cold water washed away the dirt and grime, but it couldn't wash away Catherine's fatigue or her aches and pains. With Re-bekk-ana's help, she put on her cape and wraparound skirt and hobbled to Lone Wolf's wigwam.

"Oh, Catherine," Little Flower gasped in dismay when the older woman came into the wigwam.

"Not now, Little Flower," Re-bekk-ana ordered sharply.

Her ankle throbbed too badly for Catherine to go farther. Gratefully she sank into the soft rabbit furs that carpeted the main room. Smiling weakly, she turned her bruised face to Little Flower and said, "I don't think my magic was too strong today."

"But it will be stronger tomorrow," Little Flower promised, her eyes touching every bruise.

Closing her eyes, Catherine nodded. She was too exhausted to say more, and at the time she really didn't care about tomorrow. The way she felt she wasn't sure she would see a tomorrow.

"I'm going to No-am-ee's to get some medicine," Re-bekk-ana said. "I'll be back shortly." Again Catherine nodded.

When she opened her eyes again, Re-bekk-ana was kneeling in front of the fire pit, cutting roots and herbs, dropping them into a small pot of water. Soon the water was boiling and a delicious aroma filled the room. Re-bekk-ana poured the fragrant drink into a bark cup.

"Drink this," she told Catherine. "No-am-ee said it will make you feel better."

Stiffly Catherine rolled over, finally levering herself into a sitting position. Taking the cup, she cradled it gingerly in her abraded hands. She lifted it to her mouth and slowly sipped the hot liquid. After she had drunk the entire cup, Catherine lay back down, letting the warmth of the beverage seep through her insides and dull her senses.

"Get the cornhusks," Re-bekk-ana said to Little Flower. "Catherine has twisted her ankle, and we need to

331

bind it."

The child climbed onto the platform and reached for the basket of husks. She sorted them, picking out the stronger ones which she quickly twined together. When she was through, she handed the long bandage to Re-bekk-ana who wrapped Catherine's ankle.

"There," Re-bekk-ana murmured, tying off the ends. "This will give your ankle support. By morning it will be better." As Little Flower flower cleaned up, Re-bekk-ana slipped into the sleeping room, returning with a blanket which she laid over Catherine.

"After you sleep awhile, you'll feel better," Re-bekk-ana told the dozing Catherine. "Now we must go and help No-am-ee. Will you be all right by yourself?"

Not wanting to be jarred out of her cocoon of peaceful oblivion, Catherine nodded. She folded her hands under her chin and curled into a tight ball. Her sigh of contentment eased into the even breathing of sleep. When she awakened later, she was alone, but she didn't ache anymore. She lay quietly, looking at the fire, watching the flames leap into the air. Finally she roused, pushed herself up, and walked into the sleeping room.

She knelt beside her chest and opened it, taking out her possessions one by one. Her sewing notions, her material. The books. Her writing chest. Ellen's letter. Running Bear's writing chest. She unfastened the clasp, took out the sheet of paper and unfolded it. Setting it on the floor, she hand-pressed the wrinkles and then pored over the characters he had so painstakingly written. Someday! she told herself, remembering her promise.

Her moment of introspection over, she repacked the trunk, keeping out only a nightshirt. Returning to the entry, she pulled the bark over the door and walked back to the main room. Standing in front of the fire, she pulled the cape off and dropped it at her feet. Then she untied the belt at her waist, allowing the skirt to slide down her legs. Bending, she retrieved the nightshirt, letting it dangle loosely from her right hand. Naked, she stood in front of the fire, so caught up in her own thoughts that she didn't hear the quiet shuffle at the door.

Thinking Catherine asleep and not wanting to disturb her, Lone Wolf quietly pushed the bark aside. As Wolf Friend padded to his bed, Lone Wolf laid the four rackets on the platform; then he silently moved through the entry room. Her back to him, Catherine stood facing the fire, the white linen nightshirt brushing against her legs. In one fluid motion she lifted her hands and dropped the nightshirt over her head. The soft material slid down her shoulders and back. Lone Wolf had thought Catherine beautiful the day he had seen her at the river. The night she had joined him in the forest, he had thought her a heavenly vision. But tonight he found her lovelier than ever.

As the firelight played over her slim body, his eyes moved downward following the path of the fluffy material that covered her. Shadowed back; round firm buttocks gleaming gold; long, slender legs, one ankle wrapped in cornhusks. Catherine shook her head, letting her hair flow around her shoulders.

"Catherine," he whispered, crossing the room in two long steps.

Before Catherine knew what was happening, Lone Wolf softly caught her shoulders with both hands, and he turned her to him, his eyes raking her bruised face. His breath caught in his throat, and his chest felt as if it were about to burst. At that moment her pain was his, her suffering his.

He lifted a hand and, with gentle fingers, brushed her hair from her face. Reverently he touched the lump on her forehead; he outlined the cut on her eyebrow. His eyes lowered, his finger moved, and he stroked her swollen lip. With great tenderness, Lone Wolf cupped

Catherine's face with both hands, and he tenderly feathered his lips over it.

"I'm sorry, my darling," he whispered.

Needing the comfort and the solace he offered, Catherine drew closer to him, letting him ease her into the circle of his arms. She buried her face against his chest, but when his arms closed around her and his hands touched her back, Catherine winced and groaned. Startled, Lone Wolf pulled away. He turned her around, and bunching the nightshirt in his fist, he pulled it up and looked at the angry slashes across her shoulders.

Without speaking, he eased the nightshirt over her head and dropped it at their feet. Then he delicately lifted her into his arms and carried her into the sleeping room. Gently he laid her on the rabbit-fur carpet, and he made the bed. Before he lifted her to the platform, he stood, getting a basket from the shelf above the bed. He withdrew several small clay jars from it, and kneeling on the floor beside Catherine, he turned her onto her stomach and gently smeared salve over the cuts slashing across her upper back, careful not to apply pressure.

That done, he dipped his fingers into another container and rubbed his hands together, smearing the oil over his palms. His greased hands slid down to the small of her back, and he gently kneaded the tight muscles there, his fingers splaying across her buttocks that gleamed golden in the firelight. Unable to stop himself, he lowered his head, his lips caressing the indention that ran down her back, stopping when he reached the gentle swell of hips. The medicine having taken effect, Catherine's pain had dulled. She sighed and trembled beneath his hands.

"Am I hurting you?" he asked.

"No," Catherine husked, not exactly telling the truth. His touch was excruciating agony. Forgotten were the aches and pains of the ball game. Renewed was the pain of

334

loving Lone Wolf, of knowing that she must always share his love with someone else.

He turned her over. Again he moistened a finger in the small clay jar and gently daubed the ointment over the purple lump on her forehead and on the cut above her eye. Then he stretched out beside her, his hands and his lips spreading love all over her bruised and battered body. His mouth brushed across the gentle swell of her breast, but he didn't touch the sensitive tip.

Catherine didn't want to respond, but as usual his touch brought her to life. She craved him in the deepest part of her being, his touch making her painfully aware of her need. Involuntarily she lifted her arms, her hands capping the back of his head, and when his lips traveled to the satin skin of her midriff, circling and gently caressing her navel, she sucked in her breath and moaned softly.

He lifted his face, and again he asked, "Am I hurting you?" She shook her head. His hands moved up her leg, softly feathering the inner thighs. "Do you want me to stop?" he whispered.

This was her cue, but in truth, Catherine didn't want him to stop. She wanted the fulfillment that Lone Wolf could give her; the love he offered her. Slowly she rolled her head from side to side.

"Will you stop me if I'm hurting you?"

She nodded, and he lowered his head, his lips and hands telling her of his love, igniting her desire, and making her yearn for more than mere caresses. Although Lone Wolf knew his touch excited Catherine, he was also aware that she was responding only physically. He could get total abandonment from her but never total surrender. She always held back that certain part of her self. Still, he wanted her—he wanted whatever part of her she was willing to give.

Quickly he rolled away from her and undressed without breaking the flow of their building desire. When

335

he stretched out again, he lay on his side and nestled close. Dropping his arm over her, his hand splayed against the sensitive flesh of her stomach.

"I love you," he whispered. "Without you, my darling, I have no day; I have no sunshine."

Tenderly he maneuvered her onto her side so that her buttocks were cradled in the cup of his stomach and thighs. Gently his hand stroked her rounded hips, slipping between her legs. He waited, listening for her command to stop. Instead he heard her heightened breathing; he felt her tremble. He eased one of his legs between hers, spreading her thighs apart, and his left hand moved down her stomach, his fingers gently stimulating her.

His stomach to her back, he slid down on the bed and raised her leg with his. Then he pulled her closer against his chest and stomach, his manhood sheathing itself in the warm, feminine opening. Soon they were moving in that primitive, age-old dance of love. Softly and gently, he moved within her, never touching her shoulders or her face. They moved together as the one they were.

Although the evening was chilly, Catherine's body was covered with a fine film of perspiration that reflected the glow of the fire. Her eyes were closed, and she was breathing deeply and erractically; her body was quivering, on the verge of completeness. Suddenly she cried out, and she wilted in Lone Wolf's arms. Later he turned her onto her back, and his lips softly moved over her face, thanking her for the completeness of her giving.

"I love you," he whispered, lifting his head, peering into her face.

He said no more; instead, he smiled. Her eyes were closed, and she was breathing evenly and deeply. Gently untangling himself, he picked her up and laid her on the bed. Lying down beside her, he melded his frame to hers and pulled the blanket over them.

Chapter XVI

When Catherine awakened, Little Flower had already come and gone. The morning meal simmered on the fire, and Lone Wolf, dressed in shirt, leggings, and moccasins, sat in front of the blaze, rethreading a lacrosse racket. Catherine yawned and stretched, shivering when she moved out of her cocoon of warmth. Retreating and curling into a tight ball, she closed her eyes and would have slept again, but the odor of cooking food wafted through the wigwam, tempting her to rise. Pushing the blanket aside, she touched her toes to the floor, gingerly setting her weight on the twisted ankle. The joint was stiff, but she felt no pain.

She walked to the center of the room where her nightshirt lay. Kneeling, she reached for it, her hand closing over the material as she looked through the doorway. At that moment Lone Wolf turned his head, their eyes meeting. Catherine's movements were immediately stayed; she posed as if she were a statue. Lone Wolf's fingers stilled, and his warm, liquid eyes slowly moved over her naked profile, lingering on those sensitive places. His look was a vivid touch, a splendid reminder of pleasures past. His lips, sculpted bold and firm by the Creator, now rendered soft by love, lifted in that special smile—that gesture that belonged to Catherine alone. Lowering one eyelid, he winked, the thick, dark lashes fanning across his bronzed cheek.

"Good morning, Catherine Graystone. Did Manitou bless you with sweet dreams?"

"Yes," she rasped, her only movement the slight lifting of her breasts as she caught her breath.

She wondered if she would always be so affected by the blatant virility of Lone Wolf. Just his gaze, his presence, sent warm waves of pleasure through her body. A word or a smile accelerated her heartbeat and lodged her breath in her chest. His touch awakened in her feelings hitherto unknown, a hunger for more than gazes, or words, or smiles.

Her thoughts mirrored in her eyes for the warrior to see and read, Catherine lightly ran the tip of her tongue over her lips. She smiled when Lone Wolf answered in kind, his mouth opening, his tongue peeping through parted lips. Without taking her eyes from Lone Wolf, Catherine picked up the nightshirt and held it suspended over her head. Lone Wolf, spellbound, was mesmerized by the flowing beauty of the movements of the woman he loved. He gazed adoringly at the proud arch of her back, her smooth buttocks, the thrust of her firm breasts, her flat belly, the slender grace of long, tapered legs.

The nightshirt gently slid over Catherine's body, covering her feminine contours, but she knew that she would always be naked and vulnerable to the Scupperongac war chief. He alone—of all the people in the world— had the ability to look into her soul. Shaken by the onslaught of emotions that his gaze generated, Catherine stood and moved to the platform. With trembling hands, she picked up the porcupine tail and brushed her hair. Not taking the time to braid her auburn mane, she pulled it back to the nape of her neck and tied it with one of the thongs Lone Wolf had given her. Then, slipping into a pair of fur-lined moccasins, she moved into the main

338

room for the morning meal.

A rakish grin lifted Lone Wolf's lips as his eyes swept Catherine from head to toe. "How are you feeling this morning?" His question covered much more than her aches and bruises from the ball game.

"Quite well, thank you," she returned primly, following his train of thought and inwardly shivering with pleasure at his teasing.

"Your forehead and eye are discolored," he told her, chuckling as he caught sight of her face, a bright, embarrassed red, "but the swelling has gone down." He looked at the tail of her nightshirt. "How's the ankle?"

Extending her leg, Catherine flexed her foot. "Almost as good as new. Re-bekk-ana and Little Flower did an excellent job of mending me."

"It was the least they could do since they were the ones who sent you out there so Happy Woman could do an excellent job of tearing you apart." Lone Wolf's chuckle burgeoned into soft laughter. "If you're going to play, Catherine Graystone, you're going to need—"

"I know," Catherine interjected dryly, "I heard it repeated enough yesterday. I need strong magic."

"That too," Lone Wolf agreed. "But even more you need to learn one basic strategy." Interested now, Catherine stared earnestly at him. "You can play a better game if you stay on your feet rather than on your buttocks."

Not joining in his rich, mellow laughter, not enjoying a joke at her expense, Catherine made a face and glared at him as she sat down. "You seem to think I do pretty well on my buttocks. You haven't complained about my skill so far."

Lone Wolf's laughter deepened and, laying the racket down, he dropped the unused sinew into the bowl of water. "We're talking about two different games," he replied. He reached for Catherine, pulling her into his arms. Cradling her next to his body, he cupped her

339

shoulder with his hand. "And you're right, my darling," he murmured pensively. "I have no complaints." His lips touched hers in the briefest but sweetest of kisses. "As much as I like the taste of you, and as much as I would like to linger on the sweetness of your body, I can't." He patted her playfully. "I'm starved, and Little Flower has—"

"Speaking of Little Flower," Catherine interrupted, looking around, "where is she?"

"She asked if she could go to No-am-ee's. She had a special errand to run. I gave her permission, promising her I would stop by on the way to practice, so she'll know when to return." He grinned, tweaking the tip of Catherine's nose. "And speaking of practice, it starts early in the morning, and you need plenty of it before the contest." He nodded his head toward the fire pit. "Let's hurry and eat."

Groaning her misery, Catherine pulled out of Lone Wolf's arms and turned her attention to the morning meal. Lone Wolf returned to his racket, dipping his thumb and index finger into the bowl and fishing for the moistened sinew. As he stretched it and tied it to the racket, Catherine ladled the squirrel broth and corn dumplings into the bowl.

She said, "I just hope the Turtles don't rue the day they selected me for their team."

Lone Wolf pressed the newly repaired net with his palm, testing its strength. "That will depend on what they want out of the contest," he said, his eyes on the racket. "If they're looking for a champion . . ." He shrugged the rest of the sentence, letting his words trail into eloquent silence as he twanged one of the sinews. When he was satisfied with the tautness of the string, he spoke again. "If they're looking for a good wager"—he grinned and lifted his head—"I think it's already begun."

Catherine spooned the stew into the serving bowl. "I

340

think so too," she murmured, setting the bowl in front of Lone Wolf. For the first time she looked at the racket he had restrung. "I don't remember seeing that racket before."

"You haven't," Lone Wolf answered matter-of-factly, glancing over his shoulder at it. "I won it yesterday."

Remembering the scene she had witnessed between him and Kee-lee, she said, "So that's what you and Kee-lee were talking about yesterday?"

"Yesterday's game, today's game, the contest . . . that's what everybody is talking about." Lone Wolf glossed over the incident, dipping his spoon into the rich broth.

Catherine was so inundated with curiosity she could hardly contain her questions until he had made the morning sacrifice and said the prayer. As soon as Lone Wolf ceased speaking, she asked softly, "You made a wager with Kee-lee about yesterday's game?"

"I did," he mumbled more than he spoke as he bit into the dumpling.

Her hunger forgotten, Catherine doggedly ferreted for information. "The Turtles against the Beavers?" Chewing his food, Lone Wolf shook his head. Before he could swallow, Catherine prodded unmercifully. "Me against Happy Woman?" When he nodded, Catherine screwed her face in puzzlement. "And . . . and you won?"

Lone Wolf looked up in surprise. "I never lose."

"But I didn't win," Catherine sputtered quizzically.

Lone Wolf chuckled softly. "I knew you wouldn't." Not observing Catherine's slack jaw and the disappointment in her eyes, he continued. "Kee-lee will be a great warrior one of these days; perhaps a good gambler, but he must learn to be guided by reason rather than emotion."

Catherine inhaled deeply and laid her spoon down. "You wagered Kee-lee that Happy Woman would win?"

Oblivious to Catherine's indignation, Lone Wolf nodded again, explaining, "There was no way you could

341

win, Catherine. You haven't been trained to play these games; you didn't know the first thing about them."

Again the scene came to mind, and Catherine saw Kee-lee looking at Lone Wolf's ring and the pearl necklaces. "You wagered my father's ring?"

Angry at Catherine's audacity and infuriated that she was questioning him, Lone Wolf jerked his head up. "What if I did?"

"How dare you!" Catherine screamed, jumping to her feet, knocking over the bowl of food. "I gave you my most treasured possessions and you treat them as if they are nothing."

Slowly Lone Wolf stood, facing Catherine, looking down at her. Finely tempered steel couldn't have been harder than the timbre of his voice. "Don't ever question my actions or my motives again, Catherine. You forget your position both as a woman and as a slave. I have been most tolerant of your ignorance, but it begins to grate on my nerves. I repeat, I answer to no one but my chief, my village council, and my tribal council. I'll never answer to a woman and surely not to a slave."

"I knew the village would ridicule me," Catherine whispered hoarsely, shrinking away from him, not because she feared him but because she was hurt. Always he relegated her to being a slave. "But not you. I hadn't figured on your doing this to me." Her green eyes were accusing. "I thought you loved me."

Lone Wolf breathed deeply. He reached for Catherine, but she took another step backward. "I did not ridicule you, and I do love you," he said patiently. "My wager with Kee-lee was not meant to create such doubt in you." He held his hand out, looking at the ring. "A wager is meaningless unless one bets his most prized possession." He paused, letting the meaning sink in. "You, your love, your father's ring, and your handkerchief are my most prized possessions. I could offer Kee-lee no less."

"What if I had won?" she asked, her voice hoarse.

"You couldn't have and you didn't," he returned obdurately. "I am guided by reason, not emotion, when I place my wagers."

Catherine whispered, "Just as you are guided by reason in your marriage, not by emotion."

The muscle in Lone Wolf's cheek tensed; otherwise, he didn't let Catherine know how perfectly targeted her remark was, or how hard it hit him.

"And what valuable gift did you win?" Catherine asked quietly, her tone dull and lifeless. "Two sticks with deer sinew strung across one end!"

"They are his most prized possession."

The gentle reprimand hung suspended between them. Slowly Catherine followed his gaze to the floor. For a long time she stared at the lacrosse stick. Finally she turned and walked to the platform in the sleeping room. Unbanding her hair, she picked up the porcupine tail, brushed her hair, and plaited it.

"I'm giving you fair warning," she said in that same quiet tone as she went to the clothesline, "you'd better change your wager for the festival contests. Already I have knowledge of archery and boating, and I am quickly learning double ball." Her voice was muffled as she pulled the nightshirt over her head and tossed it across her trunk. Her back to him, she jerked her buckskin dress from the line.

"Catherine . . ."

The paleface slave was an enigma to Lone Wolf. The longer he was around her, the less he understood her. Rather than lauding him for his good judgment, she censured him because he hadn't wagered foolishly. She took the wager personally.

"Our games are different," he pointed out. "You have never competed with—"

"So you've said before," Catherine snapped. "But you're soon going to learn that people are people, Lone Wolf. They are not so different from one another."

Holding her dress in front of her, Catherine spun around. "I'm going to win. I'll be Scupperong's next champion, and I'll be a warrior woman."

Lifting her arms, her dress bundled above her head, she posed naked in front of him for a second time, her breasts uplifted, her midriff stretched. Then she dropped the buckskin over her head, letting it slide down the gentle curves of her body. Leaving the cornhurk dressing on her ankle, she put on her knee-high leggings.

"I like you as you are, Catherine," he said.

"You'll like me even better as a warrior." Holding the thongs in her hands, she laced the leggings. Pausing in the midst of her task, she lifted her face and stared somberly at him. "Perhaps you'll come to respect me." Not waiting to see his reaction, she dropped her head and started threading again.

"You are being stubborn, Catherine," Lone Wolf admonished, moving into the room to stand close to her. "You're not trying to understand—"

"No," Catherine interjected, standing up and shaking her legs to let her skirt fall over her moccasins and leggings. "I'm not trying to understand." She spun around. "I'm tired of being hurt, emotionally and physically, because all of you keep pointing out that I'm different from you, because I'm paleface not Indian. You want to be guided by reason," she charged, thumping her index finger on his chest. "You're going to get it. From this minute on, Lone Wolf, war chief of the Scupperongacs, I shall be guided by reason. No more emotion. Like you, I shall be a warrior."

Catherine flounced past him, not stopping until she reached the entry. As her hand closed around the handle of her racket, Lone Wolf caught her other arm. He jerked her around, glaring angrily into her face.

"No woman has ever spoken to me like this," he accused.

"You lie," Catherine returned sharply, not a whit

344

perturbed by the fury she saw brewing in the ebony eyes. "I just did." She jerked her arm from his loose clasp. "Now leave me be. While you reason and wager, I must practice for the contest." She walked to the door. "There are those who believe in me."

"I believe in you, Catherine." The words rang with truth.

"And I, too, believe in you, Cath-er-ine." Wise One walked into the wigwam, his eyes laughing at the young warrior who had been reduced to a fool by love and misguided words. He smiled at Catherine. "I have also brought you a gift." He held out a bow and an exquisitely designed deerskin quiver filled with arrows.

"I—I couldn't take your bow and arrows," she gasped.

"You cannot refuse," he told her kindly. "It is a gift of love. Also it has much magic which you are going to need."

Taking the quiver, Catherine suddenly grinned, and her eyes twinkled as she asked, "Are you a Turtle by chance, Great Chief?"

He smiled. "I am of the Turtle Clan, my daughter." Wise One angled his head over his shoulder. "Lone Wolf, why are you glaring so?"

"I am surprised," the stunned Lone Wolf replied. "This is truly a gift of great magnitude." His eyes on the feathers, he added, "These are your finest arrows." Being a warrior himself, Lone Wolf knew how long it took to amass arrows of such quality. The making of arrows was a painstaking job, requiring great care and skill. He reached into the quiver and extracted one. "All of these are of excellent quality, my chief," Lone Wolf said. "All of them boast eagle feathers."

Catherine took the arrow from him, and she turned the shaft around in her fingers; then she ran the tip of her finger along the slender length, touching the shallow grooves. Because her arrows had been crafted for target practice only, she was unfamiliar with the notches.

"What are these?"

"Lightning marks," Wise One replied. "They allow the blood to flow from the wound of an animal. This weakens the prey and leaves a trail of blood for the hunter to follow."

His index finger touched the end. "The magic in these arrows is great, my daughter. The feathers came from the wings of the mighty eagle. Like the eagle these arrows will fly fast and sure."

Catherine's eyes ran the length of the arrow. It was fletched with three split feathers, all from the same wing of the eagle, set at equal distances around the circumference of the shaft. Fastened with glue and lashed with sinew at both ends, the middle part of the feather was free.

"Thank you, Great Chief," Catherine murmured. "I will prove myself worthy of such an honorable gift."

"The arrows you will use," Wise One said, "but not the bow. It is much too large for you. We will hang it in your house to bring you magic, and I shall take you to the best bowmaker in Scupperong—Mo-no-ta-me. He shall make one that will fit you."

"Lone Wolf," Kee-lee's voice echoed through the wigwam seconds before he materialized through the door. Seeing Catherine and Wise One, he smiled his greeting; then he fastened his gaze on Lone Wolf. "It is time for us to meet at the ball field. Practice will begin in a few minutes."

Lone Wolf nodded, softly calling the wolf to his side. To Catherine he said, "I will send Little Flower to tend the wigwam." He paused at the door, reluctant to leave. Retracing his steps and coming to stand in front of her, he said low for her ears alone. "I wish you good magic today, my darling."

Catherine nodded, emotion once again clotting in her throat and stifling her breathing. Kee-lee slipped out of the wigwam, and Wise One, his bow in hand, walked into

346

the sleeping room, leaving the two of them alone.

Lone Wolf's hands curled gently around Catherine's shoulders, and he pulled her close to him. Then he lowered his head, his lips capturing hers in a long, warm kiss. Catherine's arms slipped around his neck, and she pressed herself into him, wishing they could become one together.

"Lone Wolf"—the singsong call resounded through the lodge—"they are expecting us at the ball ground . . . today."

Lone Wolf lifted his head, smiling lazily and warmly into Catherine's face. "I must go."

"You must," Wise One barked lightly from the entrance. "If you don't, I'll never get Catherine's bow measured and made." The old man walked to the platform and picked up Lone Wolf's rackets. Extending them, he said, "Here, my love-stricken warrior. Take them and go. Your woman will be here when your day is over."

"True, my chief," Lone Wolf conceded, "but I have not much longer to spend with her before I walk the trading path."

Turning, Lone Wolf joined Kee-lee, and the two of them trotted off to the ball field, the wolf sauntering behind. Later as Wise One and Catherine walked down the main street, Catherine spied a group of strange Indians who sat with several of the village chiefs on ceremonial mats in front of the townhouse. Language flowed from their hands as they signed and bartered their goods.

"Who are they?" Catherine asked curiously, her eyes running over their clothing—the heavy thigh-length buckskin jackets, the thick leggings and moccasins, the belts that circled their waists sheathing their war clubs and their knives.

"Iroquois," Wise One said. "They are already gathering for the trading party."

347

"Iroquois," Catherine murmured. Lone Wolf's sworn enemies; yet the men with whom he must travel on the trading expedition.

"And Lenape." Wise One pointed to another group of Indians who stood next to the ceremonial wigwam. "They come from . . ."

Catherine, however, wasn't listening to Wise One. Her attention was on the Iroquis braves—on one of the Iroquois braves in particular. Separated from the rest of the group, he leaned indolently against the townhouse, his arms folded across his chest. Though lean and wiry, his gaunt features were handsome, his cheekbones high and prominent. His lips were finely shaped, beautiful in their firmness. His hawk nose was clearly defined, and his eyes, closer to chocolate brown than black, glittered with interest.

So this was Lone Wolf's paleface slave! His eyes carefully moved from the top of her head to the bottom of her feet. This was the woman he had heard so much about since he had arrived in Scupperong. She was beautiful, he thought, his gaze ascending as thoroughly as it had descended. Slender and graceful, he noticed. Fair skin, flaming hair. He could understand Lone Wolf's killing for her. He would do the same! Even now he felt a tightening in his loins, a flicker of desire running through his veins. He would enjoy having such a woman grace his long house and warm his bed.

Catherine, compelled by the magnetic quality of the brave's gaze, tilted her head slightly, her green eyes locking with his brown ones. Although she appreciated the rugged handsomeness of the man, apprehension slivered through her. Discipline shielded the man's thoughts and intents from the woman, but her perceptions easily removed that invisible cover. Catherine saw the passion that flickered to life in his fathomless brown eyes; she felt the tenseness of his desires.

Marshaling all her strength, Catherine broke the

348

binding gaze. She half-listened to Wise One discuss the coming festival and the subsequent trading expedition, but she couldn't push the image of the Iroquois brave out of her mind. She had an eerie feeling of recognition.

"Cath-er-ine, is something wrong?"

The words jarred Catherine out of her stupor, and she swallowed, hastily shaking her head. "I'm—I'm fine," she said. "I was just thinking about the contest."

"Ahhh," Wise One responded. "You will prove yourself, my daughter. You have strong magic."

When they arrived at Mo-no-ta-me's wigwam, Wise One entered. Catherine, however, hesitated and cast a last apprehensive look over her shoulder at the Iroquois brave who still stared at her. Unable to shake off her fears, she walked through the opening to stand behind Wise One.

Sitting down, the great chief spoke with the old man. "My friend, I have a favor to ask of you." Wise One held a pouch of tobacco across the fire.

Mo-no-ta-me lifted his weathered face, looked at Catherine, and motioned her to sit down. "You would have me make a bow for the paleface, my chief?"

"No other hands can do it as well as yours," Wise One replied.

"They are twisted with age and pain," Mo-no-ta-me said, lifting arthritic hands above the fire.

"Still they are the most gifted in the land of the Scupperongacs."

Mo-no-ta-me filled his pipe with the tobacco which Wise One had given him, and the two men smoked in silence. Eventually Mo-no-ta-me stood, extending one of his gnarled hands. "Come." He stiffly motioned to Catherine.

As Catherine moved across the wigwam, he reached to the rafters, unhooking a long slender buckskin case. Slowly, with labored and painful movements, he pulled out a long hickory stick that was flat and tapered at

349

the ends.

"Stretch your left arm," he ordered.

Holding the hickory stick in one hand, he measured the distance from Catherine's right shoulder across her chest, down her outstretched left arm, to the tips of the fingers on her left hand.

"Have you ever used a bow before?" the old man asked.

"Aye," Catherine replied.

"Good," Mo-no-ta-me muttered, using his flint to notch the stick at the proper length. "I shall make you a bow powerful enough to send a well-aimed arrow through the side of a deer."

"Better to go through the center of a target to defeat Happy Woman," Catherine quipped.

"What kind of design do you want on your bow?" the old man asked, grunting his approval of the paleface.

Catherine didn't ponder the question. Already she knew her mark—that of the Forest Woman. She knelt close to the fire pit, moving one of the reed mats. Picking up a twig, she drew a beautiful but simple leaf design. Mo-no-ta-me looked at the design and studied it for a long time. When he had memorized every line and curve, he pulled the mat over the exposed dirt.

Using cornhusks to protect his hands, he picked up a heated, pointed stone from the fire and traced the design on the wood. With a smaller stone, he then scraped away the charred parts.

"I will do this many times, before it is finished," he told her. "When the decoration is complete, I will fill in the indentations with red pigments. Come back before the evening meal, and your bow will be ready for you."

"Also, my friend," Wise One said, "Cath-er-ine must have a war club."

Crouching on his feet and rocking back on his heels, Mo-no-ta-me nodded. He was quicker to answer than to move. Eventually he stood. Going to the platform that circled his wigwam, he opened a large basket and extracted several war clubs which he handed to Catherine.

"Clasp each of these in your hand one at a time and see which one feels best." Following his instructions, Catherine's hand closed over one handle after the other; then she brandished the clubs in the air. Finally after she had made her selection, Mo-no-ta-me said, "I make you a gift of this, paleface. It has my marks, but they have good magic in them."

As the day passed, members of the Turtle clan showered Catherine with presents and talismans. No-am-ee gave her a flint knife; another gave her a warrior's belt. They brought food and clothes; they brought tanned and worked skins. That evening after a day's practice at the ball field, Catherine wearily trudged into the wigwam, tilting her racket against the platform in the entry room without missing a step as she headed for the main room.

"Umm," she sniffed, thankful for the cheery presence of Little Flower. "What are you cooking? It smells delicious."

"Fish stew," Little Flower replied, adding, "Lone Wolf wants you to meet him at the river immediately."

Catherine smiled and slid to the floor beside the fire pit. She laid her bow down and shrugged her shoulder, allowing the quiver strap to fall free. "He can wait a few minutes," she murmured, tugging her knife and war club from her belt, and placing them by her side. "I've got to rest."

Unknotting the belt and pulling it from around her waist, she lay down and inhaled deeply. She enjoyed the comfort of the wigwam, the soft furs beneath her body, the warmth of the fire, and the tempting aroma of the food.

"How did the practicing go today?" Little Flower asked, patting corn cakes in her palms.

"Wonderful," Catherine announced grandly. "I

tripped Happy Woman twice and almost threw her over my shoulders once."

"Cath-er-ine!"

When Catherine heard No-am-ee's voice, she flipped over on her side, and propped up on an elbow. "Yes, my grandmother."

The old woman shuffled close to the fire and sat down, splaying her hands over the blaze. "Ma-wa-ska told me that you are a fast learner and that you did well today against Happy Woman."

"Thank you, Grandmother."

"There is one more thing which you must learn in order to defeat Happy Woman."

Catherine sat up. "What now?"

"You must learn to do the Woman's Dance."

"The Woman's Dance," Catherine mimicked, her voice shrill with incredulity. "Is that another contest?"

Little Flower giggled quietly. "No, it's not a contest," No-am-ee replied. "It's our custom to use this dance to begin our harvest festival."

"Why didn't you tell me sooner?"

"There was no hurry," the old woman answered. "You had enough on your mind, and I knew there was plenty of time for you to learn the dance."

Catherine chuckled, the sound lightly hinting at sarcasm. "Tell me about the dance, Grandmother."

"Let me, Grandmother," Little Flower begged, her face glowing. When No-am-ee smiled and nodded her permission, Little Flower said, "We have this dance on the first evening of the harvest festival. The celebration continues all night with dancing, laughter, and singing." She laid the third patty on a smooth round rock in the fire. "Friends give presents to one another during this dance—a pouch of tobacco, a headband, a pair of moccasins"—Little Flower shrugged—"whatever one wishes."

"Man to woman or woman to man?" Catherine

questioned, her interest thoroughly aroused.

"Just friend to friend," Little Flower replied, innocent of the direction in which Catherine's questions were headed.

"Will Lone Wolf dance with Little Doe?" Catherine asked No-am-ee.

The old woman gazed sorrowfully into the beautiful green eyes and wished her answer could be different. "He will give her the first gift of purchase."

Catherine had never felt such despair as she did at that moment. Like a blanket it covered her entire body, denying her the radiance of happiness, the breath of life. Almost suffocating from its oppression, she closed her eyes and blinked back the tears.

No-am-ee lifted her hand and touched Catherine. "I feel your hurt, my daughter, but I would have felt it more if you did not know."

Little Flower, not understanding Catherine's anguish, broke the silence. "When you give your friend the gift, Catherine, he thanks you by dancing with you, and he returns the honor by giving you a gift of equal value."

Catherine smiled weakly and stretched out on her back, gazing through the smoke hole. "What is the use of my learning the dance?" she asked. "There is no one to dance with me."

"Oh, yes, Cath-er-ine," Little Flower hurriedly assured her. "You have many friends who will dance with you."

"It would not be unlike Happy Woman to give you a gift." No-am-ee's dry retort crackled across the fire. "If you do not thank her with a dance, you will be disgraced."

Disgraced and heartbroken in one dance! Catherine thought, stifling bitter laughter.

As if the matter were settled, No-am-ee said, "Little Flower will teach you the dance, and the secret will be ours."

Little Flower grinned, sheer devilment glowing in her eyes. "Think how surprised Happy Woman will be to find that you have outsmarted her once again!"

Catherine turned her head and gazed into the small round face. The two friends smiled at one another. Sitting up, Catherine picked up her weapons, looping her quiver strap, her belt, and her bow over one arm and holding the knife and war club in each hand.

"All right, Grandmother," she conceded, "if I must learn to dance, I must." Again she allowed her soft, melancholy laughter to blend with the child's bubbling happiness.

"We must get you many gifts, Catherine," Little Flower gurgled. "You are going to need them."

"Aye," Catherine agreed. She smiled enigmatically. "And I must get one worthy of Happy Woman." And one for Lone Wolf, she thought.

Her mood somber, Catherine walked into the sleeping room and hung her bow and quiver from the rafters. She laid her knife and war club on the shelf above their bed; then she stepped across the room and slung her belt over the clotheslines. Sighing deeply, she hunched her shoulders and arched her throat, flexing her exhausted muscles.

"Cath-er-ine, do you mind if Little Flower eats the evening meal with Re-bekk-ana and me?" No-am-ee asked.

"This is becoming a habit," Catherine called, grabbing her drying skin from the peg. "What are you doing over there that's so important, Little Flower?" She reached for her cape and wrap around skirt and reentered the main room.

"Helping Grandmother sew," Little Flower answered, her face lowered, her eyes on the fire and the pots.

"Can one old woman have that much mending?" Catherine teased.

"Not mending," Little Flower answered, looking at

354

No-am-ee and chuckling softly. "She must have a new dress for the festival, so Re-bekk-ana and I are making it for her."

Catherine smiled fondly at her small friend. "As soon as Lone Wolf and I return, you may go."

"That is good," No-am-ee replied, winking at the little girl. "I will go now, Cath-er-ine."

Saying their goodbyes, No-am-ee and Catherine scurried out of the wigwam, No-am-ee in one direction, Catherine in the other. When Catherine arrived at the waterfall, Lone Wolf was not alone. Sitting on the incline above the river, he and several other braves huddled around a canoe, the outside of which they had just covered with pine pitch to make it waterproof. Lying not far from his beloved master was Wolf Friend.

Seeing her, Lone Wolf smiled and waved. "I'll be ready to bathe in a little while," he called out, walking down the hill to the banks of the river. Stooping, he tended the fire and laid his adze on the ground.

Acknowledging his greeting with a slight nod, Catherine dropped her clothes and deerskin to the ground and scampered up the incline toward the canoe. All thoughts of the Woman's Dance and of Lone Wolf's first gift of purchase were pushed from Catherine's mind as she ran her hands lovingly over the craft. She remembered that summer in England when she had helped Running Bear and Manteo make their canoe. When she rounded the bow, she saw the mark. She couldn't believe it; she looked again. Her mark—the design she had embroidered on Lone Wolf's pouch, the one she had drawn for Mo-no-ta-me that morning. Lifting her head, she looked at Lone Wolf who now stood, hands on hips.

He nodded. "Yours for the contest."

"Mine." Catherine whooped with joy, jumping to her feet and running down the hill. "You made this for me."

She threw herself into his arms with such force that

his feet slipped on the muddy banks of the river and they tumbled into the water. The other braves laughed heartily, enjoying Catherine's exuberance. Gathering their adzes, they quietly disappeared into the forest, leaving the lovers alone. Gasping for air when he surfaced, Lone Wolf laughed.

"Is drowning the thanks I receive?" he teased.

Tossing her head to get the water off her face and out of her eyes, Catherine wrapped her arms around Lone Wolf, and she pressed her lips against his, murmuring, "This is my thanks, darling."

Without breaking the kiss, he stood waist deep in the water, holding her in his arms. She wrapped her legs around his waist, sighing when his hands cupped her buttocks and pressed her feminine inner arch closer to his body.

The kiss of thanksgiving soon burst into flames of passion, their mouths opening wider as the blaze burned hotter. Lone Wolf headed toward the shore, but his foot caught on a root, and he fell, both of them tumbling into the cool shallow water.

Lone Wolf unlaced Catherine's neckline, his hands sweeping aside the buckskin to reveal the creamy softness of her breasts. Lowering his head, his mouth brushed over the swollen incline, his hands grazing her thighs as he pushed her skirt up around her waist. With frenzied movements, Catherine's hands unknotted Lone Wolf's belt, and his breechclout fell off.

Wanting each other with a hunger that precluded all preliminaries, Catherine arched her lower body, welcoming the thrust of his manhood. She gasped with pleasure when he filled her, and she undulated her hips with a violence and force that both surprised and pleased Lone Wolf. His lunges were deep but gentle, almost as fulfilling to her as the culmination of their desire. Crying her pleasure, her hands dug into his shoulders, and she buried her face in his chest. When they had shuddered into quietness, Lone Wolf lifted her, carrying her to the waterfall, and they bathed.

Later after they dressed, Lone Wolf spread his blanket on the ground near the fire and sat down. Catherine lay beside him, and much to her surprise Wolf Friend ambled out of the forest, lying beside both of them. In utter silence, the aftermath of complete love, Lone Wolf picked up her bow and strung it. When he had finished the task, he rose to his feet.

"Come," he said, "while it's yet day, let's go practice."

Extending a hand, he helped Catherine to her feet. He drew her to the edge of the clearing, where he hunted for a thick, flat piece of bark on which he scratched circles with a sharp stone. Then he peeled the bark from the center spot and the third ring so that the darker inner bark showed. He set this target against a tree and stood back to watch. Knowing she needed practice and must become familiar with her weapons, his advice and instruction were sparse. As she shot, he collected her arrows, few of which hit the target.

When she tired of archery, Lone Wolf picked up the tomahawk and showed her how to use it. That lesson, however, was doomed from the beginning. Unaccustomed to the crude tomahawk and out of practice, Catherine was clumsy in her attempts to wield and throw it. Her grimaces and body contortions had Lone Wolf howling with laughter.

"You'll regret your laughter," Catherine stormed as she stalked away to gather her weapons. "When I become the village champion, we'll see who's laughing the loudest."

Lone Wolf quickly caught up with her. "Ah, Catherine, my love," he said, wiping tears of amusement from his eyes, "I couldn't help but laugh. The way you—" He couldn't finish his sentence. Wave after wave of quiet laughter rolled from his chest as he saw her teetering and tottering when she tried to fling the war club. Only once did it land more than a few feet in front of her.

After the evening meal, Catherine cleaned the dishes and put them away. She was too tired to work on her mending so she sorted the moccasins and leggings, putting them into a basket close to the fire. She would leave them for Little Flower to do. Glancing at Lone Wolf, she saw him band several torchlights together.

"What are you doing?" she asked.

Lighting the large torch from the fire, he beckoned her to follow him. "I need to teach you how to use the canoe."

"You don't have to—" Catherine began, but Lone Wolf cut her off.

"I don't have to, but I will. I don't want you to disgrace yourself in front of our visitors." Catherine stiffened. "Hurry," he enjoined. "We don't have much time."

Lone Wolf's laughter had chafed at Catherine that day, but she had tolerated it, thinking his motives to be pure. Indeed, she had almost confessed to him that she knew how to canoe. But this last comment cut her to the quick. Lone Wolf wasn't teaching her out of love; he was doing it because of his aversion to ridicule. Like Wise One and Sunflower Woman and No-am-ee, his purpose was totally selfish; he wanted to impress the Lumbroans. He, too, wanted to impress Little Doe.

"Go get Little Flower," Catherine said quietly, striving to project a civility she was far from feeling. "She's working at No-am-ee's. I'll meet you at the river as soon as she gets here to watch the fire."

By the time Catherine joined Lone Wolf, he was standing at the water's edge, the torch glowing from the bow of the dugout, the wolf already perched in the canoe. When Lone Wolf began to give her instructions, she said loftily, "I know something about boating."

Lone Wolf grinned and his eyebrows rose, the glow of the torch highlighting his visage. "About as much as you

358

know about throwing the war club!" He chuckled softly and picked up his paddle. Getting into the canoe first, he moved to the bow with Wolf Friend and rested his paddle in the water, waiting for Catherine. He was prepared to enjoy her spill. Anticipating his thoughts, Catherine smiled; she, too, was prepared to enjoy this lesson. She lay her paddle in the stern, gave the canoe a powerful push and jumped in, holding on to the sides. She balanced her weight evenly on the sides, and the canoe sailed smoothly away from shore. Looking at the dumfounded man, she picked up the paddle and with one powerful stroke headed the dugout into the middle of the river.

"Running Bear taught me," she quietly announced as they paddled down the river. "And please don't be concerned about my disgracing you in front of the Lumbroan chief and his daughter. I won't." Her chuckle blended with the soft ripple of the water and the dipping of the paddle.

From that day forward Catherine's routine changed. Every spare moment she practiced for the contests. In the morning she hurried to the ball field and practiced with the women. She learned to stay on her feet, to maneuver and to outmaneuver her opponents. Daily her accuracy and her speed improved; still Happy Woman always outdid her. After the games were over, Catherine slipped into the forest by herself and practiced her marksmanship with bow and arrow, war club, and knife, her skills continually improving. During the evenings she and Lone Wolf relaxed, canoeing up and down the river.

The day the festival began, Catherine stood in the clearing practicing one last time. Gracefulness had replaced her clumsiness; knowledge, her ignorance. With flowing coordination, she hurled the war club, the weapon whining through the air, the handle vibrating when the blade thwacked into the tree trunk.

"That's for you Happy Woman," Catherine gloated.

She tugged her knife loose, balancing the blade between her fingers. With a fluid movement, she spun and threw it, the blade sailing smoothly through the air to land in the center of the target. She laughed exultantly.

"And that is for you, Lone Wolf."

"What is for me?" Lone Wolf asked, walking into the clearing, holding both his rackets over one shoulder.

"That!" she cried jubilantly, pointing her finger at the knife.

Lone Wolf looked at the target, and he smiled his praise. His eyes landed on the tomahawk that protruded from the trunk. "I think Happy Woman will find you a worthy opponent, Catherine."

And I think Little Doe is going to find me a worthy adversary too, Catherine thought. She walked to the target and removed her knife. "That is all I can ask." She moved to the tree, tugging her war club loose.

"How are you doing with the bow and arrow?"

Catherine shrugged. "I'm good, but not nearly as accurate as I would be if I had the bow Father had made for me."

They fell into step and walked back to the wigwam. When they arrived, they laid their rackets and weapons on the platform in the entry room, and they entered the main room. Because they would eat with the village tonight, Little Flower had prepared no supper and as soon as they walked into the wigwam, she jumped to her feet, eager to be on her way.

Moving into the sleeping room, Catherine walked to the clothesline and looked at her new dress—the one that Cor-on-a-me had sewn for her. Slowly she took it off the line and held it as she watched Lone Wolf undress and then put on the clothes she had embroidered for him. After he had combed and braided his hair, he placed a colorful headband around his forehead and looped necklaces over his head. But something was missing. . . .

"Where are your wolf-fang necklaces?" Catherine demanded with a start.

Lone Wolf automatically lifted his hand, touching the shell necklace that had replaced his pearls. Catherine dropped her dress onto the platform and crossed to him, her gaze falling on his ringless finger. After an eternity, she lifted her face.

"Where is my father's ring?" Her voice trembled with anger.

Lone Wolf's eyes were frigid with displeasure, his voice chilly with reproof. "Have I not told you before, Catherine," he barked, "that you are not to question my actions?"

"I don't care what you've told me," Catherine hissed. "I want to know. Have you lost them in a wager?"

Without answering, Lone Wolf turned. Catherine flew at him, her fists pounding on his shoulders. Wolf Friend leaped to his feet and bared his teeth, but Catherine didn't notice. "Tell me," she cried. "What have you done with your necklaces and the ring?"

Lone Wolf spun about, his hands banding around Catherine's wrists. "That, Catherine, is my concern and mine only."

Lone Wolf's words had barely echoed into silence when Kee-lee entered the wigwam, carrying a large, lidded basket over his arm. "Here you are, Lone Wolf," he announced with a flourish, ignoring the tension between Lone Wolf and Catherine. "The gift of purchase."

Lone Wolf dropped Catherine's hands. "Thank you," he said, taking the basket and setting it on the platform. He turned to Catherine. "I would speak with Kee-lee alone." Catherine stood defiantly for a second, her silence and stance more challenging than an argument. "Go dress!"

361

His command brooked no disobedience, yet Catherine stared at him for a moment longer before she brushed past him. Her back was erect, her shoulders squared. Once inside the room, however, her defiance evaporated, and she wilted on the platform. She balled her hands together, digging her nails into the soft flesh of her palms. In the other room, Lone Wolf spoke.

"Did you have any trouble making the trade?"

"None, my brother. They are a greedy people." Kee-lee hesitated; then he said, "The palefaces think you are going to marry Catherine."

"So I am," Lone Wolf returned.

"They have no idea that you're going to marry both women," Kee-lee added. Another poignant pause. "How do you think the Lumbroans will feel about this?"

"I'm fulfilling the conditions of their agreement for peace," Lone Wolf barked, his voice on edge. "They have no right to dictate my actions."

"Our tribal council will not mind that you keep Catherine for your slave, but, my brother, even they will advise against taking her for your second bride."

Lone Wolf didn't answer Kee-lee's allegation. He knew it to be true. Already Wise One had spoken to him about the matter.

"I'm sorry," Kee-lee said. "I know where your heart lies and—"

"I don't want your pity or your sympathy." Lone Wolf covered his pain and grief with anger. "I am Lone Wolf, war chief of the Scupperongacs, and I will do what I must. My duty to my people will come first."

"I offer you no pity," Kee-lee responded quietly, "and very little sympathy." He smiled sadly. "I understand what you must do." He paused. "I am prepared to buy the paleface slave from you, Lone Wolf."

"What!" Lone Wolf thundered, his voice bellowing incredulity. At the same time that Lone Wolf spoke,

362

Catherine bolted straight up. She had always liked Kee-lee, but she had never once entertained the thought that he wanted her. She waited breathlessly for Lone Wolf's reply.

"You heard me," Kee-lee answered. "I want to buy the slave."

"You have always desired Catherine, haven't you?" Lone Wolf snarled. "From the first moment that you saw her, you wanted her in your wigwam."

Kee-lee nodded. "Yes, my brother, I have desired her from the beginning, and now that you are giving Little Doe the first gift of purchase for marriage, I am asking for Catherine."

"Why?" Lone Wolf growled.

"I want to marry her," Kee-lee returned. "I want to build her a wigwam. I want her to be my wife and the mother of my children."

"No," Lone Wolf snarled, his hands clenching into fists at his sides. "I will not part with Catherine. After I marry the Lumbroan princess, I shall marry her."

"I learned many things while I was in the paleface settlement," Kee-lee said quietly. "The palefaces do not believe in taking more than one wife. They will be most unhappy when they learn that Catherine will be your second wife."

"I don't care what they think," Lone Wolf muttered defiantly. "Catherine belongs to me, and she'll do what I tell her to do."

"Then, my friend, I do offer you pity and sympathy. You are going to need it because you're walking a difficult path. But, most of all, my brother, I understand how you feel; I know what you must do."

Lone Wolf walked to the platform and took the lid off the basket. As his fingers grazed his first gift of purchase, Lone Wolf murmured, "I just wish Catherine could understand."

Chapter XVII

Although the image of Lone Wolf dancing with Little Doe and giving her the first gift of purchase haunted Catherine, she took her time in dressing. When she finally stepped out of the wigwam, her face was beautifully made up, and her berry red lips were curved in a friendly smile. Her back was straight, and her head was tilted defiantly. Carrying a basket of gifts over her arm, she walked up the street to the side of the square where the women were grouped together. When she saw a gnarled hand waving through the air, a wrinkled face smiling, Catherine hurriedly made her way to No-am-ee. She lowered the basket to the ground; then she sat down beside the old woman. She smiled and spoke to those sitting around her.

When the greetings were over, the gossip and news shared, she allowed her eyes to sweep over the growing crowd. Her gaze landed on the handsome features of Lone Wolf who sat conversing with the tribal chiefs seated on either side of Wise One. Next to Lone Wolf sat Kee-lee, but he wasn't talking. He raised his pensive eyes and gazed across the square at her. Catherine remembered the conversation he and Lone Wolf had had, and she smiled her thanks at the young warrior. Lone Wolf caught the gesture, and he glared, first at her, then at Kee-lee.

Catherine returned the glower, never lowering her eyes or flinching from his harsh gaze. When Lone Wolf finally broke his stare to answer a question he had been asked, Catherine turned her head and looked at Little Doe who sat at the top of the square with Sunflower Woman. She is young, and she is beautiful, Catherine thought, looking at the thick, glossy braids that framed the Lumbroan princess' delicate, oval face. The buff-colored buckskin she wore enhanced her olive brown skin and her jet-black hair. Little Doe, as if feeling Catherine's visual touch, lifted her face at that moment, and the two women gazed curiously at one another across the village square.

Little Doe's almond-shaped eyes were large and winsome, her lips sensuously full. A tentative smile, Catherine noticed, lurked at the corners of her mouth, but deep in the recesses of those beautiful dark eyes Catherine could see the girl's apprehension and fear. Involuntarily Catherine responded to the sweetness of Little Doe's gaze. Despite the agony of her soul, despite her loss, she reached out to the frightened girl with a smile. Little Doe's lips twitched into a full smile just before she demurely dropped her head.

Wise One stood and walked to the huge fire in the center of the square. He dropped tobacco on the flames, offering incense to Manitou, and he lifted the sacred pipe to the heavens. When his seven chants of prayer ended, the village dancer—a member of the Wolf Clan—trotted onto the field. After he had circled the fire seven times, the men and boys of the Wolf Clan rose and followed him in single file. The women and girls of the Wolf Clan formed another circle outside that of the men, and the ritual dancing continued until each clan had followed suit, every dancer dropping his sacrifice of tobacco onto the fire.

365

When the religious ceremony ended, the people returned to their places, women and men again grouped separately. With great hilarity they feasted, talking and visiting with one another. Eventually the musicians and singers migrated to the center of the ceremonial grounds, where they began to play and sing softly. An excited hush descended on the crowd. Hurriedly the women picked up the bowls and spoons, cleaned them, and stacked them near the fire. People grabbed their baskets, enigmatic smiles hovering on their lips as they pondered the giving of gifts.

Sunflower Woman opened her basket and extracted a beautiful dress embroidered with colored quills. Standing, she moved to the center of the grounds. She looped the dress over her arm and she began to dance, circling the fire. Spellbound, Catherine watched the older woman sway back and forth, her arms and legs moving to the ever-increasing rhythm of the drums and rattles. When Sunflower Woman eventually stopped, she stood in front of Little Doe. Smiling, she handed the maiden the buckskin garment.

Little Doe took the dress from Sunflower Woman. Standing in front of the chief's wife, she looked at the buckskin, and she thanked Sunflower Woman before she laid the gift on her blanket. Then she extended her hands, and the two women danced around the fire. When the dance ended, Little Doe gave Sunflower Woman a fur cape. Caught up in the beauty of the moment, Catherine was entranced. She watched the dancers as, one by one, they rose and danced after offering and receiving their gifts.

She was so absorbed in the celebration that she momentarily forgot that Lone Wolf would be giving Little Doe his first gift of purchase. When he stood, she caught her breath, watching the glow of the fire as it painted him golden. No matter how angry she might be with him, no matter how hurt, Catherine felt a tremor of excitement ripple through her as she looked at him. He was one of the most majestic men she had ever known. Slowly he moved to the beat of the music, his lean, muscle-corded body graceful and flowing. Catherine had to admire his fluid grace. In an almost trancelike state, she heard the drums stop. She saw Lone Wolf stop in front of Little Doe, and her eyes opened in surprise when she saw him hand the young woman a white linen nightshirt. Catherine caught her breath. Her lungs hurt; her heart ached. She closed her eyes when Little Doe rose and danced with Lone Wolf. She couldn't bear to watch. Blinking back her tears, she lunged to her knees, prepared to run away, but No-am-ee's hand darted out and grasped her wrist.

"No, Catherine," she whispered, pulling her back, "you can't leave. No matter how heavy your heart, no matter how grieved you are, you must remember that you are now a warrior woman. You cannot run away. If you do, you will disgrace—"

"I know," Catherine snapped bitterly. "I will disgrace Lone Wolf in front of the Lumbroans."

The old woman shook her head, saying softly so that only the young woman she held would hear her, "No, Cath-er-ine, you would disgrace yourself in front of the Scupperongacs and the Lumbroans." No-am-ee's hand uncurled, and she lifted it to Catherine's face, wiping the tears from her cheeks. "I love you, Cath-er-ine, and I would not see you hurt." She sighed. "But I can do nothing to ease the hurt Lone Wolf's marriage to Little Doe inflicts on you. Manitou has chosen the path each of us must walk." She ran her hands down the smoothness of Catherine's braids. "But I can keep you from hurting yourself through disgrace."

Sniffling, Catherine forced a tiny smile, and she nodded her head. "I will be brave, my grandmother, and I promise that I won't disgrace you, the Turtle Clan, or myself."

"Good," the old woman declared curtly, folding her arms across her bosom. "I think perhaps it is now your time to dance."

Catherine's eyes flew open when she saw Lone Wolf dance up to her. Her jaw went slack, and she blinked in surprise. Shock had rendered her speechless. Lone Wolf was breathing raggedly, and his chest was heaving. He stood silently in front of her, holding out his hands.

Angry, quivering inside, Catherine wanted to refuse to dance with him, but she found her body responding to his silent injunction even as her brain recoiled. She slowly rose to stand before him. Then she walked by his side to the center of the square. Remembering Little Flower's instructions, she gave no indication that she knew him. He held his hands out, and she laid hers in his. He smiled into Catherine's eyes, but she was too hurt, too furious over their unfinished argument, to return the gesture. Soberly, they faced each other and slowly circled around the fire to the rhythm of the buckskin drum and the low chanting of the singers. Their eyes locked, baring their souls.

When they stopped dancing, both of them stood in the shadowed light of the fire, a fine sheen of perspiration gleaming on their faces. Lone Wolf reached for his pouch, and he untied the thongs. When he lowered his head, Catherine, caught in the magic of the moment, lowered hers also. She saw Lone Wolf thump the buckskin into his hand. Fascinated, she watched the gold band roll across his palm, waver back and forth, then finally drop to the ground. Lone Wolf picked it up between his thumb and index finger.

"This is for you," he said.

Catherine couldn't believe what was happening. He was returning her father's ring. She breathed deeply, and her body tensed. Disappointment overcame her anger. She lifted her face and stared at Lone Wolf. He curled a hand around her shoulder, and shook her gently. "Look at it," he commanded, holding the ring up so that the firelight reflected on the inscription. "Read the words to me."

Catherine reached for the ring, but he didn't turn it loose. Catching his wrist with one hand, she twisted his arm until she saw the words. Slowly she read: "To you, my darling Catherine, with all my love—Lone Wolf."

Transfixed, Catherine stared at the small band, finally noticing the beautiful design of overlapping leaves. She lifted her face, her lips tremulous, and her voice wavered with her soul-felt emotion.

"Where did you get it?" Her throat was dry; her voice a hoarse whisper.

"I traded my pearl necklaces for it," he told her. Thumping the pouch into his palm a second time, he extracted her father's ring. "So they would get the words right, I sent your father's ring with Kee-lee."

In numb silence, Catherine watched as Lone Wolf reached for the lifeless hand that hung by her side. He raised it. With one hand he parted her fingers, and with the other he slipped the ring over her fourth finger, gently snugging it in place.

"I give you this ring, Catherine Graystone, as a symbol of my undying love and commitment to you. You will always be a treasured wife of the Lone Wolf." He spoke in Scupperongac.

Catherine's eyes glittered with unshed tears. She stretched her hand out and gazed lovingly at the gold band. Finally she reached out and took her father's ring. She looked into Lone Wolf's rugged, gaunt face, and she knew at this moment her warrior was most vulnerable. In front of his people, in front of the Lumbroans, he was announcing his love for her. She might not be the first wife, but she was his first love.

Catherine slipped the ring over his fourth finger. "I gave you this ring as a gift of willing love," she whispered in Scupperongac, lifting her face to gaze into his eyes. "I put it on your hand as a symbol of my enduring love but not as a symbol of my willingness to be your slave, your concubine, or one wife of many." She whispered, "If you love me, Lone Wolf, please free me and let me return to my people. Don't keep me a slave bound to your side."

For a seemingly endless second they stared at one another.

"I repeat, Catherine. I cannot—I will not—let you go."

Lone Wolf caught her hands in his, and he began to sway to the tempo of the drums and rattles. Gracefully, Catherine swayed with him, following his movements for several circles around the fire. Then she took the lead. She smiled at his surprise as she stamped from heel to toe, leading him to where No-am-ee sat. Once they were standing by the old woman, Catherine knelt in front of her basket. She lifted the lid and pulled out the beautiful white shirt that shimmered in the golden orange of the firelight.

"As you have given me a gift," she murmured emotionessly, faultless in her adherence to Scupperon-gac custom, "so have I one for you." Shaking the wrinkles out of the shirt, she held it out to him.

Lone Wolf took it and held it up, his face brightening as he fingered the soft material. His eyes touched each dainty stitch of embroidery in the colorful design. Then he touched the lace that decorated the ruffles of the cuffs.

Because of the way she felt, Catherine couldn't fully enjoy the hushed sounds of approval from the crowd. "Put it on," she enjoined.

Not waiting for a second bidding, Lone Wolf untied his belt and dropped it to the ground. He unlaced the neckline of his buckskin shirt, and he drew it over his head. As the firelight glistened across the smooth expanse of his torso, Catherine noticed the pink scar that slashed his chest; she saw the tiny dots where the needle had pierced his skin. He slid one arm through a billowing sleeve, then the other. He pushed the buttons through the buttonholes. When he had finished, Catherine returned to her basket and lifted out a piece of vibrant red material. The crowd gasped with pleasure as she wrapped the sash around his waist.

"The shirt is for peace and friendship," she murmured. "The sash is for victory."

Lone Wolf rubbed his fingers over the silky texture of the material, and he lifted the fringed tassle that hung almost to his feet. "Thank you, Catherine," he said, his voice full of love and gratitude.

He lifted his face and gazed into Catherine's eyes, his love merging with her hurt and disappointment. They were so caught up in their own world that neither of them was aware of the pensive eyes on them. Flying Eagle and Little Doe watched this exchange with set faces, Kee-lee wistfully. While from the outer periphery, the Iroquois warrior looked on hungrily. He had admired the paleface from the first moment he had seen her, and he had wanted her. But now he found himself wanting her even more. Like everyone else, he had seen that this woman was more than a slave to the war chief of the Scupperongacs. Lone Wolf loved the paleface. The Iroquois chuckled. How complete his revenge would be!

Out of breath, Catherine sat next to No-am-ee and watched Lone Wolf make his way back to Wise One. She watched as the Indians fingered the material of his shirt and sash, but eventually she returned her attention to the square that had become a center of frenzied merriment. All around her, Indians were dancing with one another or exchanging gifts. She laughed with them, clapping her hands in time to the music and joining in the loud, lusty singing. Out of the corner of her eye she saw Happy Woman, and she laughed. She had been unprepared for Lone Wolf's gift, but she was prepared for the champion of the Beavers.

371

Catherine leaped to her feet at the same time that Happy Woman stood. The two women glared at each other across the distance that separated them. Then a slow, menacing smile quirked Happy Woman's lips, and she rubbed the palm of her hand over her copper medallion. Catherine smiled, glad she had learned the Squaw Dance. Reaching into her basket, she pulled out a beautiful chest, and she began to move her feet in rhythm to the drums and rattles. Steadily she danced toward Happy Woman.

Catherine's confidence shattered Happy Woman's moment of revenge. The Indian woman was so puzzled, she missed her footing, and she stumbled. Upon regaining her balance, she swayed from side to side, her smile sickly. Never missing a step and in perfect time with the drums, Catherine moved closer and closer to her adversary. Intent on hearing as well as seeing what was happening, the crowd hushed. They stared at the dumfounded Beaver champion. They watched the smiling Turtle champion.

"I bring you a gift," Catherine said, holding out the box. "A gift worthy of a champion." She released the small lock and set the box down in front of the Indian woman. She lifted the beautiful piece of silver. "A powder box." Taking off the lid, she dipped the puff and splattered the fine, white powder all over Happy Woman's face. "A matching brush and the mirror," she added, holding up each as she spoke.

Happy Woman reached out a tentative hand, and she ran her finger over the box. She lifted the puff to her face, and she smelled the scent. She felt the softness. Then she held the mirror up and looked in astonishment at her reflection. She touched the bristle of the brush, and she turned it over, tracing the etching. After she had looked at each piece and had touched it, she carefully replaced them in the chest. Slowly she looked at Catherine, hatred gleaming in the depths of her eyes.

"Thank you, Cath-er-ine," she said, holding her hands out.

After she and Catherine had danced around the fire seven times, Happy Woman stopped. The paleface had outsmarted her again. Now Happy Woman had to give her a gift of equal value or be ridiculed by the entire tribe. She had to give her the object that she loved most. Venomous hatred surged through Happy Woman. Never in her life had she been so disgraced and humiliated. Her arms rose, and her fingers touched the copper medallion that hung around her neck. The crowd sucked in its breath, watching the Beaver champion.

Pulling the string of shell and copper from over her head, Happy Woman walked closer to Catherine. She looped the necklace over Catherine's head. "I give you my victor's medallion," she declared. Then she spun around and returned to her seat. Her eyes glittered with hatred and her face was set in uncompromising lines, but she stared straight ahead, otherwise calm and impassive.

Suddenly boisterous shouts erupted from the crowd, and the dancing became more frenzied. Catherine returned to No-am-ee's blanket and sat down, content to watch. But within moments Little Flower approached her. The child smiled and handed Catherine a fur cape.

"This is for you when Old Man Winter comes," Little Flower said. "Grandmother helped me sew it for you."

Catherine rubbed her hands over the rich fur; then she snuggled her face into its softness.

"And this is for the contest," Little Flower continued, handing Catherine a set of leggings, a breechclout, and a shirt. Smiling, she proudly admitted, "I did the embroidery myself." She pointed to the leaves. "Lone Wolf drew the design for me."

Laughing, Catherine lifted her face. "This is what kept you at Grandmother's wigwam so much of the time?" Giggling, Little Flower bobbed her head. "Well, my little friend, I have a gift for you." Catherine lifted the lid to

373

her basket, and she brought out the cornhusk doll in her right hand. She held it out to Little Flower. Then she extended her left hand.

Little Flower gasped. Catherine had made another cornhusk doll—a man who was dressed in paleface clothes. The child's round face lit up, and she could hardly restrain her enthusiasm.

"Oh, Cath-er-ine," she squealed delightedly, "these are beautiful!"

Carrying a doll in each hand, the child ran to Cor-an-a-me. After she laid her treasures in her mother's lap, she returned to Catherine and held her hands out.

"I would thank you, Cath-er-ine."

The dancing continued throughout the night, but Catherine was too weary to stay. Tomorrow the contests would begin, and she wanted to be ready. Her arms laden with gifts of love, she finally stumbled through the entry room, past the napping wolf, into the wigwam. She set the basket on the floor, and she quickly made the bed. In the soft glow of the moonlight that came through the smoke hole, Catherine undressed, first pulling the copper medallion over her head and looking at the picture drawings.

When she had laid it on the shelf above the bed, she pulled off her pearls and wolf fangs, and she ran her fingers over the polished teeth. Time was running out. Her warrior loved her, but he intended to marry the princess first. What was she going to do? She placed the pearls on the shelf beside the medallion.

When she had slipped out of her moccasins and unlaced her leggings, she pulled her dress over her head. Too tired to care, she dropped her clothes on the floor and left them lying there as she crawled between the blankets, welcoming their warmth. She lay, wide awake and pensive, for a long time. In the background she heard the singers and the musicians, the whooping and hollering. By the time Lone Wolf came to bed and held her, she was too deep in the arms of slumber to awaken.

Little Doe sat on the floor of the guesthouse, holding the nightshirt in both hands. In the orange glow of the fire she was beautiful. When her father had told her of her coming marriage to the Scupperongac war chief, she had been devastated. She had never thought about marrying a warrior from another tribe, and certainly not of marrying the war chief of the Scupperongacs. Little Doe was aware of Lone Wolf's reputation, and she feared such a man, such a warrior, as he. Tonight she had seen the legend himself. Never had she seen such a magnificent brave. Never had any maiden received such a beautiful first gift of purchase.

She sank into the soft furs and leaned her back against the platform. At first she had been angry when she had heard rumors of Lone Wolf's paleface slave. Indeed, she had been furious when she had learned that he intended to make the slave his wife so soon after his marriage to her. That very night she had been humiliated when he had danced with the slave, and her wrath had been kindled when he'd made his declaration of love to the slave.

At the same time, Little Doe's fury as well as her fear was slightly appeased. She had immediately liked Catherine. Just as quickly she had understood that Lone Wolf loved the paleface. He was marrying Catherine because he loved her, not because he wanted to humiliate the Lumbroans. This understanding brought Little Doe a modicum of peace.

Little Doe would be proud to be the wife of Lone Wolf and to be the mother of his children. She wanted to be an instrument for peace between her people and the Scupperongacs. But being a gentle, loving soul, Little Doe feared a man like Lone Wolf, and she was wise enough to know that she would not be able to command

375

the love of such a man. When Little Doe had seen
Catherine, she had known that Catherine was a woman
who could match the hot, fiery passions of the war chief.
She and Catherine, Little Doe reasoned, would get along
very well; they could easily share a wigwam together. She
would tend the house, and Catherine would be the
warrior woman.

Valiantly fighting against the fears and apprehensions
that were closing in on her, Little Doe stood and walked
outside the wigwam. Leaving the festive sounds far
behind, she moved to the river's edge. As she watched the
silent ripples in the water, she heard a soft approach, but
she didn't turn. She was surprised; she hadn't expected
Lone Wolf to come to her.

The closer he came, the more her body trembled. She
was excited by his nearness, but she was also afraid. She
had never been touched by a man before, and her virgin
body paradoxically yearned for a man's possessive touch
yet fought against it.

"Good evening, Little Doe."

The words touched the Indian maiden; their gentle
tones caressed her soul, chasing away the final remains of
her fear. She turned around and looked the warrior full
in the face.

"You . . ." she whispered. "What are you doing
here?"

Kee-lee stopped a foot from her, and again he stared
into her face. "Forgive me," he murmured. "I didn't
mean to frighten you."

"You haven't," she replied, her beautiful lips curving
into a welcoming smile. "You just surprised me. I—I
expected—"

"I was out walking," Kee-lee told her before she could
say Lone Wolf's name. "I had many things on my mind."

Little Doe nodded. "I, too, had to get away so I could
think."

The moonlight flowed gracefully over Little Doe's

petite figure, cloaking her in a heavenly beauty that took Kee-lee's breath away. He had thought her pretty when he'd seen her earlier, but now her delicate features were softly sculpted by the moonbeams.

"I think perhaps you have the same worries and concerns that I do, my Scupperongac warrior," Little Doe said softly. Kee-lee looked down at her, his face expressive. "We are in love with people who are in love with one another."

Kee-lee opened his mouth. He wanted to deny the charge, but he couldn't. He smiled sadly and nodded his head. "How did you know?"

Little Doe chuckled quietly. "You had eyes for no one else."

"And you love Lone Wolf?" Kee-lee asked.

"I don't know whether I love him," Little Doe admitted, not stopping to wonder over confiding in a stranger, "but I don't welcome the idea of his taking a second wife immediately after marrying me."

"You don't have to accept the gift of purchase," Kee-lee pointed out. He suddenly wanted to protect this tiny woman who was being used as a pawn by the two tribes.

"Yes." She sighed. "I must accept the gift of purchase. You know that as well as I do."

Falling into step the two of them walked the bank of the river, stopping every so often to talk, their gentle laughter singing through the autumn forest.

Dressed in the clothes Little Flower had given her and haloed by the morning sunlight that spilled through the smoke hole, Catherine stood beside the platform in the sleeping room. Lifting her hands, she tied No-am-ee's headband around her forehead. Then she hooked her war club and knife in her belt, and walked to the rafter from which her quiver was suspended. She caught the wide strap in the palm of her hand and looped it over her head.

Flexing her shoulder, she adjusted Wise One's gift on her back. In her left hand she carried her bow, and when she walked through the entry room, she picked up her double-ball racket with her right. Ready now, she stood, waiting for No-am-ee to come get her.

As No-am-ee walked down the street, she saw the warrior woman standing in front of the wigwam. A sunbeam fought its way through the branches of the trees and framed Catherine in a glorious aura. No-am-ee couldn't help but catch her breath at such a vision of loveliness. The old woman's gait turned into a shuffle, and she shielded her eyes with her crippled hand. When she stood in front of the paleface, No-am-ee's weathered face crinkled in a thoughtful frown. Catherine's hair glistened as brightly as the copper medallion she wore around her neck. Her eyes, the color of the forest in springtime, glittered with challenge. Her stance bespoke her courage and confidence. The morning breeze lifted wisps of her auburn hair and fanned them across her face; her neckband thongs gently swirled.

No-am-ee had suspected from the first moment she had seen the paleface. Now she knew!

"Are you ready?" No-am-ee asked.

"I am," Catherine replied, her voice firm and steady.

"Come then." No-am-ee impatiently crooked her hand. "We have much to do if we're to be ready by the time Elder Brother, the Sun, is directly overhead."

"What is going to happen?" Catherine asked.

"We will go through the purification ceremony," No-am-ee told her, leading the way to a secluded spot in the forest. "First, I will purify the Turtle ball team; then I will dedicate you to Manitou as the Turtle champion."

Soon Catherine stood with the other members of the Turtle Clan. She watched No-am-ee shuffle to the fire and bend over the pots, muttering as she stirred her smelly concoctions. The old woman chopped more roots and herbs, dropping them into the boiling pots. Then she picked up her rattles and rose to her feet.

"Hah-yaaaaaaah! Hah-yaaaaaaah!"

No-am-ee's piercing chant shattered the tranquillity of the forest, and her feet thundered their message on the ground. She stamped heel and toe, she snorted, she cackled, she crowed. She shuffled to the left, she shuffled to the right, she shuffled all around the fire. Then with a crouch, a spring, a grunt, and a wheeze, she threw the tobacco into the fire. Her song and dance ended with the sacrifice of incense.

After the purification ritual was over, the other Turtle players withdrew to a secluded place in the forest, leaving Catherine alone with No-am-ee. Hours later, the Turtle Clan chief led the Turtles to the sacred spot, and they gathered around Catherine praying with her for victory and sharing her dance. Finally, No-am-ee walked to the stick she had inserted in the ground earlier. When she had measured the shadow, she nodded her head, and the reverent moment was over. Some laughing and talking, others jesting and wagering, the congregation boisterously moved to the Big House. Catherine, however, stayed behind with No-am-ee.

The two of them walked through the empty village to the Big House. No-am-ee and Catherine arrived at the same time that Happy Woman and her shaman did. The two old women walked to the door of the sacred house, and they waited. Wise One offered the sacrifice of tobacco, and he filled the sacred pipe, lifting it to Manitou. Then he called for Catherine and Happy Woman.

Each young woman, led by her shaman, walked to the center of the room. Wise One extended the pipe in the direction of each clan chief, and he chanted the seven prayers to Manitou. Afterward he laid the pipe on one of the smooth stones that surrounded the holy fire. Then he dipped a gourd into a boiling liquid and filled two bark cups. He handed one to Catherine, the other to Happy

379

Woman. After they had drunk, the two shamans led them out of the house.

"What contest will come first?" Catherine asked as she and No-am-ee stood on the sidelines of the ceremonial field.

"I don't know," No-am-ee returned. "The captain of the contests will announce the order."

As the people thronged onto the mounds at either end of the field and yelled their wagers across the grounds, Catherine felt moisture bead the palms of her hand. She gazed over the crowd, her eyes searching for Lone Wolf. When she found him, he was standing between Flying Eagle and Wise One. His hand was extended, and both of the older chiefs were looking at the ring. Catherine knew without hearing their conversation that Lone Wolf was laying his wager. She held her hand out, and she looked at the small gold band on her fourth finger. Her talisman of good magic.

She was so deep in thought, she didn't see Kee-lee walk onto the field. She started when she heard him shout above the crowd. "This is the order of contests for this sun: Racing, marksmanship with the knife and tomahawk, and hoop-and-pole."

When the day ended, a weary but jubilant Catherine sat between Happy Woman and Lone Wolf at the head of the ceremonial square. Together they dipped their corn patties into the bowl to sop the stew and open the banquet. Happy Woman had won the race and the tomahawk contest, but Catherine had held her own, winning at knife throwing and hoop-and-pole. Excitement was high, and wagers were growing both in number and in magnitude.

After the feast, the musicians and singers migrated to the center of the ceremonial square. Little Doe, according to custom, rose to her feet and walked to Lone

Wolf. Stoically Catherine watched the two walk toward the fire, the beautiful Lumbroan princess in the lead, the lusty war chief following. Little Doe turned and lifted her head, a soft, tentative smile curling her beautiful lips. Catherine caught her breath when Lone Wolf smiled in return. To the slow seductive beat of the drums and the wail of the reed flute, the two clasped hands and opened the dance.

Catherine felt as though someone were twisting and turning a knife in her abdomen. Tentacles of jealousy curled around her heart, constricting her breath. How could she compete with this delicate woman-child of the forest? she wondered, painfully comparing herself to the Indian woman. Little Doe was young and soft, whereas she was older and tough. She is utterly feminine, Catherine thought, lowering her head to look at the weapons that lay around her, yet I am on the way to becoming a warrior woman.

Her eyes gleaming with malicious delight, Happy Woman turned her gaze to Catherine. "Little Doe and Lone Wolf make a lovely couple, do they not?"

"Yes," Catherine returned quietly, never taking her eyes from the sensual swaying and the seductive, almost touching. Nothing more was said; nothing more had to be said.

Smiling complacently and smugly, Happy Woman rose and walked around the square, stopping when she stood in front of a warrior whom Catherine recognized but did not know. As soon as the two of them had moved into the ceremonial field, others followed, and dancing couples soon filled the square. Mothers with single daughters remained as chaperones, but others took their sleepy children under their wings and guided them to the wigwam.

All evening Catherine sat by herself. She watched Lone Wolf and Little Doe dance; she watched them sit together, laughing and talking. Although her mind whirled with doubts and questions, an invisible mask shielded Catherine's thoughts, rendering her face expressionless. Only one could read it; others merely guessed at what she was feeling. Catherine remained where she was seated and waited. Several times her eyes caught Kee-lee's, and she saw the compassion that made them soft and warm. Slowly she smiled. Tenaciously clutching the strength of his friendship, she looked at him, accepting the warmth of his understanding.

Always alert, Lone Wolf misinterpreted the gaze that passed between those two, and he was furious. Hot, molten anger billowed through his veins, pumping through his heart and destroying reason altogether. Totally forgotten was the tiny woman who sat beside him; his entire being was consumed with thoughts of Catherine. Yet Lone Wolf could not go to the woman of his choice. A prisoner of custom, he must stay with Little Doe until her chaperon deemed it time to go.

An extremely astute and wise person, Sunflower Woman noted the war chief's impatience. Glancing at Catherine, the older woman knew where his thoughts lay. She was aware also of the uncomfortable but steady gaze Flying Eagle fixed on Little Doe and Lone Wolf. She wondered about the Lumbroans. Wisely Sunflower Woman stood, silently announcing that it was time for her and Little Doe to leave. After the two women rose, Flying Eagle also retired, leaving Wise One and Kee-lee alone.

The women had hardly turned their backs and disappeared before Lone Wolf rose and strode across the square. When he stood in front of Catherine, he bent over, clamped iron-banded fingers around her shoulders, and yanked her upright, causing her to be thrust against his chest.

"What's wrong?" she cried, puzzled by his behavior.

"I'll teach you to humiliate me," he grated through clenched teeth, roughly hauling her toward the wigwam.

382

Watching the angry interchange, Kee-lee started. He had seen the results of Lone Wolf's anger, and he wanted to spare Catherine. He wanted to rush to her defense, but Wise One reached out a detaining arm and restrained the young man. "This matter is for Lone Wolf to handle, my impetuous young warrior, not you."

"But, my father," Kee-lee argued in a low voice, "can you not see what he is doing to Catherine?"

Wise One puffed on his pipe, not at all perturbed that the strained silence stretched to immeasurable length. Eventually he lowered his pipe. "Have you not seen what this is doing to him?" the old man questioned softly. "We are making him walk a hard road, my son. We must be patient if he stumbles and falters a little."

As Lone Wolf dragged Catherine behind him, she tried to free her arm from his grasp, but he didn't turn her loose. He slackened neither his grip nor his stride. Eaten up by jealousy, he now broke free of the shackles of convention. Extreme impassivity gave way to intense emotionalism. Catherine thought he was angry. Instead he was a man trembling with fear; he was afraid of losing the only woman he had ever truly loved. Ever the warrior, he was camouflaging his fears and desperation with anger.

Even the wolf was unsure of his master's temperament; therefore, he kept his distance, cautiously sidling into the wigwam ahead of Lone Wolf. His hand still banding her arm, Lone Wolf shoved Catherine inside. Releasing her, he stopped in the entry room only long enough to pull the bark over the door. Then he followed Catherine into the main room.

Shivering in the autumn coolness, Catherine knelt in front of the blackened fire pit. Under Lone Wolf's unnerving gaze, she rebuilt the fire, coaxing it from a tiny spark into a burgeoning blaze. When the warming flames leaped into the air, she rose and would have walked into the sleeping room, but Lone Wolf moved, blocking

383

her way.

At the same time that his hand rose and his fingers touched the wolf fangs, Catherine lifted her head. In pain herself, she couldn't see the despair and fear in him. Instead, she stared into the face of a stranger, and she found it hard and indomitable.

"How could you humiliate me like that?" he demanded in a voice as icy and hard as his visage.

"Humiliate you!" Catherine hissed, her eyes suddenly blazing as brightly as the fire. "Was it no humiliation for me to sit by myself while you flirted with Little Doe all evening?"

"My actions are not to be questioned," Lone Wolf thundered, disturbed because this woman had carefully insinuated herself in his heart. Again and again, she dared question him; she even hurled accusations into his face.

"No, of course not," Catherine responded, her voice silky with sarcasm. "You're the man; I'm the woman. You're the war chief; I'm the slave." All of autumn's fury raged in her eyes, and her stance signaled her anger. She dropped her hands to her hips; planting her feet firmly on the floor. "Because I'm a woman, because I'm a slave my feelings are of no consequence."

"I have explained to you—" Lone Wolf began, but Catherine would not be silenced.

"Aye," she broke in. "You've explained, and I hear your reasoning. But my heart and soul do not listen. They cannot be reasonable about such an important matter. When I saw you flirting with Little Doe," Catherine cried, "I felt as though you had stabbed me with a knife, as though you were turning and twisting the blade." She shook her head. "I can't stand it, Lone Wolf." Her voice dropped to a whisper of anguish. "I love you too much, too possessively to share you with Little Doe."

Lone Wolf's gaze moved from the wolf fangs to her

eyes that had become hollow and questioning. In the glowing light of the fire, he groaned his misery and wrapped his arms around her, cradling her to his body. He buried his head in the sweet curve of shoulder and neck.

"Catherine," he whispered incoherently, his voice thick and husky. "Catherine. I know how you feel. Believe me I know." His confession turned into an agonized plea. "But please understand, my darling."

Responding to the loving injunction, Catherine circled him in her arms, and she ran her hands up and down his back in soothing, comforting motions.

"I know how you must feel when you see me with Little Doe." He paused, his grip tightening until Catherine almost gasped. "I am eaten up with jealousy when I see you smile at Kee-lee." Again he hesitated. "But I have no choice, my darling. No choice at all."

"You seemed to be enjoying Little Doe's company."

Her muffled complaint provoked a quick response. "Nay, my love," he denied softly, resting a hand on the crown of her head. "How can I love a child when I have a woman." He pulled away. Balling one hand into a fist and placing it under her chin, he tilted her face upward. "A soft spring breeze is beautiful, my darling, but more beautiful is the raging beauty of autumn's fury. I like the sweet innocence of spring, but I prefer the hot, fiery passion of autumn."

Love pushed anger and resentment away, and with a low moan, Catherine welcomed Lone Wolf's lips. Their soft, tentative caress finally melted into a deep, warm kiss. His mouth still melded with hers, Lone Wolf's hands slipped to her waist, and he gently guided her to the floor.

The warrior, bathed in moonlight, lay on the platform, his hands locked behind his head. He stared through the smoke hole into the clear, star-decked sky. Although it was late, he couldn't sleep. Tired of tossing on his platform, Kee-lee finally rose, dressed, and threw his blanket over his shoulder. Deep in thought he began to walk, not consciously aware of the path he had taken until he caught sight of the small moon-silvered form. Aware of his presence at the same moment he sensed hers, Little Doe silently studied Kee-lee. Though he couldn't see it, a sweet smile tugged her beautiful lips, and she turned toward him.

As if in a dream, Kee-lee walked to her. When he stood before he, he felt her pain. Reaching out a hand, he tipped her chin upward, and in the pale light of the moon he saw her swollen eyes, saw the trail of tears that glimmered down her cheeks. A kindred soul, he pulled the delicate woman into his arms and cradled her close to the hard muscularity of his body. He could understand her hurt; he, too, cried for a lost love.

Two lonely people entwined in the arms of friendship, Kee-lee and Little Doe stood unmoving until her tears subsided. When Kee-lee felt her shiver, he pulled the blanket from his shoulder and wrapped it around her. Smiling, he said, "I think it's time that you were in bed."

Not wanting to be alone, Little Doe shook her head and reached out a detaining hand. "Stay a little longer and talk with me," she whispered.

Kee-lee looked at the small, slender fingers resting against his sleeve. So tiny, he thought. Yet they burned through the buckskin, singeing his flesh. Little Doe's gaze followed his, and she, too, stared at her hand. But she wasn't looking at or thinking of her hand. She marveled at the warm feeling that tingled through her body. Never had she felt this way about a man.

Puzzled by this new response, Little Doe was nonplused. Moments ago, she had thought her life was ruined; she'd felt cheated, and she'd hated Lone Wolf for loving the paleface. Now she was begging Kee-lee to stay with her. She was feeling new life stir in her body, a new awareness that dispelled earlier disappointments.

Spellbound, Kee-lee's hands lifted, cupping Little Doe's delicate oval face. He gazed into her large, somber eyes, drinking his fill of their beauty. Cautiously he moved his fingers, until the tips touched her temples. Again Little Doe trembled, but she was no longer cold. Her body was reacting to the hot, raging desire that churned in the pit of her stomach.

When Kee-lee lowered his face, his lips gently touching hers, Little Doe moaned and reached out to encircle his body. If she hadn't, she would have fallen; her knees felt so weak. When she pressed her soft curves against his hard length, Kee-lee's hands dropped to her shoulders, and his kiss deepened.

Quickly he realized that Little Doe was inexperienced, but even then he couldn't stop himself. A man caught up in the throes of passion, he didn't want to restrain himself. He slowly moved his lips on hers, guiding and tutoring her. Their mouths gradually opened, until his tongue gently nipped her inner lips. Little Doe whimpered and melded herself to Kee-lee, willingly surrendering to this pleasurable torment.

Kee-lee's hands moved over her shoulders and down her back, softly settling around her waist. He felt the thrust of her breasts against his chest, the pouting fullness of her mouth against his, and he fought the urge to lower her to the ground and to carry their lovemaking to its natural conclusion. Gently he lifted his mouth from hers.

When Little Doe looked up at him, her expression puzzled and bereft, he capped the back of her head with his hand and pressed her cheek against his chest. She listened to the heavy thudding of his heart, and she smiled. This warrior was as shaken as she—more experienced but shaken nevertheless.

"I—I didn't mean for this to happen," Kee-lee

387

whispered, his voice thick and husky.

"I'm glad it did," Little Doe softly replied, snuggling her cheek against him, ignorant of the provocativeness of her action.

"You have never been kissed before?" Kee-lee asked, a strange exhilaration running through his veins.

"Never."

"How many winters have you seen?"

"Sixteen."

"You have never been spoken for?" he asked.

"I was to have married Red Fox," Little Doe answered, the words intruding on her euphoric state.

"And now you are to marry Lone Wolf," Kee-lee said. He gently pushed Little Doe out of his arms.

"If I'm to marry Lone Wolf"—Little Doe looked at him questioningly—"why do I feel this way about you?"

Kee-lee smiled tenderly and gently pushed a wisp of hair from her face. "We are both lonely," he explained, "and vulnerable. We are susceptible." He draped an arm around her shoulder. "Come. It's time you were in your bed. The games will start as soon as Elder brother, the Sun, is midway in his journey through the sky."

"Kee-lee," Little Doe ventured tentatively as they slowly moved toward the guest wigwam. The warrior lowered his face in answer. "Have you . . . have you ever kissed the . . . the—"

Kee-lee chuckled softly, and his arm tightened about her shoulder. "No, little one, I have never kissed the paleface. She has eyes only for Lone Wolf. Never has she seen me as more than her friend."

"I fear that is the way Lone Wolf will always regard me." Little Doe sighed. "Although he spent the entire evening sitting beside me, he was never with me. His thoughts, his laughter, and his love belong to the paleface."

"Yet your father will have you marry him." It was a statement, not a question.

"Yes," Little Doe replied. "And I will marry him. At the end of the games, I will accept Lone Wolf's gift of purchase. When I have received the seventh gift, I shall give them all to my father for his approval and acceptance."

Thinking of Catherine's and Lone Wolf's anguish, remembering Little Doe's sweetness in his arms, Kee-Lee suddenly stopped walking and turned to Little Doe. "There is a way out of this, Little Doe." She peered at him questioningly. "What if another Scupperongac warrior were to give you a gift of purchase?" Little Doe started to shake her head, but Kee-Lee continued. "You can return Lone Wolf's gift and accept the other."

Although the idea appealed to Little Doe, she quickly said, "I can't."

"Yes, you can," Kee-Lee insisted. "You don't love Lone Wolf; he doesn't love you. Our marrying would solve many problems. You wouldn't be forced into a plural marriage immediately, and our tribes would still be bound together through the blood of our children."

"It cannot be," Little Doe murmured, walking again. "I would like you to give me gifts of purchase . . . but I cannot accept them. Our council demands that I wed Lone Wolf. Only by marrying the man who killed Red Fox can I bring peace to our tribes."

Long after he had left Little Doe, Kee-Lee walked through the town, moving soundlessly down the silent streets. Finally, stopping in front of his wigwam, he leaned against a large tree. Folding his arms across his chest, he lifted his eyes and gazed into the heavens. Oddly enough his thoughts were no longer filled with visions of the red-headed paleface with the sparkling green eyes. He now envisioned a delicate oval face, large somber eyes, and a gentle smile. He remembered the soft thrust of Little Doe's breasts, the gentle curves that had melded against him.

Chapter XVIII

Her toes squared to the line that she had drawn in the dirt, Catherine stood with her back to the sun, her face to the target. Never had she been as tense as she was this morning. So far, she and Happy Woman were equally matched, each having won three of the six games. This was the day of the last contest, and the outcome would determine the winner and the next village champion. Shading her eyes, Catherine saw Happy Woman standing nearby, her bow in hand. The Indian lifted her head, and the two women stared at each other for a long time.

"Come, Ca-ther-ine. Practice is over; it's time to prepare for the contest." Breaking through the small, silent ring of onlookers, Ma-wa-ska indicated that Catherine should follow her.

Catherine held Happy Woman's gaze for one more second, regretting that she must be the one to break their visual contract. Finally, however, she dropped her head, blinked, and took a deep breath. Then she trotted behind her coach to the river. In a secluded thicket, she saw No-am-ee huddled over a fire, chanting prayers and mixing potions.

"Take your bath," Ma-wa-ska instructed. "Then put on your new clothes." She pointed to the bundle of buckskins near No-am-ee.

Obeying, Catherine undressed and walked into the cold water, quickly bathing. When she had donned the buckskins, she stood quietly in front of No-am-ee while the old woman anointed her with herbs and painted her face in victory colors. When she finished her task, No-am-ee joined Ma-wa-ska, and the two of them chanted and danced for Catherine's victory.

The prayer over, the two older women opened a pouch and offered their sacrifice of tobacco to Manitou and his helpers. Then No-am-ee stooped, lifted the sacred pipe, and filled it with a special tobacco mixture. After the two Indian women had taken seven puffs each, they handed the pipe to Catherine and she did the same.

"Now, my daughter," No-am-ee said, taking the pipe from Catherine and handing it to Ma-wa-ska, "you have much magic against the Beaver champion." She lowered her head and tugged a medicine bag from her belt. Untying it, she extracted a necklace of shiny red beads which she looped around Catherine's neck. "These are for victory, Ca-ther-ine." She smiled and stepped back. "Ma-wa-ska and I must go now. Pray for strong magic while we're gone." She waved. "I will return for you when the contest begins."

Catherine picked up her quiver, slid the strap over her shoulder, and shrugged it into place. Then her fingers curved around her bow, and she lifted it, twanging the sinew with her right hand. Her heart sank. No matter how much she practiced the Indian bow was still foreign to her. Sighing deeply, she nocked an arrow and drew back the bowstring. Before she released the arrow, however, she heard the faint sounds of moccasined feet on the pathway. She whirled around to see Lone Wolf.

Glad to see him, she rushed forward. "What are you doing here?" she cried. Then, before he could answer, she added, "You know what No-am-ee will say and do if she finds you with me." Tinkling laughter followed her words.

"She won't catch me." He grinned. "And it won't matter if she does. I have strong magic for you." Noting the mysterious twinkle in his eyes, Catherine shook her head warily. Lone Wolf's grin deepened, and he reached out his hand, clasping hers. "Come see."

Carefully placing her bow and arrow on the ground, Catherine followed him into the forest, away from the river. Finally he stopped. "Stand here and close your eyes."

Giggling like a child, Catherine obeyed. She heard him walk away and return. Then he commanded softly, "Hold your hands out."

Something smooth touched Catherine's palm. As her fingers curled around the polished curve of wood, her eyes flew open; she recognized the touch. "My bow!" she cried, throwing one arm around him and jumping up and down. "You brought me my bow!" Laughing with her, Lone Wolf just nodded his head. "How did you . . ." she began, but overcome with surprise and joy, she couldn't continue. She looked at the bow; she looked at Lone Wolf. "When did you? . . ."

Still chuckling, Lone Wolf laid a finger across her mouth. "I sent a runner to the paleface settlement to ask your sister if she would send it to you."

"Why?" she asked, tears of joy glimmering in her eyes.

Lone Wolf moved closer to her. His hands gently clasping her shoulders, he slanted his head and his lips lightly brushed hers. "I have a wager to protect."

"Just a wager?" Catherine whispered, her words mingling with his breath as she lifted her face. Tightly clutching her bow, she wrapped her arms around him.

"Nay, my darling," he murmured, lowering his head and circling her body with his arms.

His lips pressed against hers in a bond of love, the kiss silencing him. Catherine's lips parted to accept the sweet thrusting invasion of his tongue. When the tip ran around the sensitive inner circle of her lips, she sighed and moved closer to him.

Eventually he raised his head and murmured, "I have our love to protect."

Catherine laid her cheek against Lone Wolf's chest, delighting in the fast, erratic pounding of his heart. Her joy couldn't have been greater. Even if she didn't win the harvest contests, she had proved herself a worthy opponent and had won the grudging respect of Happy Woman and the village. Lone Wolf had given her the ring, and now the bow. Although Little Doe would be remaining in Scupperong throughout the winter, Flying Eagle would be returning to Lumbroa on the morrow. The next few days would be hers and Lone Wolf's.

Reluctantly Lone Wolf pulled away from Catherine. He smiled. "And now I have another surprise for you." He untied his pouch and pulled out a crumpled letter. "From your sister," he said. "She sent it with the runner."

Catherine took the paper in her hands, and she held it. She wanted to open it, but she knew she didn't have time now. Hastily she shoved it into her belt. "I'll keep it with me for luck," she told Lone Wolf. "I'll read it later."

He nodded, dropping a quick kiss on the tip of her nose. "I must go, darling, before No-am-ee returns." He backed away; then stopped. "Remember, I'll be cheering you on."

When No-am-ee came for Catherine, she looked at the European bow. Without a word she reached for it, running her hand over the smooth, polished finish. When she handed it back, she said, "This is a beautiful bow, Ca-ther-ine. I have never seen it before."

"No, Grandmother," Catherine replied, her green eyes

393

never wavering from the steady gaze of the black ones, "you haven't seen it. My father had this one made for me." When No-am-ee said nothing, Catherine said defensively, "My father was a brave man, my grandmother, and the bow he gave me has great magic."

No-am-ee couldn't understand why the paleface continued to defy Scupperongac custom, but she admired Catherine's courage and confidence. She knew Manitou and his helpers would do the same. Slowly she nodded her head. "I hope so, Catherine. Surely you're going to need it this day."

Spinning on her heels, No-am-ee straightened her back as best she could, squaring her shoulders. Regally she walked through the forest; proudly she led the Turtle champion to the game field. When the crowd cheered her appearance, Catherine trotted into the center of the field, holding both arms in the air. Then she ran down the sidelines, softly chanting her song, promising victory. She smiled as new wagers were laid, and old ones were raised.

When she returned to the center of the field where No-am-ee waited, Catherine scanned the sea of faces, looking for one in particular. She saw Little Doe; she saw Sunflower Woman. Re-bekk-ana. Little Flower. Her eyes brushed across Flying Eagle's stern countenance, across Wise One's gentle, encouraging smile, and they finally landed and lingered on the rugged, indomitable face she cherished more than any other.

Her lips curved in a tremulous smile, and she lifted a hand toward Lone Wolf, her ring mirroring the noonday sun. For long, precious moments Lone Wolf didn't move. Instead he gazed at Catherine, lost in her beauty. Her hair shone like burnished copper, gleaming as brightly as the amulet that rested on her chest. Soft curls defied her braids and headband to wisp around her face, and her white buckskins, made by No-am-ee, were decorated with quills that were died in deep autumn colors. Disregarding the disapproval of several staid countenances, Lone Wolf finally raised his arm and held out his ringed hand. He remembered her gesture the day he'd run the gauntlet, and he brought his hand to his mouth, kissed it, and blew the kiss to Catherine. She did the same.

Trying to get Catherine's attention, Kee-Lee called her name several times, but she was too caught up in Lone Wolf to hear anyone else. She didn't break from her reverie until No-am-ee barked a sharp reprimand, grabbed Catherine's elbow, and gave it a tug. Laughter twittered through the crowd, and Catherine turned a hot, embarrassed face to No-am-ee and Kee-Lee. As Catherine listened to Kee-Lee's instructions, she kept her face straight ahead, avoiding Happy Woman's smug smile, ignoring her malicious chuckle.

Catherine rubbed the palm of her right hand down the side of her leggings; then she wiped the other hand. Reaching over her shoulder, she extracted an arrow. With methodical precision she angled the bow and nocked the shaft. She pulled against the taut string; she released. Then it was Happy Woman's turn.

Again and again, arrows whizzed through the air, thudding into the targets, as Catherine shot; then Happy Woman. The crowd cheered them alternately, but now a tense silence had fallen. Several braves rushed to the targets; quickly they removed them, replacing the two with one.

Happy Woman squared her feet behind the shooting line. She nocked the arrow, she released it, she waited. She heard the thwack that resounded when the flint, having pierced the center of the bark, drove into the stump against which the target leaned. She smiled, and a sigh of approval emanated from the spectators. Then everyone waited to see if the Turtle champion could outdo the Beaver.

Happy Woman lowered her bow and slowly turned, her eyes sweeping the cheering crowd before they lit on Catherine. Her lips twitched into a full smile, and her eyes danced victoriously. She has never looked more majestic or confident, Catherine thought, watching Happy Woman out of the corner of her eye as the Indian woman moved away from the shooting line.

Her eyes glued to Kee-Lee, Catherine awaited his signal. She ran her sweat-moistened hands, one by one, down the side of her leggings, wiping them dry. Lifting her arm, she drew the back of a hand over her brow. Then Kee-Lee called, and she trotted to the center of the field. She shielded her eyes with her arm and stared at the target—at the lone arrow that protruded from the center circle.

Her inspection completed, she whipped an arrow from the quiver, then nocked it against the bowstring. With calculated movements she raised the bow and aimed, but she didn't release the arrow. Instead, she turned her head. Lone Wolf, standing in the front row, gazed solemnly at her. Reading her soul and knowing what she must do, he acknowledged his faith and confidence in her. He nodded his head and smiled encouragingly. Drawing in a deep, ragged breath, Catherine nodded and returned his smile.

She turned her head and slung her braids over her shoulder. Aware of what she must do, Catherine steadied her hands and aimed again. She released the arrow and squinted her eyes, watching its winged flight through the air.

Dumfounded, the Beaver champion stared at the target. She couldn't believe her eyes. Catherine's arrow had split her arrow in two. Kee-Lee and several other braves walked onto the field. Standing next to the target, they pointed and they talked. Motioning the two women to him, Kee-Lee spoke to both of them.

"Ca-ther-ine, you and Happy Woman have been equally matched throughout the contests. The other coaches and I are having a difficult time making a decision. We have decided that in fairness, the two of you should shoot another round." Kee-Lee looked from one woman to the next. After both nodded their agreement, he said, "Ca-ther-ine, you will shoot first."

Catherine returned to the line, pulled an arrow from her quiver, and nocked it against the string. Fighting for control, she aimed and released the arrow, holding her breath until it sank into the center circle. Stepping back, she watched as Happy Woman positioned herself, aimed, and shot her arrow. In order to win, the Indian had to split Catherine's arrow.

Catherine's heartbeat accelerated until she felt blood rush to her head. She nervously opened and closed her free hand, time and time again. She squinted her eyes, never taking them off the flying arrow. The air whooshed out of her in a happy sigh as Happy Woman's arrow sank into the target next to hers. When Catherine heard the gasp of the crowd, when she heard Lone Wolf's roaring cheer above all the others, she jumped into the air and squealed with delight. She had done it! She had defeated Happy Woman.

The crowd swarmed onto the field, several of the jubilant Turtle braves hoisting Catherine onto their shoulders and parading her around the grounds. Catherine laughed joyously as she watched the boisterous throng shout congratulations and collect their wagers. Moving with the flow of the crowd, the braves carried Catherine into the village, finally setting her down at the head of the ceremonial square. Then they trotted off to collect their bets and to take their places for the banquet that would follow.

Catherine sat between Wise One and Lone Wolf, her face radiating her joy. She was too excited to eat, but

397

after Wise One had made the meat sacrifice and offered the prayer of thanksgiving, she sopped her corn patty into one of the meat dishes and lifted it to her mouth. As she took the first bite, the last-night festivities began.

When the evening shadows began to fall, people, carrying their robes and blankets, closed in around the large fire in the center of the square. Eagerly they awaited the awarding of the prizes; nothing pleased them more than to reward valor and ability.

Wise One stood and moved closer to the fire, its light creating a beautiful hue on his handsome features. He held the sacred pipe up in both hands and softly chanted.

"Aa-da-mii, Men of our Nation. Aa-da-mii. It is good to see the leaves fall and to know that we have lived yet another year. We are thankful that so many of us are alive and that we are able to meet together once more to hold our ceremony."

He paused, and the people cried in unison, "We are thankful that we have gathered here for the past seven days and prayed to Manitou, who has taught us how to pray."

Wise One continued. "Our dances and games have helped raise our prayers to him. We are glad to be together again and thankful for all Manitou and his helpers, the Manitouwuk, have done to give us everything we need to make us happy: good crops, plenty of deer and fish. We are thankful, too, that they have kept the storms away from our villages and have told floods and earthquakes to pass by us."

Everyone chorused, "We are thankful to the Manitou for all the Manitouwuk he has created to take care of us."

When his prayer died, Wise One turned and held the pipe toward Flying Eagle. The Lumbroan chief stood, took the pipe, and held it up toward the heavens. Like Wise One he lifted his voice in a short chant of thanksgiving.

Both chiefs remained standing as Wise One filled the pipe with tobacco. Then a boy scooped up a live coal on a small piece of bark, and from it Wise One lit the pipe. He took seven puffs from it, holding it toward a different clan chieftain after each puff. Afterward he handed the pipe to Flying Eagle who followed the Scupperongac's example. Wise One then opened his pouch and thumped tobacco into the palm of his hand. Lifting his voice in one last wailing chant, he threw the sacrifice into the fire. When his voice died out, he turned to No-am-ee first, then to Happy Woman who jumped to her feet instantly.

Happy Woman quickly moved through the seated crowd and knelt beside No-am-ee, helping her to rise. Wearing a long fur-lined cape over her most festive dress, the old woman draped a hand over Happy Woman's arm for support. She moved slowly, and rather than stopping in front of Wise One, she stopped in front of Catherine. Surprised, Catherine blinked her eyes and looked from No-am-ee's smiling face to Happy Woman's closed one, then to Wise One. The old chief, holding out his hand, chuckled and motioned for her to rise.

"This day, my daughter," he said proudly, "you have gained the favor of Manitou and his helpers, and you have pleased us."

When he paused, the people voiced their agreement by clapping their hands and calling, "Hear! Hear!"

No-am-ee moved closer and lifted her swollen, pain-racked hands, a copper medallion swinging from them. Catherine sucked in her breath in anticipation, and she unconsciously lowered her head. But the old woman swung toward Happy Woman, and she handed the necklace to her.

Happy Woman took the medal; then she stepped closer to Catherine. "This is the medallion of victory, Ca-ther-ine," she said, her voice, loud and clear, carrying across the ceremonial square, "which I the Beaver Champion give to you."

Before Happy Woman could loop Catherine's head with the shell chain, however, Catherine stepped back. She shook her head, and she smiled. Reaching up, her fingers curled around Happy Woman's medallion. She pulled it over her head.

"Since I am to have my own medal of honor," she said, taking a step forward, "I would like to return this medallion to its rightful owner." To the surprise of everyone, she dropped the necklace over the unsuspecting Happy Woman's head. "This belongs to the Beaver Champion."

Admiration glinted in the depths of Happy Woman's eyes, but her expression was guarded. She lifted her arms and dropped the new medallion over Catherine's head. "And this belongs to the new champion—the Turtle Champion." She backed away, and looking Catherine straight in the face, she added, "I, Happy Woman of the Beaver Clan, am now your slave, Ca-ther-ine. I am yours to command."

Catherine reached out a hand and touched Happy Woman's shoulder. "I release you from your bondage, Happy Woman," she said softly. "No person should be a slave to another." She smiled. "I would much rather have you for my friend; I would prefer that you walk by my side, not behind me."

"I owe you a debt of gratitude, Ca-ther-ine," Happy Woman said, her voice slightly thick. "You have behaved more honorably than I." She smiled tentatively and extended her hand, touching Catherine's shoulder. "I will be your friend; I will walk by your side."

The ceremony ended with whoops and hollers; then the musicians and singers positioned themselves for the last night of dancing. The evening passed entirely too quickly for Catherine, and she was surprised when Lone Wolf suggested they return to the wigwam. It seemed so early. But she didn't argue; she was willing to spend the time with him. Holding hands, they walked down the streets to the secluded wigwam, the wolf quietly and unobtrusively following at a discreet distance. When the autumn wind began to blow, Lone Wolf dropped an arm around Catherine's shoulders and drew her closer to him.

"The winter is going to be cold without you," she whispered.

"Aye, love," he returned, "I was thinking the same thing." He chuckled. "At least you'll have the wigwam for warmth. Most of the time I'll be sleeping on the ground with nothing but my blanket."

Catherine's lips curved in a smile, but her eyes and her face were sad. Tonight her soul was crying over its loss. "I'm glad we have a few days together before you go."

Lone Wolf hesitated before he said, "We don't have those days, my darling." Despite the cold wind that swirled around them, Catherine stopped and spun around. "I must leave early in the morning."

"Why?" she cried.

Lone Wolf caught her elbow in his hand and gently turned her. "Let's go inside. I'll tell you all about it."

They stooped and walked into the entry room, the wolf scurrying in behind them. Lying down on his robes in the corner and tucking his head between his extended paws, the animal watched Lone Wolf and Catherine as they moved into the sleeping room. He didn't close his eyes until a fire was lit.

Both Lone Wolf and Catherine sank into the warm furs that carpeted the floor. Because the room was still cold, they wrapped a robe around themselves, snuggled against each other, and huddled close to the fire.

"A runner came from Lumbroa today. Since Flying Eagle came here, trouble has been brewing. A group of Lumbroan warriors, wanting revenge for a past raid made

401

by the Iroquois, crossed into Iroquois territory. They looted homes and set fire to cornfields. Demanding immediate revenge, the Iroquois retaliated."

"War," Catherine whispered. "You're going to have to leave with a war party."

"That is what Flying Eagle wishes to raise," Lone Wolf stated, "but Wise One has persuaded him to take his grievance to Echota."

"What is Echota?" Catherine asked, stumbling over the unfamiliar sounds.

"A Cherokee town of sanctuary. Warriors of every tribe are safe within its palisades. Here chiefs of both nations can meet to pay fines in buckskins and corn for the damage done by their warriors."

"Why must you leave?"

"Flying Eagle will not be safe until he is within the walls of Echota and the grievance has been settled. Our land will be swarming with Iroquois war parties who will kill Flying Eagle on sight."

"And you," Catherine murmured. "They will take this opportunity to kill you, my darling."

"It will take more than an Iroquois warrior to kill me," Lone Wolf boasted, his arrogance merely a veil to cloak his anxiety from Catherine. "Because I have strong magic and because I'm the war chief, Wise One wishes me to travel with Flying Eagle, and he wants me to speak of peace and an alliance with the Cherokee council and with the chiefs who are gathering at Echota."

"What about the trading expedition?" Catherine asked.

"I will lead the expedition after I have finished my mission in Echota."

Stifling her cry of dismay, Catherine turned her head and buried it against Lone Wolf's chest. She clutched him tightly, knowing this was her last night with him, uncertain of what the future held for them. Lone Wolf draped his arms about her, and rubbed his hands up and down her back in soft, soothing motions.

He lowered his face, resting his cheek against the top of her head. When he felt her copper medallion digging into his chest, he said, "You are indeed a champion, Catherine." Too choked up to speak, Catherine said nothing. "The people saw that you are the more honorable of the two. Your actions pleased me greatly."

"Were you disappointed that I won?"

Lone Wolf barely heard the muffled words. "No, I expected you to."

Catherine turned her head, rubbing her cheek against his chest. She raised a hand and placed it on his cheek. "What about your wager?"

She felt his lips as they moved into a smile; she heard his soft chuckle. "I told you once, my darling, I'm not an emotional gambler. I study the odds and know exactly who the winner will be."

"Did you win or lose?" she asked.

Again he emitted a low, husky chuckle. "Are you going to get angry?"

Catherine reached up and caught his hand. Bringing it down so she could see, she looked at her father's ring. "Nay, I'll not be angry," she promised, running her fingertip over the small circle of gold.

"I won," he returned, mesmerized by the movement of her white hand on his copper one.

"You didn't think I could do it, did you?"

"Aye," he replied, "I knew you could." His chest rumbled with laughter. "Remember, love, I saw you fight for that chest. I knew how important it was to you."

"Oh, yes," Catherine cried, pulling away from Lone Wolf. "I almost forgot." She jumped to her feet and ran across the room. Kneeling in front of the chest, she unfastened it and lifted the lid. She reached for Little Flower's doll, holding it for a second. Lone Wolf moved

403

to the platform. Bending, he pulled out the mattress and blankets.

His voice full of amusement, he said, "You have need of a doll when you have me, Catherine?" His back to her, he stood and made the bed.

"Nay." Catherine laughed with him. "I forgot to return Little Flower's doll. She gave it to me for a good luck talisman, and I promised that I would return it to her after the contests."

Lone Wolf walked to where she sat. Kneeling beside her, he reached for the doll, gently taking it. "There will be time for you to give her that tomorrow. Tonight is ours." He laid the doll aside and placed both hands on Catherine's shoulders. "Ours alone."

"Ours alone," Catherine whispered, rising to her feet in response to the gentle guidance of his hands.

She lifted her face to his descending lips, their mouths touching lightly at first, then slanting and settling into a demanding kiss. Closer they moved, their arms banding their bodies together, love bonding their souls. Their union stirred embers of recognition deep inside each, creating an insatiable appetite and igniting the fire of desire.

Breathing deeply, Lone Wolf lifted his head, his lips nipping hot, moist trails of pleasure over Catherine's face. His hands gently but deliberately untied the belt that cinched her jacket around her waist. Unheeded and forgotten, Ellen's letter slithered to the floor. Stepping back slightly, Lone Wolf pulled the buckskin over her head, dropping it at their feet. As if he had never seen her before, he stared at her loveliness. Two hands—broad and strong—swept upward from her small waist. He cupped a breast in each, his thumbs circling the tips. Slowly, as if in agonizing torment, he lowered his head, his mouth settling on a sensitive crest. His tongue was cool to Catherine's passion-fevered flesh; his touch was light and quick. But she felt a jolt at the core of her body. Lone Wolf reveled when Catherine sharply drew in her breath, when she trembled beneath his touch. His playful swirls turned to deep tugs that rendered Catherine weak and dizzy. Her fingers bit into his shoulders, and she clung to him for support.

Again Lone Wolf lifted his head, and he looked into her face, his own gaunt with desire. He sensed Catherine's need for reassurance, and his intense gaze held hers as his voice, a low rasp, echoed through the wigwam. "I love you, Catherine."

He didn't wait for a verbal response; he needed none. Gathering her into his arms as if she were no heavier than his bundled blanket, he carried her to the bed and laid her on the soft rabbit furs. With flowing motions that were coordinated with the tide of their arousal, Lone Wolf removed his clothing; then he undressed Catherine, sitting for a moment on the edge of the platform, his eyes slowly perusing her fair-skinned beauty from head to toe.

When he looked up, he reached out to touch the copper curls that framed her face. As he ran his fingertip down her cheek and the side of her neck, he felt her small shiver of delight, and he smiled, his fingers brushing the fullness of her breasts. Then his hand moved down her midriff, the palm flattening on her stomach. Gently he kneaded the tender, sensitive skin.

"Does a baby grow in you, my darling?"

Catherine felt the import of his question, and as she shook her head, she somehow wished her answer could be different. "I have seen none of the signs." She lifted her hands and twined them together at the nape of his neck. "Do you really wish for children from me?"

Ebony eyes gazed somberly into green ones. "I want a child from you more than I want anything in this world, Catherine."

"Why?" Catherine couldn't hold back the agonized

whisper. "You'll have Little Doe, and her children will heal the breach between your people and the Lumbroans. Her children will belong to one of the seven clans; mine will be outcasts like me." She watched the pain that crossed Lone Wolf's eyes; she felt his muscles tense beneath her hands. "Why do you want me to have your child?" Before Lone Wolf could answer, Catherine continued, her voice low, "You know I love you, but perhaps you think a child will be the sinew with which to bind me to your side. Perhaps you fear that I will run away."

After her words had trailed into silence, Lone Wolf continued to look into her face. Without denying her allegation, without defending himself against such a charge, he finally repositioned himself. He stretched out beside her, and he lowered his head, pressing his cheek against her stomach, his hands sliding down to cup her hips.

"Perhaps I do seek to bind you to my side," he admitted, his breath flowing like warm maple syrup over her skin. "But more than that, Catherine, I want a child to be born out of our love—a child that is you and me."

"A boy?" Catherine husked, trembling against the sweet weight of his head as his hand trailed down her thigh.

"Or a girl," he answered. "I care not."

"Little Doe will give you the son you need."

"I need no son," Lone Wolf told her, adding softly, "You have been with us for some time, yet you do not understand. Men and women are equal in our tribe. Our child can be whatever it desires, regardless of its sex." He lifted his head and looked at her. "Understand me, Catherine. I don't need a child. I want one."

He lowered his head, his lips moving hungrily over her stomach, his hands working magic with her thighs and legs. When Catherine could stand no more torment, she

406

moaned from desire and tugged his shoulders. Lone Wolf levered himself until his head was above hers.

"I want our child because I love you."

Soft hands, hands he knew so well, reached up to cup his face. Spring green eyes voraciously devoured his gaunt and shadowed handsomeness for several seconds before Catherine brought Lone Wolf's mouth down on hers. He moved, lowering himself and stretching his frame atop hers. Catherine groaned deep in her throat. Lone Wolf tensed. He'd been so caught up in the vortex of his desires, he had forgotten: he was too heavy for her. He had hurt her.

Understanding his hesitation, Catherine shook her head, her hands cupping his head to press his lips against hers. She would not be denied the warmth of his body, the weight of his love. Her lips and hands refused to turn him loose; she even wrapped her legs around him, hugging him closer. Deeper and deeper they sank into the swirling eddy of passion. Finally Lone Wolf wrenched his mouth from Catherine's, and he pressed moist, fevered kisses over her face, down the arched column of her throat, lingering at the pulsating hollow at the base of her neck.

His hands swept up her hips and across her stomach to caress her breasts. Catherine's body tingled with anticipation as he lowered his head, his mouth gently surrounding an engorged tip. She moaned and she trembled as he gently sucked. Pleasure, like a bolt of lightning, flashed through her senses, settling in her lower stomach and again reminding her of her need. She had wanted Lone Wolf before; now she ached for him.

Her heart pounding heavily and loudly, Catherine ran her hands down his muscle-flexed back, finally cupping his tight-sinewed buttocks. She arched against the swell of Lone Wolf's passion, her sinuous movement alerting him to her immediate need. She had to have him now.

Lone Wolf quickly shifted his position, and he lovingly penetrated Catherine.

When he felt her tremble, when he heard her low growl of pleasure, Lone Wolf paused—a pause that both wanted, both appreciated. Each fully savored the moment of complete possession. They wrapped their arms around each other, holding on tightly. Eventually Lone Wolf separated himself slightly. Balancing his weight on his palms at either side of her shoulders, he looked into Catherine's passion-glazed face.

Unashamedly Catherine returned his gaze. Not knowing what the winter held for them, she determined to take as much from him as she could—as much pleasure, as much love. This might be all she would have; this might have to do her for a lifetime. His thick black hair gleamed blue in the waning firelight. His bronzed, muscled chest narrowed into a flat stomach and firm hips. As Catherine's gaze had swept downward, now it swept up to Lone Wolf's face. She felt Lone Wolf's burgeoning passion pulsate inside her.

"I love you," she whispered, the words ragged with need.

Lone Wolf eased his weight onto her, and he began to move, his deep, stroking rhythm setting Catherine afire. Slowly, deliberately, he brought her to the peak of pleasure only to withdraw, to pull away from her altogether and to begin his loving forays all over again. Then he would rise above her, penetrate her. Again and again they teased and played; they raced to the summit, only to withdraw. Finally both were breathing raggedly, and their hearts were pounding furiously.

No retreat this time. Lone Wolf gave the final thrust, and Catherine arched, receiving it, welcoming it. The deep, driving movement started an avalanche of emotions that rolled over both of them. When their spasms of ecstasy turned into the calm of complete fulfillment,

Lone Wolf rolled over, easing his weight off Catherine and lying beside her.

Long after the village quieted down, long after Lone Wolf's breathing was light and shallow, Catherine slipped off the platform so as not to awaken him. But the warrior, trained to be a light sleeper, stirred at her first movement. Opening his eyes, he watched her as she moved about the room.

Stopping in the middle of the room, Catherine added wood to the fire. That accomplished, she put on her nightshirt, and she returned to the center of the room. Bending, she picked up Ellen's letter and Little Flower's doll; then she scooted over to her chest.

She reached up and caught the lid with one hand. She was about to close it when she saw her letter box. Setting the doll aside, she opened the small leather chest and extracted Ellen's first letter. Smiling, she held both of them for a minute before she unfolded the latest one.

Dearest Kate,

I was glad to hear from Manteo that you were well and happy. I was even happier when I received your letter from Mr. Flint. Lone Wolf has invited us to celebrate the strawberry festival with you in the spring. God only knows, I hope we can!

We are quickly running out of supplies, and our only friends are the Croatoans. Otherwise, we are surrounded by enemies, the Roanoacs. Timothy Johnston was killed by the Savages only the other day. Manteo and Will encourage us to move from this island. The Indians are so proficient with their canoes and so knowledgeable of the waterways that Will claims we are prey easily caught. Ananias, however, has refused to leave thus far. He wants to wait here for the return of Governor White and the

409

supply ships.

The colonists grow more restless each day, and distrust is growing. Fear is our constant companion.

Write soon, for I love you dear sister.

Ellen

The news depressed Catherine. Knowing Ellen's propensity for exaggeration, she wondered how much of it was true and how much was a figment of her sister's fertile imagination. She frowned as she thought about the plight of the small colony.

"What's wrong, Catherine?" Lone Wolf asked.

"I just read Ellen's letter," she replied, holding the sheet of paper before her. "If she's telling the truth, the colonists are not faring too well."

Lone Wolf propped himself on one elbow, the blanket slipping down to his waist and leaving his torso naked. "Does your sister generally speak lies?"

Catherine laughed. "No, but she's a silly, spoiled child who often misinterprets what she sees and hears. She lets her emotions color her view of the truth." Catherine lifted the letter to refold it; then she reconsidered. "May I read Ellen's marks to you?" she asked.

"Only if you wish me to hear your message."

"I do." Catherine patted the floor beside her. "Come over here, closer to the fire, and I'll read it to you."

Lone Wolf pushed the blanket aside and stood, his naked body glowing handsomely in the crackling light of the fire. He bent and picked up his breechclout and belt, doning them, and sat by Catherine. Fascinated, he watched her finger move across the paper as she pointed out each group of letters that she pronounced. When she had finished speaking, he took the letter and held it, closing examining the strange marks.

410

"What do you think?" Catherine asked.

"I think Ellen is right," Lone Wolf replied slowly. "Enemies are everywhere in the Great Forest." As he talked, he carefully refolded the letter and handed it to Catherine. "About seventeen winters ago, five tribes of the far north joined together to form the League of Five Nations. Since then these tribes have grown larger in number and more ferocious in war. They have wiped out complete tribes, adopting the women and children, killing the warriors. Slowly but steadily they are moving farther and farther south. Even now they send scouts into our territory."

"That is why an alliance with the Lumbroans and the Roanoacs is so important to your people."

Lone Wolf nodded his head, his eyes watching the hypnotic dance of the flames. "That is why marriage is a duty rather than a luxury for me, Catherine."

His resigned tone touched a string of tenderness in Catherine's heart. Feeling his aloneness, she moved closer to him, laying her head against his chest. They sat, silent, for a few minutes.

"Why are the Roanoacs watching the planters?"

Lone Wolf shrugged. He had wondered about Wanchese's strange behavior and his hatred for the palefaces. "Perhaps he thinks one of the palefaces killed the peace man."

"Nay," Catherine answered. "Not one of them would have killed Running Bear."

"Not even the one called Tom Small?"

"Not even Tom Small," Catherine paused, then said, "He wouldn't . . . have killed Running Bear."

"How can you be so sure?" Lone Wolf asked. "He killed Wind Woman."

"That was different," Catherine argued. "He was frightened, and—"

"He is a coward, Catherine"—Lone Wolf interrupted

411

her firmly—"and cowards are not to be trusted."

"But Running Bear was a friend. Why would he—"

"I don't know," Lone Wolf murmured, pulling Catherine closer. "I was guessing. Let's forget it now; there's no need to worry."

"What if the warriors watching the settlement are not Roanoacs?" Catherine asked after a moment of pensive silence. "Could they"—Catherine could hardly say the words—"be Iroquois?"

Lone Wolf had been harboring the same thought, but he hesitated to admit it. "I don't know," he replied evasively. "They don't usually come this far south." Looking down at the letter she clutched tightly in her hands, he smiled. He decided to change the subject. "Put your letter away, Catherine, and let's go to sleep. Elder Brother, the Sun, will make his appearance soon."

Catherine smiled and nodded. Before she could move, however, Lone Wolf turned, reached into her chest, and extracted the brown leather writing box. He unfastened the clasp and opened it. Silently Catherine watched him curiously examine the contents: the bottles almost empty of ink, the worn quill, the folded sheet of paper with Running Bear's name in broad, black strokes.

Lone Wolf didn't touch anything; rather, he lifted his head. "These marks are not yours, Catherine. They are stronger and bolder. Whose are they?"

"This is Running Bear's writing box," Catherine answered. Laying her letter aside, she reached for Running Bear's paper. The document crackled as she unfolded it and gently laid it on the floor, hand-pressing the wrinkles and creases. She pointed to the letters, saying the sounds in English, repeating the sounds in Roanoacan. After she read the incomplete list, she said in a teary voice, "All he wanted to do was teach his people to read and to write."

Without a word Lone Wolf stood and walked across

412

the room. Catherine carefully refolded the paper. She placed it in the small leather box, and closed the lid.

"Why do you have the peace man's totem?"

Lone Wolf's angry words startled Catherine. She looked at him in surprise. "This isn't Running Bear's totem," she answered.

"You were angry about wearing my totem because it branded you a slave, because it branded you mine," Lone Wolf said accusingly. "But you've had the peace man's totem ever since you came to our village."

"Running Bear was my friend, Lone Wolf. Just a friend. And this is a token of his friendship, not a brand of ownership like your wolf fangs." Catherine smiled at Lone Wolf's jealousy, never thinking he would misinterpret her gesture.

Quickly Lone Wolf covered the space between them. He yanked the writing box from Catherine's hands. "You are mine, Catherine. I will not share you with another, dead or alive," he thundered.

"Yet you would have me share you with another for the rest of my life," Catherine responded with a calmness she was far from feeling. As she watched Lone Wolf walk to the fire, she held out her hand. "Give me the letter box, Lone Wolf." He extended his hand over the fire, the tips of the flames leaping greedily for the brown leather. "Don't you burn that," Catherine cried, running to him, grabbing for the box. "It belongs to me."

Lone Wolf caught Catherine's flailing hand in his, easily warding off her blows. "Why do you want it, Catherine? Does he mean so much to you?"

"Yes," Catherine screamed, "he means that much to me."

Lone Wolf staggered back a step, his face ashen with shock. He had accused her, he had provoked her; but he hadn't wanted to hear her make such a confession. Catherine lunged for Running Bear's box, grabbing it out of his hands. She clutched it tightly against her breast, tears running freely down her cheeks.

"Can't you understand?" she cried. "He was my friend. I was his teacher and guide in England; he was mine here. I was English; he was Indian. But we were people. We were friends, and this is all I have left of him. This paper is a legacy for his people. That's why I have it; that's why I cherish it. I want peace for our people too, Lone Wolf. I want us to live side by side, to work together, to play together." The torrent of words stopped and Catherine slumped over the box.

Lone Wolf walked out of the room, leaving her by herself. She heard the scraping of the bark as he removed it from the door, and she knew she was alone. Walking to her chest, she knelt down and replaced the writing box. Then she fumbled through the neatly stacked linen for a handkerchief. Holding the soft square of material to her face, she collapsed on the floor. Finally she wiped her eyes and sniffed one last time. She was through with self-pity.

Forgetting about the fire, Catherine ran out of the wigwam. Finding Lone Wolf would not be difficult; she knew where he was. She raced down the familiar pathway to the waterfall, and she saw him sitting on the large boulder. The wolf sat beside his master, man and beast silhouetted in the moonlight. She paused, drawing in deep gulps of air, but her warrior had already heard her coming. Lone Wolf turned. Man and woman stared at each other. As if one had spoken, as if one had given a command, Lone Wolf stood at the same moment Catherine raced from the cover of trees.

He held his arms out, catching her as she softly thudded against his chest. Tightly they clutched one another, silently conveying the depth and magnitude of their love for one another.

"I'm sorry," Catherine whispered. "I—"

"No. I am sorry, my darling," Lone Wolf murmured, sinking his face into the scented curve of neck and shoulder. "I ask from you what I'm not willing to give to you. More and more I understand the pain and agony you are suffering because of your love for me. Yet I do not know the answer . . . for you . . . for me."

Suddenly Catherine knew the answer, and she now understood her tears a few moments ago. Lone Wolf was her love and her lover, but he was also a Scupperongac war chief, a fierce and proud warrior. She knew without being told that he was agonizing, that he was in the throes of a decision. Because of his love for her, he was considering making a choice: Little Doe or her, his people or her! How clear No-am-ee's words were. Catherine could almost hear the old woman speaking.

If Lone Wolf should sacrifice his people for your love, the two of you will have gained nothing. You will have lost the man you love because he will hate himself; he will have lost his soul and his integrity.

Catherine's hand slid up his chest, and she cupped his chin with her fingers. "We have only this night left, my love, before you leave for Cherokee county. Let's have no misunderstandings or bad words between us." Catherine smiled. "I love you, and I will wait for you to return. Our love will make a way for itself."

Lone Wolf conceded to the wisdom of her words; he welcomed the solace of her promise. He knew what he must do. But he would not do it until he returned from Echota. He needed the assurance that Catherine would be waiting for him. When he returned from his trip, he promised himself, he would set Catherine free. Then she could make her choice. At the thought that she might decide to return to the palefaces, he shuddered and tightened his clasp about her.

"What is it, darling?" Catherine asked, jerking her head so that one of her braids landed against Lone Wolf's

415

chest. Relaxing his grip, he smiled grimly. He picked up the braid and absently rubbed the polished wolf fang on the thong.

"I'm already missing you."

His arms circled her body, and his hands smoothed the soft material of her nightshirt over her back, over her buttocks. Catherine shivered in his arms and lifted her mouth for his kiss.

Lone Wolf chuckled. "Are you trembling from the cold or from the fire of my love?"

"Fire!" Catherine shrieked, going stiff in his arms. "I left the wigwam unattended," she cried.

Lifting her in his arms, Lone Wolf raced through the forest as if she were no heavier than his blanket. Inside the entry room, they both breathed a sigh of relief. Then he set her down, drawing the bark over the door as she went into the sleeping room to check the blaze. Wolf Friend ambled over to his bed, lay down, and closed his eyes as Lone Wolf walked into the sleeping room. He untied his belt and dropped his breechclout at the same time that Catherine tossed her nightshirt on the floor.

Naked, they moved toward each other.

Chapter XIX

The morning sun shone brightly, but its warmth couldn't completely chase away the autumn chill. Wearing a cape, Catherine dressed a deer in front of No-am-ee's wigwam. Finished with the butchering, she draped thin slices of venison across her hand, then skirted around a stump and moved to the food line stretched between the wigwam and a tree. As she carefully hung the meat to dry, strip by strip, her eyes swept the village, taking in the antics of the boisterous children who romped through the streets with their hoops and poles, the old people who dozed in the square, and the crowd of men and women who had gathered in front of Sunflower Woman's wigwam. People were all around her, Catherine thought, but she was alone.

Like the rest of the villagers who remained in Scupperong after Lone Wolf and his braves had departed two days ago, Catherine worked, getting ready for the winter. But her heart wasn't in Scupperong; it was with the warrior who was making his way to Echota. As she gazed into the distance, she remembered the way he looked the day he left; a smile touched her lips and eyes.

Having dressed lightly because he had to travel far and fast, he'd worn a shirt, breechclout, leggings, and moccasins. He carried only the essentials for the trip, food, weapons, and extra moccasins. But the war chief had also packed into his small pouch the white linen shirt and red sash Catherine had made him. Their personal, intimate goodbyes were said in the wigwam, so when it was time for him to leave, Catherine smiled as brightly as she could.

She trembled with delight when Lone Wolf stopped at the entrance gate and turned around. He smiled at her— the special smile he reserved for her alone, the smile she remembered from her first encounter with this magnificent savage. Slowly, deliberately, he lifted his ringed hand to his lips. Never forgetting her endearing caress, he blew her a kiss. Catherine lifted her hand, sunbeams dancing off the small gold band, and she touched it to her lips. She blew him a kiss. Spiritually the two of them clung together in the timeless embrace of love; silently they declared their enduring affection. Then he turned, walking away, leading his braves to Echota. Catherine's heart swelled with pride as she watched him fade into the forest. He was a warrior, he was the war chief of the Scupperongacs; more, he was the man she loved with all her heart.

Though she kept the smile on her lips and soft words in her mouth, Catherine couldn't make her heart laugh. Loneliness shadowed her eyes which mirrored the anxiety in her soul. Today she was even quieter and more withdrawn than usual. As she listened to the animated conversation of the women who stood around Sunflower Woman and Little Doe, Catherine envied them their laughter and happiness. Sighing, she turned away, returning to the front of the wigwam.

As Catherine approached the entrance, No-am-ee walked out the door, pulling a fur-lined robe about her frail form. She squinted her eyes against the glare of the sun as she watched Catherine kneel in front of a drying frame.

"You will have enough skins to make you and Lone Wolf beautiful, new clothes for the spring festival."

"Perhaps Little Doe will be making his clothes by then," Catherine gritted out, pulling the sinew strings to stretch the skin tightly. She could hear Little Doe's laughter above the crowd's din, and its tinkling beauty irritated her . . . it was a constant reminder.

"She will probably sew him clothes for her gift of acceptance," No-am-ee agreed quietly, ignoring Catherine's tartness, "but she won't do that until he has given her the seven gifts of purchase." No-am-ee shuffled past Catherine, her movements stiff and labored. The autumn chill made her bones ache.

"Always seven," Catherine grated bitterly, running her hands over the taut skin.

No-am-ee knew Catherine's sharp replies were only a defense; therefore, the old woman continued to ignore them. "Because Manitou lives in the seventh heaven, seven is our magic number." No-am-ee sat down on the abandoned stump, squirming and adjusting her robe around herself. "In order to give the woman plenty of time to consider her marriage vows, the man gives her seven gifts. Until the woman gives all the gifts to her father and he makes an announcement of marriage to the village, the woman can change her mind."

"Can the man change his mind?" Catherine asked.

"Before the father accepts the gifts, the man can change his mind easily enough," No-am-ee replied. "He goes to the woman and tells her that he's changed his mind. Then they go to her father who publicly announces that the marriage is no longer to be."

"Does the father also publicly return all the gifts of purchase?"

No-am-ee chuckled. "No, the return of the gifts is left up to the woman. If she wishes, she can keep them." She chuckled. "In which case the brave is generally so relieved to have escaped marriage that he doesn't mind her keeping his gifts."

Still crouching, Catherine let her gaze again stray to the women and men grouped around the chief's wigwam. She lifted a hand, shading her eyes from the morning sun. "What are they doing?"

"They're going to build Little Doe a wigwam," No-am-ee answered.

"But Lone Wolf already has one," Catherine cried in surprise, spinning around on her toes so quickly she toppled to the ground.

"Aye. As a great warrior he could demand it," No-am-ee returned, "but it is not our custom for a man to have his own wigwam. The wigwam, the cornfield, and all the stored food belong to the woman." No-am-ee shook her head. "People would lose respect for any woman who consented to live in a man's wigwam."

"I have," Catherine said, her voice defiant.

"But you were a slave." The old woman quickly whittled down the defiance of the younger one. When she saw pain flicker in Catherine's eyes, however, she repented her hasty retort. Softly she added, "You had no choice in the matter, Ca-ther-ine, and now that you're the village champion, people respect you highly."

For a few minutes the two sat in silence. The one worked creases out of the deerskin, the other watched. Eventually No-am-ee said, "For too many winters Lone Wolf has refused to marry another. He has been a man possessed by his past. But now he will marry, and he will live with Little Doe in her wigwam."

Catherine's movements slowed as tentacles of despair wrapped themselves around her heart. "Will I . . . will I have to live with them?"

No-am-ee sighed deeply. If Catherine's plight had been hers, the old woman couldn't have felt the pain more.

420

This question had also haunted her thoughts recently. "I don't know. That's . . ."

No-am-ee faltered. She never told lies, but at the moment she didn't know whether Catherine could bear the truth. Also, the old woman admitted to herself, she didn't want to see the sparkle disappear from the paleface's green eyes or the smile from her beautiful face. The more No-am-ee came to love and respect Catherine the harder it was for her to watch the young woman groping with the Scupperongac traditions which were so different from her own.

"That's what?" Catherine prodded.

"Little Doe will make that decision."

"Little Doe!" Catherine exclaimed, jumping to her feet. "Why Little Doe? I'm not her slave." This was more than Catherine could tolerate.

No-am-ee's voice was soft and soothing. "The house will belong to her, Ca-ther-ine. She will decide who lives in it."

"Lone Wolf has known this?" As the question was whispered through her numbed lips it became a statement. "And he has never told me."

"Perhaps his heart is so involved, he could not speak of it to you."

Catherine had experienced loneliness and despair before, but this was the heaviest burden she had ever born. It was so heavy she didn't know what she was going to do, so heavy she murmured, "What about me?"

"If Little Doe accepts you in the house, you will live with them. If not . . ." The old woman paused. She had spent many sleepless nights pondering the situation. If Little Doe did not accept Catherine into the wigwam, what would Lone Wolf do? Anyone could tell that Lone Wolf was in love with Catherine. "If not"—No-am-ee refused to give voice to her most private thoughts and fears—"Lone Wolf makes the decision. You are

421

his slave."

"I'm a person, not chattel!" Catherine screamed in frustration. "I will not be treated like this. I have tolerated Lone Wolf, but I will not be a slave to Little Doe." She turned on her heel, fleeing to the river. She had to get away; she had to think.

No, the old woman thought, watching Catherine's retreat, you haven't tolerated Lone Wolf, Ca-ther-ine. You love him; therefore, you didn't feel the bonds of your servitude. Aware of the conflicting emotions raging in Catherine's breast, No-am-ee understood the young woman's need for solitude. She made no attempt to call her or follow her.

Catherine walked until she came to the large boulder by the river. Sitting down, she stared at the rushing waterfall. Blinded by the darkness of her despair, however, she couldn't see the splendor of nature. It is ironic, she thought, that Lone Wolf and I are both sacrificed. She must be Lone Wolf's slave and remain in Scupperong to ensure the safety of her people; Lone Wolf must marry Little Doe to preserve and ensure peace between his tribe and the Lumbroans.

Catherine could hardly believe that in so short a time so much had happened to her. Until Lone Wolf had left, she had been able to close her eyes to his forthcoming marriage; she had even pretended that it wasn't going to happen. But now . . . now she had to face it. Hearing a noise behind her, she turned to see Sunflower Woman, leading a group of women and children through the village to the river.

"Over here," Sunflower Woman called. "We build the wigwam close to the waterfall. This is one of Lone Wolf's favorite places."

Before she could be spotted, Catherine slid off the boulder and melted into the forest. Her heart felt as though it would burst, it was so full of pain. Never had she needed the reassurance of Lone Wolf's love as she did in those moments. Never had she wanted the comfort of her father's arms and the wisdom of his advice more. Deeper into the forest she burrowed, not knowing where she was going, not caring. She desired only to escape the encroachment of Little Doe. Catherine did not want to see the desecration of the place where she and Lone Wolf had made love.

"How does it make you feel to know that you're going to have your own wigwam?" Happy Woman asked, her ebony eyes dancing with excitement.

Before Little Doe could answer, another woman said with a soft chuckle, "And to think she's going to share it with Lone Wolf."

The Lumbroan's lips curved upward as gentle laughter twittered through the crowd, but she didn't smile from her soul.

"Any woman would be excited to have such a brave warrior as her husband," another well-wisher added.

The Scupperongac women continued to extol Lone Wolf's prowess as a warrior and hunter, but Little Doe didn't hear them. She was too caught up in her own thoughts. Because she was not allowed to help with the construction of her bridal wigwam, she slowly moved away from the busy crowd. She stood at the edge of the activity for a long time, but finally she strayed to the edge of the forest. Seated there on a thick mat of pine straw, she silently watched as Happy Woman and the others outlined the foundation of the wigwam—her wigwam— the wigwam she was to share with Lone Wolf.

Little Doe heard the laughter about her, but she couldn't join in. Within she cried. She longed for the familiar faces of Lumbroa; she longed to be with her people. Solemnly she watched the braves return from the forest with trimmed saplings over their shoulders. They set them in the ground, and as each sapling was staked and strapped to another, Little Doe's heart grew heavier. Her fate was being shaped and formed by men just as the wigwam was. When the house was completed, the villagers would bring her wedding gifts . . . when the house was completed, her future would be bound with Lone Wolf's.

Why, Father? she cried silently, leaning against the tree trunk and closing her eyes. Why must I marry Lone Wolf? Why does the council insist on him? But even as she mentally rehearsed the questions, Little Doe knew the answer. Only the bravest of the Scupperongac warriors could command respect and achieve peace. The mention of Lone Wolf's name was enough to put fear into the Iroquois.

Little Doe also grieved because her father had left her so suddenly. She hadn't wanted to spend the winter in Scupperong. Although she understood why her father had hastened to Echota, she still resented being left behind. The only one of Flying Eagle's children to survive, the child of his old age and of his favorite wife, Rain Cloud, Little Doe had enjoyed a relationship with her father that few children knew. After Rain Cloud's death, the old chief had defied convention which decreed that she be reared by her mother's family, and he had reared Little Doe himself, doting on her, spoiling her. Now because of the decree of the council she was bound by her father's word to marry Lone Wolf, war chief of the Scupperongacs—a man whom she feared . . . a man who loved another.

Unnoticed, Little Doe rose and meandered away from the builders. Deep in thought, she followed the winding river through the forest, moving farther and farther from the protective palisades of Scupperong. When she reached a certain spot, she stopped walking and she smiled, remembering the night she had first met Kee-Lee.

*　　*　　*

Ever since Lone Wolf, his warriors, and the trading expedition had embarked from Scupperong, the brave had waited and watched, biding his time. Now he moved stealthily and purposefully through the forest. Patiently he had awaited the moment when the woman was far enough away from the others so that her cries could not be heard, when he could safely capture her and take her to the waiting canoes without fear of immediate reprisal. He had been patient. However, he admitted to himself that at times he'd wondered how long it would take him to keep his promise to Manitou.

Now he smiled. His day had come. He would have his revenge; he would make the murderer suffer. Lone Wolf had escaped the gauntlet, but he would not escape punishment this time. Lone Wolf would pay dearly for having taken a warrior's honor and integrity. The Scupperongac would die a long, lingering death. The brave chuckled softly, his plans for revenge filling him with amusement. First he would strip the Scupperongac war chief of all he held dear. Then he would take Lone Wolf's women—the paleface and the Indian princess. He had admired Catherine since the first time that he had seen her. He was glad that she had left the paleface village. He laughed aloud, pleasure singing through his veins. He would humiliate Lone Wolf; he would bring the Scupperongac war chief to his knees.

He would make all Scupperongacs suffer, and the Lumbroans would regret that they had considered joining with the Scupperongacs. As the lone warrior boasted to himself, he lifted one hand, easing his fingers to the neckline of his leather jacket. He touched the necklace that hung about his neck, and his lips twisted into a smug smile. How carefully he had laid his plan . . . how patiently he had waited. Soon—very soon—all of it would come together. The Algonkin tribes would be fighting each other, and the Scupperongacs would attack the palefaces—the hated people from over the sea. Destroyed from within, the Scupperongacs and Lumbroans would be easy prey for stronger tribes.

Suddenly jarred from his musings, the brave dodged behind a tree. The woman had stopped walking; she was slowly moving her head from side to side and looking around, her thick, shiny braids swinging as she did so. Crouching low, her pursuer hid, hardly breathing until she sat down. When she leaned against a tree trunk and closed her eyes, he emitted a long sigh of relief.

The brave stopped at the river's edge, and he took his cosmetic pouch from his belt. He pulled the bunched buckskin open and dipped his fingers into the grease, smearing it over his face and through his cockscomb. Then he streaked colors across his countenance—bright, vivid, grotesque colors. Finally he added his deer roach and colored his hair vermillion. With luck the woman wouldn't recognize him until it was too late, until he was ready to reveal his identity.

He lifted his head and his hands to Manitou. "I will have revenge," he swore, remembering a promise he had made not many moons ago. "I will keep the Lumbroans and the Scupperongacs from making an alliance," he had sworn to his tribe. "And I will see the palefaces destroyed."

Now he was ready for victory!

The afternoon sun glared relentlessly on the small group who worked on the wigwam. The saplings were already bent and bound in place, and some of the women were shaping the dome with strips of bark while others stacked the reed mats that would be pegged over the bark. Still others brought furs for the inner lining. The children, playing games as they worked, gathered straw to line the house and to cushion the reed-mat floor. Happy Woman, wanting to know where to put the loose mats which could easily be unpegged for windowlike openings in the walls, looked about for the Lumbroan maiden.

"Where is Little Doe?" she asked one of the women nearest her.

"I don't know," the woman replied, looking about. "I haven't seen her since early morning."

Having overheard the question, Little Flower called, "I saw her walking that way." Her arms full of straw, the child jerked her head in the direction she indicated. Reaching Happy Woman, she dropped her load and pointed into the forest.

"When was that?" Happy Woman peered into the woods.

"When Elder Brother, the Sun, was still in the eastern sky," Little Flower returned.

Nodding her acknowledgment, Happy Woman took a few steps, calling Little Doe's name and straining to see into the forest. When the woman didn't answer, Happy Woman grew concerned. "Are you sure?" she asked Little Flower.

"I'm sure." The child stooped and picked up her doll, tucking it under her arm. "Follow me. I'll show you where she went." Skipping ahead of Happy Woman, Little Flower led her through the woods.

Always alert to nature and its messages, Happy Woman listened to the subtle cry of the forest. She knew something was wrong. Softly she called Little Flower to her side and took the child by the hand, slowing her steps and moving more carefully. Although she looked straight ahead, her eyes swept all around her.

Under her breath, she said, "Little Flower, I want you to return to the village. Tell Wise One that something is wrong in the forest."

Conditioned from infancy to show no outward emotion, Little Flower squeezed Happy Woman's hand to let her know that she understood.

"I will follow the river," Happy Woman said, the fingers of her other hand tightly clasping the hilt of her knife. Looking down at the small, round-faced youngster, the woman said, "Run as fast as you can, and be careful. I fear the enemy is roaming our forest."

Little Flower nodded her head. Holding the doll up, she said, "I will run fast, Happy Woman, and nothing will happen to me. I have Catherine's magic with me. It is strong."

Happy Woman smiled. "Go then."

The woman watched the retreating figure of the child; then she turned and started walking again. This time she veered from the open path, seeking safety in the shelter of the trees. Slowly and carefully she moved, her eyes looking for telltale signs: broken twigs, snagged buckskin dangling from branches, the fluttering of disturbed creatures, crushed leaves. She listened for unfamiliar sounds.

Then she spotted the footprints, the crushed leaves. Lowering her head, she followed the path through the forest. As suddenly as it had begun it ended. Puzzled, Happy Woman stooped, hoping to pick up the trail again. At the instant she realized why the trail had disappeared, she heard the noise above her. She looked up as the painted warrior jumped from the tree and landed next to her. Leaping to her feet, she swung her knife through the air, but the brave was too quick and too strong for her. With one deft blow, he knocked the weapon from her grasp and clamped his hand over her mouth, stifling her screams. His other arm held her body in an iron vise.

Gagging Happy Woman so she couldn't scream, the brave laughed softly. "Manitou is with me this day," he said.

Chapter XX

Three elm-bark canoes, each manned by two braves, sailed smoothly and quickly upriver without attracting undue attention. During the trading truce the participating tribes honored the peace agreements. As long as strangers traveled the established trading route and made no attempt to land close to an Algonkin village, they were safe.

Bound and gagged, Catherine squirmed gingerly in the bottom of one of the canoes, trying to ease her cramped and aching muscles. She squinted her eyes against the glare of the sun as she wriggled from beneath the blanket under which she had been lying since her capture. For the hundredth time since she had been thrown into the canoe, she wondered who had seized her; she wondered why she had been kidnapped. Taken by surprise when she'd been dozing, she had only once glimpsed the paint-streaked face of her captor. As he dragged her through the forest, she had felt that she knew him, but she couldn't recognize him from that quick glimpse.

She looked at the two braves in the canoe, one in the bow, the other in the stern, and she recognized neither. The one who had kidnapped her was not in the canoe. But that doesn't mean he isn't close by, Catherine thought.

Although she had been hidden from sight and had been unable to see, she knew this wasn't the only canoe. She could tell by the soft ripple of the water lapping against the sides of the craft that several more paddles were being used. The Indian who had captured her could be in one of the other canoes.

She fiddled with the thongs that bound her hands, but she couldn't loosen them. Finally she ceased fighting and lay down. They traveled a long time, day turning into night, night into day, yet none of the braves spoke. Late one evening they finally stopped. The braves deftly leaped out of the canoe, one holding it steady while the other roughly yanked Catherine onto feet that were numb from lack of circulation. She hit the shallow water with a splash, falling to her knees, and one brave growled angrily, then jerked her up and dragged her ashore.

More canoes! More Indians! Catherine thought, the grunts and splashes around her, confirming her earlier suspicions, but it was too dark for her to see. When the brave pushed her to the ground, she heard two more thuds close to her. Then she heard a soft groan that was definitely feminine. Rolling onto her backside, Catherine painstakingly pushed herself up until she was leaning against a tree. Her eyes having grown accustomed to the dark, she made out two forms. They lay nearby, but she wasn't close enough to make them out. Because she was still gagged, she couldn't talk to them.

The braves built a small fire and circled around it, forgetting about the women. They munched on their corn meal; then they talked in low grunts, laughing every once in a while. Catherine stared at them, studying their faces in the glow of the blaze, listening to their voices as they talked. Not one of them sounded like the brave who had captured her; not one of them felt or looked familiar. Eventually one of the braves came to where Catherine sat.

Crouching in front of her, he untied her gag. In sign language he said, "We are far from your village now. You can scream all you want." Then in his own language, he spoke to the other braves. "Bring them some food. Strong Hand will be angry if anything happens to the captives."

"Why should we care, Brown Hawk?" one of the braves called back, making no effort to relinquish the warmth of the fire. "They are not for our pleasure."

The warrior moved from Catherine to the other woman. "It would be better, Straight Arrow," he said, untying the second gag, "if you did not cross Strong Hand. Remember what happened the last time one of us disobeyed him. He has no mercy."

Straight Arrow grunted and stood. Untying the food sack from his belt, he moved to where Catherine sat. Pouring some corn meal into his hand, he held it under her mouth. But Catherine couldn't eat. Her tongue was blistered from the thong, and her mouth ached. Blood trickled from the corners where the leather had cut into her tender flesh. Snarling his disapproval, the brave grabbed a fistful of hair and pushed her face into his hand.

The corn meal went up Catherine's nose, and she coughed and sputtered. Eventually she managed to eat a couple of mouthfuls. Irritated because he had to tend to the captives but he could not avail himself of their bodies, Straight Arrow gave Catherine no consideration. When the palmful of meal was gone—most of it spilled on the ground—he moved to the next captive.

Her eyes accustomed to the dark by now, Catherine recognized Little Doe. Silently she watched Straight Arrow cram his palm against the Lumbroan princess' mouth. She heard her muffled cry. Turning her head, Catherine saw Brown Hawk move to the third form, the one who lay so quietly, never moving.

431

"Is she alive?" Brown Hawk grunted as he untied the gag.

"I do not know," Straight Arrow replied unconcernedly. "Nor do I care. If she's dead, that is one less burden for us to carry." He drew back his hand as if to slap Little Doe's face when she refused to eat the meal. "I hope Strong Hand knows what he is doing," he grumbled. "When Lone Wolf learns that we have his women—"

"Strong Hand knows," Brown Hawk assured the other brave. "Long and carefully, he has planned his revenge." Brown Hawk's fingers touched the wound on Happy Woman's temple. Her body twitched, and she moaned. "Good," the brave grunted, shifting her into a sitting position. "I do not want Strong Hand to be angry with me."

After Happy Woman had eaten a bite or two of the corn meal, Brown Hawk and Straight Arrow led the women to the river and they untied their captives' hands so they could get a drink of water. Knowing she must drink to survive, Catherine did so. Then she moved closer to Happy Woman so she could see how badly she was wounded. Brown Hawk noticed, however, and he jerked her away from Happy Woman, shoving her to the ground beside Little Doe.

Angry, Catherine grabbed the man by the heel and jerked him off his feet. Brown Hawk grunted his surprise as his body thwacked against the ground, and Straight Arrow, spinning around and forgetting Happy Woman, ran to Brown Hawk's rescue. He kicked Catherine aside and held out his hand to Brown Hawk.

The Iroquois slowly rose to his feet, his visage set in angry, uncompromising lines. Nothing would have given him more pleasure than to torture the paleface. Yet his fear of Strong Hand kept him from hitting her. Like Straight Arrow, Brown Hawk wished Strong Hand would arrive soon. He was tired of dealing with the captives.

Happy Woman, taking advantage of the distraction, jumped to her feet and lunged for freedom. She reached the river and managed to shove the elm-bark canoe into the water, but still dizzy from her head wound, her vision blurred and she stumbled and fell, the splash catching Straight Arrow's attention. In several long strides, he was at the canoe, hauling Happy Woman out of the water.

As he dragged her, Happy Woman, off balance, blinked her eyes, trying to clear her vision. She lifted the paddle and swung it wildly, hitting him on the shoulder. Instead of stunning him, however, the blow served only to whet his anger. Catching the flailing paddle in his hand, he jerked it out of Happy Woman's hand, and he boxed her on the side of the head in the same place she had been wounded earlier. Reeling from the blow, Happy Woman crumpled, falling to her knees.

Yanking her to her feet, Straight Arrow slapped her across the face several times. Dazed, Happy Woman momentarily drooped in his arms. One arm slung around the woman's waist, the brave grunted his satisfaction as he waded out of the water. Happy Woman felt the hilt of his knife as it gouged her arm. Moving carefully so as not to arouse his suspicion, her fingers crawled to the weapon, and before he knew what was happening she jerked it out of his embroidered belt. Suddenly, startlingly she twisted to stab him, but the brave was quicker. Instinctively he realized her intent. He dropped her and she fell, the weight of her body impaling her shoulder on the blade.

Stone-faced, Catherine and Little Doe watched Happy Woman stagger to her feet. She glared at Straight Arrow for a minute, then reached up and yanked the knife from her shoulder. When blood gushed from the wound, staining her dress, both women wanted to run to her aid. But they knew better. With hurting hearts they watched the woman warrior slowly lift her hand. With a proud arrogance Happy Woman tossed the knife into the river, and she stared defiantly at Straight Arrow as if she were not in pain.

The man's hand banded around her arm, and heedless of her wound he pulled her along behind him as he joined Brown Hawk and the captives. Laughing, the two men herded the women close to the fire and tied them together around a tree. This time, however, Brown Hawk didn't gag them.

When the braves had stalked back to the fire, Catherine softly called, "Happy Woman, are you hurt badly?"

"I don't think so," came the reply.

"Why have they taken us?" Little Doe whispered, her eyes never leaving the six braves who sat around the fire.

"Because the two of you are prisoners I would say it has something to do with Lone Wolf," Happy Woman mumbled, pain now searing through her shoulder and her arm.

"Why you?" Catherine asked.

"I"—Happy Woman leaned her throbbing head against the tree, trying to still the dizziness—"I'm not sure. I think I am an innocent victim. I must have come upon them when they were capturing the two of you." She licked her dry lips, wincing when the tip of her tongue touched the cuts at the corners of her mouth. "I was out looking for Little Doe," she said, "when I realized something was wrong."

"Will anyone know where we are and who's taken us?" Catherine asked.

"Aye," Happy Woman replied, "I sent Little Flower back to the village."

The words sent a small surge of hope through Catherine, but it quickly deserted her. All of the Scupperongac braves were with Lone Wolf, and it would

434

take a runner several days to reach him. By the time he returned to Scupperongac and gathered a war party, she would be deep in enemy territory. There was little likelihood that he would find the three of them.

The night was long and sleepless for Catherine. By morning she was chilled to the bone. She was glad when the braves hopped to their feet, untied them, and guided them to the canoes. Soon they were moving up the river. This time the braves didn't retie the women; instead they allowed them to sit up, each one in the middle of a canoe. As another day and night passed, Happy Woman's wound became infected, and her fever soared. For the most part she lay in the canoe. Catherine and Little Doe cast alert eyes along the shore, marking their way, hoping they would be able to escape and return to their own village.

The farther north they traveled, the colder it became. Although not solicitous of the captives' welfare, the braves feared Strong Hand's retaliation should anything happen to the women; therefore, they took three blankets from the bottoms of the canoes and gave one to each. Late in the afternoon of the third day, they finally reached their destination. The braves pulled ashore, and Catherine and Little Doe helped Happy Woman disembark. While the braves beached the canoes, Little Doe gathered some moss which the captives stuffed in their moccasins and knee-high leggings for added warmth.

Catherine's hands were so cold and stiff she could hardly relace her leggings. She shivered as the cold wind whipped against her face, blistering it with cold icy blasts. Straightening and pulling the blanket closer around her body, she looked around. Happy Woman, weak from the loss of blood, stumbled and fell to her knees. Quickly Catherine went to her.

"Here," she said. Gently insinuating her shoulder beneath Happy Woman's, she placed the wounded woman's arm around her neck. "Let me help you."

The warrior woman's fever-glazed eyes stared into her green ones. Only for an instant did defiance make them hard and glassy. Then a smile twitched at the Scupperongac's lips. "Thank you, Ca-ther-ine." When she lowered her weight onto Catherine, the two of them stumbled, but Catherine quickly regained her balance. "It seems"— Happy Woman drew in a deep painful gulp of air, and she closed her eyes, wishing the throbbing in her temples would stop—"that I owe you another debt."

"You owe me nothing," Catherine grunted. She was so engrossed in wrapping a blanket around Happy Woman that her own slipped unheeded to the ground. "You would do the same for me."

"Would I?" the Scupperongac asked. She paused; then said: "I am the one who started the fire and let you take the blame."

"I thought it was you," Catherine replied.

"Yet you have treated me honorably."

"I have. But if our roles had been reversed and my place in English society had been threatened by your arrival, I don't know how I would have reacted." Catherine looked around. "Now it doesn't matter. We must be friends until we can escape."

Stooping, Little Doe picked up the fallen blanket and draped it over Catherine's shoulders, holding it in place with her arm. Then Happy Woman stepped into a hole, jarring Catherine, and the three of them, entwined together, almost fell. When they regained their balance, they laughed.

"What are they going to do with us?" Catherine asked, her fingers biting into Happy Woman's waist.

"Generally they adopt the women," Little Doe ventured. "But in case of war with my father or with Lone Wolf . . ."

Her next words were whipped into oblivion by a gust of

wind, and the women quieted. Finally they arrived at a large town, built on a hill. Catherine gasped when she saw the log palisade. It was thick and ominous looking, its pointed poles spearing the air. The huge moat around the fence was filled with water.

Carefully they crossed the earthen mound that served as a bridge, and Catherine guided Happy Woman toward the gate. However, one of the braves grabbed her by the shoulder and gave her a rough shake. He then signed for them to stop. Another brave lifted his hand to his face, cupped his mouth, and made soft cooes. They waited. The brave cooed again. Catherine heard a soft bird call at the same instant that he waved his hand for them to move. They walked through the long, winding entrance, and Catherine gazed at the warriors who stood watch.

Inside the walls were a dozen or more houses that were different from the wigwams. Instead of being dome shaped, these houses were long and rectangular. Bark-covered and single-storied, they had slooping roofs and a door at each end. They were clustered around an open square in the center of the village. Unlike Scupperong, Catherine noticed, this village was noisy and untidy. Children and dogs overran the paths and open spaces, while men and women sat about, working at their tasks in the waning warmth of afternoon sun. Other women were returning from the river, water jars balanced on their heads and shoulders.

Fires blazed and people soon gathered to greet the returning warriors. Agog with curiosity, the villagers bombarded the braves with questions, and they gazed curiously at the paleface woman. Hands reached out from all sides, touching Catherine's hair. She wanted to recoil from the touching, but she stared ahead of her, ignoring the clawing fingers. Finally Brown Hawk halted the captives in front of a long house in the center of the village. Pulling the skin flap aside, he pointed through the door.

Leading the way, Catherine stopped in the small storage room which was filled with firewood. Roughly nudged on by Brown Hawk, she stumbled through the second skinned opening into a roomy and comfortable long house which was approximately fifty feet in length and about twenty-five feet wide. Catherine noticed that the long house had neither windows nor chimneys; the only light in the room filtered in through the five or six smoke holes in the ceiling. The interior was smoky and full of the strong odors of cooking, of drying meat, of skins, and of people.

Down the center of the earth floor ran a row of small fire pits, all of them burning, people crowded around each of them. Storage poles were lashed across the rafters near the roof on both sides of the long house. Strings of corn and dried meat hung from the rafters. Bunches of clean-smelling sweet grass hung from the poles. Pots and baskets of corn, dried berries, and other stored foods overflowed from the spaces under the sleeping platforms which were built along the walls a foot or two from the floor. Hanging from the walls were bows and war clubs, snowshoes, belts, charms, and pouches. Every bit of the crowded space was used. Counting the dividers between the sleeping platforms, Catherine realized there were five separate compartments.

Brown Hawk, speaking to friends as he moved, threaded his way to the other end of the long house. Behind him trailed the captives, Straight Arrow bringing up the rear. When Brown Hawk stood in front of the village chief, he stopped. Swimming Eel stared wordlessly at the braves.

During the tense silence, Catherine let her eyes sweep around the long house. The Iroquois were well-built people of medium height, she noticed. The men were rather thin, but strong and muscular. The women were

438

stouter, but they were also muscular. They were brown-eyed, with prominent cheekbones and straight black hair, and their skin was a light brown.

"Sit," Swimming Eel eventually commanded, his dour expression never changing.

Catherine watched Brown Hawk and Straight Arrow sit in front of the fire, but neither she, Little Doe, or Happy Woman moved. They remained standing. The chief's wife hastened to get the returning braves a bowl of fresh corn mush.

Catherine could hardly keep from drooling when she smelled the food. For the past three days she had lived on corn meal, and her stomach was contracting painfully at the thought of warm, cooked food. She disciplined her face, however, refusing to give the Iroquois the pleasure of seeing her hunger.

She looked at Happy Woman, then at Little Doe. With just a flicker of their eyes the three agreed to be one in purpose and resolve. Stoically they stared straight ahead, ignoring the hunger pains and the hecklers who were crowding around them.

When the prayer and sacrifice were over, Swimming Eel asked, "Why have you returned from the trading trip with captives rather than goods?" His dark brown eyes moved disapprovingly over the three women.

"These are Lone Wolf's women—his paleface slave and Flying Eagle's daughter," Brown Hawk answered, slurping his food appreciatively. "Strong Hand is following closely behind. He wanted to meet with Wanchese, war chief of the Roanoacs; then he will speak with you, Great Chief, about all he has done."

"And what will the council chiefs say when they return from Echota?" Swimming Eel exclaimed, his face still creased in a frown. "Do we prepare for war now? Do we fight both the Scupperongacs and the Lumbroans? Will the palefaces with their sticks that thunder join

439

the Algonkins?"

Brown Hawk shook his head. "Do not concern yourself, my chief. Strong Hand, my brother, has been given great wisdom by the Great Spirit. Lone Wolf will never know that we are the ones who captured his women." He chuckled as he thought of Strong Hand's plan. "His raiding party will be destroyed before he leaves his own territory."

Swimming Eel accepted Brown Hawk's report. He, too, believed in the wisdom and magic of Strong Hand. He was one of the most valiant of all Iroquois warriors, and he was destined to be one of the great tribal chiefs of the league of the Iroquois. He asked, "Will Strong Hand also bring the goods we sent you after?"

"Strong Hand promised he would get them," Brown Hawk assured the chief. "I'm sure he will bring them when he comes."

"Umph!"

Swimming Eel wasn't pleased with the outcome of the trading expedition so far. He had wanted some of the beautiful pipes only made by the Indians in the distant, southern forest. His wife had wanted buffalo robes and horns from which he could make her spoons. But the old chief said nothing. He would wait to hear Strong Hand's story. Silently he smoked his pipe, and he gazed pensively at the women while the two men ate their meal.

The paleface was unusual, he grudgingly admitted, pleased with her poise; the other two were not so exceptional; and none of them were worth jeopardizing the trading truce. But these young bucks were stubborn and headstrong—Strong Hand more so than most.

"What are you going to do with the captives?" he eventually asked.

"We would have taken no captives if the decision had been mine to make," Straight Arrow said, holding his bowl to his lips and slurping out the last of the broth.

440

"They are going to bring us nothing but trouble." Running his index finger around the inside rim of the bowl, he wiped it clean. Then he lifted his hand and licked the tasty meal off his finger.

"They are not going to bring me trouble," Brown Hawk denied with a soft chuckle. Looking at the chief, he said, "They belong to Strong Hand, my chief. They are his concern."

The old chief's displeasure seemed to grow. "Rather than the goods we wanted and needed, Strong Hand has returned with three women we can easily do without! What does he plan to do with them? Who is going to take care of them until he arrives?"

Neither Brown Hawk nor Straight Arrow answered. They hadn't given the last question any thought. Would Bluebird, Strong Hand's wife, allow him to bring the women into the long house? Brown Hawk wondered. If so, he would have to place them in her custody, and Strong Hand would not like that. Bluebird and the other women might decide to torture them rather than adopt them into the tribe, and Brown Hawk knew Strong Hand would not want that . . . not just yet.

"I will put them in one of the storage huts," Brown Hawk finally replied, and Straight Arrow grunted his approval. "When Strong Hand arrives, he can do with them what he wishes."

Swimming Eel nodded his head. "That is a wise decision, my son."

He cleaned his pipe, refilled it, and lit it. After he had taken the first puff, he handed the pipe to Brown Hawk. By the time the men had smoked, they had completed their discussion. Rising, Brown Hawk pushed the onlookers back. "Out of my way," he shouted. Grabbing Catherine by the arm, he yanked her along behind him, and he motioned for Little Doe and Happy Woman to follow.

He and Straight Arrow led the women out of the long house and through the village to a hut near the palisade. Pulling the flap aside, he pushed them roughly through the door, into the dim, musky interior. "Wait here," he said to Straight Arrow. "I'll go get Tall Tree. He can guard the women until Strong Hand arrives."

Straining her eyes to see once they were inside, Little Doe glanced around for something with which to anchor the flapping bearskin to the door frame. Her gaze landed on the ash blackened spot in the center of the hut. Quickly she moved across the room and she picked up two of the larger stones in both hands. While she worked with the door flap, Catherine threw a blanket on the earthen floor and eased Happy Woman down. By this time Little Doe was beside Catherine, helping her with Happy Woman. Cradling the wounded woman in their arms, Catherine and Little Doe removed her dress and covered her with another blanket. In the wedge of light that filtered through the crack between the flap and the door, they examined the cut.

"It is not deep," Happy Woman muttered when Catherine's fingers gently probed the wound.

"Not deep but infected," Catherine replied, her eyes tracking the red streaks that fanned from the cut. Looking at Little Doe, she said, "We need some water to clean the wound."

Pushing herself to her feet, Little Doe walked to the door and pushed the flap aside. Before she could walk through the opening, however, a scowling brave blocked her way.

Quaking inwardly but outwardly poised, Little Doe signed. "We are cold. We would like to gather some wood for a fire, and we need water."

Never acknowledging her request, Straight Arrow glared disdainfully at the Lumbroan princess. Then he lifted his eyes, his gaze sweeping the room. He looked at the paleface who knelt beside the wounded Scupperongac. Shaking his head, he dropped the flap and resumed his position in front of the hut.

Tucking the skin between the stones and the frame, Little Doe reanchored the door flap. Wrapping her arms around her shivering body, she moved restlessly around the hut. The shadows were lengthening, and the room was getting darker and colder by the minute.

Catherine lifted the third blanket and threw it around her shoulders. Looking up and catching the Lumbroan's attention, she held one arm up. "Come," she said. "Share the blanket with me."

For what seemed like hours, Catherine and Little Doe huddled together under the blanket. They talked awhile, but neither found solace in words. They had no answers for their questions, no assurances for their doubts and fears, and both were loathe to voice those fears. Finally the Lumbroan stretched on the blanket beside Happy Woman and dozed. Feeling alone and vulnerable, Catherine pulled the blanket closer around her shoulders.

As her loneliness grew, Catherine ceased to be aware of the sounds made by the Iroquois community; it silenced all the outside activity. She missed Scupperong and her wigwam. She smiled wistfully and thought of Little Flower and the cornhusk doll. This memory invited another that reminded Catherine of her captivity and of her plight in Scupperong. Pulling her legs up to her chest and lacing her arms around them, she rested her face on her knees. She closed her eyes and sighed, picturing Noam-ee's frail form hunched over the stump in front of the wigwam.

She saw Lone Wolf, standing at the gate to Scupperong, waving goodbye. She felt the touch of his kiss on her mouth, whisper soft but soul deep; she felt the warmth of his smile. Squeezing back tears and drawing a

443

long breath, she tightened her arms around her legs, trying to stop the hurt in her heart.

She started when the skin over the door flapped open, a cold gust of wind ushering in two women with burden baskets strapped to their backs. The older woman carried two cooking pots in her arms, both of which she set near the cold fire pit in the center of the room. The younger woman carried robes and blankets.

Unexpectedly a man entered the room after the women, a water jug in his arms. Because it was dark and he stood behind the women, Catherine didn't immediately notice him. Limping to the platform that stretched along one wall, he looped the thong of the jar around a peg. Turning, he silently waited for the older woman to join him. Speaking in Iroquoian, she motioned the younger woman to her side. With quick, fluid motions, the maiden slid the basket from her shoulders; then she laid a cornhusk mattress over the platform. As she stretched fur-lined blankets over the bed, the older woman and the man returned to where Catherine and Little Doe sat. Again the woman spoke, this time her eyes studied Catherine and Happy Woman.

"Yellow Corn, the older woman," the man said in faultless English, directing his words to Catherine, "would like to know who you are?"

Shocked, Catherine struggled to her feet and squinted her eyes. She stared at this man who spoke her language so smoothly it had to be his natural tongue. Not interested in the identity of the Iroquois woman, she took a step nearer him and peered into his face. She could tell from the way he spoke that he was older, but the room was too dimly lit for her to make out his features.

"I . . . I am Catherine Graystone," she murmured. "Who are you?"

"I am called Feather Man, slave to Yellow Corn," the old man replied, his gray eyes straining to see the paleface

444

about whom the entire village was talking. He pointed to Yellow Corn. "She is Strong Hand's mother, and the guard outside your door is his brother, Tall Tree."

"I'm not interested in the woman's or the guard's name," Catherine hissed. "Nor do I want to know what the Indians call you. I want to know your Christian name."

The man chuckled. Indeed rumor was right. The paleface was feisty. He would wager that Strong Hand was going to need all of his resources when dealing with this female. Not liking Strong Hand, the man was amused by this thought. Lapsing into Iroquoian, he spoke to Yellow Corn. "The paleface is called Catherine. She thanks you for your hospitality." The woman's expression never changed, but she grunted her appreciation.

"I said—" Catherine began.

"I'm John Fletcher," the man interrupted.

"John Fletcher!" Catherine exclaimed. "One of the caretakers!"

"Aye," he exclaimed. "How did you know?"

"Flint," she replied. Then, her words coming out very rapidly, she added, "Flint and Miller are living with the Scupperongacs. They didn't know what happened to you. How come you're here with the Iroquois, and why are you helping the women?"

"That's a long story, mistress, but I'll be more than happy to—"

Before Fletcher could say more, Brown Hawk came through the dancing flap, a cold gust of wind announcing his arrival. "Feather Man," he said in Iroquoian, "what are you doing here?" His voice indicated his irritation.

Yellow Corn pushed in front of Fletcher. "He is my slave," she answered firmly. "I brought him with me so he could tend to Strong Hand's captives."

"He is not to be trusted," Brown Hawk growled. "He is one of them."

445

"He can do no harm," Yellow Corn replied. She pointed to Fletcher's leg. "He is old and crippled, and he knows what Strong Hand will do to him if anything happens to these captives. Besides they are inside the palisades, surrounded by the villagers, and Tall Tree is keeping guard." Yellow Corn laughed. "Even if they escape from Fletcher and Tall Tree, they will never make it out of the village."

Brown Hawk's eyes derisively ran over the scar that stretched from Fletcher's temple to his chin. "If anything happens to them, not only Strong Hand but I will demand your life." The Indian paused meaningfully, and he stared long and hard at the paleface, willing him to remember those he had seen tortured. "Your death will be slow and painful."

Without another word Brown Hawk turned on his heel and walked out of the room, taking Straight Arrow with him. As the two men walked away, Catherine could hear their voices interspersed every so often with gusty laughter. Cold wind blew through the entrance, and Little Doe slipped across the icy room to tuck the flap between the frame and the stones once again.

In the heavy silence that settled over them after Brown Hawk's departure, Catherine watched the Iroquoian women as they efficiently turned the platforms on either side of the hut into beds and as they carefully built a fire. One of the women set two clay jugs in the flames—one filled with water, the other with corn mush. The other placed a mat by the fire, laying a bowl and three spoons on it. Then she moved to where Happy Woman lay. Not speaking a word, she pulled the blanket aside and looked at the cut. She lifted her hands and gently touched the swelling on Happy Woman's head.

Speaking Iroquoian, Yellow Corn ordered Fletcher to move Happy Woman to the platform. The younger of the two Iroquoian women filled a bark cup with water and moved to the bed. Dipping a treated skin in the water, she wet it; then she cleaned the wound. Yellow Corn walked to her burden basket and lifted out a small bark box. Opening it, she went over to Catherine and spoke. Fletcher interpreted.

"These are salves for the woman's wounds, and the cornhusks are in the basket by the platform," he explained as the woman pointed to each container. Yellow Corn held up some roots and spoke again. Fletcher said, "Boil these in water, so she can drink the tea, and she'll be better by morning."

When Catherine nodded, Yellow Corn set the salves down on the platform; then she motioned for the younger woman to follow her. The Iroquoian women slipped out of the hut, leaving Fletcher alone with the three captives. As Little Doe walked to the door, he limped to the fire. This time the Lumbroan not only secured the flap against the frame with the stones, she pegged two heavy robes over the entrance. Afterward she returned to the platform and sat beside Happy Woman while Catherine moved to the blaze in the center of the room.

Holding her hand out to Fletcher, she asked, "May I borrow your knife?" The Englishman hoisted thick silver eyebrows, and Catherine sighed. "I need to cut the roots."

"I'll cut them," he said.

Catherine laughed. "You don't trust me?"

As Fletcher moved closer to the fire, for the first time Catherine could distinguish his features. Thick brows shaded his silver gray eyes, and his white hair, parted in the middle, hung in braids.

"I trust you." He crouched in front of the blaze and took the roots from her hand. "I just don't trust your judgment at the moment." Catherine lifted her face and blinked at the top of his bowed head in surprise. "My life depends on your staying here, Mistress Graystone," he stated as bits of root splashed into the water. "So that's exactly what you will do. Now if'n you try to escape from me, I probably won't harm you, but I don't vouch for Tall Tree. He's mean, just like Strong Hand. And if'n you should get by the both of us, you'll face the whole village"—he looked up at Catherine, his eyes squarely on hers—"and the women are the worst."

"You fear for your life?" Catherine mocked.

"Maybe," he muttered.

"Or perhaps you are thinking about Yellow Corn?"

"She saved me," he answered tersely. "Them devils, her included, were killing me little by little, and they were enjoying it immensely. They broke my legs in several places, and they cut me all over. They were about ready to burn me when one of the hecklers, a small child, tripped and fell. I was so far gone that I welcomed death." Remembering the ordeal, Fletcher grimaced. "I'd . . . I'd seen what they did to other prisoners, mutilating their bodies, member by member." Unable to go on, he lapsed into painful memories.

"What happened to the child?" Catherine gently reminded him.

"The child?" he asked blankly; then he immediately said, "Oh, the child." He paused. "Yellow Corn's child." Fletcher shrugged his shoulders. "I flipped myself over and kept him from falling into the fire." He lifted his head and laughed, the sound raw and bitter. "Yellow Corn, the woman in charge of the torturing, then owed me a debt of gratitude, a debt she had to pay before I died. So she took me for her slave."

Dropping the last bit of root into the pot, he wiped his knife down one legging, his hand down the other. "Why don't you and the girl eat; then lie down and rest some. I'll care for the wounded woman."

He sidled nearer to the flame, filling the bowl with

448

mush. While the women ate, he limped to the sleeping platform and sat on the edge. Holding Happy Woman's chin with one hand, he smeared the salve on her forehead and shoulder with the other.

"I'm sorry," he murmured as his big hand gently touched the inflamed cut. "I know this must hurt."

A paleface, Happy Woman thought, a hint of a smile on her lips. He spoke the same language as Catherine. Her thick lashes lifted and her ebony eyes peered curiously at the man who dressed her wound. She wished she could see more than shadowed features. When he touched the wound, she tensed.

"Sorry," he murmured again.

"I'll feed her now," Catherine said.

"Nay." Fletcher rose and slowly moved to the fire. "Now that you women have eaten," he said, taking the bowl and spoon from Catherine, "why don't you lie down and rest. I'll feed her and give her a cup of the broth when it's brewed."

"I . . . I would like to talk with you," Catherine said, weariness settling over her now that she was warm and full.

"Nay, Mistress Graystone," Fletcher replied. "We'll have plenty of time to talk once you've rested. None of us will be going any place soon."

Offering no further argument, Catherine nodded and smiled. She put more wood on the fire. Then she and Little Doe willingly moved to the platform on the opposite side of the hut. Gratefully they slid between the fur-lined blankets.

Going to Happy Woman's platform, Fletcher set the bowl on the floor and rolled together two robes. "Here," he said, and helping Happy Woman up with one hand, he slid the bolster under her back with the other. "Let's sit up."

Following the soothing sound of his voice and the

449

guidance of his hands, Happy Woman forced herself up. She watched as the old man sat on the edge of the platform, winced, and straightened his crippled legs. He picked up the bowl of mush, and as though Happy Woman were a baby, he spooned the food into her mouth.

Afterward Fletcher pulled the furs from her back, and he eased her down onto the bed. Pulling the blanket up to her chin, he smiled. Then he slowly ambled back to the fire and lay down on a fur blanket.

Exhausted, Catherine lay on her platform, but sleep had abandoned her. She stared at the dying fire and the glowing stones that surrounded the fire pit. Shadows danced across the room, their ghostly promenade accenting her loneliness and reaffirming her helplessness.

She turned onto her back and silently cried for her Scupperongac war chief. *How I wish I could see you one more time!* She mouthed the words of her heart. *I want to hold you close; I want to tell you that I love you . . . really love you!*

Aware of Catherine's restlessness, Fletcher said, "You'd best go to sleep, missy. Just let tomorrow take care of itself."

Chapter XXI

The silence in the hut was broken only by the crackling of the flames and the angry snarl of the wind that ripped relentlessly around the building. A rope draped around her shoulders, Catherine hunched closer to the fire, seeking warmth in this cold, foreign land. Hours had passed since Yellow Corn had taken Little Doe and Happy Woman away—long, lonely hours. Catherine was getting nervous. Her solitary confinement was taking its toll, and her imagination was running wild. Lifting her head, she gazed through the smoke hole. Late afternoon, she guessed, unable to gauge the time since the sun wasn't shining. Instead thick, gray clouds were massing.

As she pulled the robe even tighter around her shoulders, her ring softly grazed her neck. Slowly she lowered her hand, and she looked at the golden band, at the intricate design of interwoven leaves—a symbol of Lone Wolf's love. Tears misted her eyes, but her heart swelled with renewed hope. He would come for her.

Lone Wolf, she cried silently, the plea coming from the depth of her soul. Hear me, my love, my darling. She tilted her head upward, her eyes closed. "Please, my darling," she whispered, the cry lost in the fury of nature that surrounded her, "please find me."

451

Her supplication over, Catherine stretched out on the thick pallet of furs and attempted to think happy thoughts. When that exercise proved futile, she reverted to the lesson her father had taught her many years ago. She began to quote her favorite poems, her favorite scriptures, her favorite hymns—those which gave her strength and courage. She said the words over and over, repeating them until she finally drifted into a state of insensibility—awake but untouchable, indifferent to her surroundings and her captors.

Then she heard the noise. Quickly she shed her indifference, and her senses were honed for acute perception. Above the clamor of the coming storm, she heard the voices. People were approaching. Hoping Fletcher was returning with Happy Woman and Little Doe, she strained to hear more clearly. Still she didn't move. But she watched. When the robes parted, she caught her breath and her heartbeat hastened until she thought surely it was a drum beating.

"Catherine."

She heard the old man's call first. When he came closer she could see him. Captive air slowly escaped from her lungs.

"You're back," she whispered, pushing herself up, slowly standing. "I'm so glad," she cried. "Yellow Corn took Little Doe and Happy Woman a—"

Before she could say more, the Englishman lifted his hand and signaled for silence. His expression was stern and closed, but his eyes were pleading for her understanding and her cooperation.

"Mistress Graystone," he said, spinning around quickly, pointing toward the door, "I would like you to meet Strong Hand, the warrior who is responsible for your abduction."

Caught off guard, Catherine's head jerked in the direction of the door. Surprise diligently tried to lift her

452

features, but Catherine had learned the lesson of impassivity too well. Lowering the invisible veil of indifference once again, she stared at the Iroquois—the man who had been in the village with the trading expedition. She had known from the beginning that this man would bring her trouble. Because his victory paint had distorted his face and body the day he had abducted her, Catherine hadn't recognized his features, but she had unconsciously recognized him—she had felt his evil presence.

"You," she whispered, her voice coarse and grating. Apprehension and fear weighed heavier on her shoulders than the bearskin robe.

"You know him?" Fletcher asked.

Catherine nodded as the painted brave arrogantly sauntered deeper into the room. "He was part of the trading party at Scupperong."

Chocolate brown eyes leisurely roamed over Catherine's figure as Strong Hand imagined the delights the buckskin hid, delights which would soon be his— delights that would be all the more enjoyable because he was taking them from Lone Wolf.

"Tell the paleface that she belongs to me now," Strong Hand said to Fletcher.

After the words were interpreted for her, Catherine shook her head. "Tell him I belong to no one but myself," she declared, defiance and hatred making her words cold and hard.

Before Fletcher's words trailed into silence, Strong Hand moved closer to Catherine, and with one hand he grasped both of her braids. He knew the paleface was a warrior woman, but he would show her who was the stronger. He would have her on her knees in front of him, cowering, begging and pleading for mercy. He yanked her face within inches of his.

"You are mine," he spat angrily. "I have taken you

453

away from the Lone Wolf." When Fletcher didn't immediately interpret the words, Strong Hand turned his head and gritted out, "Tell her what I have said." He jerked her braids again, and Catherine's eyes watered; she clenched her teeth together to keep from screaming out in pain.

After Fletcher repeated Strong Hand's words, Catherine forced herself to laugh. "What makes you think the Lone Wolf will care?" she taunted. "I'm only a slave."

Strong Hand smiled, but there was a sinister gleam in the depths of his brown eyes. "I know my adversary well," he gloated. His gaze swept to the thongs that bound her braids; then it lowered to linger on the wolf-fang necklace. "Above all else," Strong Hand said smugly, "Lone Wolf prizes his possessions. You may not mean anything to him personally, but ownership means everything to the war chief of the Scupperongac. But even if the slave means nothing to Lone Wolf"—Strong Hand shrugged unconcernedly—"his future bride will. He will come get Little Doe."

Strong Hand threw back his head and laughed, the sound booming maliciously through the hut. "Without her, the Scupperongac have no alliance with the Lumbroans." He paused, savoring the culmination of his plan. "Now the Lumbroans will be most unhappy. If the Scupperongacs were unable to protect the only daughter of the Lumbroan's great chief, how can they ensure the peace of the entire tribe." Strong Hand's voice hummed with self-satisfaction. "To redeem himself and to reestablish relations with the Lumbroans, Lone Wolf will have to come for his bride. And when he arrives, he will find that I have provided games for his entertainment"— the sinister sound of Strong Hand's laughter swelled through the hut—"games he has never thought about, and he will be the chief contestant."

As Catherine listened to Fletcher's repetition of Strong Hand's words, she shivered with fear. Under no circumstances must Lone Wolf come to this village. She must—she would—escape so she could warn him.

"I go now, paleface," Strong Hand said, giving her hair another jerk, "to meet with Swimming Eel and the village council." His lips moved toward hers, but regardless of the pain, Catherine twisted her face away. Revulsion made her stomach churn. Drawing back his arm, Strong Hand slapped Catherine across the cheek, leaving the imprint of his hand on her face. "I will teach you," he promised, his face contorting, his nostrils flaring with anger. "Don't ever turn away from me again. I will have you."

Then the Iroquois shoved Catherine so hard she fell to the floor.

"You stay," he said to Fletcher. "I will be back after the council meeting and the feast." Without a backward glance, without any concern for Catherine's well-being, Strong Hand yanked the bearskins from the door as he walked out.

A gust of wind swirled through the room, fanning the flames in all directions. Ignoring the cold and forgetting about the fire, Fletcher knelt beside Catherine, but she shook her head and gently pushed him away. "I'm fine."

Knowing she wanted time to compose herself, the Englishman stood and limped across the room. He stooped and picked up the furs, pegging them above the doorframe and anchoring them to the floor with the stones. Then he moved to the fire and sat across from Catherine. Picking up a piece of loose bark, he swept the live coals back into the fire pit. Then he nursed the flagging blaze, carefully adding more wood.

Her face turned from Fletcher, Catherine forced back tears of anger and humiliation. She fought against fear of her coming ordeal with Strong Hand, and she schemed and planned ways to escape from her fiendish captor.

Eventually she asked, "Why have they taken Happy Woman and Little Doe?"

"Strong Hand gave the order," Fletcher replied. "He wants to be alone with you tonight."

"Where has he taken them?"

"Happy Woman is in a hut not far from you," he answered, sitting back and slowly stretching his stiff legs. "Little Doe is in Yellow Corn's long house."

"What will happen to them?"

"To the Scupperongac . . . I don't know," he answered. "Little Doe will become Strong Hand's woman." He hesitated. "Maybe his wife."

Both of them lapsed into silence. After they sat pensively for a few minutes, Catherine asked, "Why did Strong Hand take us prisoners?"

"For several reasons," Fletcher said, reaching for more logs to lay on the fire. "Many years ago the Iroquois broke the trading truce and raided a Scupperongac village. In a hurry to return home before the winter snow fell and before the Scupperongacs retaliated, the raiding party killed most of the villagers—those who stayed and fought. Among those who fought were Lone Wolf's family."

Catherine could almost guess Fletcher's next words. "The following spring the young warrior led his braves in a daring raid deep into Iroquois territory to revenge the death of his family. A casualty of that battle was Strong Hand." He paused; then he said, "A deadly, living casualty."

"I suppose Lone Wolf killed Strong Hand's family in return," Catherine said, her heart revolting at such barbarism.

"I'm not sure about that," Fletcher answered. "According to what I've heard since I've been here, Lone Wolf and his party were largely outnumbered and he

456

realized his braves would all be killed. So like the courageous warrior and chief he is, he gave his braves time to escape by allowing himself to be taken captive. Instead of torturing him to death, however, Strong Hand challenged Lone Wolf to a fight with the knife. Lone Wolf won, but he didn't kill Strong Hand. He spared his life—a token of peace, Lone Wolf said. Strong Hand has been seeking revenge ever since. He wants to redeem himself in the eyes of his tribe, yet Strong Hand cannot challenge Lone Wolf because he owes him a debt of gratitude. Lone Wolf must challenge him."

Remembering Strong Hand's words, Catherine said, "Strong Hand knows his adversary well. Lone Wolf prizes his possessions above all things, and he will fight for them." Without thinking, she lifted her hand and touched the wolf fangs that banded her braid. "Lone Wolf will come after us, and he will challenge Strong Hand."

She thought for a minute; then she looked pleadingly at Fletcher. "Let's escape, Fletcher." She reached out and touched him. "You can return to the settlers, or you can come home with me."

So caught up was she in persuading Fletcher to join her in escape, Catherine never noticed her choice of words. At the moment she was speaking from her heart.

Deep in thought, Fletcher lifted his hand to his mouth and tapped a nail against his teeth. "I would like to go with you, lass," he eventually murmured, "but I'm an old man, and—"

"If we plan it well, Fletcher," Catherine interrupted, reassuring him, "we can make it." She smiled. "There's a risk involved but we must take it."

Fletcher ran a hand through his gray hair, contemplating her words. "These Indians don't trust me not to help you; they're watching me like a hawk watches his prey. Don't be foolish, woman."

457

"I'm not. But I suspect the Iroquois are foolish enough not to think that I'll try to escape." Before Fletcher could argue with her, Catherine schemed. "The best time to escape will be after the feast when Strong Hand and his braves are telling their tale of valor, bragging about the way they took us out from under Lone Wolf's nose." As she looked across the flames at Fletcher, the fire cast a golden shadow over her face. "Surely they won't have more than one guard on us during that time, and the villagers will be too caught up in the celebration to think about us."

"Aye," Fletcher said, running his hand down the scar.

She laughed softly. "And when Strong Hand comes to take Lone Wolf's slave, he will find the hut empty."

"These be fierce Indians, mistress," Fletcher warned her, his hand again going to his face. "You don't want to trifle with them."

Catherine saw the pain stirring in the old man's eyes, and she hurt for him. "I can understand if you don't take the chance," she told him, "but I must. I can't let Strong Hand's obsession with revenge destroy all that Wise One and Lone Wolf have been working for. As long as the Lumbroans and the Scupperongacs fight each other, the Iroquois are happy. Their expansion is made that much easier. Besides," Catherine added, "I must think about our people, Fletcher. Until they have made other provisions their only alliances are with the Croatoans and the Scupperongacs."

Fletcher nodded his acknowledgment. Standing, he hobbled to the door. "I will go now, Catherine. If it's"— he shook his head—"if it's possible, I will bring you some weapons and help you escape."

The hours dragged by. Afternoon turned into evening, evening into night, and still Fletcher did not return. Nervous and apprehensive about being caught, Catherine paced back and forth, carefully planning her escape. Her greatest concern was her ignorance of the territory, her greatest fear that she would not make good her escape.

Throughout the night she heard the celebration in the village. She knew there was only one guard outside the hut, but she also knew that he was alert to her every movement. She waited; she paced more; finally weary from worry she lay down. Just as she gave up hoping for Fletcher's return, the flap and the bearskin blankets were pushed aside. Expectantly Catherine leaped to her feet, a greeting on her lips. But the sound died prematurely, and she backed farther into the room.

Washed clean of his victory paint, Strong Hand swaggered into the hut, his chest swelled with pride. His story was told, his valor lauded, and his victory danced. He was drunk with overconfidence. Tonight he would take Lone Wolf's slave; tomorrow night he would take his bride-to-be. After the degradation of Lone Wolf's women, the war chief of the Scupperongacs would have no choice but to issue a challenge. If he did not, he would be ridiculed. He would have to fight for the honor of his women. Even then, the women would never be the same again. Every time Lone Wolf touched one of them, he would know that Strong Hand had been with them.

A cunning, menacing smile curved Strong Hand's lips as he looked at Catherine. Slowly his gaze swept down her figure; slowly it swept upward. "I have waited a long time for this," he said in Iroquoian as he walked to the platform. "I saw you several moons ago when I was scouting in Scupperongac territory." His smile widened at the memory. "Had I not been on an important mission I would have taken you then, but my pleasure would not have been as great." He walked across the hut, soft laughter following him. "I didn't know at the time that you belonged to Lone Wolf. Knowing this makes my possession of you all the more pleasing."

He stopped speaking and hooked his bow on one of the rafters. As he slumped a shoulder to slide out of his quiver, and as he laid it on the lower platform, his eyes never left Catherine's face. He pulled his knife and war club from his belt. Placing them next to his quiver, he smiled sardonically as he watched her gaze fasten on the weapons.

"You may be heralded as the village champion, paleface," he taunted, "but you're not a warrior. You're a woman, and I am about to prove that."

Sitting on the edge of the platform, he unlaced his leggings and moccasins. When he began to unlace his shirt, Catherine dropped her head, unwilling to look on his nakedness. She heard a soft thud as buckskin landed on the floor at her feet. She saw the movement of his hands and knew they were going to his breechclout.

Before she could turn her back on him, his arms shot out and he darted across the room, his sudden movement shaking the platform. The knife thudded to the floor and slithered across the damp dirt, but the Iroquois was too consumed with anger to worry about the knife.

"No, paleface," he grated. "You will look at me. You will know my nakedness, and I will shame you by looking at yours."

He caught Catherine by the shoulders, and he hauled the twisting, fighting woman against the solid wall of his chest. His eyes glowed with malicious intent, his nostrils flared, and his face was uncompromising and hard. Then he turned her loose, his hands gripping the neckline of her dress so tightly he was choking her as he pulled her face close to his.

"I will make you beg for mercy. You will cry and plead with me to stop."

Catherine heard the mockery; she heard the meaning. Repulsed by his touch, she glared at him, her eyes never leaving his face. "Given the chance, I will kill you, you

460

cur," she spat out venomously.

Strong Hand didn't understand her words; but he saw the defiance in her eyes, he felt the challenge in her stand. She angered him almost as much as Lone Wolf did. Suddenly the brave's arms circled the paleface, his arms banding around her body like a moist thong that shrinks as it dries. He held her so tightly, she couldn't get her breath. Her head began to spin, and she gasped for air. Finally she collapsed in his arms. He laughed as he threw her to the ground. Winded, Catherine lay on the cold soil, frantically sucking air into her body but never getting it to her lungs. She cried aloud with pain as her chest constricted, as her heart raced with fear—fear that she'd never draw another breath.

Strong Hand straddled Catherine's body, and he stood watching her, laughing as she struggled for life. Slowly he untied the breechclout and let it drop across her body. Catherine felt the skin as it hit her, and the woman in her rebelled at seeing his nakedness. But the warrior in her refused to quell before an adversary. Angry because she was so strong, because she continued to defy him, Strong Hand lifted his foot and kicked Catherine. She tensed at the impact, but she didn't cry aloud nor did her face mirror her pain. Out of the corner of her eye, she saw the knife. At that moment she made up her mind to get it.

Tiring of his game, the Iroquois dropped to his knees, pinning her arms to her sides. He caught Catherine's face in his hand, his fingers biting into the tender flesh of her cheeks. "I will have you," he muttered savagely. "And when I'm through with you, I'll give you back to Lone Wolf." Hideous laughter boomed through the hut. "But he'll have no desire for you then."

Angry because Catherine refused to rise to his baiting and because she did not whimper or beg for mercy, he slapped her. Spitting into his face, she yanked one arm free, balled her hand, and slammed it against the side of

461

his face. Howling with rage, Strong Hand struck her soundly, knocking her insensible; then he caught her wrist and dragged her across the cold ground until they were close to the fire. Feeling the heat and looking at the flames that leaped into the air, Catherine knew what he was planning.

"I'll give you something to think about," he taunted. Pushing her cheek down until it almost touched the hot stones that surrounded the fire pit, he said mockingly, "Now be brave, paleface."

Without understanding a word he was saying, Catherine stared into his demonic face. When he breathed in deeply, his necklaces moved on his chest. The movement caught Catherine's attention, and her gaze lowered to fasten on the shining bead and shell ornaments that circled his neck. Then she saw it—the one that glittered gold in the firelight. Slowly she exhaled, and in the wake of discovery all fight oozed out of her. She wilted, and as if in a trance she lifted a hand, reaching for the necklace. As her fingers touched the small round object, torrents of hatred flooded through her body.

The locket she had given to Running Bear. The locket he would have taken off for no one. It hadn't been buried with him as she had supposed. His murderer had stolen it!

Feeling the resistance ebb from her tense body, Strong Hand lowered his face, his eyes following the path of her gaze. Resting his chin on his chest, he laughed as he ran his fingertips over the locket. "Yes," he replied in answer to her silent query, "I took this from the peace man after I killed him." Inebriated with his victory, he boasted more. "I couldn't let him bring peace among the Algonkins, nor could I let him find alliances for the palefaces. That would have destroyed everything I had worked for."

Exalted, triumph racing through his veins, Strong

Hand continued. "When I yanked Lone Wolf's totem from around Running Bear's neck, I found this." He rubbed the locket between his fingers. "I liked it, so I took it. Then I placed Lone Wolf's broken necklace in Running Bear's hand, hoping the blame for the peace man's death would be placed on Lone Wolf or on the cowardly paleface." He paused reflectively for a moment, looking at the strange marks.

Catherine had ceased to hear the foreign sounds. She saw nothing but Running Bear and his gentle obsidian eyes; she heard nothing but his soft words of peace. Rage began to build up in her, billowing through her body, filling her with a furious, blind resolve. In the face of such anger, her fear and apprehension faded into oblivion. Angrily she began to kick and to flail her arms, catching the unsuspecting warrior off guard.

Her every movement was calculated to bring her closer to the knife. If she reached it—no! When she reached it—she would show this savage who was master of her destiny. Strong Hand rammed his fist into Catherine's jaw, the force of the blow knocking her head against the floor. Breathing deeply, she frantically, valiantly fought her way back to full consciousness. She had to think clearly, she had to . . . or she couldn't defeat this man, couldn't warn Lone Wolf.

She clamped her free hand onto the floor at her side, the tips of her fingers walking across the dirt, touching the icy flint. Thinking Catherine to be stunned, Strong Hand gloated over his victory. He picked the locket up again and studied the writing. Catherine stretched her hand, her fingertips reaching . . . grasping. . . . Then the balls of her fingers tapped the blade of Strong Hand's knife. Victory softly hissed through her lips as she expelled the air she had been holding captive. Almost . . . she almost had it. Slowly, so as not to warn Strong Hand, Catherine's fingers inched farther, finally curling around the hilt of the knife.

Strong Hand shifted his weight, the movement sliding Catherine's dress above her thighs. As his naked flesh touched hers, she burned with shame and she felt degraded. Catherine wanted to scream out her protest, but she bit back her cries. She lay still, passive under his touch. He grunted his approval, bending his torso so he could stretch out.

Then when Strong Hand least suspected it, Catherine turned, the sudden movement toppling him over. Bringing the knife up, its hilt planted against her chest, she lunged for him, and the weight of her body pushed the flint under his sternum into his heart. The warrior grunted his pain, and his eyes rounded with disbelief. Death gurgled through his throat, and blood trickled from the corner of his mouth. Then his body jerked convulsively before he lay still.

Catherine jumped to her feet, quickly pulling her dress down. Knowing she would need warm clothes for her journey to Scupperong, she picked up Strong Hand's shirt and pulled it over her head. As she tied his belt around her waist, she ran across the room to the platform. She pulled his quiver strap over her arm, shifting her shoulders until it rested comfortably on her back. Then she slipped the war club into her belt, and she grabbed the bow in her left hand. Finally, moving across the wigwam, she knelt by the dead warrior, and she pulled the knife from his chest.

As she looked into his face, she shuddered, but she had no time for recriminations. She cleaned the knife, wiping the blade back and forth across his leggings. Then she slipped the weapon into her belt. Quickly she unfastened the chain around Strong Hand's neck and clasped it about her own.

Her senses heightened, she heard the quiet movement outside the wigwam. Stealthily she moved to one side of

464

the door, and pulling the war club from her belt, she stood, holding it above her head. She had killed once, and she would do it again. She had to get Little Doe out of here; she had to save Lone Wolf—no matter what the cost.

The man hesitated. He heard no noises from within. Gently he eased the flap aside; cautiously he pushed his hand between the furs and the doorframe. Through the crack he saw Strong Hand asleep on the floor. He couldn't see the woman. He pushed his arm through the opening; then his body.

"Catherine." Fletcher whispered her name before Catherine could bring the war club down on his head.

"Fletcher," she gasped, her hand instantly dropping to her side. She saw the woman slip into the room behind him. "Happy Woman!" Catherine said softly, and she hugged her.

The Englishman hobbled across the hut and looked down at Strong Hand.

"How's your arm?" Catherine asked Happy Woman.

"It hurts a little," the Scupperongac confessed, "but I can use it."

"He's dead," Fletcher announced flatly.

Catherine nodded, slipping her weapon into her belt. "I gave up on you."

"I was at the council meeting. I couldn't leave without arousing suspicion," he replied. "Afterward I had to figure a way to slip you weapons without anyone knowing."

"Are you coming with us?"

"Aye," he said. "Don't reckon I have much choice." Catherine looked at him curiously. "We must get back to the settlement as quickly as possible. Strong Hand laid a trap for the settlers."

"What kind?" Catherine asked.

"One of the settlers was away from the fort, and

465

Strong Hand's braves captured and killed him. Using his weapons, they also killed two Roanoac braves. They set it up to look as though he was in league with the Scupperongacs." Fletcher paused reflectively. "Funny thing, missy. The Englishman had a pearl and wolf-fang necklace on, like the one Lone Wolf wears."

"No," Catherine said dully, "it's not so funny." She held her hand out so Fletcher could see the gold band. "Lone Wolf traded his necklace to one of the settlers in exchange for this ring."

"Ahhh." Fletcher rubbed his hand over his face and nodded his head. "Strong Hand used the necklace to his advantage. Wanchese thinks Lone Wolf and the settlers are plotting against the Roanoacs." He clucked his tongue disapprovingly.

"We must get back," she muttered, nodding her head. "Where is Yellow Corn's long house?"

Fletcher shook his head, reading her thoughts. "That'd be too dangerous, missy."

"We've got to get her out."

"We're not going into that long house," he said firmly. "We'll be fortunate to get out of the village as it is. It'll soon be dawn, and we can't afford to waste anymore time."

"I'm not leaving without Little Doe," Catherine maintained. "If no one else escapes, she must."

"I don't have time to argue with you, woman." Fletcher grabbed Catherine by the arm. "We've got to be on our way."

Catherine broke free of his grip. "Tell me where she is," she demanded. "I'm going to get her."

"Why are you so adamant about taking her with us?" the old man barked. "Can't you see you're jeopardizing our only chances of getting away."

Before Catherine could answer, Happy Woman broke in. "Why are you arguing?" When Catherine told her, she said, "No, Ca-ther-ine, you can't. You'll be captured again."

"We're taking her back," Catherine announced flatly, first in Scupperongac and then in English.

"In God's name, why?" Fletcher thundered. "What does this damned Lumbroan mean to you? Why are you willing to risk your life and ours for hers?"

Like an erupting volcano, Catherine's anger spewed out, her words spilling over Fletcher and Happy Woman like hot, thick lava. "Don't you think I want to forget about her?" she screamed. "I do. There's nothing I would like better than to leave her." The realization of what she had said sobered Catherine, and as suddenly as she had begun her tirade, she stopped, again hiding her feelings behind a veneer of calmness. "We're going to get her."

"Miss"—Fletcher's tone was soft and sympathetic— "it's gonne be nigh to impossible to rescue that little girl. Six families live in that long house and if we get her out of there, we've got to make it through the village and out the gate." The man paused, letting the weight of his words sink in. "Remember, the exit walkway is lined with guards."

It is too difficult, Catherine thought, pacing the room. Fletcher is right: Should I jeopardize the chance we have? Is one person worth it? A person I'm not sure we can free? How easy it would be, how convenient, to escape without Little Doe, she thought. No one would blame me . . . no one but me!

She stopped pacing in front of Fletcher. Looking him directly in the eyes, she said, "Faced with such great odds, Mr. Fletcher, I suggest we formulate a plan of some kind."

Chapter XXII

Hiding behind the stack of firewood, her bow in her hand, an arrow nocked, Catherine tensely waited behind Yellow Corn's long house for Fletcher and Little Doe. Her eyes moved in all directions; her ears strained for the least sound. Her only protection was the darkness and the Iroquois' total absorption with the celebration. When she heard the slither of the deerskin flap and saw the man come out, Catherine crouched until she could barely see above the pile of wood.

Although Catherine had no difficulty identifying Fletcher's unmistakable gait, she didn't disclose her whereabouts by speaking. Instead, she quietly waited for him and Little Doe to approach, her bow poised for immediate action.

"Here she be," Fletcher whispered as he and the Lumbroan rounded the woodpile.

"Ca-ther-ine," Little Doe exclaimed under her breath, "you rescued me."

Catherine lowered the bow. Dropping an arm around the young woman's shoulder, she hugged her. "Not quite." She grinned. "The worst is yet to come."

"No time for talking," Fletcher said, limping toward the gate. "It won't be long before they discover that Little

Doe is gone."

They hadn't taken many steps, however, before a brave materialized from the darkness. Recognizing Fletcher but not yet seeing the women, the Iroquois continued to walk toward them. Immediately, Catherine fell behind Little Doe, dropped to one knee, and nocked an arrow. By this time the brave saw Little Doe. His eyes widened in surpise, and he opened his mouth to give warning. No sound came. Catherine's arrow had pierced his heart. With a soft cry, he lurched foward and fell to the ground. After Catherine and Fletcher dragged his body behind the woodpile, the three hurried to the gate where Happy Woman waited for them.

"How many?" Catherine asked in Scupperongac as she squatted beside the woman.

"Four," Happy Woman replied. "Two at this end of the corridor; two at the other. Evidently they are expecting Lone Wolf."

"Too many." Fletcher crouched near them, shaking his head. "We must silence all four at the same time. Otherwise, they'll warn the village, and there's no way we can do that."

Catherine stared at the gate to freedom. Never had an exit seemed so formidable. A sure pathway to death, she thought, looking at the circular hallway walled with thick palisades of logs. Double guards—acutely alert because they expected trouble.

"Can we"—her eyes scaled the spiked poles, the ramp that circled the inside wall, and the ladder—"climb over the fence?"

Feltcher didn't answer immediately. He shifted his weight from one leg to the other, his eyes running the length and the breadth of the palisade. "Maybe," he said, pulling his robe closer around him as the wind whipped against him. "If someone keeps the guards occupied." He chuckled softly. "And that shouldn't be difficult to do

469

since they're expecting the enemy to come in, not go out." He looked around for a minute, then pointed to a ladder set some feet from the gate. "Move over there. You'll be close enough to hear and see but far enough away so they can't hear you if they're talking. Once I get the guards' attention, climb the ladder and drop over the fence."

"What are you going to do?" Catherine asked.

"Don't worry, miss," Fletcher assured her. "I'll be coming with you. With Strong Hand dead, I can't stay behind." His chuckle grew into laughter. "Right now, I think Yellow Corn wants some water, so she'll be sending her slave for it."

Fletcher hurriedly limped back into the village, returning shortly with a water jug. As he walked through the gate, a guard stopped him.

"Where are you going, Feather Man?"

"To get some water," he replied.

"Can't that wait until morning?"

"Could," Fletcher answered, "but I shouldn't like for it to." He leaned nearer the guard. "You see, I don't want to be out in the forest in the morning. I think Lone Wolf and the Scupperongacs are going to come get the paleface slave and the Lumbroan princess."

The guards laughed, and one of them scoffed. "I think you are frightened for nothing, old man. Strong Hand said Lone Wolf would be coming alone."

"Besides Lone Wolf couldn't get here so quickly," another added.

"I don't know about that." Fletcher scratched his chin. "If he had any idea what Strong Hand is doing with that woman right now . . . through the slit in the flap I saw . . ." The braves were forced closer and closer as Fletcher kept lowering his voice.

Their duty temporarily forgotten, the guards listened attentively, and the women quietly scampered up the ladder. Carefully they eased themselves over the spiked poles, and holding on with both hands, they slowly let their bodies down. Little Doe lightly dropped the few feet to the ground; then she helped Happy Woman ease down quietly. Together they held Catherine as she slid down.

Following the path to the river, Happy Woman and Little Doe pushed the canoes into the current, except for the one they would use. This done, the three of them waited for Fletcher. When Happy Woman finally heard the soft uneven thud of moccasins, she tensed and touched Catherine on the shoulder. Hardly daring to breathe, the three women stared at the pathway.

"That's Fletcher," Happy Woman whispered, relief in her voice.

"Are there more?" Catherine asked.

"I don't think so," Happy Woman replied, cupping her ear to the ground.

When Fletcher limped to the canoe and softly called their names, the three of them rushed from their hiding place. Quickly they hopped into the elm-bark canoe, and they shoved off. With Fletcher in the stern and Catherine in the bow, they paddled downstream, making good time.

No one talked as they traveled; each one concentrated on watching the shore and on paddling swiftly. They knew the Iroquois were not far behind them. As dawn brought the misty gray of early morning, Fletcher guided the canoe to shore.

"What's wrong?" Catherine asked, thankful for the rest but concerned about stopping. She laid her paddle across the canoe.

"Nothing," Fletcher replied, squinting his eyes and peering into the forest for signs of unfriendly Indians. "We need to change rivers," he said, treading water with his paddle to steady the canoe while the others disembarked. "We'll carry the canoe and walk a ways."

"Will the Iroquois know that we've taken this trail?" Hopping out, Catherine held the canoe steady as Happy Woman and Little Doe waded ashore.

"Aye," Fletcher called from behind. He hoisted the canoe onto his shoulder and shoved past the women. "This is the only trail that leads south, but"—he flashed a toothy grin—"instead of picking up the river again as they'll suppose, we'll go a little farther and take the creek."

Fletcher in the lead, the three women following in a single file, they moved noiselessly through the gray-misted forest. When they reached a fork in the trail, Fletcher stopped. He lowered the canoe and gently set it down. Using his hand as a broom, he swept the ground in front of him clean, and he picked up a twig.

Motioning to the women around him, he said, "As I give you the directions, you translate for them." He looked at Catherine who nodded; then he began. "Here's the way to get back to Scupperongac territory." He drew in the dirt. "You're to take this trail for about a mile, so it'll look like you're headed for the river. Instead you're to leave the trail and head east. You'll run into a creek. Once you get there, paddle downstream as fast as you can. The creek ends, but . . ." Talking quickly, Fletcher finished giving Catherine directions. "When those devils find out what you've done, they'll be on you before you can blink your eyes." He stood and wiped his hands on the sides of his leggings. "Think you can follow those directions?"

"I can," Catherine replied, handing him her paddle, "but I won't."

"What do you mean?" he barked.

"It'll be up to you, Fletcher, to guide them. I'm staying right here."

Fletcher shook his head vigorously. "No, you're not. If anyone is staying, then it'll be me." He caught her

472

shoulders and pushed her in the direction he had pointed out. "I'll only serve to slow you down. I'll wait here, and when the Iroquois come, I'll hold them off as long as I can." He smiled. "That'll give you a pretty good head start."

"You can't outrun the Iroquois because you're crippled, and Happy Woman is too weak." Turning to Happy Woman, Catherine said in Scupperongac, "Fletcher will take you to Scupperong. I'm going to stay here to give you a better headstart."

"I will stay, Catherine. You must return with Little Doe."

"No," Little Doe cried, rushing forward, "I will stay."

Happy Woman laid a detaining hand on Little Doe's arm. "Let me stay, Ca-ther-ine. This will be my opportunity to repay my debt of gratitude."

"Yes," Catherine mused, recalling how important repaying a debt of honor was to the Indians. "Yes, you are right."

"I will stay then."

"No," Catherine barked. "Fletcher will warn the settlers, and you will repay your debt of gratitude by seeing that Little Doe is returned safely to Scupperong and to Lone Wolf."

Happy Woman opened her mouth to protest, but Catherine said, "I have spoken." Happy Woman nodded, and Catherine turned to Fletcher. "It's settled. I will stay. You and Happy Woman will go." She smiled, her eyes moving hungrily over each visage as she committed it to memory. "Now! No more arguing. Leave." A teary catch in her voice, Catherine said, "Take care of them, Fletcher. See that both of them get home safely."

"Aye." The old man's eyes were bright with unshed tears.

Happy Woman stood a minute longer, looking at Catherine. She looked at Strong Hand's bow and knew

473

that it was too big and strong for Catherine. "I am better with an Indian's bow than you are, Ca-ther-ine."

Her eyes misting with liquid love, Catherine nodded her agreement and spoke in Scupperongac. "That you are, Happy Woman, but at the moment I am the stronger. With your wounded shoulder you wouldn't be able to hold the Iroquois back long enough to give us a good head start."

In deep thought, Happy Woman looked at Catherine. Finally she propped her paddle against a tree and stripped her victor's medal from her neck.

"Please wear this," she said, walking toward Catherine. "It has much magic, and it will protect you."

Catherine ducked her head, letting the Scupperongac put the copper medallion on her.

"Here," Fletcher said when Catherine lifted her face. "Take my quiver of arrows. You'll need them lass." Grateful for his thoughtfulness, Catherine reached for the beautiful case. "Remember," he enjoined gruffly, "watch where the arrows land. Keep picking them up and keep running. Stay ahead of the varmints."

Smiling, Little Doe walked to Catherine and put her arms around her, hugging her tightly. "Thank you, Ca-ther-ine. I can understand why the Lone Wolf loves you. You are a brave and honorable woman."

Catherine watched the three until they disappeared into the forest. She followed them a short distance; then she looked around for a place to make a stand. When she found the large fallen tree, she knelt behind it, standing Fletcher's quiver of arrows upright against the trunk. She pulled her jacket more closely around her, and she settled down to wait. When the sun shone brightly and morning was fully come, Catherine heard the changing sounds of the forest. She knew the Iroquois were coming.

She peered over the log, watching as five braves, Brown Hawk and Straight Arrow in the lead, moved in

474

single file through the forest. Catherine turned, resting on her knees. Positioning the bow, she nocked one of Fletcher's arrows. The element of surprise on her side, Catherine sent arrow after arrow in their direction. Her first shot killed one of the Iroquois, and the others dashed for cover, their chase temporarily halted.

Soon the Iroquois were shooting at Catherine, but their aim was short. Eventually a daring brave, scooting from behind the shelter of a tree, eased his way toward Catherine. Having seen him, she lifted her bow and shot another arrow which sent the man sprawling on the ground. In the confusion that followed Catherine quickly gathered the Iroquois arrows close to her and sprinted down the trail.

In a minute the Iroquois were after her. When she came to another place where she could shield herself, she took a stand once more and began to shoot at the Iroquois with their own arrows. Several times she gathered up the arrows around her, fled to a new position, and held the enemy off.

But Catherine knew time was running out. Her arms ached from using the strong bow, her supply of arrows was depleted, and she was gasping for breath. Each time she ran, the Iroquois moved in closer, their arrows barely missing her now. Closing her eyes and gasping for air, she nocked another arrow. Rising onto one knee, she balanced her body with the other foot, and she aimed at Straight Arrow who was coming, his war club raised in the air, a menacing howl bursting from his lungs. For one second Catherine was transplanted in time and place.

She remembered the day, so long ago, when Red Fox had captured her. Suddenly Straight Arrow and Red Fox merged, becoming one—a visage distorted by anger and paint. Catherine's palms began to perspire, and she trembled. The war cry sent chills of fear down her spine, then she felt a sharp stab of pain. An arrowhead had

475

pierced her chest. Tottering, almost falling, she cried aloud. A flame burned in her chest and along her arm. Her first instinct was to grab the shaft and pull the arrow from her chest, but she didn't.

Swallowing her pain, she repositioned the bow and aimed. She blinked her eyes, trying to clear her vision, and she pulled the bowstring and let go, her arrow piercing the Iroquois who was rushing toward her. Blindly she groped for another arrow when two more braves, one of them Brown Hawk, exposed themselves. She didn't have time. The men rushed her, Brown Hawk's war club knocking her unconscious as it landed against the side of her head. Slowly she toppled to the ground, the bow dropping next to her.

Kneeling beside her, Brown Hawk dug his fingers into her rich, auburn hair with one hand, and he raised the other, brandishing his war club in the air. He would take the warrior woman's scalp back; his wife would sing and dance his victory tonight. The thought had barely entered his mind, he had just opened his mouth to voice his victor's prayer when he heard an unfamiliar sound. His companion grunted and clutched the arrow that pierced his chest. Turning his head, Brown Hawk watched the brave drop to the ground. Then he heard another sound—a sound that belonged to none other than the war chief of the Scupperongacs.

Turning Catherine loose, he spun around, but it was too late to run. His eyes widened in fright, and his victory whoop died on his tongue. Wolf Friend sailed through the air, his hackles raised, his teeth bared. His front paws landed on Brown Hawk's chest, the momentum and weight of the wolf knocking the Indian over. Growling and snarling his anger, the wolf tore into the Iroquois. Withstanding the futile blows of the war club, the wolf didn't stop fighting until all life had ebbed out of Brown Hawk.

476

Then Wolf Friend trotted to the wounded woman; he sniffed, and with a gentleness that was diametrically opposed to the viciousness he'd displayed only moments ago, Wolf Friend nuzzled her cheek. He licked her face before he lay by her side, whimpering softly.

Lone Wolf dropped his war club and bow as he fell to his knees beside the prostrate body of the warrior woman. The color that smeared his face accented his anger. Oddly enough, though his body was tense with rage, his hands trembled as they reverently touched the woman who had wreaked such havoc with the Iroquois . . . the woman who had wreaked such havoc with his life. Around her unconscious body lay three dead. The one she had killed. The one he had killed. The one Wolf Friend had killed.

He picked up one of the Iroquois' arrows, his fingers touching the loosly attached arrowhead. A war arrow, he thought. And most deadly! One that would come off in her shoulder when he pulled the shaft. It had probably been dipped in poison. He broke the shaft close to her shoulder, but he didn't attempt to pull the arrowhead out.

Gently Lone Wolf lifted Catherine and cradled her next to his firm chest. Tears ran down his cheeks, dropping onto her lovely face. Although he carried Catherine, the warrior moved quickly through the forest, the brindled wolf at his side. One of Lone Wolf's braves stooped and picked up the war chief's discarded weapons. Then he and the remainder of the war party trotted behind their chief.

Oblivious of his surroundings and of his braves, Lone Wolf lifted his face to the heavens and cried out to Manitou.

Chapter XXIII

Neither Lone Wolf, who sat on a stump beside the sleeping platform, nor the wolf, who lay at his feet, noticed that night had descended. The warrior hadn't left the wigwam since he'd returned with Catherine. For him, time had ceased to exist. Sensing his master's grief, Wolf Friend never left Lone Wolf's side.

Catherine moaned, and she tried to turn her body, but she couldn't. Because No-am-ee was going to remove the arrowhead from Catherine's shoulder, Lone Wolf had strapped Catherine to the platform. Now he removed the small square of buckskin from her fevered brow and dipped it into a bowl of water; he wrung it out and replaced it.

"Will she live, Grandmother?" Lone Wolf spoke to No-am-ee who sat beside the fire pit, praying and meditating, but he didn't take his eyes off Catherine.

"Only Manitou knows whether she will walk the path to Summerland, my son. Let us hope the arrowhead is not poisoned."

The stones around the pit glowed red in the dark wigwam, and they cast black shadows on the curved ceiling and across No-am-ee's countenance. Every breath of air shifted the dancing shadows and changed their shapes. At times the old woman thought death was creeping through the room. Fearful, she would pile wood on the fire until the blaze burgeoned, flooding the wigwam with light.

Without moving, she settled her gaze on the Scupperongac warrior. She watched his tender ministrations to the paleface, and she noted the tears that coursed down his cheeks. Sighing, she lowered her head. She wished she could carry his load of grief. Somehow old shoulders seemed more suited for sorrow and grief than young ones.

Rising, she moved across the room. She lit two torches and hung them at the top of the platform. Then she returned to the fire and stirred the root tea she was brewing. "It would be better if you left now," No-am-ee said. "Re-bekk-ana and Little Flower can help me."

"No," Lone Wolf said. "I will stay."

No-am-ee returned to the platform. She pulled the cover aside and removed the cornhusk bandages. For several moments she stared at the raw, jagged flesh. Then, with tender fingers, she probed around the wound. Catherine squirmed. When No-am-ee dropped an herbal lotion on the inflamed area, Catherine sucked in her breath, opened her eyes, and looked wildly around the room.

Catherine thought Lone Wolf was speaking, but he sounded different. His voice was far away, and it sounded old and tired.

"I have done all I can," she heard No-am-ee reply. "Only Manitou knows whether she will walk the path to Summerland or not."

No, Catherine thought, *I'm not going to Summerland. I've just come from there.* It's a beautiful place, but this is home.

She was where she belonged—in Lone Wolf's wigwam, in his bed. Breathing deeply, she snuggled under the cover, smiled a secret smile, and settled into a peaceful sleep. Unconsciously she rubbed her cheek against the precious face that lay so close to hers, and when she moved her hand, her fingers intertwined with Lone Wolf's.

"Grandmother," Lone Wolf whispered, raising his head and looking at Catherine's face, "she moved."

"She's moved before," No-am-ee responded, then she returned, quietly keeping her vigil in front of the fire.

"Not like this," Lone Wolf declared excitedly, holding their locked hands up for No-am-ee to see. "And she's smiling."

The old woman stood and hobbled to the platform. She looked at Catherine. Carefully she pulled back the cover and lifted the cornhusk bandages to study the wound. "We are blessed that the arrow was not poison-tipped, my son."

Lone Wolf nodded. "Manitou has breathed the blessing of life on us, my grandmother."

"That he has," No-am-ee agreed thankfully.

She returned to the center of the wigwam, stretched her hands to a rafter, and took down the long, buckskin pouch. Pulling the string, she extracted her beautiful hand-carved pipe. Then she crumbled tobacco from the gift pouch into the bowl, and raking a live coal onto a small piece of bark, she lit the pipe. After she had taken seven puffs, she lifted her head and looked through the smoke hole. Lifting her voice, she chanted her thanks to Manitou for guiding Catherine's spirit back to her body.

Catherine didn't know how long she had slept, but she felt the sun as it gently touched her face, covering her with brightness and warmth. Her lashes fluttered open, and she slowly looked around the room, her eyes lighting on the old woman who sat in front of the fire pit. She stared until No-am-ee felt the younger woman's visual touch. The grizzled head turned, the wrinkled face smiled, and tears coursed down the weathered cheeks.

Then the old woman stood and slowly limped out of the wigwam to Wise One's lodge. Happily she spread the good news: Catherine was awake.

Catherine's gaze fastened on the platform above the bed. She saw all the magic amulets—tokens of love and concern. Happy Woman's copper medallion, Little Flower's dolls, Wise One's bow and quiver, No-am-ee's headband, Ho-sa-eeth's medicine bag, Running Bear's writing case. Her eyes brimmed with tears. Thinking it had great magic, Lone Wolf had brought the paper with Running Bear's writing.

Catherine knew Lone Wolf was sitting beside her. She heard his even breathing, and she felt the warmth of his body, the weight of his head on one side of her chest. She squirmed. When she moved her right arm and shoulder, she moaned. Instantly, Lone Wolf's head jerked up, and Catherine found herself staring into his gaunt, sorrow-ravaged face. She found herself searching the ebony eyes that were dull with worry.

"I knew you would come for me," she whispered, the words barely audible.

"Catherine," Lone Wolf whispered, tears flowing down his face. He lifted his large, strong hands to her face. They trembled. "Catherine, my love."

Catherine smiled, and she lifted her hand, grazing Lone Wolf's cheek with the back of it. "Why are you crying?"

Lone Wolf turned his head, his lips touching the tips of her fingers. "Because I'm so happy." He caught her hand in his, and he pressed the palm against his lips, his tears mingling with the caress.

"I knew you would come," she murmured. "I knew you would." She licked her dry, cracked lips. "Little Doe and Happy Woman?"

"Both of them are safe, and they're here," Lone Wolf answered, squeezing drops of water out of a buckskin onto her mouth. Before Catherine could ask, he added,

481

"The paleface reached the settlement in time to warn them of Wanchese's attack."

"Is . . . is Fletcher all right?"

Lone Wolf nodded his head. "For the time being. The settlers abandoned the island, but they refused to come this far inland. They have taken refuge with the Croatoans."

"Ellen?"

"I sent for her when I brought you home." Lone Wolf smiled. "I'll let her talk with you later," he promised. "But now I want you to myself."

Catherine nodded and smiled, her lids drooping over her eyes. Holding her hand, Lone Wolf sat by her side until No-am-ee returned.

"You may leave," she announced. "I am going to feed Catherine, wash her hair, and give her a bath."

Lone Wolf shook his head. "Thank you, Grandmother, for your kindness and your ministrations, but I will nurse Catherine."

"You know it is not our custom for—"

"Surely you must know, Grandmother, that where Catherine is concerned I make my own customs."

No-am-ee snorted her disapproval, but she couldn't hide the small smile that twitched at the corners of her mouth. She limped to the platform and pressed an arthritic hand against Catherine's brow. "The fever is gone, my son. Catherine will be fine."

As soon as No-am-ee had walked out of the wigwam, Lone Wolf went to the entry and pulled the bark across the opening. By the time he returned to the sleeping room, Wolf Friend was sniffing around the platform. He pressed his wet nose against Catherine's face, and he nuzzled her cheek. When she lifted a hand and rubbed his head, he whimpered softly and padded back to his bed and lay down.

Lone Wolf filled a bowl with water and moved it close

to the platform. Next he added more wood to the fire, so that it blazed higher and warmed the room. Then he lay several furs on the floor close to the fire. That done, he dipped the small piece of deerskin into the water, wet it, and wrung it out. Pulling the fur-lined robe from Catherine, he tenderly washed her body and hair. After he had dried her, he gently picked her up and laid her on the pallet while he changed the bedding on the platform.

When he had tucked her back into bed, he ladled out a bowl of meat broth and sat on the edge of the platform, spooning it to her as if she were a baby. After the third spoonful, she closed her eyes and shook her head.

"I'm full," she declared, almost yawning the words.

Lone Wolf set the bowl on the floor and tucked the blanket under her chin. "Go to sleep, my darling," he murmured, leaning down to kiss her forehead. Then he stood and walked to the fire pit.

Catherine forced her heavy eyelids up, and she tried to focus her gaze on Lone Wolf, but she couldn't find him. "Lone Wolf," she cried, sitting up in bed, pain jolting through her body. "Where are you?"

"I'm right here," he reassured her, rushing to her side and easing her down. "I'm right here."

"Don't leave me," she whispered. "Please don't leave me."

"I won't," he promised her. "I'll be on the platform across the room."

"No," Catherine whispered, pulling his hand to her lips and nibbling at the ring, "I want you to sleep with me."

"What about your wounds?"

"What about them?"

"I . . . I may roll over and hurt you."

"Nay," Catherine told him. "You'll hurt me far worse if you don't sleep beside me."

Chapter XXIV

"This will ease the pain enough for you to attend the council meeting," No-am-ee said, handing Catherine the root tea. "Drink it. Then lie down until I get dressed."

Grateful for the old woman's ministrations and concern, Catherine reached for the bark cup, and she gulped the bitter concoction down. "Why must I attend the council meeting?" she asked as she lay back on the platform.

No-am-ee chuckled. "You are not only a champion, Ca-ther-ine. You are now a warrior with a tale of valor and adventure. Wise One and the tribal council would hear you speak."

"I am a woman of valor because I killed three men," Catherine murmured, her eyes closing of their own volition. She hadn't realized how weak she was. She was exhausted, and all she had done was put on her clothes. She didn't know whether she had the strength to walk under the weight of her weapons, but No-am-ee had insisted that she wear them.

"You did more than most women would have done in the same situation," No-am-ee responded.

"I had to," Catherine mumbled, wishing she could sleep for a while.

"Don't go to sleep," No-am-ee admonished. "It is time for us to go to the Big House."

Catherine's lashes fluttered up, and she gazed at No-am-ee. "Where is Lone Wolf?" she asked.

"He is with Wise One and Flying Eagle," No-am-ee replied.

"Discussing the wedding," Catherine muttered, swallowing her bitterness.

No-am-ee nodded her head and held out her hand. "Come. We must go."

Walking beside No-am-ee, Catherine moved down the streets of Scupperong into the Big House, past the brindled wolf who lay outside the door. Although her shoulder was tender, she held her back erect, never flinching from the weight of her quiver. In the belt around her waist she carried her knife and war club. In her left hand she carried the bow her father had given her.

When they entered the Big House, No-am-ee guided Catherine to the raised platform where the guests of honor sat. Sunflower Woman moved to Catherine's side and helped her to her seat.

"Pssst. Kate!"

Catherine looked around, her gaze finally settling on Ellen and Will who sat on the straw-covered floor below the platform. She waved at them. Then she looked around for Lone Wolf, but she didn't find him. She tried to catch No-am-ee's eye to ask where he was, but the old woman never looked in her direction.

The village council entered the room, as did the Scupperongac tribal council, the Lumbroan tribal council, and Flying Eagle, and Little Doe. Then Wise One and Lone Wolf entered, Wise One walking to the center of the room, Lone Wolf to the platform. All movement, all talking ceased. Moving to the fire, the chief threw some tobacco leaves into the blaze, their sweet aroma permeating the lodge. Then he lit his pipe, took several puffs, and blew the smoke in the direction of each village clan chief. Finally, holding his pipe with both

485

hands and extending his arms above his head, Wise One began to pray, the soft chant sounding through the room. The prayer over, he laid his pipe on one of the seven large, smooth stones which circled the fire.

All the grievances were heard first. As she had before, Catherine enjoyed listening to both sides of the issue. She was delighted that the women had such an open voice in their community and government. Finally, however, local business was over.

"Now we will hear our brother, Flying Eagle, speak."

Flying Eagle stood and walked to the center of the lodge. He took the pipe from Wise One and smoked it. After he returned it to Wise One, he walked to where Lone Wolf sat.

"War chief of the Scupperongacs, you have asked permission to marry my daughter, Little Doe?"

"I have." Lone Wolf's answer resounded through the quiet lodge.

"The wedding is to take place during the strawberry festival in the spring?"

Lone Wolf nodded his head.

"And you have given my daughter the first gift of purchase?" Flying Eagle held up the linen nightshirt for all to see.

"I have."

Flying Eagle returned to the platform, and he looked at the tribal council. "This marriage between my daughter, Little Doe, and the war chief of the Scupperongacs will tie the sinew of friendship between your tribe and mine. You have spoken; our council has spoken."

The spokesman for the Scupperongac council, No-am-ee, nodded her head. One of the members of the Lumbroan council also nodded affirmation.

Flying Eagle walked to the platform, and he laid the nightshirt in front of Little Doe. When he returned to the center of the room, he said, "My council demanded that Little Doe marry an honorable, valiant warrior, a warrior

486

whose fame struck fear into the hearts of our enemies. Their first choice was Red Fox, but when he was killed in an honorable battle to the knife, the council chose Lone Wolf."

The spokesman for the Lumbroan council rose. "You have spoken the truth, Great Werowance. We chose Lone Wolf because he is the only warrior whom the Iroquois truly respect."

"That may have been true at one time, Great Werowance Flying Eagle of the Lumbroans, but it is no longer so." Kee-Lee stood to his feet and moved to the center of the room. "May I speak?"

Tension and silence stretched tautly in the Big House. Catherine pushed to the edge of the bench. Caught up in the tenseness of the moment, she eagerly awaited Flying Eagle's response to Kee-Lee.

"You may speak."

After Kee-Lee had smoked the sacred pipe, he walked to the platform, and he addressed the tribal council. "I will be the first to admit Lone Wolf is one of the most valiant Scupperongac warriors, and he is to be respected. He is a mighty war chief, but he is not the only brave who can strike fear into the hearts of our enemies."

"And what would a boy know about such valor?" No-am-ee taunted, following the custom for initiating a young warrior into the office of war chief.

"I have not been a boy for many winters, my Grandmother," Kee-Lee returned respectfully. "When I was sixteen winters, I proved myself a brave warrior. I earned my first feather." He turned around. "Now you will see many feathers decorate my hair." He held one up in his hand. "These are the last three feathers I have earned—the ones I earned when I saved Werowance Flying Eagle's life."

"Do you have a story of valor to tell us?" No-am-ee asked even though she had already heard his story.

"I have a tale of bravery and adventure to share with

487

you," he acknowledged.

"Then tell us."

The people craned their necks and strained to hear. They never tired of hearing tales of courage.

Kee-Lee's deep voice flowed through the building, and although he was extolling his own bravery, his story was one of confidence and valor. Conceit and bravado were not traits of his.

"When the runner came with the news that Catherine, Little Doe, and Happy Woman had been taken prisoners by the Iroquois, our party had not reached the safety of Echota. Lone Wolf and his braves left to rescue the women. I and my braves were to conduct Flying Eagle safely to Echota where he was to meet with the Iroquois chiefs. Before we arrived at the protective palisades of the city, however, we were attacked by an Iroquois war party, led by Strong Hand. My braves and I defeated the Iroquois"—he paused, looking into the face of each council member—"I alone saved Flying Eagle from an Iroquois poisoned arrow." He brandished his bow and war club through the air. "Now Kee-Lee's name is feared among the Iroquois. To save Flying Eagle I killed three Iroquois braves."

"Hear! Hear!" The people chanted their praise and admiration for the valor of their warrior.

"Now my chief"—although Kee-Lee addressed the chief, he looked first at Catherine and smiled; then he looked at Little Doe—"I would like to ask permission to marry your daughter, Little Doe."

"Why do you wish to marry my daughter?"

Kee-Lee didn't immediately answer. First, he looked at Catherine again and then at Little Doe. At one time he had thought he would be happy with no other woman but the paleface. Now he knew differently. Since the night he had kissed Little Doe, he had known that she was his woman. He smiled at the Lumbroan princess.

"I love your daughter." Kee-Lee's declaration rang

through the Big House.

"I cannot give you permission," Flying Eagle declared. "My daughter is to marry Lone Wolf."

Lone Wolf stood and moved to the fire. He smoked the sacred pipe with Wise One, and then he said, "Great Werowance Flying Eagle, I respect you like my father. You are a wise and great leader." Lone Wolf turned to Wise One. "And you, my werowance, are a father to me. I love no man as I love you." His words walked the tightrope of silence that stretched from one side of the wigwam to the other. The villagers watched closely. Lone Wolf moved the length of the house until he stood in front of Catherine, but he continued to speak to the council. "Disciplined to be a warrior, I promised the tribal council that I would do whatever was necessary for the welfare of my people. I agreed to marry Little Doe." He looked at Catherine, at her dark-circled eyes, her pale cheeks. "But now, my fathers and elders, I ask to be released from this promise." He held his hand out to Catherine. Dumfounded, she sat, staring at him. "I would marry this woman and her alone. I love her more than life itself. Without her I have no life." He motioned for Catherine to join him. Then he walked with her to where Little Doe sat. Lone Wolf said, "Little Doe, I would like to be released from the promise of marriage."

"I release you," Little Doe said, reaching for the nightshirt. "And I return to you the first gift of purchase."

Lone Wolf stepped forward and took the bundle from Little Doe. He walked to the Scupperongac tribal council. "Grandmother, I would like to be released from my promise to the council."

No-am-ee looked at the other five members. Clustering together, they talked quietly. Eventually No-am-ee said, "You are free, my son."

Lone Wolf held his hand out to Little Flower who came running with a basket. "I have a gift of gratitude for each of you." Taking off the lid, he gave each of the men a pouch of tobacco, to the women he gave a linen handkerchief.

Lone Wolf led Catherine to the fire in the center of the building. "Catherine Graystone," he said loudly and clearly, "I release you from your bondage to Lone Wolf, war chief of the Scupperongacs. You are now free to return to your people."

Catherine stared into the depths of those obsidian eyes, and she saw the fear, the uncertainly. "Thank you," she whispered.

Lone Wolf then walked to Flying Eagle. "I give up my claim to your daughter."

"So be it," Flying Eagle declared. As he approached the Lumbroan council, Lone Wolf and Catherine returned to their seats. "You have heard, and you have seen," Flying Eagle said to his council. "What is your judgment?"

Quietly the tribal chiefs conferred among themselves. Finally one stood. "We are in agreement, Great Werowance. A marriage between Little Doe of the Lumbroans and Kee-Lee of the Scupperongacs will tie the sinew of peace and friendship between us."

Nodding his head, Flying Eagle looked at Kee-Lee. "Do you have the first gift of purchase?"

A quiet joy surged through Kee-Lee's veins. He was now counted a village war chief, and his valor had won him the respect of the Lumbroans. He returned to his seat, opened a basket, and drew from it a small box, which he handed to Little Doe. As they looked into each other's eyes, embers of love ignited into flames of passion. The warrior swallowed hard as the heat of Little Doe's love swept over him. Both were jarred out of their reverie when people began to clamor for Little Doe to open her gift. Laughing, she lifted the lid of the box and she held up the brush and comb for everyone to see.

"It is beautiful," she murmured, pleasure painting her

490

cheeks pink.

"I traded with the settlers," Kee-Lee announced proudly.

After everyone was seated, Wise One rose. The moment everyone had been waiting for had arrived. "Now, my people, we will hear from our Turtle champion, our warrior woman." The chief of the Scupperongacs smiled at Catherine, and he waited until she stood in front of the sacred fire before he sat down. Lone Wolf moved to where Ellen and Will sat, so he could interpret for them.

Her voice strong and clear, Catherine related the story of her capture and escape. Throughout the telling, she had to stop because the villagers interrupted her so frequently with their cries of "Hear! Hear!" When she was through, she walked to the sacred fire.

"Great Werowance, Wise One of the Scupperongacs," she said, "I am honored to be the Turtle champion, and I am proud to be a warrior of the Scupperongacs. But my vision is not to kill and to take life. My vision is to give life. From this day forward I walk the path of peace."

"Will you wear the Coat of Peace, my daughter?"

Remembering Running Bear's words to her, Catherine said, "The Coat of Peace is hard to wear, my father, because it is a garment of love and understanding. The Coat of War can be worn by anyone because it is hastily sewn together, bound by the threads of impulsiveness and misunderstanding. Hatred grows more easily than love because it is wild and unruly; love is difficult because it must be tenderly nurtured. Love is like our corn, hatred like the weeds that spoil our crops. Winning feathers in war is much easier and more glorious."

"All this I know, my daughter. My question is: Will you willingly take the coat and wear it?"

Catherine looked at Wise One. "Yes, my chief, I will gladly wear the Coat of Peace."

"So be it," he said, standing. "You are Ca-ther-ine

491

Gray Stone, daughter of the Turtles, peace woman of the Scupperongacs."

"No, my father," Catherine corrected him. "I am Autumn Woman, daughter of the Turtles, peace woman of the Scupperongacs." She smiled. "My eyes are the color of the forest in the springtime; my hair is the golden fire of the autumn forest."

Wise One nodded, peace filling his soul. "You have had your vision?" he asked. Catherine nodded. "At the strawberry festival you will share it with our people."

"I will." She turned to the people, holding her hands out imploringly. "Share the vision of peace with me. Let us walk the road of friendship together. Walk with us," she implored, directing her last words to the Lumbroan council.

Then Catherine turned and walked to Kee-Lee. "I give this knife and war club to you, Kee-Lee. They have great magic for the warrior."

"I accept, Autumn Woman," Kee-Lee said. "Little Doe and I count you as one of our dearest friends."

"And to you, my friend," Catherine said to Mo-no-ta-me, walking toward him, "I give you one of the most precious gifts I possess." She handed him the bow her father had given to her. "It is a woman's bow and is too small for you to use, but I treasure it greatly because it is a work of art. I know you will appreciate it." A gnarled hand reached for the bow, and soft sighs of appreciation echoed through the townhouse.

"My chief," Catherine said, moving to Wise One, and slipping the quiver from her shoulder and laying it in front of the fire. "I will keep the quiver and the bow you gave me. They will always grace my house, reminding me of your honor and wisdom."

Catherine looked at Ma-wa-ska and smiled. "I have need of your racket, Turtle Coach. I intend to compete with Happy Woman again." The villagers laughed and cheered.

Catherine moved to the Beaver section. "And to you, Happy Woman, I would like to give these earrings and the necklace I brought from my homeland."

Surprised, Happy Woman rose, extending her hand for the jewelry. "These are beautiful," she murmured, too dumbfounded to say more. She lifted her head and stared into Catherine's face. "Thank you, my friend."

Catherine returned to the sacred fire. She picked up the rattles and began to shake them, stamping her feet in slow rhythm. The musicians, in their corner, began to beat the drums. Catherine danced until she stood in front of Lone Wolf. Wrapping her blanket over her shoulder, she extended her arm.

For breathless seconds Lone Wolf stared at her. Then he slowly stood and joined her in the ceremonial ring. When he slid an arm around her waist, she dropped the blanket over him so both of them were covered. Joyously they began to dance, their eyes glowing with excitement, promise . . . sensuality.

Hand in hand, Catherine and Lone Wolf walked to the wigwam, Wolf Friend trotting behind. "You do not wish to join your people at the village of the Croatoans?" he asked. Catherine shook her head. "And you do not want to go with your sister to the other paleface colony to the south?"

Again Catherine shook her head. "I'm going to miss Ellen and Will," she confessed, "but I have no desire to return to England." She paused reflectively a moment before she said, "I hope the Spaniards at St. Elena receive her and Will."

"There is doubt?"

Catherine nodded. "Our world is no different from yours, my darling. Like the Scupperongacs and the Iroquois, the English and the Spanish have been enemies for years."

"Ellen knows this?"

"She knows, but she's willing to take the risk to get back to England."

"What will happen to the warrior?" Lone Wolf asked.

"I'm not sure," Catherine mused, then she added as they walked into the wigwam, "But that's his story and his life, my darling."

Catherine walked through the house as Wolf Friend padded to the corner and lay down. By the time Lone Wolf had drawn the bark over the door and reached the sleeping area, Catherine's clothes were piling up in the center of the room. Divesting her dress, she stood naked.

"I'm more concerned about you, my darling. You're my story and my life."

Lone Wolf's jacket landed on the floor, then his moccasins and leggings and his breechclout. Walking to Catherine, he murmured, "I never wanted you for a slave, my darling. I only wanted you to be part of my life." He pulled her into his arms. "But I feared losing you, so I didn't set you free. I was afraid you would return to your people, I sought ways to bind you to my side."

"As a slave I could never be bound to you, my warrior. No commitment goes with slavery, only servitude. As a free woman I bind myself to you, in love, for life. Only so can two individuals really be bound together."

Catherine's words blended into the essence of a kiss, and her arms slid up Lone Wolf's chest, her hands locking at the nape of his neck. She moaned softly when he lifted her into his arms and carried her to the bed.

"Am I hurting you?" he whispered solicitously.

"Aye." She laughed softly. "My body is aching for you, my love."

Wolf Friend cocked one eye open and disinterestedly looked at the couple on the platform. Yawning, he moved his head, settling it more comfortably between his outstretched paws; then he closed his eyes.

494

Epilogue

Lone Wolf and Catherine stood side by side in the Big House in front of the ceremonial fire. Catherine looked at her husband. How handsome he was: the new moccasins and buckskin leggings; the beautiful breechclout she had just made for him, striped with colored bands of porcupine quills that shone yellow, red, and purple; the white linen shirt and the red sash. She thought him to be the most magnificent man she had ever seen in her life.

And the war chief of the Scupperongacs was equally pleased with his wife. She wore a white buckskin dress. The form-fitting bodice molded her breasts, and the belt accented her small waist. The three-quarter-length sleeves billowed into fringes that hung the length of the garment. The full skirt swirled softly around her legs, hanging well below the leggings that were laced to her knees. Her shining auburn hair hung down her back in a single braid.

Both of them beamed when No-am-ee entered the lodge, carrying a cradleboard. As the old woman walked to the center of the room, Catherine smiled at Lone Wolf. She couldn't have been happier. As No-am-ee lifted the baby toward heaven and Wise One made the dedication, Catherine closed her eyes and thanked God for his many blessings.

When the prayer was over, Wise One asked, "Who will name the baby?"

Lone Wolf stepped forward. "We would have you name the child, Grandmother."

No-am-ee turned, placing the baby in Lone Wolf's arms. She moved to the fire, opened her pouch of tobacco, and threw some crumbled leaves into the flames. In a low monotone she chanted her prayer. Finally she walked to Lone Wolf and took the baby from his arms. She held up the firstborn and named him and dedicated him as Gray Stone. Then Sunflower Woman entered the lodge, carrying another cradleboard. After the prayer and ritual, she held the secondborn up to the heaven, naming her and dedicating her as Kate.

Simultaneously the two women turned, No-am-ee placing Gray Stone in Lone Wolf's arms, Sunflower Woman handing Kate to Catherine. The proud parents looked at the tiny babies for a moment; then they lifted their heads and looked at each other. From the depths of their eyes, the wellsprings of their souls, they declared their love for one another.